THE GIRL ON THE BURNING BOAT

GREGG DUNNETT

Old Map Books

PROLOGUE

By the time the lights went off, the man concealed in the front garden had been there two hours.

Just watching. And getting excited, about what he was planning to do.

It was ten forty five on a Thursday night. Right when he expected her to go to bed. Because this wasn't the first time he'd watched her. Oh no. He'd been here many times. Checking where the shadows lay. Where he couldn't be seen by the neighbours. Staring in through the windows while she was at work. Wondering if he was really going to do it.

It was amazing how much you could tell about a person - just from looking through their windows. The single wine glass on the coffee table. She lived alone. The tiny kitchen and cosy lounge always neat, just the one small sofa, a pile of documents on one side, a blanket on the other. A professional woman, early in her career. Little time for visitors.

A photograph on the wall showed her graduation. Posing in her academic gown. She was pretty. But looked the shy type. A few close friends. No boyfriend.

Why is that Emily? The man had mused, gazing in. There was a cat though. Sometimes it came over to the window and arched its back at the man, as if it wanted him to scratch its ears. Sometimes he laid his gloved hand against the glass.

Soon. I'll see you soon, he would whisper at the animal.

Now of course, everything in the room was hidden. By the curtains, and now by darkness. But the bathroom window was bright now. He watched the shape of her, behind the obscured glass. Cleaning her teeth. Taking off her makeup and - ahhh - removing her contact lenses.

Don't worry Emily. You'll still see me.

There was the sound of the toilet flushing. Then the light went out. Just a dim glow, showing how she'd moved to the bedroom, which over-looked the back garden. He walked lightly to the side of the house. He had to be cautious here, it was the only place on the property where he might be seen from the road. He had considered knocking out the bulb in the lamp-post closest to the front of the house, but decided that would only serve to draw attention to the cottage. He checked the road. Empty. All the neighbours were comfortable behind their curtains. Unthinking. This was a quiet area. A safe area. No reason to keep an eye out here. He smiled.

The gate was as tall as he was. Had it been locked it might have slowed him down, but he'd been watching once when she put the bins out. Seen how the key was hung on the hook inside. He only had to reach over and flick it off, and unlock it from the outside. It took seconds. Then he slipped through the opening and shut the gate again, disap-pearing into the darkness behind.

The back garden was small. Very private. No light from the bedroom window above. She must have gone straight to sleep. There was a tiny patio. French doors - no curtains - led into the little dining area. He didn't try the doors. Not yet. Give her a few minutes to drop off. He prac-tised slowing his heart rate. After a while there was a soft alert from his mobile phone. He pulled it out and checked the screen. An email from work. He smiled at that, then answered it. He put the phone into silent mode before slipping it back into his pocket. No mistakes now.

He waited as long as he could, then stood again. He made his way to the French doors and stared into the dark interior. Softly, he tried to tug it open. The door was locked. He reached to his brow and clicked on a lamp. It shone a tight, focused beam which he shone upon the outer mechanism of the lock. Thinking. Then he unzipped his jacket and pulled out a leather case. He selected a half-diamond pick and a torsion wrench with a wrist strap. He pushed the pick into the key shaft. It resisted at first, but then the tool slid inside. The wrench too. His fingers flexed confidently as they operated the tools, carefully releasing each of the three pins that secured the door. As each gave way he maintained the pressure on them with the wrench, ensuring the springs inside the lock couldn't snap back and return him to the start of the process. For a few moments he forgot why he was even there. He was simply enjoying the challenge of beating the mechanism. And then, with a final soft click, the lock drew back. He pressed down on the door lever, and with a small rush of warm air from inside, the door slipped open.

The man put his tools away and slid the case back inside his jacket. Then he softly entered the house. He pulled the door closed behind him.

It felt totally different inside. It always did. The air was drier. There was an oiliness to it - she had been burning a perfumed candle he remembered. There was the buzz of the fridge, oblivious and uncaring that an intruder had gained entry. The heating system, now off, was settling down, the flow of hot water around the radiators slowing to a stop. Like the blood in a body settling once the heart could no longer pump it around. The man listened. He switched off his headlight, then waited a few moments for his eyes to adjust again. He saw the knife rack. Hesitated. Then he slipped one out. A chopping knife, slim bladed but sharp. He pulled another, this looked like the knife used in *Psycho*. He liked that more but took both with him, slipping one into a pocket and holding the bigger one with the steel blade flat against his wrist. He stepped quietly towards the stairs.

He had to concentrate to keep his breathing quiet as he climbed up, keeping his weight on the outsides of the treads, listening for any creaking that might give him away. He reached the top without any noise at all. He looked around. The bathroom door was open, the only other room had the door closed.

He opened the other door.

Ahead of him, in a small double bed, the girl lay asleep. Her hair was ruffled up around her head. There was a shoulder strap visible from her nightdress. One hand was slipped under her pillow, placed as if she were using it to cradle her head. He watched in the darkness for a few minutes.

Suddenly he noticed a pair of eyes glowing at him in the darkness. The surprise hit him like a punch to the chest. He didn't move, but the cat did. It got up and arched its back. Began to purr. The man let out a breath. He reached out and stroked the animal with two fingers, the rest were still holding the handle of the knife against his palm.

Hello pussycat, he said. He watched it carefully, as if unsure whether he could trust it, but it seemed entirely unconcerned at his presence.

For a very long time he simply stood there, stroking the cat and watching the girl. Then, when the animal finally settled back down to sleep, he withdrew his hand, noticing it shook a little now. He was getting nervous. He focused his mind. She deserved this. This wasn't his fault. Before he could lose his nerve he moved quickly. He opened his jacket again and slipped out the phone. He slid it off silent, then opened the timer app. He set it for one minute, the alarm to *'fire engine bell'*, the volume to *'extra loud'*. His eyes went wide with anticipation. He hit *start* and watched the seconds begin to count down. The milliseconds flying faster than his eyes could see.

Then he set the phone on the dressing table at the end of the girl's bed. The seconds still ticking away. The screen still alight. It was now facing where she slept. When she sat up in bed, in about forty seconds time, it would be the first thing she saw. Then he changed his grip on the knife so that he held it like a dagger. He knelt down by the foot of the bed. Dropping low to the carpet. And he counted down the final few seconds.

PART I

1

There was no reason for Jamie Weston to expect, as he waited outside that chilly spring morning, that the coming day was the beginning of anything. Much less the beginning of the end. No clue, in the quiet streets around, that the events that day would spark a chain of actions and reactions leading to just one place. But then there never is. Few of us wake up on the day of our death and recognise that day for what it is. It's just another ordinary day. Until it isn't. The moments marking the beginnings of our entry and exit to this planet are like ghosts, sometimes sensed but never seen.

But the clues *were* there, if only you knew where to look.

Jamie Weston was twenty-three years old. He had just three months to live.

What breeze there was that day was light and came from the sea, carrying with it a taste of salt. It was cold. Jamie stuffed his hands deeper into his pockets, wishing he'd taken a warmer jacket. Mostly though he regretted ever taking this job. He had essays to write, examinations to study for. Things to do that were more important than earning this bit of extra cash. He considered turning around and going back inside. But he needed the money. And the man who offered him the job seemed like a nice guy. Jamie didn't feel like letting him down. Instead he breathed out hard in the cold air, creating his own little cloud of mist.

A Volkswagen panel van turned the corner of the road, its paintwork new and lacquered. The driver slowed as they read the numbers of the flats. *Too late now*, Jamie thought, and he stretched out an arm in greeting. The driver saw, then cruised to a stop alongside. The window purred down.

"Made it out of bed then?" The driver had the rough voice of a long-term smoker but there was a friendliness as well. He had the worn, lined skin of someone who'd worked hard all their life. "It's Jamie isn't it? I'm Len, we spoke on the phone."

They shook hands through the window. Then Jamie hesitated.

"Well come on then. It's cold out there. Jump in."

Jamie did what he was told, walking around the front of the van to the passenger door. A younger man was already sitting in the window seat, wearing a bulky set of red headphones. The family resemblance was unmistakable. Wordlessly the young man unclipped his seatbelt and slipped out onto the pavement, allowing Jamie to climb in and sit in the middle seat where there was less legroom. The young man then climbed in again and slammed the door shut behind him. Throughout the process he maintained a constant nodding of his head to whatever music he was listening to.

"That's Stevie," Len said with a sigh. "My son." He went on, speaking across Jamie and nearly shouting. "*Stevie, this is Jamie, he's helping us out this week.*"

Stevie moved his head but said nothing. It might have been a greeting, or it might have just been in time to the music. Then he turned away again.

"Stevie's not really a morning person." Len said. For a moment he looked disappointed. Then he pulled away.

Len threaded the van through the one-way system and down the road by the harbour. This early in the morning the traffic was still light, and the off-licences and betting shops near where Jamie was picked up soon gave way to long driveways and substantial homes, glimpsed behind high walls and thick hedges. They passed through a suburb with shops, which seemed to be mostly wine bars, the offices of financial advisers and tanning clinics. Then the road dropped down to the waterside. On one side, small fishing boats and yachts waited obediently at their moorings. On the other, Jamie caught sight of more water - this time blue flashes of the ocean in the narrow gaps between the buildings. The homes here had two faces, one looking out over the harbour, the other over the beach, and each building seemed to rival itself in an effort to appear more grand, more self-important. There were thrusting balconies, soaring roofs, glass and steel sun decks. Here and there a porthole window had been added, a small concession to help them fit into their waterfront setting, but the architectural arms race made fitting in forlorn hope. These homes weren't built to take in the view, they were designed to *be* the view.

"What'd you say you were studying? " Len asked suddenly. "Something useful I hope?"

"Medicine," Jamie replied.

Len nodded approvingly.

"Sensible young man." He glanced across at Stevie, who ignored him.

Len rolled his eyes at Jamie, then decided to change the subject.

"You ever been into one of these places?" He nodded to the house they were just passing. Crisp white render and smoked glass windows rose above them like the bridge of a cruise liner.

"No."

"Just you wait. That'll be an education that will."

Jamie didn't answer, but turned to the window and watched the homes slipping by.

A little further down the road Len pulled on the indicator and slowed the van. Ahead of them a heavy steel gate blocked their way. Len fumbled in the pockets of his overalls and pulled out a small black remote control. He aimed it at the gate and pressed the button. Nothing happened for a second and then the gate began to split in two. One part swung out of their way, but the site was too tight for the other half to do the same, so it sank into its concrete base.

They drove in, and at once Stevie opened the van door and jumped out. Jamie followed him and gazed up at the three stories. They were standing at the foot of an angled white block, above them a large concrete balcony was cantilevered out from the top floor. It looked like a fortress.

Len held up another device. This one looked like a credit card but thicker. As they approached the front door a noise of rapid beeping sounded from somewhere, and a CCTV camera angled down to view them. Len stood in front of it and tilted his head back. He waited a moment and a light switched from red to green.

"It's all automatic. There's no one home," he said to no one in particular.

There was the noise of heavy bolts sliding back. And when Len pushed on the door it swung open, revealing a set of stairs leading upwards.

"This is the reason we've got you in son," Len continued, still talking to Jamie. "We're up on the third floor and there's no lift."

Jamie glanced around. It seemed the whole of the ground floor was given over to a kind of boat house. There was a giant RIB on a trailer, with absurdly large twin outboards hanging off the stern. There were racks filled with surfboards and canoes, bikes and diving equipment. A pair of jet skis lurked in a corner. Jamie didn't have time to see more, as Len led them quickly up the stairs. He didn't stop on the first floor, where a generous hallway had various doors leading off - all shut. Len kept climbing, puffing slightly from the effort.

At the top of the third flight of stairs Jamie stopped, stunned. The entire top floor was one giant open space, perhaps sixty foot long. At each end the walls were glass, one looked out over the harbour, with its green islands, its stretches of sparkling water, and the hills behind. The other side gave a view of the ocean as if the building were a ship out at sea. Behind the glass an enormous sun deck jutted out right over the beach. At one end of the deck a wooden hot tub bubbled away, its cover half open and steam rising gently into the blue sky.

Inside, the vast room was divided into three by careful zoning and use of furniture - no walls were permitted to clutter the pristine space. The part nearest to the ocean was given over to the kitchen, three times the size of any Jamie had been in before. The rest of the room was split between a sitting area, with white leather sofas and a white steel log burner, and a dining area big enough to house a green glass dining table and ten glass and steel chairs. Above it all ran a full length roof lantern through which light poured into the room.

"Wow." Jamie said when he'd taken it in. Even Stevie pulled his headphones off.

Len grinned. "I did tell you didn't I?" He shook his head. Then he walked over into the kitchen area. He ran his hand over the marble worktop "Seems a shame to rip this all out, but... Best get started."

Stevie followed him and opened some cupboards at random. They were full. Crockery and thin necked champagne glasses. "It's got all the stuff in it still." He sounded annoyed.

"Well, that'll be your first job then won't it? Go get the boxes from the van."

Jamie went back down with him to help. While he was there a lorry turned up and delivered a skip. Then he went back upstairs and the three of them began to pack away the kitchen. The brands in the cupboards were unfamiliar to Jamie. It was all Fortnum and Mason. Harrods. It seemed to be mostly biscuits and condiments.

"Normally we'd ask the client to empty all the cupboards before we come in, but I guess when you're rich enough to own all this..." Len said after a while. He sounded apologetic.

Jamie shrugged. It made little difference to him what he was being paid to do.

"Who lives here anyway?" He asked instead. "Who can afford all this?"

Len paused for a second, leaning over one of the boxes. "Does the name Belhaven mean anything to you?"

Jamie thought, then shook his head. "No. Should it?"

"Probably not. Not unless you've got a few hundred grand to invest." Len waved his hand as if to dismiss what he'd said.

"The bloke who lives here runs some sort of investment fund. I don't understand. All I know is this isn't even the main house. The family spend most of their time up in London. They've got an even bigger house there I heard."

"What kind of investments?"

Len shrugged. "Don't ask me. I just fit kitchens. Or take them out. It's the wife who wants this one taken out. Not fashionable enough for her apparently. Different world isn't it?" He smiled at Jamie, his eyes twinkling. Jamie just looked around the huge space again.

"Anyway," Len said. "Time for my cancer break." He pulled out a packet of rolling tobacco and some papers and expertly made a cigarette.

As soon as Stevie noticed what he was doing, he pulled out a chair, sat on it, and began studying his phone. Jamie realised this was an official break in the proceedings. He watched as Len stepped outside onto the big balcony that overlooked the ocean. He cupped his hands in front of him and lit up.

Since he didn't want to join Stevie, Jamie walked towards the other end of the room. One of the side walls was given over to a display of photographs, artfully arranged in white frames. There were typical family scenes, just not - Jamie thought - showing a very typical family. Mostly they were of a couple, handsome and tanned. They were embracing in ski wear, a sunny alpine backdrop behind them. They stood on tropical beaches - where he looked fit and muscled, she pouted, curvy but slim, her hair glossy. There were more - posing in evening wear, on a red carpet somewhere. Shaking hands with people that looked familiar - perhaps a Hollywood actor, Jamie wasn't sure. But in between these shots were other images just of the man. In these he seemed to be some sort of adventurer. In some he was climbing mountains, with a full backpack and an ice axe in each hand. There was another where he was grinning through a thick frosty beard in front of a pack of huskies and a sled.

As Jamie worked his way along the wall, new images appeared. Children. Two girls. Little blond things that mostly seemed to feature in the background at first. As Jamie moved along he realised the display was in order. The children grew older, became schoolgirls in prim uniforms, presumably of some exclusive private school. Then older still, no longer children but young women pushing their way to the front of the images. And understandably so. The mother was good looking, Jamie had noted that, with an Eastern European or Russian look to her features - but the daughters were something else. They were stunning. The older one - Jamie supposed she was older - seemed to take after the mother more, with Slavic looks and a model's pout. But this was absent on the younger daughter. She shared her father's eyes, sparkling and somehow filled with humour. She seemed to smirk at the camera lens. Jamie leaned in to get a better view.

Near the end of the display Jamie found himself particularly drawn to one photograph of the younger daughter. It was a close up, and presumably taken recently. The girl was perhaps twenty years old, steering the same RIB he'd seen downstairs. Her hair, cut quite short, streamed out behind her. The wind blew her blouse hard against her body. She drove casually, one hand on the wheel even though a long line of creamy wake showed how fast she was going. She had her head slightly tilted to one side, her eyes on whoever was taking the photograph, giving them what looked to be a cool sarcastic smile. Jamie tried to pull his eyes away, but something about the image was captivating. There was something, perhaps in the proportions of her face, the way the sun lit up her skin. The more he tried to look away, the more the image drew him in. He stared at her face. He realised it was simply beauty. He wondered if he had ever seen a more beautiful girl.

"She's alright ain't she?" Stevie said, from behind him, making him jump. The spell was broken and Jamie spun around. But Stevie was pointing at a different picture, this one of the other daughter, standing on a beach in a red swimsuit with a motor yacht in the background. Jamie looked at it and didn't disagree. In the image the woman was standing with one hand on her hip, her long blond hair wet and piled over one shoulder. She pushed her chest out, as if trying to emulate the photographs that filled fashion magazines. But Jamie's eye moved easily away, there was something too obvious about the looks of the second girl. It was the other photograph that drew Jamie's eye. The girl driving the boat. She wasn't just beautiful, he decided, there was something more. Her character seemed to come through, a spirit, an enthusiasm for life that she wore on her face. Again he found himself unable to look away.

"Totally out of your league though," Stevie went on.

"Thanks." Jamie replied.

"No problem mate." Stevie slapped him on the back and moved away.

Jamie hardly noticed. He stared at the image of the girl driving the boat. Trying to read what that expression meant.

For a long time he stood there. There was nothing else he could do. She had a look - a quirkiness - some combination of features and smile and beauty that just *floored him*. Every time he tried to look away he found he couldn't. It was like her eyes were literally on his. Compelling him to look. Forcing him to feel things that made no sense.

Jamie, a young man who studied medicine, who until that moment had never even considered the concept of love at first sight, felt the almost physical sensation of the bottom dropping out of his world. That this girl existed in the world - and he couldn't have her, would never even *see* her for real - caused him a sickening feeling.

Jamie Weston's world would not, could not, ever be the same again.

2
_____

They stopped work at four. Len offered to drop Jamie back at his flat, but instead Jamie walked to the bus stop and went to the library. He only meant to spend a couple of hours, but once he got started the time flew by. When he finally got back it was dark, and he had difficulty fitting the key into the lock. He trudged up the stairs and called out to see if anyone was home.

From the kitchen a pretty, blond-haired girl called out to him. She was standing up, phone in one hand, the other holding a slice of pizza that she'd just taken from a box on the worktop. She wore a short black dress smoothed down over sheer tights. Her makeup was tinged with silver and purple.

"Hey you," the girl said as Jamie walked in. Her dark eyes twinkled behind purple eye shadow.

"Hi," Jamie said.

"We're going to that new club in town tonight. You fancy coming?" There was a note of hope in her voice, but not too much.

"I can't tonight," Jamie replied. "I've got to study. And I'm working early again tomorrow." Jamie didn't mean to, but his eyes dropped down to the pizza box. He still hadn't eaten.

At once she pushed the box towards him.

"You want a piece?" She said, "I'm not going to eat all this anyway."

"No..."

"Go on..." She smiled when Jamie took a slice, like this was a small victory.

"Thanks Laura," Jamie said. He cradled it with two hands and took a bite.

"You sure I can't tempt you out?" She dropped her head on to one side and watched him eat.

"I'm sorry Laura. I'm just really tired." Jamie said.

She looked away, as if pretending to be insulted, but she didn't hold the pose for long. "How did it go today anyway?" Laura asked suddenly. "You were in one of those mega seafront houses weren't you? Anyone famous?"

"I don't think so." Jamie looked at her and shrugged. She tried to hold his gaze for a moment but he looked away. She slid the pizza box back under his nose.

"Well anyone interesting then?"

"Just some finance guy. Don't think there's anything interesting about him."

"Huh," she huffed a little. "I bet there is. You have to do something dodgy to make that sort of money."

"Maybe," Jamie replied. He felt strange. While he was studying, and now here, having this conversation, his mind was still picturing the girl in the photograph.

"Here, have another slice," Laura told him.

"I can't, it's yours..." Jamie replied.

"It's only going to go in the bin. I told you, I'm full." As if to demonstrate, Laura ran her hands over her flat belly, watching his reaction as she did so. Jamie's eyes stayed on the pizza box.

"You sure?" Jamie asked.

"Of course." A note of petulance entered her voice.

"Thanks Laura," Jamie picked up the box. "Have a good night." He carried it out of the kitchen.

She watched him leave. Her face was wistful as he walked away.

Tom was in his usual place on the sofa, midway through his usual four-pack of lager. As ever his smoking paraphernalia laid out in front of him too. The TV was on, the remote control balanced by his side. Jamie dropped down onto the other end of the sofa and picked out another slice of pizza.

"You indulging?"

Jamie looked up to see him brandishing a newly rolled joint in the air.

"No thanks mate. I might try and do a bit more work."

Tom raised his eyebrows.

"Serious?"

"Yeah, I've got exams coming up, I've got to do the work." Jamie grimaced and glanced over at the corner of the room where a pile of text books was neatly stacked. Next to them was a kit bag, roughly packed with a sleeping bag and a pillow on top.

"Shit," Tom said. Then he lit the end of his joint, sucked in a few half-breaths and finally one deep breath. When he exhaled a large cloud of smoke billowed out into the room.

"What?" Jamie replied, when he'd finished.

"Just *shit*. You work too hard *shit*. I've smoked too much *shit*. You know? That *shit*."

Jamie spent a moment trying to decode this. He failed, but a thought occurred to him.

"Is it getting annoying, me staying here? I can always arrange to stay somewhere else. If it is."

"No, no. *No. No way man*," Tom sounded suddenly worried. "I didn't mean that. You stay here as long as you like. We like having you here. You redress the male to female imbalance in the house. It's all cool." He took another puff. Sent another cloud out into the room.

"And anyway, the girls' friends seem to hang around here a lot more with you here." Tom smiled at him and held out the joint. "Come on. Keep me company."

"No I've really got to work."

Tom seemed to think for a moment and then he shrugged.

"Laura looks hot tonight." He slid a sideways glance over at Jamie. "You noticed at all?"

"Yeah. I guess so." Jamie replied without really thinking about it.

"You're not tempted there?"

Jamie's brow crinkled in confusion. "*Tempted?*"

"Dude she's *all over you*. Don't tell me you haven't noticed."

"No she's not."

"Her and Karen are going out clubbing. It's a girls night. Then she invites you?" He raised his eyebrows. "I didn't get an invite."

Jamie thought before answering. "Well that's because you prefer sitting here getting stoned to leaving the house. She knows what the answer's going to be."

"That may be the case, but..." Tom held the joint with its glowing tip vertical, as if this somehow proved his point. Jamie sat for a moment, thinking. Laura took some of the same lectures as him, and it was she who first suggested that Jamie move in. It was just for a few months while he had nowhere else to stay. There was no spare room, so he'd had to inhabit the lounge - waiting every night until Tom had smoked enough to drag himself off to bed. Jamie had believed she was just being friendly. The thought there might be more to it hadn't occurred to him.

He didn't get long to brood however, as another girl slid into the chair next to him. She was tall and had red hair that cascaded down her bare back. She wore a sparkly silver top and black trousers. Jamie liked Karen a lot. She was straightforward.

"Give me a bit of that," she said to Tom. She reached forward and plucked the joint from his fingers. She took a couple of hits and then offered it to Jamie. When he declined she shrugged and held onto it instead.

"How was it today? You were in that big house weren't you? By the harbour?"

"Yeah," Jamie replied. But once again, at the mention of the house, the image of the girl in the photograph appeared unbidden in his mind. He remembered the physical elements, the way the light fell on the exposed skin of her shoulders and neck, and how her hair curled away from the base of her ears. But more than that, he thought of the expression she wore on her face, a knowing smile. A touch of humour in the absurdity of life.

"*Jamie!*" Karen's voice brought him back to the room.

"You sure you haven't been smoking that stuff?" Jamie refocused to see her getting up.

"Taxi's here. We're going to that new club if you change your mind and want to come along," Karen gave him a look. "I'm sure Laura wouldn't mind." She touched Jamie on the shoulder, and Jamie watched as she slid from the room.

3

The next day they began taking out the old kitchen. Jamie found himself trekking down the stairs with awkward armfuls of dismantled cabinets, and dropping them into the skip. On each trip back up he would pass Stevie on his way down, carrying rather less.

"Hey Jamie," Len said, sometime around mid-morning.

"Yeah?"

"Come here a minute, I need your help."

Jamie walked over to where Len lay on the floor, reaching for something out of view under the revealed carcass of a cabinet. Len pulled his arms out and got to his feet.

"You've got longer arms than me. And younger ones." He offered Jamie a screwdriver. "There's a screw under there I can't reach. You mind?"

Jamie lay down on the floor and peered into the darkness under the cabinet. He saw the screw which held the unit to the wall.

"You want it all the way out?" he asked, but before Len could answer his mobile phone rang. Jamie waited while Len took the call.

Rather than get up, Jamie stayed where he was, half listening as Len discussed when he might be available for another job. Jamie idly considering the strange perspective he had of cabinet legs and the dust balls that had gathered under this family's feet. Then he noticed something strange.

Right at the back of the cupboard, Jamie saw that a short length of one of the floorboards was loose. He moved his hand to bang it into place. But as he did so, the other end lifted even higher. He shifted position to have another go, but all he achieved was to move the first end up again. There seemed to be something there that was preventing it from lying flat. He banged the other end again, harder this time, but instead of solving the problem, the board jumped completely out of its space in the floor and banged into the cupboard's base above him. As it did so it revealed the cavity below, and what was preventing the board from going flat.

Hidden inside was a slim black rectangle. It was smartly covered with leather stitched into place. He couldn't see what it was, but it looked very out of place.

"Hey, look at this," he called out to Len, forgetting he was on the phone. But the older man didn't hear anyway, having retreated out to the sun deck to finish his call.

So Jamie was unobserved when he reached in and picked up the item. Then he reversed out from under the cabinet and stood up. For a while he still didn't understand what he was looking at, but then he saw one end held a cap, and when he pulled this off he realised it was a USB stick. He had several himself, for storing his work when using the university computers. But the ones he had were cheap, plastic items, this was different. Embossed into the leather were the letters CB in gold. Jamie looked up, expecting to see Len about to ask what he had found. But he was still outside, one hand clamping his phone to his ear, the other gesticulating as if the person on the other end of the phone were standing opposite him. Stevie was downstairs, probably skiving. Jamie looked back under the cabinet at where he'd found it. The space seemed to have been made for the drive. Crudely made, to be sure, but it seemed to be a tiny secret hiding place, hidden underneath the floor at the back of the cabinets. He wondered if it could have fallen there by accident. It seemed unlikely. Impossible even.

His first thought was to put it back. It looked like Len was finishing his call, and Stevie would be back upstairs at any moment. But if he was quick he could hide it again. But what if Len then found it? Or Stevie? It wasn't the sort of thing you could just dismiss. Len would probably want to give it back to the family. And if that happened Jamie would never know what was on it.

He knew it wasn't the right thing to do. But something made him act. Instead of putting it back where he found it, or telling the others what he'd found, he put the cap back onto the USB drive, and as Len stepped back into the room, he slipped it into his pocket.

"What was that?" said Len.

"What was what?" said Jamie, too quickly.

"You wanted something?"

"Oh," Jamie remembered how he had called out to Len. "Nothing. Just a loose floorboard, I wanted you to hand me a hammer."

Len grunted. "You want me to do it?"

"No, I'll get it." Jamie grabbed a hammer and nails and crawled quickly back under the cabinet, feeling the USB drive press against his leg. Before nailing the board down he looked carefully into and around the hole, in case there was anything else hidden there that he'd missed. But it was empty. He nailed the hiding place closed, and slipped out again.

"Come on. Let's get this bloody thing out." Len said, lifting one end of the cabinet.

His next moment to himself was when he took another load down to the skip. Jamie reflected on what he had just done. He didn't exactly understand what had made him take the USB drive, but he was sure it had something to do with the crazy way he was still feeling about the girl in the photograph. Somehow the hold she had cast over him had made him act the way he had. He decided that once he went back upstairs he would show Len what he had found and let him deal with it. If it really had been hidden under the floorboards there must be some reason for it - and whatever that reason might be, it certainly had nothing to do with Jamie. It was none of his business.

He was thinking this as he walked out of the open front door, just as the steel entrance gate separating the property from the street was once again descending into the ground. A white Range Rover sat waiting for it, its orange indicator light blinking. And through the windscreen Jamie instantly recognised the two women sitting in the front seats.

4

The mother - less Eastern-European looking in life than in the many photographs upstairs - climbed out from behind the wheel. She was tall, and held herself erect. Her face was tight, as if she had undergone significant surgery, but she was still strikingly attractive, and impeccably dressed. She seemed to notice Jamie, but ignored him and instead continued talking with a girl, exiting from the passenger side. She was beautiful too, and family resemblance was clear both in her face and her poise. She was obviously the first woman's daughter. But she was the wrong daughter.

"Look all I know is it's not at the hotel." The daughter said. "And I need it today." She stared at her mother, that slight pout that Jamie had seen from the images. The mother let out a weary sigh.

"Well I hope it is. That's all I'm saying," the mother replied. She slammed shut the car door behind her.

At seeing the family here, in real life, Jamie was hit by a sense of shock. Until that moment it was as if they existed only in the abstract. Some sort of theoretical example of perfection unspoilt by the imperfections of actual people. But here they were - living, breathing people. But the rush of elation this revelation provoked disappeared just as quickly as it had arrived. *She* wasn't there. His girl wasn't with them. He had time to register just how much that hurt before the mother paused, then called out to someone still inside the vehicle.

"Stay in the car, we won't be a moment." She said.

The side windows of the car were tinted, meaning Jamie couldn't see who the mother was talking to in the back, but somehow he already knew. And he didn't have to wait long to confirm it. At that moment the back door of the car swung open and a third figure emerged. In life she was even more beautiful than in the images. It physically took Jamie's breath away.

"No I'm coming up." She said. Her voice was like music. "I want to see what they're doing."

As the younger daughter got out of the car, she noticed Jamie. In truth it was hard not to, he was standing in her doorway with an armful of dismantled kitchen furniture. As her gaze swung over him, she seemed to absorb him for what he was - just a labourer come to fit a new kitchen in one of her parent's homes - but there was a hesitation as her eyes panned. A hint of a smile. Or perhaps he only imagined that part.

"It's not anything exciting dear," the mother said. "It's just workmen doing... Whatever they're doing."

"I don't care. I'm not waiting in the car. I'm not a *dog*." She wore flip flops beneath dark blue shorts revealing slim tanned legs. Her blond hair fell onto bare shoulders and a white top. Jamie fought to take his eyes off her but failed.

The mother looked frustrated."We're only going to be a moment," she said, but the girl had already shut her door too.

Jamie hurriedly moved out of the way as the mother moved to enter the house. She didn't say a word to him as she passed. Neither did the older sister, who went second. But when the younger girl walked past she turned to where he was standing.

"Hello." She said. The word hit Jamie like an electric shock. She gave him an ironic smile - almost a smirk, then disappeared inside.

For Jamie, as soon as she was out of sight, it was like someone had switched off the sun. Like the parts of the world without her in it were just dimmer. He wasn't thinking straight, he knew that. He found himself climbing the stairs behind them, following the scent of her perfume.

Then he realised he still had the wood in his arms. He turned again and hurried out to the skip where he dropped it in and then went back up the stairs. He had no plan, he just knew he had to set eyes on the girl again.

On the first floor he peered around to see if any of the doors were open, they weren't, so he continued up, then stood by the top of the stairs.

"So Joanne, where *exactly* did you leave it?" the mother was interrogating the other daughter still.

"It was right here on the table. I'm *sure* it was." The elder girl - Joanne, Jamie filed away the name - glanced distrustfully at the workmen.

"Mr White," the mother sighed, turning to Len. "Have you moved a catalogue by any chance. It's a wedding catalogue."

Len's face crunched up into a deep frown. He turned to Stevie. "Have you..?" he asked, then when Stevie shook his head he turned back to the mother. "I'm sorry no." He said it as if it were a matter of grave importance.

This seemed to irritate the mother. "Are you quite sure? It's rather important..." She spoke as if Len might be simple, and Joanne broke in at the word *important,* as if it were nowhere near strong enough.

"I'm getting married next month. It's absolutely essential that I get that catalogue back."

Len's mouth dropped open but he shook his head again.

"Well what about him? Has he seen it?" Irritated, the mother flapped a hand in Jamie's direction without actually looking at him. Eventually Len got the idea that he was supposed to ask on her behalf.

"Son, have you seen a wedding catalogue?" Len asked.

It flashed through Jamie's mind that this was his opportunity. If he could locate the missing catalogue the family would somehow be so pleased he could get talking to the girl. The only problem was he hadn't seen any catalogues. His eyes flashed around the room before he answered. "No, sorry."

"He hasn't seen it either," Len fed the bad news back, though this seemed to further irritate both mother and elder daughter. Jamie's girl watched with a cool indifference. Jamie had to fight to not stare at her.

The mother sighed again.

"Well we may as well go. If we set off for London now we may find another one..." Suddenly Jamie cut her off.

There was no plan to what he said. The words just came out. Unbidden.

"Maybe it's in her room?" He said.

The mother looked shocked. "Excuse me?"

"Her room, maybe it's in Joanne's room..."

"What would you know of Joanne's room?" the mother demanded. Suddenly everyone in the room was staring at Jamie. There was a second of silence that felt like a minute.

"Nothing, I was just... When you lose things you have to look everywhere properly."

With another sigh the mother turned to the elder daughter. "Joanne. Have you looked in your room?"

"Of course not," she replied, her voice indignant. "I left it right here."

"Well would you mind just satisfying this young detective here and going and having a look? Before we drive all the way to London for nothing?"

Joanne's nose wrinkled with irritation "If I really have to. But it's not there." She walked to the stairs and disappeared down.

Suddenly there was an awkward silence. The mother eventually chose to break.

"So is it going... well?" She asked.

Len began a brief summary of their progress, but she didn't seem to listen, interrupting almost at once.

"Oh, " she said. When you change the fridge, you will be careful of the walls of the stairway won't you?"

Len hesitated. The fridge was a giant American two-door affair that would take the three of them to lift. Len had already explained how a mini crane was coming to hoist it down from the balcony.

"We'll move it down the front of the house, when we get the new worktop in," Len explained, but the mother wasn't really listening. Jamie wasn't either. His eyes were fixed upon the younger daughter. Jamie noticed that the girl had the same quizzical look on her face that she had in the photographs. It was a half smile, as if she perpetually found the world amusing. He was powerless to look away. Eventually she seemed to register that he was staring at her, and she raised a curious eyebrow at him, as if she now couldn't work out what was so fascinating. Jamie held her gaze for a second, in which the world around them seemed to shrink away to nothing. Then she seemed to tire of observing him, and suddenly strode into the kitchen area.

"So what exactly are you doing?" she asked Len. She stood so close to him that Jamie felt a pang of jealousy.

"Do you just - take it all out and put a new one in?"

When she spoke she seemed to command the room. Stevie had slipped off his headphones. Suddenly it seemed everyone - even the mother - was interested in how the refit of the kitchen was going.

"Yeah, that's mostly it," Len said. He looked uncomfortable at her proximity, as if her beauty were something to be feared.

"Obviously there's a few changes to where things are going, so we have to move the water and the gas..." She listened carefully to what he said, her eyes flicked around the room as she took in what he was saying. Jamie found his jealousy intensify.

"I didn't think there was much wrong with the old kitchen," the girl said.

Len hesitated to reply, even though he'd been saying the same for two days.

"Oh don't be silly Alice," the mother said.

Alice.

Suddenly Alice was the most beautiful name Jamie had ever heard. He repeated it silently to himself, his pulse quickening with each repetition. Then finally, after nearly a full minute of ignoring him, she glanced over, as if checking he was still watching her.

There was a call from down the stairs.

"We can go now."

The mother made a face. "So it was in your room after all?"

The older sister didn't reappear but they all heard her.

"Yes but Maria must have put it there." Her mother started descending the stairs.

"Well at least we can go now." She began. She kept talking as she passed out of sight, but Jamie couldn't hear what it was.

Alice didn't follow her mother at once, but her face once again wore its amused half-smile.

"Maria's our cleaner." She explained. "She does tend to move things about."

It felt to Jamie like the comment was directed entirely at him, and he answered before he could stop himself. "It's hard to get good staff these days."

Alice bit her lip and contemplated Jamie for a while. He thought she was going to reply, but in the end she simply smiled.

"Alice!" The mother's shout carried up the stairs, annoyed. "Hurry up. We're going."

For a moment Alice didn't move, then she turned to Len.

"Well I guess we've found what we came here for. We'll leave you to it. So sorry to disturb."

She shone a full beam smile at Len and he nearly crumbled in response. He managed a mumbled reply, and as she walked it wasn't just Jamie but the two other workers who followed her every move. But as she disappeared down she turned to Jamie again and hesitated just for a moment. Her eyes met his, her face set serious. Then she looked away, smiled and descended out of view.

5

Laura and Karen were out again when Jamie got back to the house. The cinema this time, according to Tom, who was in his normal spot, drinking his usual beers and rolling his usual joints. Again Tom asked him if he wanted to smoke, again Jamie declined. Then Tom asked if he was hungry but Jamie said no again. The truth was he didn't feel anything, didn't want anything. Other than the space to relive the moments he had spent in the company of Alice earlier that day. They sat watching some comedy, Tom snorting with suppressed laughter at the jokes, but Jamie hardly noticed. In his mind he was replaying every word she had said, every expression on her face. Each time he did so she seemed to become more beautiful, more captivating. More perfect.

And behind these thoughts lay the USB drive. Seeing Alice in person had relegated the mystery of its appearance to a distant second place, but it occurred to him it might reveal information about her. Just the thought of it somehow connected him to her, and he felt it burning in his pocket, challenging him to open it.

On the other hand, the last thing he wanted to do was open it in front of Tom. So he decided to wait until his flatmate had gone to bed and he would have the lounge to himself. But then another thought occurred to him. Perhaps the USB drive even had photographs of her. And once that thought became lodged it was more than he could do to wait. Besides

Tom looked set in for the evening, and already stoned. Quietly Jamie pulled out his laptop computer and opened the lid. Tom said nothing but flicked through the endless channels with the remote control.

When the computer booted Jamie pulled out the USB drive and pulled off the cap. He looked at the end, suddenly nervous about what he would find. He thought again at how this had been hidden - or was it hidden? Could it have simply fallen down the back of the worktop? With all that had happened since, he wasn't so sure now.

His screen went black, and then came back, this time showing an image of a yacht, sitting at anchor on a misty sea: Jamie's desktop image. Jamie plugged the drive in.

Almost in a mockery of Jamie's nerves, nothing at all happened. He had forgotten to find the drive and click it to open. When he did so he noticed the drive had a name.

F: Aphrodite

He clicked it. The computer whirred for a while. Then it demanded a password.

Jamie stared at the screen for a long while. He realised he was utterly defeated at the very first hurdle. Possibilities appeared hopefully in his mind. The girl's names? Joanne? *Alice?* His stomach lurched at the thought of her name. What was happening to him? He had to make an effort to concentrate again - it wouldn't be their names, that was too simple. Their dates of birth? Maybe, but he didn't know what they were. He realised he had no chance.

"Yo dude. What you doing?" Tom's voice interrupted him. Evidently there was nothing on any of the four hundred channels he'd tried. The screen was pointed away from his friend, so Jamie nonchalantly flipped it down.

"Nothing much."

"You working again?"

"No. I mean I was going to. Not sure now."

"What's that?" Tom pointed to the drive, which was still plugged into the side of the laptop.

"Just a USB drive." Jamie replied.

"No it's not." Tom said.

Jamie looked up at his friend part worried part confused.

"It's not *just* a USB drive. It's a *leather-bound* USB drive. You posh bastard." Tom went on. It was one of his favourite themes for winding Jamie up. That the reason Jamie never had any cash - and was sleeping on the couch in their house - was that he had some secret life he never told them about, with expensive tastes. He said it with compassion though. Everyone knew how hard Jamie worked, and how tough his background had been.

"Honestly dude, you can get plastic ones of those. Save you a fortune."

Jamie smiled. Something about Tom's friendly tone made him want to talk about the drive anyway. Or more correctly, to talk about the girl.

"It's not mine anyway."

Tom waved the excuse away as if it didn't affect his argument.

"I found it at the house I was in today. You know the big one by the beach?

This made Tom sit up a little straighter on the sofa. But only a little. "You found it? What, they give it to you?"

"No. I found it. I think it must have slipped down the back of the kitchen top. I kind of picked it up, by accident."

Tom frowned. "You picked it up *by accident?*" Tom wore a delighted smile now. "You mean you nicked it."

"No, it wasn't like that," Jamie stopped, a little confused now about *how* it had been. "I was distracted. You see there was this girl. She's one of the daughters that lives there and she came by..."

"What's on it?"

Jamie stopped talking. "I don't know. It's protected by a password. But this girl. She's really, *really* hot. I mean like nothing you've ever seen before. And I was kind of worried that the drive might contain something private about the family. So I wanted to see it before the other guys there did. Just to make sure it was nothing..."

Tom held up a hand, and eventually Jamie stopped talking.

"Whoa there Jamie. What the *hell* are you on about?" Tom stared at him for a moment. Then he shifted closer on the sofa and pulled open the screen on the computer.

"So just to be clear, you stole a computer drive from a multimillionaire whose daughter you want to bone? Any idea what the password is?"

Jamie was about to question the accuracy of the summary but he decided it was kind of fair.

"No."

Tom found the drive from the computer's menu and clicked it. Again the dialogue box came up, the word 'password' blinking in the centre of the screen.

"What's her name? This girl?" he said. "Alice." Jamie replied. As he spoke he realised it was the first time he had said the name out loud. The word felt strange and exotic in his mouth.

"Alice what?" It didn't sound quite as special when Tom said it.

"Belhaven, I think." Jamie considered for the first time the possibility that the girl was married. But no, she hadn't been wearing a ring, he'd noticed her bare hands. Slim, elegant fingers.

"But that's not going to be the password, and you might end up locking it." Jamie reached out to pull the laptop away from Tom, but he was too slow and Tom slid it away from him.

"I'm not trying to break the password you moron. I'm googling her. You said she was hot."

He stared at the screen for a few moments, his forehead furrowed as he worked. Then he sat back. He whistled.

"This her?" He turned to screen to Jamie. He'd selected one photograph from a Google image search. It showed the family dressed up for some business occasion. The father seemed to be accepting some award, but the photographer had made sure that the daughters were prominent in the shot. Alice and her sister stood beside him, smiling and wearing summer dresses.

"Actually which one is she? They're both hot."

This time Jamie felt genuinely surprised. To him it seemed impossible that anyone could question which of the two girls was the one that had caught his imagination.

"The younger one..." He leaned in, realising this was a rich source of information that he had so far overlooked. "What does it say about her?"

But Tom had already clicked onto a new browser window and his fingers turned to a blur while he typed something else.

"Here we go," he said, a second later.

"What? What are you doing Tom?"

"Wow, her dad's on the *Sunday Times* Rich List. Pretty hot wife too." He whistled.

"Let me see," Jamie tried again, but again Tom moved the laptop out of his grasp.

"Oh hang on, scrap that."

Jamie gave up asking and shifted closer on the sofa so he could see the screen as well.

"That should be *was* on the Rich List."

Jamie leaned in closer. Tom had pulled up another image, this one from the local online newspaper. It showed the girls again, this time standing front row, dressed in black at a graveside. The headline read:

Family grieve as local businessman's body finally released for burial

"He's dead. You can tell the quality of a bird though, from how well they scrub up for a funeral."

Jamie tugged the laptop from his friend's grip and ignored him, reading the rest of the article.

6

It was fate that played the next part. Or plain luck. Good or bad, depending upon your point of view.

It was more than a week after Jamie had finished the kitchen fitting job, he was sitting behind the till at the Shell petrol station that led out of town. It was past midnight and he had his text books open in front of him. Although it had been busier earlier, for the last quarter of an hour there had been no customers at all, and he had made good progress on the essay he was writing. He sipped coffee from a cardboard Costa cup as he typed into his laptop. His attention was half-taken by the till beeping as a customer pulled up at one of the pumps outside. He didn't even look up before pressing the button that released the fuel. A few minutes later a different beep sounded, this time from the door, indicating the customer had finished fuelling, and had now come in to pay. Still Jamie didn't look up. His peripheral vision - and the experience of many nights such as this - told him the customer, a woman, wasn't coming directly to pay but browsing the magazines. So he finished the sentence he was writing. And only when he sensed she was standing in front of the desk, ready to pay, did he pull his attention off the books.

Neither Alice, nor her mother or sister returned to the beach house after that one visit, although Jamie found himself lingering by the photo wall, and hoping to see their white Range Rover every time he walked downstairs. As the days passed it began to feel like he may never have actually seen her at all. It took the shape of a dream.

And so now, he felt a jolt run through his body. Like he'd been snapped instantly back into that dream. But it wasn't a dream, that much was also clear. There was no mistaking the reality of it. Her blond hair, the shape of her face. That half-smile. For a second he wondered if she might not recognise him. He almost hoped she wouldn't. But there was nowhere to hide. She had to pay for her fuel, he had to take the payment. They were forced to meet.

And the next moment he saw the recognition in her eyes. Her mouth fell a little open in surprise. He saw the tip of her tongue. For a long second their eyes stayed locked on each other. Then she recovered.

"Well, well," Alice said cocking her head on to one side now. She did nothing to hide the full smile that now emerged on her lips.

"Hello," said Jamie. It wasn't the greatest opening line but her sudden appearance was so unexpected, and the reaffirmation of her beauty so overpowering, he couldn't think of anything else to say.

"So you work here as well?" Alice said, raising one eyebrow. He managed to confirm that he did with a nod, and then there was a short silence. It wasn't awkward though. Alice kept her eyes on Jamie and he let his gaze rest on her face too. Then he thought he ought to think of something else to say.

"How's the kitchen?"

"Oh it's wonderful. *So* much better than that terrible old one." Alice replied. The touch of irony was light. "I don't know how we coped before."

Jamie grinned at her, but didn't know what to say next. Neither, it turned out, did she.

"I'm just putting some petrol in mum's car." Jamie glanced outside now and saw the Range Rover parked by pump number two.

"Obviously I wouldn't drive that myself by choice," Alice said "You know I'd have a Lamborghini, or - I don't know - a Jaguar." Alice already had her credit card in her hand and she held it up for Jamie. She wrinkled her nose. "Obviously I'm joking, and I don't even know about cars. It wouldn't be a Jaguar would it? That's what old men drive."

"Probably," Jamie said.

"You don't know much about cars then?"

"Not really."

"I don't actually have one at all," she went on. She liked to fill silences, Jamie decided. "I do need to buy one though, I can't keep being driven around by mum my whole life."

Alice seemed to stop herself with an effort. Then she shrugged then smiled again. Jamie was reminded of how she'd smiled in the beach house, how it had lit up that already beautifully decorated room.

"So this is your place then? I love the way you've done it. Chocolate aisles are so *in* these days." Her eyes twinkled with fun, and he began to relax.

"Feel free to wander around, enjoy the ambiance. Maybe get some ideas for your next room makeover," he said, but she didn't move. Instead she cocked her head onto one side. Jamie decided it was perhaps the most endearing thing he'd ever seen.

Then she screwed up her face. "Are you here all night? Don't you get bored? What do you *do* all night?" Alice asked, and she leaned over the counter. Her eyes alighted on the computer and the books Jamie had open. Jamie tried to cover them quickly but he was too slow.

"Whoa," Alice said. "What is that? What are you hiding?"

He tried to keep them covered, but she teased him some more.

"Come on, let me see."

He moved his arms. " They're just books. Textbooks," Jamie said.

Alice's eyebrow rose a fraction higher. She turned her head to help her read the title of the topmost book.

"*Textbook of...* Move your arm will you." Jamie did what she said, letting her see the full title. "*Medical Physiology*. What's that?" Her brow wrinkling slightly again. The contrast of her smooth skin and that crinkle made her look even more attractive.

"Medical textbooks? Why are you reading those?" She paused just long enough to change course. "Stupid question. Obviously you're reading them for fun because that's what *everyone* does. Are you a student?"

Jamie smiled. "I'm a medical student. I've got exams coming up in a couple of weeks. I've not had much chance to study recently."

"Because you were fitting Mum's new kitchen, which she didn't even need? And now you're working here as well. God how *unworthy* does that make me feel?" Jamie realised Alice was looking closely at his face.

"You're really studying medicine? I thought you were just..." She stopped.

"Sorry," she said. "I'm such a snob."

Jamie smiled.

"That's OK." He took in her face, her bright, clear eyes. Her clothes expensive and elegant. The luxury car parked on the station forecourt outside, and he thought of what Steve had said when they saw her photograph together.

She's out of your league mate.

"You know I did think there was a little more to you than just a kitchen fitter," Alice said, as if she had been reading his thoughts. Jamie didn't know how to reply.

But then she held up her card, as if to remind him he needed to process the sale. And Jamie knew that the moment they finished she would turn around and walk out of his life. And that whatever chance or fate had brought them together had done its best, and now it was up to him. Unless he did something, unless he said something *right now*, he would never see her again. As he rang through the sale his mind raced. For a desperate second he thought about telling her about the memory stick he had taken from her house, but he stopped himself - aware of how that would look.

No. There had to be something else. He thought about the house. The photographs on the walls. The images of the man climbing the mountains, steering the yachts. He thought about what he had discovered online.

"I'm really sorry about your dad," he said.

He sensed her stiffening. As if, despite the flirtatious nature of their encounters so far, he'd crossed a line by broaching this topic.

"I'm sorry, it's none of my business." Jamie went on quickly. "It's just... it's just my parents died too and I know what it's like. No one knows what to say so they don't say anything." He held up his hands, so they wouldn't automatically press the button to process the sale. "But it's not my business."

He sensed her relax a little. "That's OK. How did you know?"

Jamie hesitated for a split second, then improvised. "Len told me," he said.

She frowned in confusion.

"The old guy who was working in the kitchen last week. He told me. I was asking him about the family who lived in such a beautiful house."

She smiled again as she accepted the explanation. But it was a sad smile, like bright lights turned low with a dimmer switch.

"What happened?" she asked. "To your parents I mean."

His gaze dropped from her face for a moment. This time Jamie hesitated for a different reason, as if to find the fewest words to explain his story.

"We lived out in Kinshasa when I was little. Mum and Dad were both doctors out there, working for a charity. One day they were flying to one of the remote tribes, you know, to vaccinate the kids. But their plane crashed as it took off." Jamie stopped. He shrugged. "No one on board survived." He glanced up at her again, then looked away and bit his lip.

"Oh shit," Alice said. "I'm so sorry."

"It's OK," He looked back. "It was a long time ago."

"How long ago. How old were you?"

"Seven."

Alice thought about that for a while.

"So what happened to you? Who did you live with?"

"My uncle. He didn't have any kids of his own. He was kind of the black sheep of the family. But he took me on. I came back to England, lived with him." Jamie shrugged like there was nothing more to say.

"I'm sorry..." Alice said again.

They looked at each other for a long moment.

"How about your dad? What happened there?" Jamie asked, although he already knew by then. This time Alice looked down.

"He was washed off a yacht." She seemed to force herself to look him in the eye. "He was doing a round the world yacht race. They were just out of Cape Town. In the Southern Ocean. He was washed overboard."

"I'm sorry," Jamie said. Their eyes stayed locked on each other. It was the first time Jamie had seen her looking serious.

"Mmmm." She said, a moment later, forcing herself to break whatever spell had been cast.

"Anyway. We're still running around after Joanne's wedding. We've got an appointment to look at *table centrepieces* tomorrow. For some reason we need to drive nearly halfway to Scotland to find any that are worthy of my sister." Alice rolled her eyes as she tucked her credit card away in her purse. She half-turned to go, but then seemed reluctant for a second. The thought flashed into Jamie's mind that he should ask for her number, try and do something to meet her again. But it seemed inappropriate, after what they'd both just said.

"When is the wedding?" he asked instead. The lightness that had returned to his voice seemed to mock him. To show how now that they had returned to inconsequential small talk, the opportunity was missed.

Alice's hesitation seemed to confirm this wasn't the topic she was hoping to finish on either, but she answered anyway.

"Next month." She said, turning slowly away. "And I better go. Mum's waiting up for me, she gets worried I've crashed, or been kidnapped." She rolled her eyes again.

And with a final smile she began walking out of the petrol station. She pulled open the door and it beeped in such a jovial way as to be completely inappropriate for how Jamie was feeling.

"Nice to bump into you again..." she said, and she paused, "Jamie isn't it?"

"Yeah," he said.

"I'm Alice," she said. He wondered for a moment if she might return, to shake his hand or offer her cheek, but she didn't. Instead she walked out of the door, glancing back once as she crossed the forecourt. She climbed into the Range Rover. With its blacked-out rear windows, he didn't even have the chance of a final glimpse of her as she drove away.

"Nice to meet you Alice," he said out loud.

And once she was gone he realised he hadn't even noted down the registration number of the car.

7

For the next two weeks Jamie tried to forget her. They moved in different worlds. There was no chance of them coming into contact again. And even if they did meet - perhaps passing in the street near the beach house - nothing would come of it. It was ridiculous to think otherwise. With everything else Jamie had going on, it was stupid to waste time even thinking of her.

But it was so easy to investigate her further online, that the temptation was overwhelming. And thus he discovered how she lived the life of a wealthy young socialite. Part of an exclusive set that included names he recognised - the grown-up children of businessmen, actors and politicians. Minor celebrities purely because of who their parents were. Their names - and that of Alice Belhaven - appeared regularly on the invite lists of the most fashionable and exclusive parties and events. Their photographs sometimes appeared days later in the society pages of the tabloids. Yet while some seemed to court the media, or perhaps didn't care when they were photographed looking drunk or dishevelled, Alice always avoided this. When she was faced with a camera she always maintained her dignity. Classy. Well-dressed. A little aloof perhaps, but still heart-breakingly beautiful.

And staring at such images did little to help Jamie forget her. Nor to improve his mood. She was beautiful. Rich. Well-connected. And him? He was a nobody.

So he tried to forget her. He tried to focus instead on his studies. His final exams were coming up that summer, and there was no question that he was behind where he should have been. In part this could be blamed upon his other work commitments, and his tutors understood this, but there were other reasons too, which were more difficult to talk about.

Yet the harder he tried to forget, the more he found himself thinking about her. His mind replayed the few words they had exchanged, and how things might have developed differently if he had chosen other words. If only he had asked for her number. If only he could see her again.

What he found most frustrating, most difficult to take, was his sense that they had *connected* on some level. Despite the gulf between them. Despite the walls of privilege and privacy the rich erected around themselves to keep out people like him, he knew she liked him. And miracles could happen. Eventually he gave up and let himself return to those online images again and again. He would stare at the photographs. Absorbing the way she looked. Allowing an alternate reality to build up in his mind. A world where a boy like him could end up with a girl like her. The problem at its root was simple. Deep down he knew he would never find anyone else as perfect as Alice Belhaven.

And slowly an idea formed. Or half-formed. Calling it a plan at this stage was probably too grand a word, since the chances of it working were slim, at best. But it was a practical plan, and doing something felt a lot better than doing nothing.

Since finishing the job in Alice's kitchen, the only paid work Jamie had done was his regular two nights a week in the petrol station. So when, in his online research, he discovered the name of the catering firm chosen to cover Joanne Belhaven's wedding, it was only a short leap to checking whether that firm needed staff. From there, it was almost no leap at all to filling in an application form on the firm's website.

As he sent the form away he quelled any disquiet he felt in what he was doing. It was just a job. He needed the money, and the chances of him actually attending the wedding were tiny.

And with the form sent off Jamie rediscovered a sense of balance in his life. It wasn't that he forgot about Alice. It was more that, now he had set in motion a chain of events that could - if fate so decided - bring them together again, it was out of his hands. If it was meant to happen it would. And if not, well that was obviously meant to be too.

He could live with that.

8

Jill Carrington, the owner-founder of Carrington Commercial Caterers, was an entrepreneurial woman in her late forties. She didn't need to work, financially speaking. Her husband was one of the top heart surgeons in the country, and his salary provided enough for the family to live very comfortably. But once the children were established in school she had become bored with the endless coffee mornings, yoga classes and otherwise empty hours between drop off and pick up. And motherhood had given her a taste for organisation. Now, ten years later, Jill's business brought in considerably more than her husband managed. She enjoyed pointing this out by driving a slightly more expensive Porsche than he did.

But she worked hard for it. For example, she was always on the lookout for presentable young people. Especially those prepared to work long, irregular hours for the minimum wage. And she liked to meet them in person. So when Jamie arrived for his interview with the firm, dressed in a suit and with his blond hair neatly combed, the interview took over an hour. But then Jill found herself enjoying speaking with Jamie.

* * *

He worked on two weddings before the marriage of Jonathan Heathcote-

Smyth and Joanne Belhaven. These happy events for the brides, grooms their families and guests proved hard work for Jamie. Partly this was because Jill expected a lot from her staff. Partly though it was because Jamie had exaggerated the extent of his experience in similar jobs. But Jamie performed at his best when put on the spot. When put under pressure.

So when, six weeks later, Jamie found himself travelling up to Oxford in a minibus to serve at one of *the* society events of the summer, he had already proved his worth and been promoted to team leader. Jill drove up herself in her yellow Porsche Carrera convertible.

The marriage service was held in a small private chapel in the grounds of a former stately home, now converted to a hotel. In this Jamie played no part. He was kept busy organising the set-out of nearly three-hundred seating places in a giant marquee nearby. But when the room was ready, he was dispatched to help the team serving canapés.

For Jamie this was the first possibility to actually see Alice for nearly two months. And despite the effort he had put into engineering it, he had been kept so busy he hadn't actually considered how it might go. As he walked across the closely mown lawn he began to wonder. How she would react when she saw him? *If* she saw him. Would she think it creepy him being here? Would he be able to pass it off as just another chance meeting? Should he even try?

The whole thing almost felt now like an unwelcome distraction. He was enjoying the job - the pressure and the running around. He even enjoyed working with Jill - or more precisely, working with a team of young people who held her in the same contempt that he did. And this particular wedding had an additional element to it - the high profile nature of many of the guests lent the event a buzz he had not experienced before. There were undercover security guards, recognisable by the discreet earpieces they wore, and their overly muscular necks. An explosives dog patrolled the car park, where bullet-proof limousines outnumbered the supercars. Some guests had arrived by helicopter. Just being there was exciting. So he calmed himself by deciding he didn't care if he saw Alice or not. Yet when he did see her, that would all change.

It was a warm day, a bright blue sky uncluttered by clouds. The ball-room, where the post ceremony drinks were being served, opened out onto steps that led down to the lawn. And the guests that began to gather there looked splendid in their fine suits, their colourful dresses and hats. At first glance it might have passed for almost any wedding - any extravagant wedding. But there were giveaways that this was a more exclusive affair. There were faces in the crowd that Jamie recognised. Politicians, actors and actresses, a few he could have named, but many who had that strange quality of looking familiar, even though Jamie had never met them. Jamie passed among them unknown and not really seen. Just another waiter with his tray of champagne flutes, his smart white shirt, his straight back and his polite smile. Until eventually he saw her.

Alice Belhaven was wearing a plum-coloured bridesmaid dress. It was easily the worst outfit of any young woman at the event, yet Jamie felt the breath physically knocked out of him as she came into view. And when she did, *any* sense that he was simply there to work vanished. The idea that it wouldn't matter if they didn't talk evaporated into the rarefied atmosphere. His thumping heart told him exactly what he had come for, and he wanted it so much he could barely breathe.

She was standing with her mother, some way away on the lawn. They seemed to be arguing quietly. He stopped dead, his silver tray still containing two crystal flutes of Champagne. For a second he thought she must see him, but then she turned the other way, so all he could see was her back, her hair heaped up on top of her head exposing the nape of her neck. For a moment he was unsure what to do, but then he realised it exposed something else too - the mother's glass was nearly empty. The opportunity he had worked towards for so long was suddenly here. His demeanour suddenly changed. As if running on some internal instinct he slowed his suddenly racing heart, he set his face back to a relaxed pose. And he began to walk forward towards her. But before he could go three steps someone stopped him.

"Excuse me? Could I take those?" A middle-aged woman appeared from nowhere, squeezed into a shimmering green silk dress. She smiled warmly, breathing fumes of alcohol and caviar.

"Hello? You seem a little distant. Are they working you too hard?" The woman lifted the two glasses from his tray and winked at him. Then another man deposited two empty ones without even acknowledging him. Jamie blinked twice, to bring him back into the present. He stared back at the woman, who still hadn't moved.

"You know when I was younger I used to work at weddings too," she said, in a conspiratorial tone. She went on, mouthing the words quietly "I married into all this."

She tilted her head to one side, watching how Jamie reacted to this. When he said nothing she went on.

"I never liked it much, all these preening peacocks walking around," she smiled again and turned a little, drawing attention to her ample cleavage.

"I do hope you're having a glass of that every time you go back to the kitchens."

Alice and her mother were moving away now, and Jamie couldn't help but look at them. The pathway he had seen through the crowd was closing. The woman followed his eyes with her own.

"Oh," she said. She sounded both disappointed yet intrigued. "Oh, it's like that is it? Well she is a pretty one I suppose. Even in that dress." Jamie dragged his gaze away from Alice and back to the woman's face, resisting the temptation to glance down. They gazed at each other for a few moments, and it felt to Jamie that she was reading his innermost thoughts as effortlessly as if they had been projected onto his forehead.

"Well *I'd* better let you get back to work. Or whatever it is you're doing here." Her lips slowly drew up into a smile. She held up one of the glasses, as if to toast Jamie, but didn't turn away.

"If you change your mind about her, do come and find me," she said, then suddenly she leaned in close and whispered in his ear. "People like us need to stick together sometimes." Then finally she did turn away. He watched her go, her behind swaying as she walked, sheathed in green silk. When Jamie looked away to find Alice again, she was gone.

* * *

Jamie's team was given five tables on the left-hand side of the marquee, too far from the top table, where Alice was sitting, for Jamie to have any reasonable reason to go near it. She was sat next to her mother, with a man on her other side that Jamie didn't recognise. The bride and groom sat in the centre, Joanne Belhaven's expression alternated between a hawk-like scanning of the room, and a fake, pouting smile whenever anyone caught her doing so. Beyond establishing that, Jamie was kept too busy to observe much. The wedding's guests were kept busy too, as a series of courses were brought out to them, the work of a chef who had his own TV series. Finally though, the dessert plates were cleared away, coffee and more Champagne was served, and the speeches got under way. This was the cue for Jamie and the other staff to be given their break, and some food of their own. When that was finished, and the plates washed and stacked away, about half of the catering staff gathered their things together and made their way out to the minibuses. But Jamie had already been asked to stay longer, to ensure the flow of drinks to the guests wasn't interrupted. And it was during this part of the evening, when the tables he was tending to had expanded to half of the marquee, that finally something happened.

It was the part of the evening when the guests were feeling full, in some cases a little drunk, and beginning to move more freely around the room. Jamie was among them, ensuring no one was without a drink. Then he saw her. Walking quite deliberately towards him, her eyes locked onto his. So he waited, his heart once again quietened in his chest. Time seemed to slow. As she came closer it felt as if the rest of the room were dropping away, the clatter of glasses and crockery, the buzz of a thousand conversations disappearing, as if someone had twisted a dial to fade them out.

"So..." She began. "You fit kitchens. You work in a petrol station. You're going to be a doctor *and* you wait tables at weddings?" She wasn't smiling, but arching one eyebrow. Jamie was hit by the scent of her perfume. He had to resist breathing in deeply.

"If I didn't know better I might think you were following me." She raised the other brow, putting two perfect creases in her forehead.

He waited a few beats before replying.

"You know I was thinking the same thing." Jamie said. "Here I am just trying to earn some cash and you keep turning up."

Her eyebrows rose even higher.

"I'm joking," Jamie went on. "The firm your sister used was advertising locally. They needed extra people for such a big event."

"Did they indeed?"

"Yeah," Jamie said. "I did wonder if I might see you."

Alice seemed to contemplate this for a while, unsure how to take it.

"Well now you have," she said at last. As she spoke her lips began to part in a smile. It was almost more than Jamie could take.

"You look beautiful," Jamie said.

The compliment seemed to take Alice completely by surprise. "In this dress?" She asked, her composure suddenly gone. "Joanne spent ages finding the ugliest one ever made."

"I've seen worse," Jamie replied. "At other weddings I mean."

Alice seemed to think about that. "Have you done a lot of weddings?" She asked.

"Yeah. I've done a few."

There was a moment when they were both quiet. Just a few seconds. For Jamie the sense of everything else around them dropping away was heightened. The only thing he saw was her face, the only thing he smelt was her perfume. The only thing that mattered was her. She smiled at him again - happier now. A quirky, lopsided smile.

"Well what do you think of this one?" Alice asked him, then grimaced as she glanced around the marquee. "Ridiculous? My sister being completely over the top?"

Jamie shrugged.

"It's her special day. Isn't she allowed to go a little over the top?"

"What did you think about the food? You wouldn't believe how much it cost. Did they give you any? I quite enjoyed the quail soup."

Jamie shook his head. "They gave me a jacket potato."

Alice's face lit up in delighted shock. "Oh my God. I can't believe it. I've discovered where my sister has actually *saved* money." She touched an arm to his shoulder.

"I'm so sorry you didn't get to try the soup."

"It's OK. I stuck a finger in as I was bringing it out."

Alice burst out laughing.

"What did you think?"

"It was a bit quail-ey."

Alice laughed again, this time tilting her head so that one earring rested on her neck and the other swung freely, the diamond catching the light. Somehow, beyond this captivating sight, Jamie registered that Alice's mother was coming over to where they stood. She seemed to be arriving from a different universe.

"Alice dear! What *are* you doing? Joanne is going to cut the cake." Jamie felt her mother look him up and down, and then dismiss him within the same glance. "*Now*." She smiled at Jamie, a blank look, then she turned to Alice and went on, more quietly. "It's not really the time to be chatting up the staff."

Alice's mother put her arm around Alice and began to lead her away. Alice did nothing to resist, but as she went she turned towards Jamie and rolled her eyes. There was a message in the look. Jamie had little doubt they would talk again.

Another hour passed, the dancing got under way, and there was less and less need for Jamie to be in the marquee. He rested in the staff area, listening to the thud of the beat and wondering if he might have miscalculated. Around him the rest of the catering staff were getting their things together. But then one of the waitresses came up to him.

"You're Jamie aren't you?" The girl asked, Jamie didn't know her name. "There's a woman asking for you, she said she'd meet you outside, by the fountain."

"Who is it?" Jamie asked, but the girl shrugged.

"I don't know."

"Young or old?" Jamie asked, remembering the woman in the green silk.

"I don't know," the girl said again, this time sounding annoyed, as if it wasn't her job to pass on messages to the other staff. "She's waiting for you now."

Jamie didn't bother thanking the girl in his sudden hurry. He got up and began to walk out, but then grabbed another bottle of champagne and glasses, so he could pass himself off as busy if he was challenged. Then he walked through the party to the door of the marquee and went outside. The air here was cool and fresh, the night pricked with stars and just a sliver of moon. He peered into the darkness, hoping not to see a flash of green. The sounds of the party were dimmed now.

"Hello again," she said from the shadows. She was sitting on the rim of a large stone fountain, her legs crossed, shapely and slim. "You're very busy aren't you. It's really hard to get a quiet moment with you."

Jamie smiled, intensely relieved. "They're working us hard."

"That seems to be the story of your life. Is that bottle open?"

"It can be." Jamie said.

Alice patted the stone beside her.

"Here let me open it. Give you a break."

When he hesitated she said it again.

"Come on. Sit."

Jamie did so, setting the tray down beside him. Alice picked up the bottle. Expertly she stripped off the foil and cage, and fired the cork high into the night sky. He didn't see where it landed, she didn't seem to care. She filled the two glasses he had brought, before presenting one to Jamie.

"I'm not supposed to drink," Jamie said.

"I," Alice began, "am a *very* important guest at this wedding. And you are being paid to make sure people like me have a wonderful time. Which means you have to do just about anything I want. And I want someone *normal* to have a drink with. Not Joanne's friends and all these awful hangers on. Here." She thrust the glass into his hand and picked up her own. Then she gave him a smug look. They touched the rims of their glasses and Jamie took a sip. The bubbles fizzed against his tongue.

"I've got a boyfriend." Alice said suddenly. Unexpectedly. "A fiancé actually. You should probably know that if we're going to do this." Jamie didn't reply, although he wanted to ask *what* it was they were doing.

"He's not here though," she went on. "He's working. He couldn't get away." She turned to him. "Isn't that ridiculous? They wouldn't give him time off even though we're practically *family*." She looked at him, tilting her head onto one side again.

Jamie wasn't sure how to answer. It felt like she had given him hope and dashed it all in the one sentence. He recognised it was the pattern of someone drunk.

"What does he do?" He asked eventually.

Alice took her time in replying. She held up her champagne flute with one hand and ran her finger up and down the stem with the other. Jamie watched.

"He's in the army," she said. "They're on manoeuvres somewhere. I'm not allowed to tell you." She smiled knowingly.

"It's a secret."

"How long have you been together?" Jamie asked. He didn't know where this was going, but he sensed he should keep her talking.

"Oh just about forever." Alice said, and again they sat there in silence.

Jamie thought of the distance between his thigh and hers. When he'd sat down that inch of space felt intimate. Suddenly it felt like a mile.

"And now that my sister is married off," Alice's voice was bright again. She spoke quickly and with forced upbeat tone, "I guess everyone's attention will be on *my* wedding."

In turn Jamie tried to force himself to sound happier than he felt.

"Are you planning a lavish affair like this one?"

"I can't think of anything worse." Alice took a long drink from her champagne. "Can you? Anyway. Let's talk about something else. Why do you want to be a doctor?"

Jamie was so surprised by the sudden shift he answered at once. Before he'd had a chance to think about it.

"I've always wanted to be a doctor." He said. "Ever since I was little."

"Why?" Alice asked at once. "Do you like ill people?"

Jamie laughed without a moment's thought. "No. Not particularly," he said, when he recovered. Perhaps she wasn't drunk. Perhaps this was just how she was.

"Then why be a doctor? When you're going to be surrounded by them?"

This time Jamie took a second to think before answering."I suppose I just like the idea of it." Jamie said. "When I was young I liked the idea of going round people's houses with my brown medical bag. Just going into their lives to help them a little bit and then going away again."

"You're funny." Alice said. That doesn't even happen anymore."

"I know."

She gave him a quizzical look. "I can't imagine what you must think of me and my family." Alice said suddenly. "With our ridiculous homes, and our ludicrous weddings."

"I don't think anything about your family."

"Liar," she said. "It's alright. I'd think the same if I was in your position."

There was a silence. Jamie took another sip from his own glass. He glanced across at Alice, enjoying the sensation of her sitting there, and no one else around. He wanted to ask her what she'd meant.

If we're going to do this.

"I saw you talking to Melanie Smithe-Jones," Alice said, not looking at him.

"Who?"

"The woman in the green dress. Flashing her boobs at you. You should be careful with her."

Jamie turned to Alice, his mouth open in surprise. "Why?"

"She's a psychopath, that's why. Twice married, to some of the richest men in the country. Now twice *widowed*." She smiled sardonically. "Her husbands keep having accidents. They say she's on the prowl for a new one. Doesn't need the money this time. So just a friendly warning."

Jamie laughed again.

"You don't think..."

But he didn't finish the sentence. Because at that moment he sensed Alice stiffen a little. A man had appeared in the illuminated doorway of the marquee. He stood for a moment, looking around. Then he seemed to notice them in the darkness. But he didn't move, instead standing awkwardly. Then he pulled out a cigar from his jacket pocket and began to light it with a gold lighter. When he was done puffing out clouds of smoke, he glanced across again at Alice and Jamie, but this time he raised a hand in recognition and began to walk towards them. When he came close Alice dropped lightly off the stone seat and allowed him to kiss her on the cheek.

"Hello Peter," she said. "You look a little lost."

He smiled. "No, not lost, just needed some air." He held up the cigar and then looked at Jamie. His eyes narrowed a little and a confident smile spread across his lips. "And you must be...?"

"This is Jamie," Alice said quickly. "He's an old school friend." She turned to Jamie and continued. "This is my Uncle Peter. He's a *very good* friend of the family." She held his gaze for long enough to send a message into Jamie's eyes.

The smile on the man's lips thinned. "*School friend?*" He peered closely at Jamie. Unseen in the darkness she nudged him with an elbow.

"That's right." Jamie said.

"You were at Abingdon College?" The man went on. He sounded more confused than disbelieving, but there was a challenge in his words as well. Alice turned towards Jamie too, waiting to see what he'd say.

"I..." Jamie began. "Yeah, that's right."

The man turned back to Alice. "I didn't know they'd opened it up to boys?"

Alice giggled.

"*He* didn't go to Abingdon, silly. I was good friends with his sister. Wasn't I Jamie?"

"Yeah." Jamie replied slowly, watching her smile. "That's right. Georgina. Georgie."

The man didn't seem to know if he was being pranked or not.

"I see," he said. He looked again at Jamie, this time taking in the waiter's outfit. He flashed Alice a questioning, slightly indulgent look. Alice beamed back at him, as if demanding he make the next move.

"Well, don't stay outside too long. You don't want to catch a cold." He seemed to delay for a moment. He held out a hand to Jamie. "Jamie," he said, puffing again on his cigar. "

Jamie shook the hand.

"I won't," Alice said. "We're just catching up a bit."

The man moved away, only glancing back once before disappearing back into the marquee.

"He's mum's spy." Alice said, once he was out of sight.

Not knowing how to take this, Jamie stayed quiet.

"And what's with *Georgie*?" Alice went on. "You could have picked a more common name. He'll probably have his people check Abingdon's records and discover there's never been a Georgina there. Then he'll know I'm lying." She gave Jamie a shove.

"What do you mean his people?" Jamie asked.

Alice looked at him as if the question surprised her.

"Do you know who that was?" she asked.

Jamie thought for a second. "No. Should I?"

Alice seemed delighted by his answer. Her face broke again into a wide smile.

"He did look a bit familiar," Jamie went on.

Alice mimicked what he said. "*He did look a bit familiar?* He will the next time you see him."

Jamie stared at her, waiting. "Aren't you gonna tell me?"

"No I'm bloody well not going to tell you." Alice tilted her head back and put her nose high in the air. "Figure it out for yourself." Then she smiled and pushed him playfully.

"Anyway, I don't want to talk about him. Or about my stupid fiancé who he came out to remind me of. In fact I don't think I want to talk at all."

He blinked at her, she was hard to follow.

"And since my mother and Uncle Peter already think I'm having an illicit affair, I might as well have an illicit affair. What do you think?" She watched him as she spoke, gauging his reaction.

"What?"

"You heard me."

Jamie stared. "I..." he began, but she interrupted him.

"When do you finish?"

"When do I finish? We pretty much *are* finished. There's a minibus to take us all back at 2 AM."

"A minibus. That sounds horrible. I've got a room here. Why don't you join me instead?"

Jamie blinked at her again.

"I'm in room 12," she stopped, thought for a second. "I *think* it's 12. It's got a brown door anyway, you can't miss it. Meet me there in..." she broke off again and checked a slim silver watch, holding her wrist up to the dim moonlight to read it. "One hour? But be discreet won't you?"

Jamie found himself nodding. Alice leaned in and kissed him on the cheek. Her lips felt soft against his skin. Then she set down her champagne flute and slipped off the stone seat again.

"Good." She sounded satisfied. "Well I'll go and convince my mother there's nothing for her to worry about. And I'll see you upstairs."

She smiled a final time and walked away.

9

Exactly one hour later Jamie stood in the corridor outside a brown wooden door with the number 12 stencilled on it. He felt nervous. A little disbelieving. Like his feet were floating just above the thick red carpet rather than sinking into it. He thought of her parting words.

I think it's room 12.

He looked around up and down the corridor in both directions. There were plenty of other doors. All solid, creamy walnut. All brown.

Downstairs the core of the party - the sister's closer friends - were dancing to a DJ that Jamie recognised from the radio. But the majority of the guests had either left, or in some cases, retired to the rooms offered by the hotel. The rooms which Jamie now stood in front of. He tried to think what he could say if he knocked on the wrong door. Room Service? But he had nothing to bring. *Fuck it*, he thought, and knocked anyway.

"Yes, who is it?" It was a woman's voice, annoyed. Clearly older than Alice.

Oh shit. Jamie dropped his head into one hand.

"I'm terribly sorry. I think I've got the wrong room," he replied, backing away before the door could open, but he was too late.

"I sincerely hope you haven't."

Alice dropped the fake voice and beckoned him with one finger.

"Well don't hang around you idiot. Someone'll see you." As if pulled on an invisible string, Jamie walked into the room, and when he was inside she pushed the door shut with a bare foot. She was still dressed though, he noticed her shoes kicked off on the floor. He felt nervous again, unsure what exactly would happen next. He didn't look at her, instead he glanced around at the rest of the room, although the only interesting thing about it was her. The only light on was one of the bedside lamps, casting a deep shadow into the room, making her face hard to read.

"Do you want a drink?" Alice said, watching him coolly.

Now he looked at her. She stood by the foot of the bed. He followed her eyes to the glass-fronted door of a small fridge. It was stocked with mini bottles of champagne, and spirits. "I'm not having one. I think I've had enough." She wobbled her head to mime being drunk.

"I'm fine, thanks." Jamie said.

"That's good, because I don't feel like waiting." Alice said. She stepped closer to him, so that he could feel her breath as she spoke. She lifted a hand and ran it slowly down the front of his shirt, as if choosing which button to undo first. When she selected one she let her fingers brush against his skin as she loosened it.

"You really did want an illicit affair then?" he said.

"Of course." She pressed herself up onto her tip toes and kissed him now. Lightly at first, but soon deeper, her tongue probing into his mouth. She tasted of alcohol. For a little while they stayed like this, her slowly unbuttoning his shirt and pulling his mouth hard against hers. Then when his shirt was fully undone her hand slid down to his belt. Suddenly she pushed away.

"I don't always take the piss you know," she said.

She reached behind to unzip her dress. She had to wriggle to escape from the plum fabric and she grimaced as she did so. Jamie eyes were drawn to her breasts, cupped in matching plum-coloured bra, then knickers. He felt his breath escape.

"Would you?" she asked. She stepped closer to him again, and placed one of his hands on her back. Their bare stomachs touched. He held his breath as he felt for the clasp, fumbled for a moment, then exhaled as his fingers managed to free it. He heard himself gasp as the bra slipped down, and he touched the warmth of her breast.

"I do take the piss *quite often* though. You should know that, if we're going to do this," she said. She rolled away from him again, and kicked the dress away from where it lay, entangled in her feet.

"I don't think I'll bother hanging that up," she said. "I'm not sure it's my colour."

"I *was* lying earlier," Jamie said. "I haven't seen any worse brides-maids' dresses in all the weddings I've done."

"I knew it," she replied, sounding delighted. "I can always tell when people are lying to me." She gave him a look, then leaned in and kissed him again. Then she pulled on his trousers, so they came halfway down his legs and he fell on top of her on the bed. She laughed, until they found a way to lie that was comfortable.

"And in all the weddings you've done, exactly how many times have you ended up fucking the bridesmaid?" She propped up her head on her arm.

"Oh about one in three I'd say." Jamie replied.

As they made love Jamie's nerves disappeared. She seemed to know what she wanted and he let her take the lead, marvelling at the feel of her body against his. The sound of her giggling and gasping. He tried to last as long as he could, and by the end she had thrown her head back and convulsed against him on two occasions, so he could only hope she was sated. This close, he couldn't read her. The feeling of unreality he had felt in the corridor was heightened. It was only in the details that the experience differed from his dreams and fantasies. The tang of alcohol on her breath, the softness of her skin, the music of her laugh.

When they were finished Alice leaned out of the bed and reached for a small bag that was up against the wall. Jamie watched her, marvelling at the shape of her back, and how it rose up into her buttocks. She slipped back into the bed beside him holding a packet of cigarettes. Without asking she lit two and passed one to him.

"I like to smoke after sex," she said. "It's intimate. Isn't it?"

As far as the cigarette would let her she snuggled down into the bed and watched him, a satisfied smile rested on her face. Jamie didn't smoke but he found himself enjoying how the filtered cigarette drew smoothly as he pulled the air through it. He listened to the rasping sound as the fire consumed the end. Then he became aware of the noise of music, still coming from downstairs.

"Sounds like the party's still going on," he said.

"Mmmmm. My family does like a good party." Alice replied, taking a quick puff and blowing the smoke away from Jamie. "Especially Dad." She turned and looked into his face. "He'd have been down there, dancing away till dawn." She smiled a little sadly. Jamie got the sense she wanted to talk about him.

"What was he like? Your Dad?"

Alice looked away again, she seemed happy that he'd understood.

"He was... He was *fun*." She said it like this was the greatest compliment there could be. "When Dad was younger, he and Mum used to host these amazing parties." She glanced at Jamie again, her voice animated once more.

"Like really wild. Dad had a motor yacht and he'd fill it with booze and not let anyone off until they'd drunk it all."

She smiled at the thought. Then she leaned away from him for a moment. Even though it wasn't finished she crushed out her cigarette in an ashtray, then she took Jamie's, took a final drag from that too, and stubbed it out into the remains of hers. Then she rolled over back on top of him.

"I think I inherited some of Dad's appetites," she said. Then she began kissing him hard on the mouth. Jamie's tongue was still numb from the cigarette, but he felt the wetness at the top of her legs rubbing against his thighs and belly, and he felt himself hardening again.

* * *

Jamie woke slowly as the warmth of the sunshine climbed into the room. It felt nice, even if he was too asleep to realise why. It was partly the lack of something - the grotty sofa he normally slept on, with its odours of spilled beer and spliffs, and partly the thick cotton sheets and the feather duvet that seemed to float above him. But mostly it was Alice, her naked form curled next to him in the bed, her chest rising and falling slowly with her breaths. He felt at home.

As his eyes opened wider, he saw her watching him, her blue eyes wide and clear. He held her gaze a moment, then took in the golden mane of hair ruffled around her head. She looked incredible. Unreal even.

"Good morning handsome boy." Alice said.

Jamie didn't reply. He just let himself fall into the beauty of her face.

She reached out and traced her hand down his face. Watching him as she did it.

"What are you doing?" Jamie said.

"I just want to remember this moment."

At first he smiled. Then something about the word she had used caught against the perfection of the moment.

"Remember?"

"Mmmm. My final fling."

Jamie felt his body tense up.

"Final fling?" The words caught in his throat.

"Before a lifetime of fidelity." She did her eye roll again, then smiled. "Believe it or not, I do intend to be a good wife" The smile fell off her face. "I don't do this all the time. I've never been unfaithful before."

So soon after waking, Jamie had no idea if she was joking or not.

"You don't have to..." he began, but he was interrupted by a mobile phone buzzing from a table over by the window. She rolled away to see where it was, then groaned and pulled the duvet with her as she stood up to fetch it. It left Jamie uncovered on the bed, with a view of her back and behind. She swore when she saw who it was, then answered anyway.

"Hi babe, how are you?" She said, her voice sounded natural and enthusiastic. Without looking at Jamie she walked into the bathroom and shut the door behind her.

Jamie could hear her speaking now but not what was being said. He soon felt awkward lying naked on the bed, so he swung his legs down and found his clothes, then pulled them on. Then he lay back down on the bed and waited. As he lay there he realised the warm glow he had felt on waking had all but evaporated.

When Alice came out of the bathroom, she gave him a look he couldn't read. She put the phone back down on the table and walked across to him. She was still wrapped in the duvet.

"So you can guess who that was," she said.

"Your boyfriend?"

"Fiancé. You forgot?"

He had. Jamie didn't know what to say next so he said nothing, and a silence stretched out between them, long enough to feel awkward. Jamie could feel the pinch of sadness on his features.

"Hey cheer up," she said. "We had fun." She flashed a smile, then lay down on the bed beside him. With one hand she gently pushed his cheek around so that they were facing one another again.

"You're dressed already? I was hoping we could maybe take a shower."

She shrugged her shoulders, and the duvet she still wore slipped down the bed, so that one of her breasts was uncovered. She leaned forward so that the tip of her nipple brushed against where his shirt lay open. She didn't notice, or pretended not to, but to Jamie the touch was electric. Yet the messages it sent him were confused now. What was this? The beginning of something, or the end?

"Come on. I'm not married yet," she said. "And I need warming up."

She led him to the shower, leaving the duvet on the bed. She set the water running, then took her time undressing him again. She pushed him under the water, and then followed him in. She held out her hand and emptied a little hotel bottle of soap onto her palm, then began to rub it onto his chest and the rest of his body. But she didn't talk. The one time Jamie opened his mouth to speak she put a finger to his lips and shook her head.

"Don't," she said. This time she didn't smile.

Left with only the sensation of her hands on his body, and the fizzing of the water, Jamie's mind began to roam. To probe around the hidden details of the world around him. He could sense the emotion in her actions so clearly it almost had a physical element. It was regret. Not regret at what they were doing, or what they had done. But regret at how they wouldn't do it again.

When Alice had cleaned Jamie, she invited him to do the same. She giggled when the little soap bottle slipped from his hands, and clattered onto the plastic tray, but it sounded forced. There was none of the easy laughter of the night before. Jamie tried to force his mind to remember the feeling of spreading the soap on her skin, but it felt impossible, and like the act of trying to remember, took away from the doing.

Before he had even finished Alice moved his hands off her, and let out a long sigh.

"Thank you," she said, with her eyes closed.

"I haven't finished yet," he responded. He picked up the shampoo bottle, to show he wanted to wash her hair as well.

"Mmmmm. I know, but I have to go." She opened her eyes, but only held his gaze for a second. "I'm sorry."

Then she leaned down and turned the water off.

"Besides," she said. "I don't really want to use that shampoo. It dries my hair out." She opened the door of the cubicle and stepped out, quickly pulling one towel around her, and wrapping her hair in another. Jamie watched her and then reached for a towel himself.

"You have to go?" he said, as she left the bathroom.

"Yeah. I have to go to the wedding breakfast," she called out from the room. "It's just a family thing. The happy couple are going to the airport straight afterwards."

"Can't you skip it?" Jamie heard himself asking. He regretted it at once.

"Not really," she at least had the decency to sound disappointed. "I'm already late."

By the time Jamie left the bathroom she was already dressed, in jeans that clung tight to her legs and a silk blouse. She was towelling off her hair. He stood in the doorway, his towel around his waist.

"Are you hungry? I can call room service if you like? You can stay for a bit?"

"What about you? Will you come back?

She glanced at him, then looked away.

"Well?" he pressed. He knew he was beginning to sound petulant, but he couldn't help himself. For a moment he wondered if her face might suddenly burst into a smile to say she was going to rebel. To say they'd have lunch together, to spend the afternoon in bed.

"I don't think I'll get the chance. But I think I have the room all day. You can stay for a while."

Suddenly Jamie knew that her leaving him there in the room would be somehow devastating. He shook his head, and quickly dressed again. She saw what he was doing.

"How will you get home?" she said. "Is there a train or something?"

"Yeah. I think so," Jamie replied, although he had no idea. He forced a brightness into his voice that he didn't feel.

Alice nodded this time, then she turned back to the mirror, and began applying makeup.

Even though they were still together, a chasm had opened up between them. It was as if they had already parted. Her mind was on what happened next. What she was going to say to her mother, how she was going to pretend nothing had happened. What she was going to say to her fiancé.

"Well I suppose I'd better go," Alice said, a few empty moments later. "Before Mum starts hammering on the door." She smiled. She looked fantastic, Jamie realised. There was no hint that she had been drinking. Nothing to give away how he had thrust his fingers through her hair. Or anything else he had done to her the night before. Suddenly she came right up to him. They stood together, not touching, but letting the air from their breaths run together. She stood an inch or two shorter, looking up into his eyes. The door loomed off to the right. Seconds passed. For Jamie each one felt like an opportunity he didn't know how to grasp.

"Thank you Jamie. For a most memorable night." She smiled at him, a mischievous smile, but measured too. She was in damage control mode, not wanting to lead him on. To give him the wrong idea. "It was a lot of fun."

Despite himself Jamie leapt at the words.

"Can I see you again?" he asked. He immediately regretted it.

She didn't answer at first, but eventually she looked down at the floor. And when she looked back at him the smile was gone.

"I don't think that's a good idea, do you?"

"Why not?"

This time she laughed. "Err... Engaged? Remember?" She waved her hand at him. To his surprise Jamie saw she now wore a diamond engagement ring. She must have put it on when he was still in the bathroom. She pushed herself up on tip toes so that she was able to plant a gentle kiss on his lips.

"No," Jamie said when she moved away from him again. "I want to see you again. I *have* to see you again."

"Oh Jamie," she said, she looked disappointed. He felt her hand on his. "Look, you're sweet. You really are. If things were different... If the world was different..." She looked away and fell silent for a second.

"But it isn't. Is it? We've got to be realistic."

She stopped talking. She stared deeply into his face. He felt like he was falling into the intense blue light that shone from her eyes. The intensity of it left him almost unable to breathe.

Then Alice's phone rang again, killing it all. She broke away from him, looking at the screen.

"Mum," she said. She pressed the button to answer the call.

"I'm *coming*. I'm literally standing at the door." Alice listened for a moment. Jamie couldn't make out the words being spoken but the tone was obvious.

"No, don't come up... Well if you *shut up* I can get there quicker, can't I..? I'm coming now." She killed the call, and then gave her eye roll one final time.

"I really do have to go Jamie," she said.

He nodded. He knew there was nothing more to be said. He was lost. He felt the pressure of tears behind his eyes and he turned away at that moment so that she wouldn't see. He opened the door, he stepped out and he walked down the corridor away from her and out of her life.

PART II

10

A lice checked her watch. "Mum, we're going to be late," she said.
Lena Belhaven ignored her daughter and continued flicking through the racks of clothes in the dressing room adjacent to Alice's bedroom. They were in the London house. The third floor. Above them two more floors lay, hardly ever used. When they were there they mostly lived below ground. Just below street level a large basement stretched out the full length of the house. Below that, a giant pool room had been hollowed out of the earth beneath the road.

"How about this one? This is more you."

Alice looked at it.

"More prostitute you mean."

"I think you'll find prostitutes don't wear *Versace* darling." Lena's voice rose to indicate her sarcasm, but Alice's matched it at once.

"I think you'll find some do mother."

Lena Belhaven stopped what she was doing to arch an eyebrow at her daughter, then went back to browsing. Alice sighed. It was three weeks since Joanne's wedding. Given how much they argued, Alice was surprised how much she missed her. But then it was the second sudden void in the family in two years. First Dad, now Joanne.

"Alright. If it'll make you happy." Alice began pulling her top over her head.

"It's not me who I want to be happy..." Lena began, but then stopped. Her eyes had caught sight of Alice's slim belly. Her smooth, young skin. Lena's face darkened into an expression of almost open envy. Alice saw the look, but just tossed the top on the bed and held out her hand.

"I said hand it over Mum," she snapped. "The taxi will be here any second."

Her mother abruptly looked away, and passed the hanger to her daughter. She went back to her browsing for a moment, as if to hide what she had been thinking.

"I do wish you wouldn't be so difficult all the time Alice," Lena said. "You haven't seen Andrew for a long time and it's important to look nice."

At the mention of her boyfriend's name Alice felt a confusing pulse of emotions. Anxiety seemed to lead the pack, though self-loathing wasn't far behind. Andy had been overseas working so hard and how had she repaid him? By having a one night stand with a waiter. Alice's nervousness, her bad mood, could be traced back to one thing - she felt rotten about the whole thing.

"Sorry mum," she said, in a rare moment of contrition.

Her mother didn't seem to hear her though. She turned her attention to accessories.

"You've got that nice Dior bag somewhere. That would go really well. You remember? The one I bought for your birthday." She began rooting around a tall pile of boxes that Alice had never put away properly. Alice watched her for a moment, and then slithered into the top her mother had suggested - a one shoulder lace top with a nude lining that was actually very beautiful. An image flashed through her mind. Jamie's hands stroking her through the silk. She stopped and shook her head lightly.

Where did that come from? She thought. She bit her lip, concerned. Jamie wasn't the first boy she had slept with while seeing Andy. But the others all happened during an earlier stage of their relationship. Their on-off phase - when they weren't *really* together because Andy hadn't wanted to commit. And he certainly hadn't held back in those days. Andy had slept with two of Alice's friends that she knew of, and she suspected there were others. Since then they'd been - stable. Happy. Or happy enough. And then, in those horrible weeks after Dad had died, Andy had gone down on one knee and presented her with a diamond so big she hadn't known what to say. And when he took that for a yes she hadn't stopped him. Instead he'd secretly filmed the whole thing, then put it on his facebook page for the world to see.

And if the earlier flings had been nothing to feel guilty for, they had also been easy to forget. For her at least. Less so for the boys involved. Each one had plagued her with calls begging to see her again. But with Jamie - nothing. He'd walked out that morning and she'd never heard from him again. Perhaps that contributed to her bad mood. To her anxiety. She didn't *want* him to call, but she had expected him to try anyway.

"That's better," Lena stepped behind her. "Much more sexy."

"Sexy?" Alice was shaken again from her thoughts. "We're having lunch with *Uncle Peter*. We're not having sex."

Her mother ignored her again. She continued to inspect Alice's reflection for a moment, making small adjustments. She went to push Alice's breasts closer together, to make more of her cleavage, but Alice slapped her hand away.

"It's fine, Mum."

There was the sound of a taxi horn from outside.

"Well I hope so," her mother said, still looking dissatisfied.

Inside the cab Alice sat in silence as the streets of West London crawled by. She ignored her mother as Lena gave a monologue on the posts of her facebook page, competition results from the doubles rota of the tennis club, photographs from a dinner party to which Lena hadn't been, and claimed she didn't want to be, invited. Alice stared out of the window, trying not to think about whether she would be able to meet Andrew's cool dark eyes.

Ping

Her phone was in the Dior bag. Automatically she opened the clasp, pulled it out, and saw she had a facebook message of her own. She got scores every day, inane chatter from her friends. She almost slipped the phone back without checking it, but habit forced her on. And when she saw the screen, it was like a kick of adrenaline.

Message from Jamie Weston

Her eyes widened in surprise. She glanced at her mother, but she was still blathering away. Alice angled the screen so that Lena couldn't see, and opened the message.

Alice, I know you said not to contact you again. I wanted to respect

your wishes. But there's something I need to speak to you about. Something important. Please get back to me.

Jamie

Alice felt her face flush. She glanced around again, this time noticing the driver checking her out in the rear view mirror, but as she looked up his eyes flicked back on the road and stayed there, embarrassed he'd been caught.

Jamie? She bit her lip again, enjoying the way the word sounded in her mind. The thought that he was somewhere *right this moment* thinking about her. It made her heart beat faster. She just wasn't sure why. Quickly she typed out a reply.

What's so serious? And how did you find me?

She hit send. She placed her palm over the phone's screen and looked up. The driver was now fastidiously keeping his eyes on the road. Her mother was still miles away.

The phone pinged again.

You're the third Alice Belhaven I've tried on facebook. Sorry...

Alice smiled. She could almost picture Jamie searching for her on facebook. Then she remembered where she was going, and who she was supposed to be seeing. Another message appeared on her screen.

Is this a good time to talk?

In reply her thumb flew over the keys.

Hardly. About to meet my boyfriend for lunch. Talk about what?

She waited, watching the phone, expecting to see his reply, but it didn't come. Instead she felt the cab slowing abruptly and swinging over to the side of the road. A bus behind them sounded its horn in anger. Alice looked up and saw they were there. Their driver tutted as the bus went past, deliberately leaving almost no gap and papping its horn again.

The restaurant had a four week waiting list for its high visibility tables, behind the plate-glass windows and in full view of the street. But it also had more secluded tables towards the rear. There was no waiting list to join to gain access to these, it was about who you knew, or who you were.

Alice pushed the taxi's door open and stepped outside. There was the usual sudden assault of noise and fumes. She checked her phone again while her mother paid the driver, but there was still no reply from Jamie.

"Alice? Are you coming?" Lena had brushed herself down and was ready to make her entrance. They stepped off the street and into the soft quiet of the restaurant's interior.

Alice noticed Andy at once, and her heart leapt in the confused, conflicted way it always did. Straight-backed and square jawed, he looked like a Greek statue come to life. He had his jacket slung over the back of his chair, his shirt sleeves rolled up, the upper parts tight against his muscular arms. He held a glass of wine in one hand, and was grinning broadly as he spoke with Peter. By his body language he was every bit the equal of the older man. When they noticed Alice and her mother, Peter pushed his chair back at once to rise, Andy was slower to do so, and when he did, it was a lazy movement, as if it wasn't quite worth his effort.

"Alice! Lena! How lovely to see you both. You look beautiful, you both do." Peter Rice-Evans held out his hands, embraced Lena lightly and kissed her on both cheeks. Alice waited, keeping her attention on him rather than risk looking at Andy. An uncomfortable memory surfaced in her mind, the way she had drunkenly teased Peter at the wedding.

"Uncle Peter," Alice said, when it was her turn. She didn't quite meet his eye, but he held her in his arms, as if to look at her better, and he gave her the subtlest of winks, like he was promising not to tell. Then he gently propelled her towards Andrew.

And for a second it was as if they were there alone.

"Hi babe," Andy said, his large, handsome head set on one side, pulling the muscles of his neck out of shape. She looked at him, his dark curly hair neatly cut. Her heart was still beating fast. She still didn't really understand why.

"So. You miss me?" he asked. Then without waiting for a reply he went on.

"Come here."

She stepped forward and he put his hands on her shoulders, one of them bare, the other sheathed in silk. She felt his fingers move slightly against the material. She saw his pupils dilate. "Well? Did you?"

"Yeah," she replied. "Of course I did,"

Ping

Her phone was still clasped in her hand, so she felt the message hit as well as heard it. She felt an overwhelming urge to check it at once, but of course she couldn't. Not then, not there.

"Of course I missed you, you big dummy," she said again, and then she leaned in, intending to give him a kiss on his cheek, but he tightened his grip, pulling her closer and kissing her, a little roughly, on the mouth. He tasted of the wine he'd been drinking. And just as Alice felt herself stiffen in resistance, he released her, stepping away to greet Lena, leaving Alice standing there.

"So," Peter said when they had all sat down. "It's so lovely to see you all. Especially to see Alice and Andrew together, after he was unlucky in missing the wedding."

Lena was the first to answer. She turned to Peter, her voice flirty, mock serious. "I still can't believe you couldn't do something about that. Brought him home early?"

He laughed. "I told you. I can't offer any special treatment. There are limits to my power I'm afraid," he replied.

Lena made a dismissive noise and turned to Andrew. "Well at least you could tell us *what* you've been doing. Have you really been to the North Pole? Or was that some form of disinformation campaign? Designed to trick us civilians?"

Andrew smiled confidently. He sat back in his chair, testing the strength of his shirt buttons.

"We didn't quite get that far north Mrs Belhaven. It was Greenland. But we certainly saw some snow."

"And what exactly were you were doing there?"

He took a moment to answer. Checked around the room to see who else might be listening. "We were arctic warfare training. Cold weather survival skills, weapons handling, that sort of thing." He shrugged, like it wasn't something he was able to talk about, but then he went on anyway.

"My section got the highest marks of anyone this year. That's why it was impossible for me to get back. The guys are relying on me now."

Lena simpered visibly at the thought of this. Peter nodded approvingly.

"Andrew's been telling me he has to be back at Sandhurst tomorrow morning," Peter said, mostly to Alice. "So hopefully you two can spend a little time together this afternoon." Then he turned to Lena. "And I'm afraid I do have to be back in an hour, meetings all afternoon." He made a face, then picked up the menu. A shadow passed over Lena's face, but she did the same.

When Lena first heard of Alice getting together with Andy she'd been thrilled. He was almost absurdly handsome, and he came from a very good family. Both his grandfather and father had served in the army before moving into politics - both serving in the Cabinet. Andy had been to the right schools and excelled. It seemed a given his career would follow a similar course.

Charlie Belhaven had been less convinced, initially at least. Partly this was due to his feeling - perhaps in common to many fathers of unusually beautiful daughters - that no man could ever be good enough. But there was also something else. Andy had never been able to pull off his arrogant confidence in the presence of Alice's father. It was like they were two alpha animals - the younger knowing he was seeking to steal from the elder his most prized possession. But then Charlie had died so unexpectedly, and this somehow allowed Andy to relax. He became a comfortable visitor at the Belhavens. Along with Peter Rice-Evans - who came frequently to console Lena.

"How *was* the wedding?" Andy asked. "Alice hasn't told me much."

"Oh it was wonderful, thank you." Lena said, casting a quick, disparaging glance at her daughter. "Joanne looked absolutely beautiful. It was just the perfect day." She smiled at the memory, but then her face dropped a little. "Or it would have been if you had come too."

Alice looked up sharply.

"Or if Dad had been there," she said.

A look of irritation flashed across Lena's face.

"Of course." She smiled again. "That goes without saying."

Alice had scallops as a starter, and a sea bream baked in cream for her main. Peter chose the wine, ordering a 1998 bottle of Pierre Lacasse Chardonnay for her and her mother, while he and Andy finished the red they were already drinking. It was all delicious, but Alice found herself eating mechanically, turned off from the conversation, not really enjoying the rich food.

The conversation left her cold as well. While they ate they talked about Andy's progress at Sandhurst, and what he would do once he graduated. Peter, who knew more than most about these things, felt Andy would probably not get sent out to Afghanistan, but would need to do a year in Germany. They discussed how this would impact upon the timing of Alice and Andy's wedding. Alice didn't contribute much beyond interrupting at one point to remind everyone that they were in no hurry. She had put her phone back in her bag, fearing it might light up and show another message from Jamie. But her mind was on what it might already say.

Eventually she made an excuse and pushed herself back from the table, hoping her mother wouldn't insist upon following her to the toilet.

When she got to the marble-lined restroom she shut herself in a cubicle and pulled out her phone. There were three messages, all from Jamie.

It's about your dad.

It's about how he died.

Alice I need to talk to you. It's important.

Alice stared at the screen for a long time. She felt a chill creep across her body. Sometime later - she didn't know how much time had passed - she heard another woman enter the restroom. Hastily she replied:

Call me tomorrow.

She added her number. She pressed send and put the phone back into her bag. Then she walked back out to her mother and her boyfriend and her Uncle Peter, and she tried to smile.

11

Andy didn't have to return to Sandhurst until the following morning, so he stayed the night. As soon as the Belhaven girls turned sixteen, Charlie and Lena had been relaxed about boyfriends staying. More so usually than the young men themselves. In those early encounters they were typically stilted and awkward - frozen with fright that the opportunity to sleep with one of the beautiful Belhaven sisters was being dangled in front of them, and all they had to do was get through a family dinner, complete with Charles Belhaven's loaded questions.

These days it was easier. Lena gave them the privacy of the top floor of the townhouse all to themselves.

Alice checked her phone constantly but Jamie didn't send any more messages. And Alice found - as she always did on actually spending time with Andy - that she warmed to him again. Beneath the arrogance, beneath the sense of superiority and self-entitlement he was fundamentally kind. He was generous. He could even laugh at himself. She found herself relaxing, enjoying his stories of what they had got up to on manoeuvres. And when they had made love, and she lay tracing the smooth lines of the muscles on his chest, she considered her future with this man. She could do worse, she knew. In the morning she was sad to see him go. But he told her this was the last time. Soon he would finish his training, and they would see each other more often than a few times a month.

And once Andy had left, after she had eaten breakfast with her mother, it was Jamie who Alice felt herself feeling aggrieved towards. He still hadn't phoned, or sent another message, and somehow that felt like a betrayal. Like he was messing her around. She kept her phone with her all morning, and checked it regularly, but there was nothing. She found herself wondering if maybe her phone wasn't working properly - she had noticed it was behaving a little odd recently, the battery would suddenly die, or calls would be hard to hear. But whenever she checked, it was fine. And when Lena went out for the afternoon and he *still* hadn't made contact, Alice messaged Jamie again. It went unanswered.

Finally, in the middle of the afternoon, and when it felt to Alice like she'd waited in all day, her mobile chirped at her.

"Yes?" She answered the phone with her voice sharp.

"Alice, it's me," Jamie began, he sounded quiet and tentative.

"I know." Alice didn't tone her voice down. She was alone in the house, her mother still out.

"Are you OK?"

"Yes, I'm OK. What do you want? Why are you contacting me. What's so important?"

There was a long pause.

"You sound angry. Has anything happened?"

"No. Nothing's happened. Apart from you stalking me on facebook."

"I'm not... I didn't..." Jamie sounded concerned. "It was the only way I could think to contact you."

"And what do you need to contact me *about*? I told you what happened between us was just a fling. I told you I'm *engaged*."

Another pause. When Jamie spoke again his voice sounded wary. Perhaps wounded.

"I know you did. This isn't about that."

Alice found herself taking a deep breath.

"I'm sorry," she said. "I'm in a funny mood. I shouldn't take it out on you."

"Are you thinking about your dad?" Jamie asked. "It can take a long time to get over something like that."

Alice let out a sort of laugh, a bitter exasperated sound. "No. It's not about Dad." She remembered Jamie's message. "At least, I don't think it is. But maybe you should just tell me?"

At the other end of the line she heard him hesitate again. "OK, but it's not an easy thing to say." He stalled again. "Where are you?"

"What does it matter where I am?"

"Can we meet I mean? It's really difficult to say this over the phone."

She thought for a second. "Why?"

"It's difficult to say that too."

"Jamie. Can you just tell me, please?"

"It might not be safe."

Those words had a strange effect on Alice. They both enhanced the sense of anger she felt, yet cut through it as well.

"What do you mean?" she asked slowly.

"I'm sorry. I know that sounds ridiculous. It's just... Look, if we can just meet, I can explain all this."

This time it was Alice who hesitated.

"No. I don't think so."

"Where are you?" Jamie asked again. It was like he hadn't heard.

"I'm at home. In London. Why..."

"When are you next down here?"

"*Jamie*, you're not listening. Just tell me what this is about."

"I told you, I can't. Not on the phone."

"*Jamie!*"

There was a long pause before Jamie spoke again.

"OK. OK. I'm sorry. I'll tell you," he said at last. But then he stopped talking.

"What?" Alice said.

"I've discovered something," Jamie said slowly. "About your father. It might be important, or it might not be. I don't know. But I think I need to show it to you."

It took Alice several moments to realise he wasn't going to say any more.

"What something?"

Jamie didn't reply.

"Tell me Jamie. Just tell me."

She heard him sigh over the phone.

"Jamie, what the hell..."

"OK," he cut her off. "OK. Look I found something. When we were fitting out your kitchen. Something I think your dad had hidden there. It's... *sensitive.* I can't explain over the phone. I need you to see it."

She heard the sound of him breathing down the phone. Suddenly her patience went and she snapped.

"Jamie, what the fuck is this all about? This is my dad you're talking about. My dad who died."

"I know. I know. I'm sorry. I wouldn't have tried to contact you if this wasn't important. Really I wouldn't." He sounded miserable, but there was a determination in his voice as well, it was enough to pull her back from the brink.

She sighed a couple more times. "OK. *What* did you find?"

Now Jamie answered at once. "That's what I don't want to... Not on the phone."

Alice thought hard.

"Jamie if you don't tell me right now I'm going to hang up and block your number. I don't need this in my life."

For a second all Alice could hear was the sound of her own breathing. Then Jamie's voice cut in again.

"I found a computer drive. A USB pen drive thing. You know the things used to store files."

"I know what they are. What was on it?"

"No. Not on the phone Alice. I need to show you."

Alice was interrupted by the sound of the key in the lock outside. Then her mother's footsteps descending the short flight of steps into the basement. She walked into the room, shopping bags hung from each hand.

"Hello Alice," Lena said, before she noticed her daughter was on the phone. "I'm going to make tea. Do you want one?"

Alice responded by moving away, to the front window where light streamed down from the pavement above. She lowered her voice.

"You're really not going to tell me?"

"Alice I can't..." his voice began, but Alice cut him off.

"OK, where? Mum's going down to the beach this weekend, I can come with her. Where do you want to meet?"

He hesitated for a second. As if he wasn't sure if she was serious.

"Along the road from your house, there's a café, by the harbour. It's got a grey roof, and an Italian name, Ve..."

"Vesuvios. I know it."

"Can we meet there? Say Saturday at ten?"

"OK," Alice said. There was no enthusiasm in her voice. "Vesuvios this Saturday. Ten am. I'll see you there, and this better not be a wind up." Alice killed the call without saying goodbye. Then she let out a small frustrated scream. She put the phone down on the windowsill, a little too hard, then put both hands to her head, gripping her hair.

"Are you alright darling?" Her mother asked.

Alice brought her hands back down, and stared at her mother through darkened eyes.

"Yes."

"Who was that dear?" her mother asked.

"No one. No one important." Alice calmed herself down. She went to pick up her phone again, but then an idea struck her. She swung around and asked her mother a question of her own.

"Mum, Dad never mentioned losing a USB drive did he? With something important on it?"

Lena narrowed her eyes at her daughter. "I don't think so. Why do you ask?"

"I don't know. But it would have been somewhere in the beach house?"

"Alice, what are you talking about?"

"Nothing... Nothing." Alice waved her hand to dismiss the question. "Forget I asked. I'm just... I'm going to go upstairs for a bit."

Lena watched her climb the stairs. And only when she'd left the room did she notice that Alice had left her mobile phone perched on the window sill. Still frowning, Lena walked over to pick it up.

12

The man on the telephone was mid-forties. He wore an expensive suit over a lean, hard body. And though he was handsome when he smiled, he rarely did. Preferring to allow his features to take on an impassive set, which best served as a mask for the calculations going on underneath. The title on the door of his office said he was a partner in law, but in practice his work was more wide-ranging than that.

The office was satisfactorily high up, with views over the Thames and its network of bridges and roads that stretched out into the City and Westminster, as if they were the roots of some huge plant. When he had first moved in he might have pondered that. These days he looked but didn't really see.

"You don't have a name you say?" when he spoke his voice was rich, public-school diction. There was a pause while he listened to the reply on the other end of the telephone.

"But you do know the firm he works for? Let me have that." He listened again, and jotted down three words on a yellow legal notepad in front of him.

"Can you give me a description?" Another pause.

"Good looking? Well that doesn't surprise me!" He laughed quickly, then became serious again.

"And you'd recognise him? If we could get you a photograph?"

He nodded, mirroring the reply he'd just heard through the telephone.

Although he kept listening, his mind turned towards lunch. He was due to meet with Rachel. An intern he'd been boffing for a few weeks. He felt like booking a hotel room for the afternoon. He wondered what colour underwear she was wearing today.

"Well I shouldn't worry," he heard himself say. "We should be able to sort something out." He listened again for a short while then laughed again. This time there was little humour in it.

"I understand perfectly - it's just a precaution, and I think you're being sensible. And look, I'm busy this afternoon but have some time now. I'll get started, then when we've identified him we'll put someone on it."

Another pause, then another laugh.

"That's why we're here. To put your mind at ease." He said goodbye and replaced the receiver. Then sat looking at his pad for a time. He rubbed his chin, clean shaven, and stayed like that for a while, deep in thought. Then he snapped open the lid of an ultra-thin laptop that sat on the surface of the desk. The lid was fashioned from a sheet of carbon fibre and would have looked more suited to a race car control room than his traditionally decorated office. He typed a few words into a web browser and scrolled through the results. Then he took a sip of water, and picked up the telephone again.

"Carrington Commercial Caterers." The voice that answered this time was female, middle aged. She had a no-nonsense edge.

"Hello, I wonder if you can help me..." The man's voice had undergone a revolutionary change in its tone and texture. Now it was honey-thick and warm. "I understand you specialise in weddings? I've heard very good things about you."

"Oh. Well that's nice to know. Thank you." The woman's voice brightened somewhat in response.

"Tell me, are you by any chance the owner of the company? My reason for calling is a little unusual you see..."

The woman hesitated now. "Yes, I'm Jill Carrington. I own the business."

"Excellent. Excellent. Jill." He repeated the name again, as if admiring how it sounded. "Thank you." The man took a deep breath and began.

"Jill my name is James Collins. I'm a lawyer. I've just been contacted by a client who has asked me to track down a young man who apparently works for you. It seems he and my client formed something of a connection at a wedding you ran recently. My client is interested to develop that connection further." The man didn't hesitate at all. He didn't allow Jill Carrington any space to reply.

"Now I don't want to alarm you - it's nothing to be concerned about, in fact it's something beneficial to the young man in question. And it's nothing that will impact upon his employment with yourself. It's just a rather unusual matter." The man calling himself Jim Collins suddenly stopped talking. He began silently counting the seconds until the Carrington woman replied.

"I see," she said at last. As he'd expected her voice was thick with suspicion. "What exactly is it about?"

The man laughed warmly. "That's where this becomes a little delicate. I cannot say too much about it I'm afraid - I'm sure you'll understand." The man stopped again. He began doodling on his pad, his pen strokes light.

"Well I'm afraid if you can't tell me that, I'm not going to be able to help you."

The man stopped doodling. "Mmmm." He mused.

"OK. Look I'm probably able to give you some idea.... In essence the young man in question is rather handsome. He and my client discussed the possibility of him sitting for a series of photographs. I understand it's an opportunity the young man was favourable to, but they weren't able to exchange contact details." The man stopped now, allowing his story to sink in.

"I see," Jill replied. "Do you have his name?"

"That's the issue we have," the man replied. He laughed, a warm, friendly sound. "I'm afraid your hospitality at the event was rather too good. My client is unable to recall the young man's name. But he does assure me he would recognise him if you had photographic records of your staff... I know this is an irregular request but there you go. Sometimes I get asked to do the strangest things, I'm sure it's the same for you?"

Jill Carrington hesitated.

"Who is your client please?" she asked.

The man's grip on his fountain pen tightened just a little. But his voice didn't change at all.

"Ah. That I'm not able to reveal. And I understand this request will put you in similar territory vis-a-vis giving out the names of your employees, which gives us both a little problem to solve. Hence my calling you personally in an effort to bridge an impasse before it becomes a gulf - so to speak." He smiled and knew she could hear it on the other end of the line.

"Are you asking for all of my staff records..? I couldn't possibly..." The man cut her off.

"No. *Absolutely not.* I was hoping there might be a much easier way. I was thinking that if I passed along my client's description of the young man, then perhaps you would recognise it, and be able to help that way. He sounds quite striking from what I'm told."

Already in her mind, before she'd even heard the details, Jill Carrington was picturing Jamie Weston.

"I wouldn't be keen for..." She thought for a moment, searching for a way to phrase what she was thinking. "For your client to go poaching my staff."

"Oh *Good Lord* no." The man did a convincing act of sounding horrified. "I assure you that's not something that could happen here. We're talking about a day, two days at the most. No follow up, but very much something the young man expressed an interest in doing." He lowered his voice. "I should add, my client also has a daughter who's just got engaged, the eldest of three girls. As we stand they are also reviewing firms to cater for the event. And it'll be rather large no doubt." He chuckled.

"My client is understandably keen to look towards your company following the success of the wedding he attended. I..." He paused, as if the next part were delicate. "Your ability to help in this small matter of course is *entirely* unconnected, but knowing my client rather well, they are disposed to remember the smaller matters. I'm sure you understand."

Jill Carrington hesitated. It was the invitation the man was looking for.

"The young man in question is about six feet tall. Blond hair, blue eyes, around twenty-four years old, and as I say rather strikingly good looking. Does that ring any bells? Ding any dongs? Shake any apples loose?" He laughed again.

This time Jill laughed along with him, still reluctantly at first, but feeling better as she let her face relax.

"Well I think I probably know *who* it is. But would it be better for me to pass on a message, perhaps to contact you? It's such an unusual request...?"

The man sucked in air over his teeth. "Jill you *could* do that - you could. But there's another issue there. The err... The photographs they discussed are not of a commercial nature as such. More of a personal nature - nothing sordid, nothing unpleasant - but perhaps the sort of thing both parties would prefer to keep private. I'm sure you understand. Perhaps if you could just give me the details, then I could pass those on, and avoid any unnecessary embarrassment?"

Jill thought for a moment. Suddenly this was something she didn't want to be involved in. On top of that, Jamie Weston had already emailed her to say he wouldn't be able to work anymore weekends because he was falling behind with his medical degree work.

"Can you hold on," she said. The line went quiet for a while. The man waited, doodling again on his legal pad while he did so, his lightness of touch had returned. He had to hold for quite some time, and by the time Jill came back to him he had sketched a neat picture of a man standing on a gallows. Instead of a face he'd drawn a question mark. The other part missing was the rope leading to the man's neck.

"I have his CV in front of me." Jill Carrington said. She hesitated. "He actually doesn't work for me any more anyway... Look are you sure this is nothing dodgy?"

"Absolutely. You have my word." The man said, his voice still entirely reasonable.

"Jamie," Jill said, hearing the word come out before she really meant it to.

"Jamie Weston."

The man's fingers abandoned the drawing in a flash and his pen scratched out the name.

"Thank you Jill," the man said. His voice was still warm and friendly, but already the smile had dropped from his face. The view of the river and the city skyline was reflected in the flat blackness of his eyes.

"And any contact details you have?" Again the nib of the pen scratched across the yellow paper as she gave him a mobile number and a c/o address.

"Thank you so much," he said. Jill said something else but he hardly heard it, he was already replacing the receiver. Then, once the call had ended he put the telephone back to his ear, waited a beat and spoke again.

"Can you open me a file on one Jamie Weston? Put Kenning on it. Tell him to get started right away. Just surveillance. For now at least. Oh - and book me a hotel room for this afternoon will you?"

He waited a beat, then put the phone down a second time.

The man who called himself James Collins took a moment to fill in the last part of his sketch, adding features to the face of the man he'd drawn, and then drawing a neat rope from the gallows down to the man's neck.

13

———

The café was so busy Alice almost didn't spot Jamie. Then she saw him, sitting at the back, wearing a baseball cap and sunglasses, and looking uncomfortable. He must have been looking out for her though, since at that moment he lowered the sunglasses and half-raised his arm.

She walked over and sat down opposite. He had an untouched cappuccino in front of him and held his hands clasped on the table top.

"Hi," Jamie said, removing the sunglasses now. His voice sounded different to how she remembered it. Hesitant. Much less sure of himself than she remembered.

"Hi," she replied.

He smiled weakly. "Thanks for coming. It's nice to see you."

She shrugged, and was about to reply when a waitress came up to the table, notebook in her hand. She was a pretty girl, Alice saw. She saw her glance admiringly at Jamie before taking Alice's order.

Alice asked for a cappuccino, then watched as the girl wrote it down. Then she flicked her hair to try and make Jamie notice her, and walked away. Jamie seemed oblivious though, he kept his eyes on Alice, or glanced around the room. When he did so Alice took the opportunity to inspect his face. He hadn't shaved in a while - there was a shadow of blond stubble across the lower half of his face, but it suited him. She wondered for a moment how they looked, right now, as a couple. The thought alarmed her. She *knew* people around here. She suddenly hoped no one would bump into them.

"What's so important that you couldn't tell me over the phone?" She decided to get it over and done with.

"Would it be so bad if it was just an excuse to see you again?" he gave a half smile.

"Yeah, it would be. What's all this about?"

The smile on Jamie's lips faded but didn't fully disappear. "Sorry. It's just nice to see you again," he said. He opened his mouth to go on, but then stopped. At the bar the waitress was loading Alice's drink onto a tray. He looked back at Alice. *Hold on*, his eyes seemed to say. When the waitress put the coffee down she spilt some of it into the saucer. But with her eyes on Jamie she didn't appear to notice.

Bitch, Alice thought.

"So what's this about my dad?" she said again as soon as she'd left.

"OK," Jamie nodded. "OK. I'd better tell you."

But he looked around again first. Then he sighed. Alice just waited.

"Do you remember, when you told me what happened to him?"

The mental image of them lying together in bed flashed through Alice's mind. God she'd been pissed.

"Yes. Of course I remember."

"Well. The way you said it happened. I thought it was odd. You know?"

Alice watched him for a moment.

"Odd?" She said.

"Yeah. Was there ever an investigation? A proper one I mean. With the police? Because I couldn't find anything about one online."

"Why would there be a police investigation?" Alice said. "And why would you be looking into it online?"

"I'm just trying to understand. Because of *where* it was, how can you be sure what really happened out there?"

She stared at him. "Jamie, what the fuck is this all about? You said you found something. Some files? Some computer disk? Because I don't appreciate this." She glared at him until he looked down at the table.

"I'm sorry," he said again. He puffed out his cheeks.

"Look Alice, this is really hard to explain. I did something really stupid OK? Really bad."

"What?"

He sighed. Glanced at her again, then resumed staring at the table between them.

"That first time we met, I was helping fit the new kitchen in your house. Your beach house. Well, I was ripping out the old cabinets. And I found something."

"The computer thing?"

"Yeah. A pen drive. USB stick - whatever you call them. I hardly thought anything of it at the time. I just supposed it had been lost, or not important anyway." Jamie said. "I didn't mean to take it. I don't know why I did.... I literally found it just before I met you, and I think you messed up my brain a little bit." Jamie flashed her a smile but she didn't respond.

"You stole it from my house?"

"No. Not... Not *stole*, I just... Well, maybe I did, I don't know. I didn't exactly mean to. I was dumping the wood in the skip when I saw it. I was going to take it back upstairs, but then you turned up, and I forgot about it."

Alice considered the explanation, and then let it pass. For now at least. "Well what was on it?"

"That's just the thing, there was nothing on it. Or nothing I could see. I did plug it in to my computer that night, but I didn't see anything, I thought it was empty. And then... Well then things happened with you and I literally forgot all about it."

Jamie took a gulp of his coffee. Alice left hers alone and watched him.

"So it was empty? That's what you called me here for?"

"No. No, that's just the thing. It *wasn't* empty." He put the cup down and leaned in close to her. "The other day, I was moving all my stuff back onto my boat and I saw it again. I was going to throw it away, because I don't have much space, but for some reason I tried it again, and this time I realised it *wasn't* empty, the files were just locked." Jamie looked at her nervously, like he was trying to gauge how she was taking this.

"You live on a boat?" Alice asked.

Jamie seemed confused that she had picked up this point. "Yeah, a small yacht. It's cheaper than a flat," he shook his head like he wanted to get back to the point. "I know I shouldn't have, but I looked online, for how to crack open locked files."

Alice was frowning now, her brow creased.

"And what did you find?"

Instead of answering her question, Jamie looked around again. There was a woman, sat at the bar, that seemed to particularly trouble him. He shifted in his chair so that his body would block any view of their faces.

"What did you find?" She said again.

"Oh there's tons of stuff. Loads of software and hacks and things. There's whole forums of people dedicated to that kind of thing." He was swivelling again, watching as a man joined the woman at the bar.

"That's not what I meant Jamie. I meant what did you find on the USB drive?"

"Sorry," he turned back to her. "I thought you meant..." he stopped. He wrung his hands nervously together again. "Look I'm a bit confused about what's going on here. That woman at the bar... I know this sounds crazy, but I keep seeing her around. Her and that guy. Sometimes they're together, sometimes not, but I keep seeing them."

"So?"

"Do you recognise them? Take a look, but be careful they don't notice."

Alice looked casually over her shoulder. She saw a middle aged couple together. She didn't know them.

"What is it? You think they're following you or something?"

"I don't know. Does that sound completely insane?"

Alice frowned at him. Had it not been for the times she had spoken with this boy before she would have walked away right then. But before he hadn't seemed crazy.

"Yeah. It does."

Jamie screwed up his face at this, then leaned in close to her.

"Look can I just show you? What's on the drive? It's easier that way." he said. "But not here. It's on the boat. I can show you there and no one can overhear us."

Alice sat back in her chair. She pushed her sunglasses up into her hair and rubbed at her eyes. She didn't know what to think.

"OK," she said. "So where's this boat?"

14

"I bought her when I turned eighteen," Jamie explained as he helped Alice down into a white fibreglass dinghy. Outside of the café he seemed much more relaxed. He was much more like she remembered him.

"Mind your feet, the floor's a bit wet."

Alice sat down carefully in the front of the boat, facing the back, where she watched Jamie lower the motor into the water. When it was locked in place he pushed the starter on the motor and it sprang into life at once with a quiet purr.

"When my parents died, I went to live with my grandfather, he was a nice old guy but not exactly a good influence, if you know what I mean. Then when he died a few years ago, I got left some money. Not much. Not enough to buy a house, but enough to buy a boat. I thought I'd be able to live on her, and save money." He shrugged.

"I didn't have anyone left to tell me it was a stupid idea. So I bought her - could you untie us?" Jamie interrupted himself. The little boat's painter was looped around the ring on the concrete hard. Alice unwound the bowline and pulled the rope back into the boat. Jamie pushed off with one hand and steered expertly through the maze of moored boats and mooring buoys. He kept talking as he drove.

"I didn't know much about boats of course. She needed loads of work, which I ignored. So last autumn she had to come out of the water for repairs."

Alice watched him, sitting in the back of the boat, one hand on the steering arm of the engine, the other stretched out towards her and gripping hold of the boat's side.

"So that's why I've been working so many jobs. To get the cash to get the boat sorted so I could move back aboard. So I don't have to sleep on friends sofas anymore." Jamie said. He smiled.

Alice didn't reply. She didn't know what to say. She turned now, twisting her body so that she was facing forward, looking where they were going. To one side of her she saw the thick woods of one of the islands in the harbour, to the other were a fleet of yachts, lying on mooring buoys, their names emblazoned upon their sides.

"Is it one of those?"

"No. She's further out." Jamie said. "The moorings are cheaper out there." He seemed to remember who he was speaking to, or at least how much money her family had. "It's quieter too," he added, as if this were a factor as well.

When they cleared the boats he opened up the power on the engine and the boat surged onto a plane over the flat water. Now it was too loud to talk and she sat quietly, still irritated at what was happening, but less so. It was a beautiful day, and she had always enjoyed getting out on the water. With Dad gone, she hadn't been able to get out much. She watched as the wake from the little tender fanned out behind them. The only wave on the otherwise mirror-like water. They travelled a little further and then Jamie pushed the helm over so that the little dinghy turned sharply towards the island and a creek that snaked into its interior. The mast of a yacht became visible from around the corner, its hull still hidden by the land. Jamie throttled back and boat slowed.

"There she is," he said.

Alice was no expert on sailing yachts either, but she saw at once that this one was beautiful. She was about thirty feet long with a tall, single mast. She was built from wood, with her hull painted dark blue and her decks freshly-sanded and gleaming in the sunlight. The name *Phoenix* was painted on her stern. Jamie slowed the little boat further and made a turn so as to come in behind her. Alice picked up the painter again and readied herself to fend off as they came close.

"Here, let me," Jamie said. He took the rope from her and manoeuvred the dinghy so they came alongside without even a bump. He quickly looped the line onto a cleat. Then he stood up in the dinghy and held out his hand to support her.

"Go on up," he said.

There was a ladder hanging off the stern and Alice used it to climb aboard. She found herself in a compact cockpit, again made of wood, with soft, weathered edges, faded by the sun. The hatch to the boat's cabin was open. There was a slow, relaxed rock to the yacht under her feet, which felt different to the ungainly little dinghy. *Phoenix* felt capable, secure. Every little bit of her looked lovingly cared for.

"She's stunning," Alice said, despite herself. The enthusiasm in Jamie's voice, the way his eyes danced as he talked about the boat, had improved her mood. But even so, she still wanted to know what this was all about.

Jamie climbed up the ladder behind her.

"I've had her out of the water all winter - a lot of work. But I guess you can see. She's done now," he smiled. He looked happy.

"Oh..." He said suddenly, his face dropping.

"What is it?"

Jamie didn't answer. Instead he moved past her, hesitated on the companionway steps, then disappeared down into the yacht's cabin.

"What?" She asked again, louder, but he didn't reply. So she followed him down. It took a moment for her eyes to adjust to the relative darkness. But when they did, she understood.

The cabin of the yacht was a mess. It was only a small space, but every part of it seemed to have been turned upside down. The floor was covered in everything from oily tools to cereal. Alice felt it crunching under her feet as she moved around. Jamie was hardly moving at all. He was stood still, looking confused. Horrified. But then, moving like he were in some sort of trance, he walked over to a locker and pulled open the wooden door. Inside Alice could see medical books and charts, and Jamie pulled them out, slowly at first and then much quicker, leaving them in a haphazard pile on the saloon table. Soon the cupboard was empty.

"It's not here. I left it in here. Someone's taken it." Now Jamie stuck his hand right into the cupboard, feeling around even though it was plainly empty. He stared at Alice and repeated what he just said. "My laptop, the USB drive. Everything. It was all in that locker. Someone's broken in. Someone's taken it."

Alice felt compelled to walk over to the locker and have a look for herself. It was only a small opening, built into the headlining of the yacht, and there was no question it was empty. She swung the door closed on its little brass hinges. There was no lock, and no sign it had been forced.

"The door was locked? Of the whole boat I mean?"

Jamie said nothing. He seemed to be dazed by what had happened.

"Was it locked Jamie? The boat?"

"The main hatch was." He moved to look, as if he suddenly doubted himself.

"Look, someone's smashed it." He stepped back to allow her to see. The wooden hatch cover had a Yale lock built into it, just like any front door, but the wood around the lock was smashed. The fresh yellow-white splinters of the wood showed it was newly broken.

He seemed to stare at the lock for a long while, so that Alice felt she should say something, just to snap him out of it, when he suddenly stared at her, and held a finger to his lips.

She froze, her mouth open, and watched as he began creeping past her. He walked to the front cabin, where the door was shut, and he suddenly burst it open. He disappeared from sight for a moment, but then reappeared.

"No one there. I just thought for a minute they might still be on board."

That gave her a creepy feeling. She looked around, there seemed to be other possible hiding places if he seriously thought a burglar might still be on board. But he returned to the cupboard. He seemed to be looking into it from different angles, to check it was still empty.

She felt faintly lost. She knew it was a stupid question before she even asked it, but it seemed like Jamie had forgotten she was there, and saying something seemed the only way to bring him back. "And you definitely had the USB drive in that cupboard?"

Jamie looked at her and swallowed. He nodded.

"And you didn't take any copies or anything?"

Jamie just breathed for a few moments, but then he nodded again.

"OK. So where are the copies?"

"I saved them onto my laptop."

Alice put two fingers to the side of her head and squeezed her eyes shut, as if she was struggling to process this information.

"But you said the laptop's gone as well?"

Jamie nodded again slowly, this time watching her as he did so. Then he stood up again. He walked the length of the saloon then turned around and walked back. Alice persevered.

"You must have saved them online somewhere as well? You can't *not* save things online these days."

Jamie put one elbow on the table and let his head rest in his palm. He screwed up his face like he wanted to punish himself for his stupidity.

"I don't have the Internet out here. Only on my phone. I haven't had a chance to back it up yet."

Suddenly, Alice felt like she didn't want to be there. She turned away and climbed back up the small wooden ladder until she stood alone, in the cockpit. The morning sunshine felt warm on her face, and the harbour looked beautiful. The steep-wooded sides of the nearby island shone a deep, dark green as it plunged into the water of the creek.

She tried to think. To make sense of what she had learnt this morning. Jamie didn't follow her up into the cockpit, but she heard noises coming from down below. Eventually she climbed back down. She found him kneeling on the floor of the saloon, his head inside one of the cupboards. He had pushed all the rubbish on the floor to one side so that it was easier to move around.

"What are you doing?"

Jamie didn't respond.

"Jamie!" Slowly he pulled his head out of the cupboard and looked at her.

"I said what are you doing?"

"I'm looking for it. There's a gap, in the cupboard here. There's a gap in the back. Sometimes things fall down into this cupboard. Maybe the USB stick fell through?"

Alice felt a strange surge of hope. "Has it? Can you see it?"

Jamie hesitated. His shoulders slumped. "No."

The hope Alice had felt faded just as fast as it had arrived. Now she looked around again. To her right there was a small kitchen area - a galley, her dad had always insisted she call it. A cooker hung on its gimbals. A strange contraption which she knew would let it swing as the boat heeled.

"Can you make coffee on that?" She asked.

Jamie looked at her as if he didn't quite understand the question. She stepped over into the galley and began opening cupboards. Although some of them had been emptied onto the floor, most still seemed to be full.

"On your cooker. Does it... Cook? Can you make coffee?"

"Yeah."

"Well come on then. Since you didn't let me drink one in the café you can make me one."

15

Martin Kenning had served thirty years in the Metropolitan police when he was offered early retirement. He didn't want to accept - it wasn't the way he envisaged his career ending - but it clear that if he didn't, he'd find himself fired anyway.

None of his colleagues had any sympathy for the man who raised the complaint against Kenning. If he hadn't robbed the particular bank in question, he'd certainly robbed others. But they had little sympathy for Kenning either. His treatment of the man had been unnecessarily heavy handed, and was only the latest in a long pattern of behaviour. There was only so many times Kenning's superiors were willing to cover for him. Kenning might be a good investigator, but times were changing. Everything got recorded on smartphones these days, you just couldn't go around beating confessions out of people anymore.

But the incident, when combined with Kenning's otherwise solid career, was enough to flag the former policeman as a potential candidate before he even left the force. He was given a few months - time to realise that a life spent golfing and catching up with DIY was going to seem very empty. Then the offer was made.

The invitation to attend an interview was made in person - a pretty young lawyer knocked on his door with the letter. The envelope also contained generous interview expenses, in cash - a hint at how lucrative the opportunity might be. There were relatively few details as to what the job itself actually entailed however. That was left deliberately vague so that, when he walked into the lobby of the beautiful tower near the river, his understanding of why he was there would be mostly furnished by his own imagination.

He went to the interview of course. On a cold winter day with light snow falling softly from the grey London sky.

The man who met with Kenning first discussed the nature of the job - it was work that would make use of the expertise in investigations Kenning had built up over his career. He would work alone, or with a partner, provided by the firm, depending upon the requirements of the case involved. The methods he used would be his own business, but if an order was made, they would expect it be carried out promptly, professionally, and with absolutely no way that it could be traced back to them. They were very clear on that.

His proposed remuneration package was outlined. The offer was for a generous monthly retainer, with additional payments made when he was actually asked to carry out any task. The money would be paid through an intermediary company into an account hosted offshore. There wouldn't be any tax to worry about. When combined with Kenning's police pension, this would make a very significant difference to the lifestyle he would be able to enjoy. Although they were never mentioned in the discussion, a number of travel brochures and magazines had been left on the coffee table between the two men. One was for a Caribbean cruising company. Poking out from underneath it, a copy of *Classic Car Magazine*, with a photograph of a British Racing Green MkI just visible on the cover. None of these were there by accident, instead they had been chosen as a result of a report into the former policeman's internet search history. In the last month these revealed that two holiday bookings had been initiated - but then abandoned at the point the full prices had been shown on the screen. It was thought these had been carried out by Kenning's wife. Kenning himself appeared to have spent his time in front of a webpage called *Classic Jaguar Cars*. Indeed this was the second most visited website on his home computer. Although the number of hits it had received fell some way behind the pornography site *Barely Legal Babes*.

How did Kenning like the sound of the offer so far, the man asked. Kenning didn't say so right way, but this was pretty much his dream job.

That was five years ago now. And most of the work that Kenning had been asked to do since was easy enough. And quite enjoyable. He found he preferred being left to his own devices. No begging courts for warrants or permissions, no chains of command. And although there was no obvious career ladder he could climb, it was obvious that his new employer had come to trust and rely on him in a way the Metropolitan Police never had. The scope of his work increased. His employers became less cautious with what they asked him to do. But they never kept him too busy either. He found time to buy himself a beautiful example of a MkII Jag. His wife took to enjoying cruises. Often alone.

So when he got the file on Jamie Weston, he cancelled his plans (a golfing holiday in the Algarve), hired a car, and drove it down to the south coast. Now he sat, two days later, sipping an Americano in a café on the waterfront. His face wore a frown of concentration - reflecting, he hoped - his attention on the crossword in the newspaper in front of him. Every now and then he remembered to nod his head to the music he was pretending to listen to on the headphones fixed into his ears. They were actually linked to an electronic directional listening device that was concealed in the newspaper's folds. It was pointed at the table where the target - Jamie Weston - was sitting, looking uncomfortable in a baseball cap and sunglasses. And as Kenning watched and listened, the girl joined him now, a little later than planned. He listened. The audio was coming through clearly enough, except when they really lowered their voices. He frowned again, and in his crossword - as if he had thought of a solution to a clue - he jotted down his notes.

16

A few minutes later Alice put two steaming mugs onto the saloon table and slipped herself onto the bench seat. While the coffee had been brewing Jamie had tidied up a little, so at least there was somewhere to sit down. But now he was back to searching the locker, as if the contents might have magically reappeared.

"Hey," she said. "*Hey*. Stop and drink this."

He stopped and sat opposite her. She pushed one of the mugs over to him.

"So what was on this disk thing anyway?"

"USB stick, it wasn't a disk."

"Whatever. What was on it? You said you thought it was connected to Dad's death."

Jamie gave her a long look before answering.

"Yeah." He said at last. Then he paused again.

"Look this isn't easy to say. That's why I wanted to show you."

She waited. "OK." He took a deep breath.

"Your dad..." He glanced at her then looked away. He patted his hand four times on the table top.

"Your dad had a file of compromising videos that he kept on people. I believe he used them to blackmail people."

"*What?*" Alice replied. "That's ridiculous."

Jamie didn't say anything. He just waited.

"What kind of compromising videos?"

"Sex." Jamie said. "They were sex tapes."

"*Sex tapes?* What like, pornography?"

He shook his head. "No. No not like pornography. The people in them, they weren't acting. And they didn't look like they knew they were being filmed. They were just - you know. Doing it. "

For a very long time, Alice simply stared at Jamie, as if she couldn't believe what she was hearing.

"*Sex tapes?*" she said again. "Of Dad?"

"No. Not *of* your dad. At least, I don't think so. I didn't recognise him in any of the videos. Tapes of other people."

Alice stared at him still. "What other people?" she asked at last.

Jamie rubbed his face before answering. "I don't know. I didn't recognise them. To be honest I didn't look too hard. Once I saw what they were I mean." He stopped for a moment. Watching her reaction.

"This is why I didn't want to tell you in the café. Or worse, show you. The videos, they were..." Jamie left a gap for her to speak but she said nothing.

"Graphic," he finished.

Finally she shook her head.

"Why?"

"Why what?"

"Why are you telling me? What the hell is it to you if Dad wanted to watch that sort of thing? It's disgusting but - lots of men like that sort of thing."

Jamie thought before replying. Then he shrugged. "I almost didn't. I almost just threw it away. I don't know, maybe I should have done. But I thought of you, and I thought..." He stopped.

"It's your *family*. I thought you had the right to know. Or I thought maybe you already knew, and were worried about where the drive had got to..."

She looked at him like he was mad.

"You thought I already knew? That Dad was into weird pornography?"

"No Alice, you're not understanding. You're not getting this. It *wasn't* pornography. This was..." He stopped.

"What?"

Jamie took a couple of deep breaths.

"It was a blackmail file Alice. And the way it was hidden. It was like your father expected that someone might come looking for it. Like it had to be hidden where no one would ever think to look. That's the only reason I found it, because I was literally tearing your kitchen out." He was breathing hard now, they both were.

"How do you know it was Dad's?" Alice asked suddenly, feeling a burst of hope flare inside her. Jamie stared right back at her for a moment, then shrugged again.

"I guessed," he said. "C. A. B."

What?" She said.

"They're your dad's initials right? They were embossed into the leather."

Alice dropped her head into her hands and squeezed her temples. She knocked the coffee with her elbow, then angrily pushed it further away. Some of the hot liquid swilled out of the mug and onto the table top. Jamie's eyes followed the spillage but neither of them did anything to clean it up.

Alice looked up again. "Back up. Back up a moment." She said. "You're saying you found this thing in my house. And on top of that, someone broke into your boat *this morning*, and stole it?"

He hesitated, glanced around them before answering.

"I don't know... I guess..." Jamie was about to go on but Alice interrupted him.

"No. Stop this. There must be some mistake. Dad *wouldn't do this*. He didn't need to. He runs..." she corrected herself automatically. "He *ran* a highly successful investment portfolio. He had plenty of money, more than he knew what to do with."

"Well maybe it wasn't money he was after? Maybe it was information. What to invest in? Wouldn't that be important to someone like him?"

Alice was silent again at this. She put her hand over her mouth and looked away.

When she turned back her voice was quite different. Quieter, more accepting.

"What was on the tapes exactly? What are we talking about here?" He seemed a little less anxious, now he had finally revealed the secret.

"I didn't watch them all. Once I saw what they were I mean. That's when I contacted you. I found your facebook profile and I sent you that message... I hope it was the right..."

"Yeah," she nodded, interrupting him. "Tell me about what you did see though."

Jamie took a moment to think. "They looked old. The videos I mean. Like an old movie, it wasn't good quality footage. And the people's hairstyles and clothes - when they were wearing any - it looked, I don't know, 80s, 90s?"

Alice considered this. "Go on."

Jamie screwed up his face, like it was hard to remember. "The camera was quite high up, it was pointed down at a big bed. It was curved. There was a red headboard. It looked like the walls were panelled. Like lined with wood." He shrugged. "Quite a small room."

"How about the people? Did you recognise any of them?"

"No. The women looked like..." Jamie paused, looking uncomfortable again. "They looked like maybe they were prostitutes. They were wearing, you know, suspenders. That sort of thing. And they looked younger than the men. And the way they were talking..."

"The videos had sound?"

"Yeah. But mostly it was just... Grunts and that."

They were both silent for a moment.

"Do you remember anything else?"

Jamie scratched his head. "Not really. Like I said I didn't really watch them. Not once I'd seen what they were." Then his face brightened. "There was one other thing."

"What?"

"The name of the folder. All the files were inside a folder. That's why I didn't notice they were even there the first time I looked."

"What was the name?"

Jamie screwed up his eyes again. "*Aphrodite*. It was called *the Aphrodite file*."

Once again Alice's hand went up to cover her mouth. Her eyes widened and she stared at him.

"Oh my God," she said.

17

"What? What is it? Does that mean anything to you?"

Alice stared at him, not speaking. Her eyes were wide, disbelieving.

"Tell me... What is it?"

She took a deep breath. Before she went on she pushed the loose strands of her hair behind her ears.

"*Aphrodite* was the name of Mum and Dad's boat. Dad's boat really..." She hesitated, then looked around. "Not like this one. It was a motor yacht. I told you about it."

At once Jamie's brow creased in confusion. "I don't..." he began, but she cut him off.

"I thought I did anyway - at Joanne's wedding - but it doesn't matter." She waved the distraction aside.

"We don't have it any more, but for years it was Dad's pride and joy. There used to be a big curved bed in the stateroom. It's where Mum and Dad slept when we took it out for weekends." She hesitated. "It had a red headboard. I remember it." Alice covered her whole face with her hands now.

"Alice..." Jamie interrupted her, a few moments later.

"I used to play on that bed. When I was a kid. Me and Joanne would sleep in it when we did long trips, over to France or down to the Med.

And he was..." Suddenly she pushed her hands up onto her head, pushing her hair back. She stared at him, the pain obvious in her wide eyes.

"Fucking prostitutes on it at the same time."

"It wasn't your dad in the videos," Jamie answered carefully.

"OK," Alice said, moments later, recovering some of her poise. "It's just a bit of a shock to discover your father was a blackmailer." She laughed, then took a sip of the coffee. She'd made it strong and the only milk on board had been thrown on the floor, so they were drinking it black. "But we need to think about this. We need to work out what to do. What else do you remember?"

Jamie watched her for a second, then shook his head. "Like I said, once I saw what it was, I just wanted to tell you. I thought it wasn't my business. Just you ought to know. That it was better if you knew."

Alice sighed. She laughed again. "Dad was blackmailing people! Why do I want to know that?" She shook her head and suddenly looked around the interior of the yacht. It felt for a second like this was a dream. She even reached out and touched the polished wood of the tabletop, as if checking it was real.

"I want to go back to a time when I never met you. That's what I want to do."

She saw the immediate hurt on his face.

"I'm sorry," she said at once. "That's not fair. I'm shooting the messenger. You did the right thing."

The hurt look on his face melted away into a grateful half-smile.

"I just kinda wish you hadn't."

They sat for a while in silence. Alice drank more of her coffee, feeling the rush of caffeine around her body.

"So, what do we do now? Do we call the police?"

Jamie looked around before answering. "From what I can see, the only thing missing is my laptop, and the USB drive. And apart from the lock on the hatch, nothing else even looks that damaged. So I guess it's up to you."

"Up to me?"

"Yeah."

She looked up. "Why?"

Jamie shrugged. "Because this isn't about me."

She narrowed her eyes, trying to think.

"You reckon whoever broke in here did so just to get this file? You think they knew what they were looking for?"

"Yes." Jamie said bluntly. Alice didn't answer for a while.

"But. How would they know you had it?"

Jamie took a breath and held it in.

"In the café," Alice said suddenly. "There was that woman? You said you thought she was watching you?" Alice remembering how Jamie had kept glancing at the woman. And how a man had joined her. Had he just returned from burgling the boat? She struggled to picture what they had looked like, but only a general impression came to mind.

Jamie put up a hand to his mouth. He rubbed his hand against the stubble on his chin.

"I've kept seeing them, whenever I've been ashore. And they seemed like an odd couple. He was older than she was."

Alice thought back. Jamie was right, he had been older. She snapped back to Jamie, who was still talking.

"I saw him in the supermarket the other day. And when I walked into town last night, she walked behind me. The exact same route. I even took a bit of a detour to see if she'd follow."

"Well who are they?"

Jamie shrugged. "I've got no idea."

Alice fell silent again.

"Well then you've *got* to go to the police. I mean... These people are..." She didn't finish the sentence. She had no idea what to say.

Jamie nodded slowly. "I will if you want me to."

Alice looked up sharply. "If *I* want you to?"

"Yeah. Alice, this thing they stole... I don't know if it's something you want to be drawing to the attention of the authorities. If you know what I mean."

She stared at him. "Shit," she said at last. "You're right. Of course you are. Shit."

"And these people, it looks like they were professional. They'd probably have used gloves and everything. I don't know whether the police would even be able to do anything." Jamie was about to say something else when Alice interrupted him.

"I don't want to call them. Not without speaking to Mum. Oh my

God. How am I going to tell Mum?" Alice looked at Jamie again, her face now set in misery and shock.

"How the hell am I going to tell Mum?"

They both stayed silent for a moment, then Jamie suddenly stood up, moved across the cabin and sat next to her. He put his arms around her shoulders and pulled her gently towards him. For a long while he held her, stroking her hair with one hand while she pressed her face into his shirt. When she had recovered, he released his grip but still held her.

Alice didn't cry, just let him hold her and sat in silence.

"Alice I think you need to be very, very careful who you speak to about this. You don't know who might be involved. And you don't know what they'll do to keep this quiet. They've already shown they're prepared to break the law."

Alice pushed herself away. Her voice sounded robotic.

"I have to tell Mum. I can't keep this from her."

A shadow passed over Jamie's face, a look of doubt. But he nodded. "OK. OK if you think that's right." He hesitated again.

"Alice, there's something else I have to ask. Have you told anyone about coming here? About what I found?"

She shook her head.

"No one. I didn't even know myself what this was about. Not until we met this morning, at the café."

Jamie thought for a moment.

"No, that's not right. I told you on the phone. I told you I'd found a USB at the beach house. Did you mention that to anyone? It's important."

Alice shook her head again. "No." But then she closed her eyes. "Mum. I asked Mum if Dad had ever lost anything like that."

Jamie's voice was icy cold.

"What did she say?"

"*Nothing!* She didn't know what I was talking about." Alice's hand suddenly went up in front of her mouth, stopped her saying anything else. She stayed still for a long while.

"And you haven't told anyone else? No one at all?"

She shook her head again. Jamie took in a deep breath, then exhaled slowly.

"Alice I haven't told *anyone*. Except for you. I think we have to consider the possibility your mother is involved in some way."

Alice suddenly realised she was crying. Tears were flowing down her face. She tried to wipe them away.

"Christ. Haven't you got a tissue or anything on this boat?"

Jamie got up at once. He went to a drawer underneath the chart table and pulled out a packet of tissues. He passed one to Alice who used it to dry her face.

"You think Mum..." Her voice broke and she started again. "You think my mother broke in here to recover my father's blackmail videos?" She smiled through her tears and then began to laugh again. "This is crazy. This is fucking crazy."

"I don't know Alice. I'm as much in the dark here as you are."

Suddenly Alice pulled out her phone. "Well let's find out. I'm going to ask her. Straight up. I can't bear this not knowing." She began flicking through her contacts. When she found her mother's number she pressed the green telephone button to connect the call. Jamie watched her, not moving. They both heard the sound of the dialling tone in the small cabin. The only other sound was the gurgling of water outside the hull.

Suddenly Jamie spoke. "Alice hang up." She looked at him, not ending the call.

"I don't think you should tell her."

"Why not?" Alice sniffed. Still the phone rang. Three times, four times.

"Because of what happened to your dad."

Her eyes flicked onto his face.

"What do you mean?"

"Alice. Your father was blackmailing people. Last year he died in an unusual accident. Don't you think those things might be connected?"

Five rings. On the sixth there was the beginnings of a voice. But Alice's thumb snapped onto the other button to kill the call. She dropped the phone onto the saloon table like it was red-hot, and they both stared at it for a moment. A few seconds later it began to vibrate and ring. The caller ID showed the word: Mum.

"Oh shit." Alice said.

Jamie didn't answer, and eventually Alice looked at him, tears bubbling up in her eyes again.

"What the hell am I supposed to do then?"

18

"What's got into you this weekend?" Lena Belhaven asked her daughter the next day. "You've barely said a word all day."

Alice looked up from the huge white sofa where she sat with her knees pulled up underneath her. The TV flickered in front of her, some game show or another, the sound down. The coffee table was strewn with empty plates and mugs. Alice didn't reply and turned back to the TV.

"Are you missing Andy? Is that what this is?"

Slowly Alice turned to look at her mother, her eyes red and haunted. This time she shrugged her shoulders.

"Because I know it's hard, with him being away so much, but you can't just mope around. You need to pull yourself together." Lena was busying herself ironing a tablecloth which she thought Maria hadn't done properly. Lena went on in a quieter voice "If you don't shape up you might find Andy isn't that interested when he does come back."

"It's not Andy." Alice said quietly.

"What?"

"I said it's not Andy." Alice said, raising her voice. "It's Dad." She watched for the reaction on her mother's face, but Lena simply turned away.

"Well even more so then. Can you imagine your father letting you flop around the house like this?" Lena didn't wait for a reply.

"No neither can I. What you need to do is get yourself busy. Go and see some of your friends. Your girlfriends. Maybe even get yourself a job. I can understand you wanting to take some time after your father, but it's been over a year now. And I know you've had offers. There's Jeremy and his marketing company. Or modelling. You'd be good at that."

Alice didn't reply.

"Well *something* then. You can't just let life pass you by Alice. You're a bright girl. You must be able to find something you want to do."

Still Alice stayed quiet, and Lena let it drop.

"Anyway, we're going back to London this evening. I want to avoid the traffic. Can you make sure you're ready please."

Lena went back to her tablecloth, still tutting at the cleaner's failure to have it ready. Alice turned to watch her. She tried to stare into her mother's mind. To see if she was still the person she believed her to be.

"I'm not coming back with you tonight. I've got a few things to do here." Alice said.

"What things?" Lena said, without looking up. Then she did so, as if suddenly suspicious. "There's no-one down here during the week. It's not the summer yet."

"I know." Alice replied, keeping her eyes on her mother still, but Lena had already turned away.

"And we've got that show this week. I've bought tickets... What's it called? The one with the..?"

"I don't want to watch any shows. I need some space. To think."

"What do you need to think about?"

"You've just told me I'm wasting my life. Maybe I want to think about that?" Alice nearly shouted her reply.

In response Lena's eyebrows rose up in mock surprise.

"OK, OK. There's no need to take that attitude. I'm just trying to help," she said. She kept on ironing for a few moments.

"How will you get back? When you've thought about whatever you suddenly need to think about?"

Alice stared at her mother, trying to read if there was anything she was hiding. It was impossible.

Since Jamie had explained what was on the USB drive Alice had found her mind swinging from believing the worst about her mother - whatever that was - to being certain that everything Jamie had told her was somehow one big mistake. As she looked at her mother now, her expression muted by the nips and tucks she'd had done to her face, holding the steaming iron in front of her breasts that she knew were fake, Alice felt stuck in the middle, unable to decide either way.

"It's nothing Mum," she added, her voice softened. "I just need a few days. I'll get the train up if I decide my life is so empty I've got nothing to think about." She smiled at her mother for the first time that day.

* * *

Later that evening Lena carried her Louis Vuitton holdall down the stairs and wished her daughter a productive few days. Alice walked out onto the balcony that hung out over the back of the property, and she watched the white Range Rover pull into the light evening traffic and head east. Then she went back inside, pulling the big sliding door shut behind her, since the air was cooling now. She walked down the first flight of stairs. She opened the door at the end of the corridor and paused on the threshold. It was a small room, on the ocean side of the property, and with the sun sliding towards the water it was filled with light. She went to the window and adjusted the blinds, so that the ocean was first sliced into yellow-blue stripes and then hidden completely. There was a large desk and filing cabinets. A computer sat on the desk. An iMac. The room had been her father's office. Now Lena had all but taken it over.

Alice sat down at the desk and looked around. There were a few papers piled up to one side, she glanced through them but found nothing of interest. She pressed the power button on the computer. When the screen loaded up she typed her father's password in and began to glance through his files. There were hundreds of folders, emails, photographs - a lifetime of business and adventures, a full life too. She knew that Dad had things set up so he could work from anywhere, so long as he had his laptop and an internet connection. She also knew that he had stepped back from the direct management of the investment fund, to allow him the time to take on his challenge of racing around the world. What she didn't know was what it was she was looking for. Forcing herself to think, she typed the word *Aphrodite* into the computer's search bar. It returned a slew of results.

Alice looked through them for an hour. There were repair bills, marina fees, insurance premiums, emails - messages from friends about trips, photographs from on board. Most recently of course was the correspondence with the claims adjuster, the salvage team that had been contracted to try and recover her. But there was nothing that suggested hidden files. No pornographic images or videos. No secret folders. At least - none she could find. But then what was she expecting? Dad's computer had never been off-limits to Alice or her sister. The whole family knew his password. If he was going to hide something like that, he certainly wouldn't use this computer. He would hide it somewhere completely separate. Like under the floor in the kitchen.

She puffed out her cheeks, then went back upstairs and stood in the kitchen for a long time. She made herself a coffee, and then stood looking at it, not drinking it. Then she dropped to her knees and began to inspect the floor. She wished she'd asked Jamie exactly where he had found the drive. It was obvious it wasn't on the exposed part of the floor, it had to be underneath the cabinets somewhere. There was a gap below the doors of the cabinets, a wooden strip concealing the space underneath. Now, she pressed against it. It was fixed firmly in place. Sitting down now, she used her foot to kick at one end. This time it seemed to give a little, so she kicked it harder, then harder again, and finally the other end popped out of place. She saw it was held in position by plastic clips. For a moment she stared at them, surprised at how cheap they looked. But then she pulled against the board and moved it fully out of the way. Now the whole of the underside of the cabinets was exposed, and underneath them, the kitchen's marble tiles stopped, giving way to floorboards. She crawled underneath as best she could, her head and shoulders just about fit, but in the darkness it was hard to see anything. She pulled herself out and began searching for a torch. There was none to be found, until she remembered the boat downstairs had an emergency pack stashed in a locker. She walked all the way down to the ground floor, into the boat house, grabbed the torch and came back up. This time when she slipped back under the cabinets she was able to inspect the floorboards carefully under the torch light. But not having really seen floorboards before - or at least, never having studied them this close up - she wasn't sure what she was looking for. She wasn't even sure they *were* floorboards, or at least not normal ones. She didn't find a space. No secret hole where the USB drive had been hidden.

Eventually she gave up. Leaving the wooden plank that concealed the gap in the middle of the floor, she returned to her dead father's office. She sat down in her father's leather chair and dialled Jamie's number on her phone.

"Alice."

"I can't find anything. I can't find anything unusual in Dad's stuff. I can't find this secret compartment. None of this makes sense."

He didn't answer. She wasn't sure if he was still there.

"Jamie?"

"I'm here. I'm thinking."

"I just don't think this fits. I don't think Dad would do this. There must be some other explanation."

"OK." He sounded reasonable. "What?"

"*I don't know.* You tell me. You're the one who came up with all this."

"I just found the USB drive Alice. That's all. I can't think of any other explanation."

Now she was silent.

"Look it's your life," Jamie said a moment later. "I've had my hatch smashed in and my laptop stolen. But I can fix that. I can forget this. It's up to you. You choose what you want to do next. It's your family."

Alice thought hard as she listened to him. It wasn't what she wanted to hear. She took a few deep breaths.

"Where is the hole? I can't even see the hole where this stupid drive was supposed to be hidden. Can you show me?"

"Come to the house?"

"Yeah."

"Now?"

"Yeah."

"OK."

19

"Thank you for coming so fast," Alice said when she opened the front door.

"I was ashore anyway. I usually work Sunday nights in the library." Jamie replied. He was about to say something else when he was interrupted by an urgent beeping sound. Alice swore and quickly tapped a six-digit code into an iPad that was set into the wall by the front door. Jamie looked at her, uncertain.

"Intruder alarm." She smiled at him. "We got targeted by burglars a while back so Dad had this lot installed. There's cameras, motion alarms. The whole works. Anyway. Come upstairs. Let me get you a drink."

Neither of them spoke as Alice led the way up the stairs, and it was long enough that Alice began to feel something. Anxious maybe? She wasn't sure. She had called him here to help answer the questions about her father, but the moment she had opened the door she felt something else. Before she could decide what it was, they stepped out on the huge top floor.

"Excuse the mess," she said, walking straight into the kitchen area. "I've been undoing all your hard work."

She flashed him a smile again, and realised what the issue was. She felt nervous because the last time she had been alone with him at night was the night of the wedding. When she'd given herself to him completely. And now he was here she realised, with something of a surprise, that she still liked him. He was dressed simply, in jeans and a t-shirt. His arms were brown and strong. His blue eyes seemed brighter and deeper than earlier, when he had been so shocked. She looked away, telling herself not to notice. Why did the person who found this stupid file also have to be the one person she'd had an affair with? Why did life have to be so complicated?

Jamie didn't reply, and she wondered whether he was thinking the same sorts of things. She caught sight of her reflection in the glass doors that led to the balcony. Her hair was tied behind her head, her face looked drawn. For a moment she wished she'd taken a moment to fix it.

"Are you OK?" Jamie interrupted her flow of thoughts. Alice gave a start.

"Yeah." She shook her head. "Yeah. I'm fine."

"It's the other side." Jamie said, his blue eyes still watching her anxiously. "The hole, I mean. Here."

Jamie got down on his knees and began gently loosening the base panel from the other side of the kitchen. He did it much more expertly than the one she had done, his fingers feeling for the catches. Alice watched, her eyes drawn to the way the muscles in his arms flexed as he moved. With his attention elsewhere Alice felt free to watch him.

Jamie jumped back to his feet. His hand reached out to grab the torch on the work top, but he hesitated.

"Can I?"

"Sure," Alice replied, shaking her head again, telling herself again to focus.

Jamie flicked the torch on, and this time he laid on his belly on the floor. After a moment's hesitation Alice joined him, lying close enough that she could breathe in his smell - soap and something else. She wasn't sure what. She followed where he was pointing the torch beam. A small section of floorboard had been sawn so that it could be removed without taking the entire length out.

"It's there," Jamie said. "I nailed it back in place. There's nothing in it now, but I can open it again if you'd like? So you can see."

Alice reached in and ran her fingers over the wood. The cut wasn't recent, but it wasn't old either. But then nothing in this house was that old. She pulled her arm out, stood up, and brushed the dust from her top. Then she shook her hair free and retied it.

"No. It's OK." She sat on a stool and watched while Jamie refitted the panels they'd removed. She thought hard. It couldn't be helped, she decided, what she was doing now. What happened at Joanne's wedding had been a mistake. A drunken, terrible mistake that she would never repeat. But that had nothing to do with this. Sleeping with Jamie had been a betrayal, but this wasn't. She had to find out what this was all about, and Jamie was the only person who could help her with that.

"Do you want to see her?" She said when he had finished.

"Who?"

"*Aphrodite.*"

20

Alice led him down the stairs and into the room at the end of the corridor.

"This was Dad's study," she said, going straight to a custom-built bookshelf. "Mum's kind of taken over since he died, but most of Dad's things are still here."

She began pulling out leather-bound boxes from recesses in the shelving, she pulled the top off each one and dug inside the contents until she found what she wanted.

"Here we go," she said. With both hands, she pulled out several old photograph albums, the types where you slipped printed photographs into cellophane sleeves.

"Mum used to make these when we were kids. It gave her something to do I suppose."

There was a small leather sofa against one of the walls, and they sat together, nearly touching - though Alice hardly noticed. It was a long time since she had looked through these albums, yet they always absorbed her. She pulled the top album onto her knees and lifted open the cover. She started flicking through the photos, snatches of the Belhaven family life. There were skiing holidays. Parties. Weddings. Fast cars that her dad had owned. Even helicopters, from when he had learnt to fly them.

"It's a bit different to my childhood," Jamie said, after a while. She glanced up at him. She'd almost forgotten he was there.

"It wasn't all like this," she said. "Just because we had money..." But she stopped herself. She remembered how she had seen him in the petrol station. Working nights and studying at the same time. "But yeah. I guess we were lucky."

She kept flicking through until she found what she was looking for.

"Here. This is her. This is *Aphrodite*."

Jamie leaned in to look. The photograph was of a sleek, luxurious motor yacht. It was big, perhaps seventy-foot long. It wasn't quite the super yacht of a billionaire - there was no heliport, no open-air swimming pool on the deck. But it was certainly way beyond what most people would have ever dreamed of owning. Jamie's reaction reminded her of this.

"Wow," he said.

"Dad bought her when the business took off. At least I think so - it was before I was born. Here." Alice pointed at another photograph which showed a younger version of Lena Belhaven smiling and cradling a baby. She was standing inside what could have been an expensive hotel suite. The table was set with croissants and orange juice. A bottle of champagne was open too.

"That's me." Alice pointed at the baby.

"Wow," Jamie said again.

"Cute huh?" She grinned at him.

"Maybe," he said. "Big ears though."

She gave him a shove, but smiled nonetheless.

"Here." She flicked on a few pages. There were other photographs of the boat. At anchor in a bright blue bay, a young and beautiful Lena Belhaven sunbathing on the foredeck in a swimsuit. A beaming toddler sitting in the captain's seat, two hands on the steering wheel.

"That's Joanne," Alice said. "I'm sure there's a photo from the state room somewhere." She frowned as she flicked through the album, then found the shot she was looking for.

"That's it." Alice said. She sat back, looking nervous now. The album lay open on a shot of the master cabin of the yacht. Charlie Belhaven was lying back on a double bed, dressed in white shorts and a shirt with dark blue epaulettes, like he was some sort of naval captain. His arms were stretched out over the headboard, his exposed legs tanned and strong, filling his tight shorts.

"Well?" Alice asked. "Do you recognise the room? Is this where the tapes were filmed?"

Jamie leaned in closer for a better look. He looked closely at the decorations and furniture. When he spoke his voice was hesitant.

"I guess so. I mean. It looks like it *could* be." He nodded as he spoke, then he turned a few pages on the album hunting for other images, until he returned to the one she had shown him. "Yeah. I think so. I don't recognise the bedspread, but the panelling on the walls, the little porthole windows. I think I remember those."

The confirmation did something to Alice. She pushed herself up from the sofa, walked over to the window and used her fingers to pull the blinds apart. She looked out over the ocean, dark now that the sun had sunk beyond the horizon. Finally she stepped away, letting the blinds mask the darkness once again.

"Where is she now?" Jamie asked.

Alice turned to look at him, confused. "Who?"

"*Aphrodite*," Jamie said. "Your dad was into hidden compartments. Maybe we can find the one he used to make the videos? At least then we'll have some actual evidence."

Alice didn't answer for a long time. When she did her voice had taken on a distant tone.

"I don't think that's going to be possible." Alice said.

Jamie waited for her to go on. When she didn't he prompted her.

"Why not?"

In response she just looked at him. "Come upstairs. I'll get you that drink."

They both returned to the kitchen but Jamie refused everything except water, so Alice poured them each a glass from a bottle in the fridge. They took them out onto the balcony and set them down on the table. It was fresh out there. A beautiful quiet evening, with the last streaks of daylight fading from the sky. The first stars beginning to appear. It seemed a better place to tell the story, rather than the dim, claustrophobic light of her father's little office.

"This was a couple of years ago," Alice said, once they'd both sat down. "Maybe three years? Anyway, it doesn't matter. Me and Joanne had flown out to Majorca to meet Dad and the boat. He had already been there for a week, cruising around with a friend." She stopped, pushed her hair out of her eyes and realised owning a motor yacht wasn't the norm. She checked in his face to see if he was following.

"Sometimes we kept the boat in the Med over the winter. Dad would use her for impressing clients. You know - 'invest with me, and see the lifestyle you could live' - that sort of thing." She flashed him a smile, but then her face darkened as she realised she would have to reassess quite what her father had been showing his guests aboard.

"Anyway," she went on. "We were going to join him. You know. For a bit of Daddy and daughters time." She gave a grim smile at the memory.

"We took a taxi from the airport down to the port. We were trying to call Dad the whole time, but he wasn't answering. Joanne got into one of her moods because she didn't want to end up waiting for him on the dockside. It was hot, and the flight had already been delayed." Alice glanced up at Jamie's face.

"EasyJet. If you're wondering. We don't have our own plane, or anything like that."

He was listening attentively in the semi-dark.

"I wasn't wondering."

She looked away again, staring over her glass and out over the dark water.

"Anyway. Sure enough, as we came down the hill, we could see that Aphrodite wasn't there. Wasn't in the marina. She was so big you couldn't ever miss her. Unless she was in Monaco or something. It was odd because Dad was never late for us. And then, once the taxi had dropped us off, Dad called and said he was just on his way in. He sounded..." She stopped. "I don't know. Stressed maybe. Different to how he normally sounded. You know, we'd been looking forward to getting away."

"Anyway, then we saw her, a couple of miles out, but coming in quite fast, so we didn't think too much about it. But then she stopped..." Alice stopped again too. She shrugged.

"And suddenly we could see the smoke. Just a little at first, but then more. And then there was massive explosion and suddenly the whole boat was on fire. I don't know, it must have been the petrol, but there were clouds of smoke. I remember it was such a clear blue day. It was like a bomb had gone off. We were panicking - you know, we thought Dad had just been blown up in front of our eyes. And there were people all around the marina pointing and screaming. But then someone who had binoculars saw a little dinghy. And there was Dad. He was OK. Everyone was OK. Except for *Aphrodite*. She wasn't. She burned for about an hour, just sitting out there. It was a calm day, no wind at all, she didn't even drift. She just burned, *pouring* smoke up into the sky. Until. Until her bow rose up in the air, and began sinking. It only took a minute or so. And then the smoke just stopped. *Aphrodite* disappeared into the water."

For a long time Jamie didn't reply. She could see him thinking.

"What did your dad say happened?" he asked at last.

"Engine fire. He said he tried to fight it with an extinguisher, but it burned too fast."

"But you don't believe that. "

Alice's eyes flicked onto Jamie's then narrowed. "Why do you say that?"

"I can see it in your face."

Alice frowned. She tried to reset her features.

"Well no. Not really. I never did." Alice shook her head. "We all thought... I was worried at the time because I thought it might be an insurance job. I thought maybe it meant the business was in trouble. Funds like Dad's - he invested other people's money. Sometimes that can go wrong. If you put too much into something risky and it goes against you... You know, you can make millions, but you can also *lose* millions." Alice felt herself gazing earnestly at Jamie, willing him to understand this. Because so few people had ever understood what her dad did.

"And Dad *liked* risk. That's why he was always climbing mountains or buying old racing cars. He got a thrill from it. It was easy to believe he might have got burned."

Jamie watched her for a moment, then nodded.

"Was she insured? Did they pay up?"

"Yes and no. But that was the other thing. We've got lawyers. The family I mean. We've got very good lawyers." She turned to Jamie and gave him a wistful smile. "You'd be amazed what sorts of things my family uses lawyers for." She rolled her eyes.

"The insurance company came up with a massive list of questions. Standard delaying tactics these people use. Had the engine been properly maintained? Did the boat have a fire protection system? Had Dad been driving her too fast? All that. And normally Dad would be all over it, you know? He'd want to make sure he got paid. And probably more than the boat was worth. But this time he wasn't bothered. He kept saying it was just one of those things. That it wouldn't be easy to prove either way." Alice laughed suddenly. "The Mediterranean gets deep there very quickly. She sank in five hundred metres of water. Way beyond what you can send divers down to investigate."

"Yes and no? You said yes and no."

Alice looked at him for a second, confused.

"Oh, they ended up settling on something. But Dad definitely didn't get the whole amount."

Jamie didn't reply.

Alice sat back in her chair. The air was cold now and she hugged her arms. She noticed that Jamie was still sitting in his t-shirt.

"I can show you all the papers if you like?"

They went inside and back downstairs to the little office. This time they both sat at the desk. At first Alice clicked open the files and emails that had dealt with the insurance claim, but soon Jamie took over. He seemed able to pick things up quickly. His eyes scanning the screen as he speed read the documents. It was still recent enough to Alice that they were familiar to her - the veiled accusations that Charlie Belhaven might have deliberately rigged the yacht to catch fire and sink. The angry push back from the family's lawyers. The settlement, acknowledging that there wasn't, and would never be, conclusive proof either way. The final assessment that the lower financial risk for the insurer was to pay a proportion of the cost of the yacht's loss. Cheaper than continuing to tangle with the Belhaven family lawyers. But running all the way through the thread of documents, Charlie Belhaven's fatalistic insistence that they shouldn't push too hard. That there was no point trying to investigate too closely.

Since they were already at the computer they moved on, Alice tried to explain to him what it was her father had done for a living. She showed him the fund, smiling as he whistled at the sheer amount of money invested each year. His eyes were round as he asked if it all belonged to the family.

"No. It belongs to the investors," she told him. "A lot of it is pension funds, wealthy individuals, even other fund managers. They all feed off each other. Dad just got a percentage of the total amount."

"But that was still enough to buy all this?" Jamie said, looking around the room, and the photo albums with the boats, and the holidays, and the cars.

"The total amount is enormous," Alice told him. "And it's quite a good percentage."

"Can I ask," Jamie said a while later, after Alice had finished her explanations of how her father had acquired so much wealth, "Do you mind me asking I mean. But who stood to benefit from your father's death? Who inherits all his money? Now he's gone?"

Alice took a little while to answer. When she did she felt uncomfortable.

"We do. We all do, the family. Mum got the houses - all the physical assets. Joanne and me just got..." She stopped.

"I'm sorry, it's none of my business," Jamie said. "I shouldn't be asking. I'm just... I'm just trying to understand what we're dealing with here. This is not really a world I'm used to."

"No it's okay." Alice took a breath. "Here, I'll show you." She took over the keyboard and logged onto her own email service. She searched until she found another set of emails from the family's lawyers.

"This is all quite recent. Dad had a will of course, but his affairs were really complicated and it was only finalised a few months ago. Here." She read from the email quickly. "Joanne and me each got shares. They're worth about two million. Mum got everything else. This house, the house in London. Dad's cars. There's also a ski chalet out in Austria." She smiled at him. "Maybe I should take you there one day?"

The mood brightened for a moment. "That would be nice. But you'd have to teach me to ski first."

"You can't ski?" Alice smiled, suddenly enjoying teasing him. "What kind of a childhood did you have?"

She only meant it as a joke, but he surprised her by answering.

"Mum and Dad didn't really go in for holidays much," Jamie said, his voice serious, but not bitter. "And after they died and I went to stay with my uncle, the only holidays we ever took were in a static caravan he had in Wales." He turned to her and smiled. "There's not much skiing to be had in Wales."

Alice thought for a moment. It was weird just how different their lives were - no - that wasn't it. What was strange was how comfortable she felt with him *despite* their differences. She dismissed the thought. It wasn't welcome in what they were doing. It had no relevance. Then she went on.

"The point is, Mum had all that anyway. She didn't need Dad dead to get it."

Jamie sat back in the chair and thought for a moment.

"She had it? Or she had *access* to it, if he let her? They're not quite the same thing."

Alice frowned, considering what he had said. "The latter I suppose. Dad controlled everything. But even so..."

There was a silence.

"You know, I don't see how any of this is relevant anyway." Jamie said. His voice sounded bright, a little bit over-cheerful. "The key to all this has to be finding out *who* it was your dad was blackmailing. Who the men were in the videos. And that definitely *wasn't* your mum. Maybe you can see your dad's bank statements? Can we see a list of all the payments made to him? Anything like that?"

Alice shook her head. "No. I mean I'm sure they exist. But I don't know how to see them. We've got accountants for all that. Through the lawyers again."

Jamie was still sat back in his chair, deep in thought. He tipped his head back and sighed. Alice watched him, waiting for his thoughts on what to do next. Then from downstairs came the sound of the front door opening.

21

"Shit!" Alice was the first to react. "That must be Mum. She must have forgotten something."

"Do you want me to hide?"

"No... *Yes*." Alice swung her eyes around the room, trying to think fast. There was nowhere to hide in the small study with its minimalist decoration.

"Go into my room. Mum won't go in there...." But as she spoke it was already too late. Whoever was coming upstairs was doing so fast. Worse still, the study door was still open to the hallway, so as soon as they got to the landing they would see straight into the room.

"*Shit*," Alice said again, realising they were going to be caught.

"Helloooo? Anyone here? *Alice*?" A voice called out, a woman's voice.

Jamie was watching her, uncertainty on his face. The only chance of hiding now was under the desk. Alice saw him looking at it.

"No. Don't bother." she said. She got up and walked towards the door, glancing behind her while the footsteps continued. "It's not Mum, it's my sister."

"Oh, Alice. You are here." Joanne Belhaven began speaking the moment she saw her sister. "Mum said you were. She said you didn't want to go home because you wanted to be *alone*?" She said the last word as if it were the preserve of the certifiably crazy. But she didn't stop what she was saying. "What's all *that* about? You're not ill or something?"

Then Joanne must have noticed Jamie in the study behind Alice because she came to an abrupt stop.

"Oh." Joanne said, glancing back at Alice, but then looking back at Jamie with open curiosity. "Oh, I see."

Eventually she turned again to her sister, her eyes full of questions.

"It's *that* sort of alone..." She seemed thrown for a few seconds, but quickly recovered.

"In *that* case I won't disturb you for long. I just have to grab a few things and then I'll be out of your way..." she gave Alice another look and slipped her bag off her shoulder, as if she would fill it at once. "Then I'll leave you. *Alone.* She sneaked another glance at Jamie. Then she seemed to change her mind.

"Actually don't you want to introduce us?" she asked suddenly, smiling coyly at Jamie.

"It's not what you think." Alice said.

"I'm *sure* it's not," Joanne replied, her voice even heavier now with sarcasm. She turned to Alice again. "You're here late at night with some guy who isn't your fiancé. But it's not what I think..." But then the smile dropped from her face. Something else seemed to occur to her.

"What are you doing in Dad's office?"

"It's not what you think." Alice said again, her face set in a look so serious that Joanne now seemed truly confused. The elder sister looked past them both, towards where the computer screen was still on. Two chairs pulled up close to the desk. Papers strewn across it.

"What's going on Alice? What are you doing in there?"

"We need to talk Joanne. We need to talk now."

"*Talk?*"

"Come with me. Both of you." Alice said.

The three of them walked upstairs in silence. As if guided by some invisible sibling telepathy, Alice and Joanne went straight into the kitchen and leaned against the breakfast bar.

"So, aren't you going to introduce us?" Joanne said again.

Alice glanced at Jamie, who had held back. He seemed as unsure as Joanne was.

"Joanne this is Jamie. Jamie, this is my sister," Alice said. Jamie nodded but didn't move. Joanne looked as if she were expecting a little more. She rose her eyebrows.

"Enchanted," she said.

"Maybe you remember him?"

This threw Joanne for a second or two. She narrowed her eyes and inspected Jamie's face, but it was obvious she had no recollection. She shrugged and waited.

"He found your wedding catalogue. Do you remember? When the new kitchen was being fitted? We stopped off here to find it."

Joanne still didn't seem to remember. She continued studying Jamie, but then shrugged again.

"Jamie was working here, fitting the kitchen." Alice said.

Joanne tried to hide it, but her face lit up a little. "Oh my *God* Alice. So he's one of the *tradesmen*?" Her eyes widened and then she broke into a smile that almost looked genuine.

"*I see.* Well you're right. I wasn't expecting *that*." Her eyes flicked across to Jamie again. Then she turned to him properly, really beginning to enjoy herself now.

"So Jamie. I assume you're here to make sure everything is okay with the installation?" She looked back at Alice triumphantly. "Quite the guarantee you offer..."

"Shut up Joanne," Alice interrupted her. "Just *shut up*. I told you it's not what you think." Alice's voice was harsh. But the anger in Alice was suddenly present in Joanne too. A lifetime of finely matched tempers that both snapped at once.

"*Well what is it then*?" Joanne spat back. "And what were you doing in Dad's study?"

For a moment the two sisters stood there, squared up against one another. But then Alice backed down.

"It's complicated. It's a long story."

There was silence for a moment and then Jamie began to speak. It was the first words he had spoken since Joanne Belhaven had arrived.

"It's my fault," he said. "I discovered something about your father. I told Alice about it."

Very slowly Joanne shifted her gaze from her younger sister and onto Jamie.

"You discovered something about my father?" her expression had shifted from delight to contempt, and she did nothing to disguise it.

"*What?*"

Jamie took a deep breath before going on. "When we were taking the kitchen out I found a computer drive, a pen drive, hidden under the floorboards." He pointed. "Just over there. It was none of my business, I shouldn't have looked at it but somehow I ended up taking it home, and I plugged it into my computer." Jamie swallowed.

"It contained..." He seemed to be losing his momentum. Maybe losing his nerve. "What it had on it was..."

Alice interrupted him, speaking sharply. "Dad was blackmailing people. He had tapes of people having sex on *Aphrodite*. He was using them to blackmail people. That's what Jamie discovered."

For a long while Joanne said nothing but stared at each of them in turn. Finally she settled on her sister.

"Have you gone completely stark-raving mad?"

Alice shook her head.

"I wish."

"What are you *talking about*? Dad would never do that. Dad didn't *need* to do that." Joanne stared at her sister now. The anger was gone, replaced by disbelief.

"*Sex tapes? Dad?*"

This time Alice nodded.

"What kind of sex tapes?"

Alice didn't reply.

"*Oh my God.*" Joanne went on anyway. The smile had crept back onto her lips. "Who was in them?" Her eyes suddenly went wide. "Is that what you were looking at on Dad's computer?"

"We don't know who was in them," Alice said.

Joanne's face creased into a frown. "Why not?"

This time Alice hesitated. "We don't have the tapes any more. They were stolen, from Jamie's yacht."

There was a pause. A palpable wave of confusion rolled through the room. Joanne gave a tiny shake of her head.

"What were they doing on his *yacht*? Actually, why does he even *have* a yacht? If he's just a tradesman?" Joanne seemed to realise the crudeness of this, but she didn't apologise.

"No, forget that - who *stole* them?" She screwed up her face. "What the hell is all this about?"

"That's what we're trying to find out," Alice said. "That's what we were doing on Dad's computer. Going through his old records trying to find anything that might explain what was going on."

"Oh my God!" Joanne said again. She smiled suddenly, relief showing on her face. "I thought you two were..." She didn't finish the sentence. Instead she looked at her sister and raised her eyebrows again. "I thought there was something going on between you two." Joanne smiled towards Jamie again. It was an automatic gesture. As if, now she knew he and Alice weren't involved, it couldn't hurt to flutter her pretty eyelids in his direction. In doing so Joanne missed how Alice Belhaven dropped her eyes to the floor. And therefore missed seeing how close to the mark she had been first time around.

The moment passed almost as soon as it happened. Joanne's mind returning to the topic that now seemed to fill the room like a fog.

"You think Dad was blackmailing people?" Joanne said again.

"That's what it looks like." Alice replied.

"But why?" Joanne said. "Dad was a bit dodgy but he'd never do anything like that."

"How do we know he wouldn't?" Alice fixed her eyes on Joanne. "Dad always made a lot of money. The fund always performed so well. Always better than the market - isn't that what people said? What if that was because he had some kind of advantage? What if he had people giving him inside information? You've got to admit, it sounds like the sort of thing he'd do."

"No it doesn't!" Joanne's voice rose in outrage. "That doesn't sound like Dad at all. Dad would never do that. Not blackmail."

They stood in silence for a moment, the darkness of the ocean looming on one side, the pretty lights of the harbour twinkling on the other. Photographs of Charlie Belhaven smiled back from the walls. Charlie climbing mountains, Charlie driving sports cars, Charlie smiling, shaking hands with smiling politicians.

"Dad would never go *that* far!"

"Wouldn't he?" Alice asked. "If he could get away with it?"

Joanne opened her mouth to speak but changed her mind. She walked away from them, right over to the window overlooking the harbour. Alice and Jamie watched her, and then exchanged a look.

"He's not a *criminal* Alice." Joanne called out to them. "Dad wasn't a criminal."

When Alice replied her voice was softer, the anger gone. "What about the *Aphrodite*? You remember when she sank? You said straight away Dad did it for the insurance."

"That's different."

"Why? Why is it different? It's still against the law. You think Dad was happy to break some laws but had this moral code that made him stop at others? Admit it Joanne, this is *exactly* like Dad. It's *exactly* the sort of thing he'd do." She sounded eager now, keen for her sister to accept the truth. For her to not be the only one.

"Where were they filmed? How did he do it?" Joanne asked again. She was quieter now too.

"On *Aphrodite*. I showed Jamie some photos from the stateroom. He recognised the bed."

"Mum and Dad's bed?" Joanne said. "He made sex tapes on Mum's..."

"Yeah." Alice interrupted her. "But they were old. Jamie says it looked like the 1980s or 90s, from the quality, and people's haircuts and things."

"You watched them all?" Joanne said to Jamie now. He hesitated before replying.

"Not exactly. I watched enough to see what they were. Then I found a way to contact Alice. To let her know."

Joanne nodded, then thought for a moment.

"The *Aphrodite* parties," Joanne said, looking at her sister. "Mum and Dad always used to go on about the parties they had on *Aphrodite*. You remember?"

"Yeah. I remember." Alice replied. Joanne turned to Jamie.

"When we started going out - to clubs and things like that - Mum and Dad always said there was nothing we could get up to that they hadn't done when they were young." She bit her lower lip. Jamie's face didn't move.

"I guess they were right." Alice said.

When Jamie spoke next his voice sounded strange. Deep and masculine. Strangely in control.

"What exactly did they say happened?"

It was Joanne who answered him. "They never really gave specifics. They had this joke, if you can remember the *Aphrodite* parties, you weren't really there." She thought for a moment. "I think they stole that from somewhere." She screwed up her face, thinking. Then Alice interrupted her.

"But you *were* there," she said. "They were still doing the parties when I was born, and you were loads older."

Joanne bristled visibly at the implication.

"I'm not loads..." she shook her head, glancing at Jamie. "I was a baby too. Anyway, the parties had calmed down by then."

"You were *five*. That's not a baby," Alice kept on. "You must remember something. Like who was there?"

Joanne glowered at her, looking ready to argue the point, but she evidently decided against it. She shook her head. "I really don't remember anything specific. There were loads of people. I remember the music, people laughing. Looking back there were definitely drugs, I didn't know that at the time, but..."

"Were there any prostitutes?" Alice asked.

"Only if you count Mum and her friends." From the tone of her voice it was clear Joanne intended the comment to be sarcastic. But it stopped both of them in their tracks.

"What do you mean?" Jamie asked again, into the sudden silence.

Whatever had passed between the sisters seemed to change the atmosphere in the room, like all the air had been sucked out and replaced and every molecule was now differently charged. It was visible on Jamie's face too, he looked suddenly confused, out of step.

"So why exactly is he here now?" Joanne asked suddenly, ignoring Jamie's question and turning to Alice. "I mean, apart from finding this tape thing, what exactly has this got to do with him?"

It took a while for Alice to find an answer.

"He's just helping, that's all."

Joanne continued to stare at her. "Why? He's actually nothing to do with this. He's just a kitchen fitter."

But this brought back Alice's anger. "No he's not," she snapped. "He's actually a doctor, or at least he's training to be one. And he can't *help* being involved. He could have gone straight to the police and then where would we be?"

Jamie opened his mouth to speak, but then seemed to change his mind. He still looked like he hadn't adjusted to the shift in the conversation. In the end he just raised his arms in a shrug, as if that was all he had to offer.

Joanne considered this for a long moment. She nodded, like she accepted what Alice had said. But then something else occurred to her.

"Why Alice?" She said to Jamie. "Why did you bring it to Alice? I mean, surely it would have been more normal to tell Mum directly? She did all the ordering for the kitchen after all. She must have booked it?"

Jamie still didn't answer.

"How did you even know who Alice was?"

It was Alice herself who ended up answering.

"I saw him again at the wedding. He was working there as a waiter," Alice told her. "It was just a coincidence that's all. We got chatting."

"*My* wedding?"

"Has there ever been another?"

Joanne ignored the barb. "Hang on. You said he was a *kitchen fitter* a moment ago."

"He was. He does loads of jobs. I told you, he has to pay for medical school." Alice said. "Not everyone's like us Joanne."

Joanne shot her sister a filthy look but returned at once to her line of questioning. Alice felt increasingly uncomfortable.

"So you got... *chatting?*" Joanne said. "Then what?" A smile was blooming on her face again.

"Then nothing." Alice said firmly, but she wasn't able to maintain eye contact and this time Joanne saw enough to understand.

"Oh Alice..." She turned to Jamie. "Did she tell you she's *engaged?*" When he didn't reply she rolled her eyes.

"How could you? At *my* wedding!"

No one spoke for a moment. Then Joanne turned again to Jamie.

"Our mother originally came to the UK from Yugoslavia, the part that's now Slovenia. She had no legal right to work here so she ended up in some sleazy bar in Soho. The clients of the bar used to pay her, and her friends, to go to parties with them." She smiled at Jamie, but it was a nasty smile. "That's how Mum and Dad got together. That's why we call her a prostitute." She fired a nasty, sarcastic smile towards her sister, then looked back at Jamie. "Another dirty little family secret for you to file away."

Jamie replied cautiously, as if he didn't want to raise her anger again. "I'm sorry Joanne. I really am. I was just trying to help. But if you think I should go..." He looked at Alice. She looked at Joanne. Who rolled her eyes this time, like it wasn't up to her.

Jamie seemed to take this as an invitation to continue. Still keeping his voice level, treading carefully, he went on.

"But what you're saying is your mum might... She might have *known people* who could have been involved in something like this?" He looked at Alice but she blanked him, so he turned his attention to Joanne.

"Prostitutes? Are you asking if Mum knew prostitutes?" She left just enough pause to suggest this wasn't even a valid question. "Of course she bloody did."

They all looked down at the floor for a moment. It was Joanne who looked up first.

"Hey, you're not going to go to the police with all this, are you?" She asked Jamie.

"No." He sounded firm again, relieved even. "Or at least, not if you don't want me to. It's like you say, none of this has got anything to do with me." Jamie looked at them both, but neither met his gaze.

A moment later he went on. "Look, maybe I *should* just go?" he turned to Alice, his voice even and reasonable again. "Now your sister's here. You can work out what to do together." He began to move, as if to leave right away.

Alice felt an immediate wave of panic. She didn't know what was supposed to happen next, but she knew it wouldn't be any easier if it was just her and her sister deciding. Jamie was the only one who she could really trust in all this.

"No. No, don't go." She said. She tried to keep how desperate she was out of her voice. "Please."

Joanne just continued to stare at him for a long time. Eventually she spoke as well.

"What was it you said about a yacht? These sex tapes got stolen from a yacht? What the hell were they doing there?"

"It's where he lives." Alice leapt in, relieved that the subject had moved on from Jamie's leaving.

"He has a yacht moored out in the harbour, near the island. He took me out there this morning to see the videos on his computer. But when we got there we found someone had broken in. They nearly wrecked the inside, but when we looked the only thing missing was the USB drive and his computer."

Joanne listened, but it was unclear if she'd really heard.

"I need to sit down," she said, suddenly. "This is too much. This is too fucking much." She walked past them both and pulled out one of the chairs around the big dining table. She was so white, so looked ill.

"I'm going to make some tea. Sweet tea," Jamie said. He must have noticed too. "It's good for shock."

Alice stared at him in surprise as he walked back into the kitchen and picked up the kettle.

"Oh fuck that," Joanne called out to him. "Get me a glass of fucking wine."

Jamie froze, kettle in hand, and Alice suddenly laughed.

"In the cooler. It's next to..." She stopped. "Oh, you probably know where it is." Then they were all smiling.

No one spoke for a long time. Alice sat opposite her sister, watching Jamie as he opened the wine cooler and read out the labels, until Joanne told him to just open the coldest bottle of white he could find. He searched through the drawers to find a corkscrew, then carefully pulled the cork and poured three glasses. He carried the three together and set them on the smoked-glass top of the table. Then he sat down as well, next to Alice. Joanne picked up her glass and took a big slug of the wine.

"You didn't back them up? The videos? You didn't make copies?" Joanne asked, her voice was quiet now, calm.

"No." Jamie replied. "I don't have internet on my boat."

"And they're definitely gone? I mean you couldn't have just... Lost them?"

"The hatch was smashed in. It looked like they'd searched the cabin for them."

Joanne took another slug of wine.

"Would you recognise the people in the videos again?"

"That's what we were doing earlier. Alice was showing me photos of people it might have been."

"And? Did you recognise any?"

Jamie shrugged. "Maybe. I don't know. No. Not really."

"And you don't know who broke in, to this boat of yours?"

"No."

Joanne's flow of questions faded out. Jamie waited, silent, like he was waiting for her to reload. But Joanne just stayed silent, staring down at the table top.

"Jamie didn't speak to anyone about what he found. Not anyone," Alice spoke into the silence. Her voice was suddenly heavy with meaning, her eyes fixed on her sister. "And I've only spoken to one person. So there's only one person who could have known where the tapes were. Just one person."

The implication of what Alice was saying registered in Joanne's features. She hesitated before answering, as if she were reluctant to know.

"Who?"

Alice swallowed. "Mum."

"*Mum?*"

Alice nodded.

"Oh Jesus." Joanne said. Her face was as white as it had been. She took another gulp of the wine.

"There's one more thing," Alice said.

"Oh go on. Don't hold back. This is already the worst night of my life, why not make it worse?"

"We think all this might be related to Dad's death. Someone could have killed him to stop the blackmail."

Joanne opened her mouth to reply. But she closed it again.

22

Joanne took another sip from her wine, much smaller this time, like she was savouring a quality vintage. Then she set the glass down carefully on the table and stared at her sister for a long time.

"Are you saying what I think you're saying?"

"I don't know. We don't know." Alice replied.

"You think Mum *killed* Dad? Had Dad killed I mean?" Suddenly she broke down into near-hysterical laughing.

"You think Mum had Dad killed? *Jesus Christ Alice*. This is insane."

This time Alice didn't reply. Weakly she shrugged her shoulders.

"How?" Joanne demanded. "How did she do it? Did she fly out to South Africa when we weren't looking? Did she... I don't know? *Sneak onto a nuclear submarine and stalk Dad's yacht*? Alice, Dad fell off a bloody boat in the middle of a storm. No one killed him."

"I'm not saying Mum *did* anything. At least... Of course I don't think that."

"Good, because it's *fucking ridiculous*. This whole thing is fucking ridiculous. I mean, it's insane." Joanne stood up and walked to the kitchen, where she had earlier slung her handbag on the worktop.

"I'm going to call her now. I'm going to put an end to this nonsense." Joanne Belhaven fumbled inside the bag for a moment. Then she pulled out an iPhone in a gold case. She unlocked it and gave a deep sigh. She began dialling. Alice raised a hand, like she wanted to tell her sister to stop. But she didn't get up. Instead she looked at Jamie, as if he might be able to regain the control they had just lost. But Jamie seemed held in some trance. He said nothing.

Joanne ignored them both. She held the phone to her ear.

"Joanne," Alice began at last. "I don't think you should..."

"Mum," Joanne said into the mouthpiece, her call had connected. "Mum it's me. Listen I need to ask you something. It's a bit strange. Are you alone?"

There was a heavy silence, the only sound Alice could hear was the small sound of her mother's voice through the phone, the words too indistinct to hear from where she stood.

"Yeah." Joanne went on. "Yeah, listen are you sitting down? I think you need to be."

"Joanne...!" Alice heard herself saying, but her sister glared at her. Joanne covered the mouthpiece for a second and shouted.

"I'm putting an end to this nonsense right now." She lifted her hand from the phone again. "Yeah I'm here. With Alice. And Alice's *friend*. Listen Mum I'm going to put you on speaker. Hold on."

Joanne dropped the phone from her ear and pressed a button on the screen. Suddenly Alice heard her mother's voice coming through louder, clear enough to hear this time. Joanne placed the phone on the dining table.

"...Is all this about? I thought Alice wanted some time to think?"

"Yeah - Mum. *Shut up* will you. I need to ask you a question." Joanne interrupted her. There was silence for a moment.

"OK," Lena's voice eventually came through.

"Thanks. So..." Joanne laughed again, it still had an edge of hysteria. "OK. So there's no easy way to ask this, so I'm just going to come out with it," Joanne said. But she didn't go on at once. It was like her subconscious knew this was a line that, once crossed, could not be uncrossed. She hesitated, then crossed it.

"Have you and Dad spent years blackmailing people with sex tapes? Oh, and when he died, was that because you had him killed?"

However awkward the conversation had felt before was nothing to how it suddenly was now. Alice realised she had both her hands clasped over her mouth. She waited, unable to take them down. Slowly her eyes shifted from the silent gold telephone to her sister. Joanne wore a self-satisfied expression that was gradually morphing into one of horror. Eventually their mother's voice came through again on the phone.

"What did you say?"

Joanne waited a beat, but she knew she was committed now.

"I asked if you were a blackmailer Mother. Because Alice here thinks you might be. And that maybe you had Dad killed?"

Another long pause.

"What's going on? Is this some sort of joke?"

"No. Well, maybe." Joanne's manic laugh rang out again. "No. Alice looks quite serious." Joanne shot a look at Alice to check. "No, she's here with a friend who says he found a secret tape hidden inside the kitchen. It was a sex tape. They think Dad was using it to blackmail people. We were just wondering if you knew anything about that?"

Again Lena waited a long time before replying. "A sex tape?" There was a pause. "Joanne, what are you talking about? What sex tape? What is all this about?"

"That's what I'm asking you Mum." There was impatience in Joanne's voice now. "I think it's a complete load of rubbish but I was wondering if you might know something about it."

"I don't have a clue what you're talking about."

Joanne snatched the phone from the tabletop and held it up triumphantly. But she carried on speaking to her mother.

"So you don't know anything about a blackmail tape?"

"Of course not."

"And you didn't have Dad murdered?"

"*Joanne!*" Lena replied. "What is this?"

There was silence again.

"Joanne, I don't know what this is about but please stop it at once."

"It's not *me* Mum," Joanne said. "This isn't *my* idea." She gave a deep sigh of the hard done-by.

No one spoke for a moment. Then Lena's voice came through again.

"Who are you there with? Is Alice there? And who is this *friend* you're talking about? What was he doing in our kitchen?"

Joanne was still shaking her head. She glanced across at Jamie before replying.

"His name's *Jamie*. He was one of the workmen who put the new kitchen in. He says he found the tapes hidden somewhere. In a secret compartment."

"*Jamie?* Jamie..." Lena's voice cut out suddenly. There was another silence, like the phone's signal had been interrupted, or their mother had meant to say something then stopped herself. "One of the workmen?"

"Yeah," Joanne took up the explanation seamlessly. "*Obviously* he should have handed anything he found to you immediately, but instead he took it home. He bloody watched it." She sent another angry look in Jamie's direction.

There was a beat or two of silence before Lena replied.

"Well it's obviously nothing to do with us. It must have been left there by someone else. The people who had the house before maybe. Or whoever put the kitchen in."

"So Dad wasn't blackmailing people?"

"Joanne! Of course he wasn't. You know your father. He would never do anything like that."

"And you weren't videoing people having sex on *Aphrodite*? Or making sex tapes? On all those parties you used to tell us about?"

Lena hesitated but didn't answer the question.

"What's *Aphrodite* got to do with this?"

"That's where the videos were filmed. Or that's what Alice and her *friend* think. He recognised the cabin apparently. Your cabin."

It seemed to take an age for Lena to answer. When she did her voice was different.

"Where is this tape now?"

Joanne didn't seem to pick up on her mother's change of tone.

"It's gone. Someone broke into Jamie's boat and stole in. They think that was you as well, by the way."

Another silence stretched out.

"Well who has it now?" There was a clear element of alarm in Lena's voice. "Who else knows about this? You haven't called the police have you?"

"No of course not Mother," Joanne said.

"Well don't. This is all nonsense but it's the sort of thing that could easily be misinterpreted. I'm going to call Jonathan. He'll know what to do. Don't go anywhere. Don't speak to anyone."

"Mum," Alice interrupted, the first time she'd spoken in the conversation. "Mum - do you think it's possible that Dad recorded people on *Aphrodite*. Without you knowing about it?"

Alice listened to silence as her mother considered what to say. When she eventually replied her tone was much more conciliatory.

"Well it's *possible* I suppose. But he certainly wasn't blackmailing people. I'd have known. Your father wouldn't have done that. He didn't need to." She stopped. Alice felt her insides hollow out. Mum's reaction was the same as Joanne's, exactly the same as her own. First there was denial that her father could have done something like this, followed by accepting that it was exactly the sort of thing he could have done. And finally the defence that it didn't happen because he didn't *need to*. Because he was already rich. But how did they get so rich? She braced herself for her next question.

"You didn't speak to anyone?" Alice asked her mother. "In London. When I asked you about a USB drive that Dad might have lost in the beach house?"

There was no hesitation this time.

"You didn't ask me."

"I did. Earlier this week? I asked you."

"I don't know what you're talking about Alice. You never told me about any USB drive."

Alice thought back, doubting herself now. Had she told her mother? What exactly had she said? There was silence as Alice tried to think, but she couldn't remember. It was Lena who spoke next.

"Look, if this *Jamie* character's boat *was* burgled, might that just be a coincidence? There's been a spate of burglaries on boats in the harbour recently. I saw Jeremy the other week and he was telling me all about it. It's a real problem." She paused. Joanne looked at Jamie and mouthed an explanation.

"Jeremy is the president of the yacht club. Silly old bastard who's always trying to get into Mum's knickers." Her eyebrows rose up her forehead.

"And the house was targeted the other year." Lena went on, from the telephone. "Do you remember?"

"When Dad had all the extra security fitted." Joanne's eyebrows rose knowingly, an I-told-you-this-was-all-nonsense kind of look. Abruptly she stalked back into the kitchen where Jamie had left the wine bottle. She refilled her glass, almost to the rim. She didn't ask anyone else.

"I guess..." Alice said at last. She had watched her sister, trying to make sense of what was going on.

"Whatever this is, it's not what you think" Lena's voice came through the phone.

"OK. I believe you Mum." Alice heard herself say.

"Good," Lena paused. "Do you want me to come back down? I can get in the car first thing in the morning. Whatever this is, we can work it out." Lena said.

"Are you going to tell Jonathan?" Alice asked.

Lena sighed. "I don't know. Not yet. I don't think there's anything to tell him. Is there?"

Joanne was back now, and she picked up the phone as if the others had no place listening in. She turned off the speaker and walked away to the other end of the room, speaking quietly to her mother as she did so. Eventually she came back, but by then the call was finished.

"Well," she said, taking a big sip of her wine. "I think that clears things up a little at least."

When neither Jamie nor Alice answered her, she put down the drink and informed them she had to go to the bathroom.

23

"Who's Jonathan? Jamie asked when Joanne had left the room.

"*Jonathan*?" Alice frowned. "Oh, he's our lawyer. The one I told you about."

Jamie nodded, then was silent.

"He'll offer you money. That's the way he operates."

"That's not why I'm here Alice, I don't want..." Jamie began, but Alice interrupted him.

"I'm not saying you do. I'm just saying that's what will happen if Mum talks to him. That's how this family deals with shit like this." She turned away.

"Whatever this is."

Jamie waited a beat before speaking again.

"Do you believe her? That your mum doesn't know anything about this?"

"I don't know," she said quickly, then turned back to face him.

"Yes and no. Mum's always known about the money. It's something to do with where she's from, there was so much corruption there it wrecked the whole country. So Mum likes to keep an eye on things. You know, the accountants, the lawyers..." Alice let her voice fade out, and only continued when she saw Jamie looking at her, not following.

"I'm just saying, if Dad was blackmailing people, there's a good chance she'd know about it. And she seemed surprised. She sounded surprised."

"But what about the break in? On *Phoenix*?"

For a moment Alice was confused by the name of Jamie's yacht. When she realised what he meant she shrugged. "It could be a coincidence?"

A look passed over Jamie's face. Incredulity? Disbelief? It didn't last long enough for her to be sure.

"I guess so," he mused. "I suppose they might just have grabbed whatever looked valuable. There wasn't much besides the laptop. All the navigation equipment is fitted. You'd need tools to take them out." He seemed to be justifying it to himself. "And if they did just grab the laptop in a hurry, maybe they just picked up the USB drive as well." He thought for a moment, then brightened.

"You know, if that's the case. They wouldn't be able to read it. Even if they bothered to plug it in, they'd either think it was empty - like I did at first, or they'd see it was locked and give up on it. I only persevered because I saw where your dad had hidden it. Ordinary thieves wouldn't have any reason to suppose it had anything valuable on it."

Alice felt herself clutch at this logic. Jamie looked at her, his eyes widening.

"So all this is nothing then?" He asked.

Instead of answering him, Alice got up and fetched the wine from the kitchen. She carried it back to the table and topped up both their glasses.

"It's not quite nothing is it? Dad was making sex tapes of people. Even if he wasn't using them, he *had* them. Even if there wasn't any actual blackmail and they were just - I don't know - *insurance*."

Joanne appeared back in the room. She noticed the wine had been moved and picked up her own glass.

"Well," she said, raising it in the air. "Cheers and all that."

Suddenly Alice turned on her.

"You *stupid, selfish-fucking-bitch*," Alice said. She surprised herself with the force of her words, and once she'd begun she seemed unable to stop herself.

"You *bitch*. What the hell did you do that for? You just told Mum I thought she had Dad *killed*? How fucking could you?"

Again Joanne's anger seemed to rise at once to match her sister's. She shouted back at once.

"*Well you're the one who came up with it? What else was I supposed to do?*"

"We were handling it! We would have found out it wasn't true. And *she* didn't need to know. Mum didn't need to know. Now what's she going to think of me? How could you?"

"Oh it's all about *you* isn't it? Just like everything else? All about *pretty little Alice*. You're such a *fucking drama queen*. Little melodramatic Alice. At least *I* got it sorted out. Maybe you should be thanking me?"

Joanne glared at her sister. But then the anger seemed to evaporate from Alice as fast as it had come on. She shook her head at her sister, then tipped her head back and stared at the ceiling. Again it was like they were linked by some cable that kept their emotions precisely matched.

"You realise that Dad did make the tapes?" Joanne asked, calmly. "Even though Mum says he didn't?"

Alice hesitated but then started to nod her head.

"Yeah, probably." She shrugged. "Maybe Mum was even *in* them. I wouldn't put it past them."

Joanne burst out laughing suddenly. "Can you imagine?"

"I'm almost glad the tape got stolen before I had to watch *that*."

Gradually the smile on Alice's face disappeared. "So what do we do now?"

Joanne finished her wine. Eventually she shrugged again.

"Nothing. There's nothing to do." She glanced again at Jamie, as if he were the only loose end yet to be decided. "So Dad made some tapes. It's not against the law. Maybe it was a coincidence that someone took them. Maybe it wasn't. It doesn't matter either way. It's not connected to what happened to Dad is it?"

24

Jamie left soon afterwards, leaving Joanne - who by then had drunk too much to drive home to her new husband - to stay with Alice. But the next morning she left early, so that Alice awoke to an empty house that echoed to her calls.

It was a beautiful morning, calm and with just a few fluffy clouds announcing that the air was still right the way up through the atmosphere. Alice made coffee and took it out onto the front balcony, which got the early morning sun. She looked out over the harbour, still thinking of everything that had happened yesterday. And as she looked she realised she could just make out the mast of Jamie's yacht. She fetched the pair of binoculars that Charlie kept in his office, and focused them on the island, looking for the creek where Jamie kept the boat. They were a powerful set, and they cut down the distance so that she seemed to be able to peer into the thickly wooded sides of the island. Then she saw it, the deep blue paintwork, the little yacht's elegant lines. And once she had the glasses settled, resting on the steel handrail of the balcony, she noticed there was a figure in the cockpit. Jamie was up, she realised, drinking his coffee at the same time.

Smiling, she reached for her phone, dialled, and attempted to balance the binoculars again while the phone connected.

"Alice?" She watched him answer. There was a half second delay between the image and the sound.

"How's your coffee?" Alice asked.

"What?" Jamie replied. She watched him through the lenses. It was too far away to see really, but she fancied she caught his face screwing up in confusion.

"And that t-shirt suits you." She said. "Matches your eyes."

"*What?*" Jamie said again. He began turning around, as if expecting to see her, spying on him.

"Give me a wave," Alice said, letting him off. "I can see you from the balcony."

There was a moment's pause, then the binoculars slipped and Alice lost sight of him, catching instead a jerky snatch of woods and diamond-jewelled water.

"Really?" Jamie's voice sounded relaxed. "You can see me from your house?"

"Yeah. We could send smoke signals," Alice said. Then without thinking she added. "Do you want to come over? Get some breakfast? We could go for a walk on the beach. It's a lovely day." She gave up trying to find him again through the binoculars - it was too hard to do that and hold the phone.

"Yeah OK." Jamie said slowly. He sounded surprised.

"Actually it's lovely out here on the water. And it's a good forecast - I was just checking." he said suddenly. "If you liked, we could go out, on the boat? If we go now we could make a day of it."

It was Alice's turn to sound surprised. "Yeah. OK. Yeah let's do that."

An hour later, Alice found the little tender at the dockside, then Jamie waved to her from across the road clutching a groceries bag. Moments later they were clattering their way across the flat water of the harbour towards *Phoenix*. Jamie drove the little boat fast enough that it was too loud to talk, and Alice felt the tension slipping from her shoulders as the wind blew her hair out behind her. It was a stunning day now, the sky a deep blue already, the morning sun warm on her face. As she neared the yacht she wondered about her mother's theory for the burglary. *Phoenix* was a long way from the other moored yachts in the harbour. If there was a gang breaking into boats in the harbour, this one would certainly be an easy target.

This time, when they got on board, Jamie moved quickly and lightly around the boat. He removed the cover from the mainsail and unlashed the tiller. When he went below Alice noted that he had already fixed the broken lock - a neat new section of wood had been added on top of where the previous lock had been smashed. Moments later the boat began to throb gently underneath her as its diesel engine turned slowly over. The warm, evocative smell of marine diesel floating on the still air. Jamie came back on deck and smiled at her.

"Do you want to cast us off?" He asked.

Alice made her way carefully to the front of the boat. The walkways either side of the cabin roof were narrow, and she had to hold on to the shrouds that held up the mast. When she got to the bow she leaned out and saw the mooring line looped through an eye on the top of the buoy and then back to a cleat. Here she uncoiled the rope and let it slip out, releasing them into the light pull of the tide.

"She's clear!" Alice called back. He raised a hand in recognition, and Alice felt the revolutions of the engine increase as Jamie pushed the throttle forwards.

She stayed there for a while, at the very front of the yacht, as they made a tight circle and began cutting a sharp groove through the still water. She paused for a while, watching a wave roll away on either side of them. Watching the steep green sides of the island slip by, and Jamie's little creek fell behind them and disappeared. They began to pass through other yachts, tied up on more expensive moorings but obviously empty from their tightly tied sail covers and boarded up hatches. They passed the marina where *Aphrodite* had had her berth - more expensive still. She remembered walking out on the pontoon to reach her, her father laughing as they walked, arm in arm. She shook her head to bring herself back to the present. Jamie was steering a practised path, keeping to the channel marked out by the red and green buoys in some places, cutting a corner where he knew there was enough depth in others. There wasn't any wind to ruffle the surface of the water, only the pull of the tide draining it slowly from the wide harbour.

"We'll just take her out through the mouth," Jamie said, as Alice climbed back to join him. "There'll be a little more wind out there, then we can get the engine off and relax."

"I am relaxed," she said, smiling. "It's beautiful to be out here."

He returned the smile, but his was doubtful, rueful, almost apologetic. "I always prefer to get the sails up." he said. "It's so much more peaceful under sail."

They fell into a comfortable silence, giving Alice more space to think. She had taken boats in and out of this harbour her whole life. With her father on *Aphrodite*, with boys her own age too, trying to impress her with the size of their craft, the power of the engines. Getting out through the harbour with them always felt like trying to navigate rush-hour traffic. This felt smoother, more relaxed. She rather liked it.

"Would you mind steering for a bit?" Jamie asked, breaking into her thoughts.

"Oh - no, sure."

Alice stepped over and took the helm of the little yacht. She gave a little experimental waggle to the tiller, and felt how it turned them, first one way, then the other.

"I'm a little more used to wheel steering," she said.

"I bet you're used to a little more power as well?" Jamie said and he grinned. "She's a bit stately, is *Phoenix*," he said. Alice had the sensation that he had just been reading her mind.

"You know where to head for?" Jamie asked. They were coming up to the harbour mouth, where the land closed in on both sides and boats had to thread their way through a narrow channel. Alice nodded without saying anything.

He watched her for a while, seeing how she was lining up the two beacons. When he seemed satisfied he went forward and readied the sails.

Alice had to concentrate, taking the yacht through the entrance. The water here churned as the tide flowed through the narrow gap. It wasn't uncommon that inexperienced sailors got into trouble here, either running their vessels into the landing stages that cut out from the mansions on the left bank, or worse, getting themselves in the way of the chain ferry that plied back and forth across the gap. But Alice steered a path just to the left of the middle of the channel, feeling how the little yacht cut a secure path through the water. Stately she might be, but she felt solid and capable too.

And when they were through, he signalled for her to turn the yacht into the wind. When she did so he released the main halyard from its cleat, then leaned back, pulling handfuls of the rope behind him as he did so. Quickly and smartly the mainsail ran up the mast. Above her, Alice saw the big sail flogging lightly as they motored into the wind.

"Let her off a little," Jamie said, and Alice pushed the tiller over until the sail filled with wind. As she did that Jamie came back into the cockpit and released another rope. This one allowed the yacht's foresail to unfurl from where it was wrapped around itself at the bow. Jamie grabbed a winch handle to wind it tight. Alice noticed how the muscles in his back showed through the thin fabric of his shirt. Then he went below. The noise from the engine stopped. At once the motion of the yacht changed. It was no longer pushed along from behind, now it leaned lightly with the wind and began kissing its way forward through the gentle swell.

Five minutes later smells began wafting up from below. There was the noise of boiling water, and then Jamie appeared again from the hatch. He held two mugs of coffee, steam blowing off the top, and tin plates with croissants on them, warmed from the yacht's little oven. He climbed out into the cockpit and handed one to Alice.

"Breakfast," he said. She smiled, impressed.

"So where do you want to go? He asked, squinting into the sunlight.

"Anywhere. I don't mind," she said. "It's just nice to be out here." She took a sip of the coffee. It was strong and hot.

"There's a bay, around beyond the headland. It's a beautiful place. We can even go for a swim." Jamie said. He pointed to the west, and Alice nodded.

"I know it," she said. "I've been there a few times with Dad."

"Sorry I forgot," Jamie said. "I guess you know everywhere around here, you grew up here."

Alice smiled. "There's not many places I haven't been to." Suddenly she felt that she had dismissed his suggestion too easily. "But it is a beautiful place, and I've never sailed there in a yacht this beautiful."

Jamie smiled deeply. The pride in how she had described his boat was written clearly on his face. He said nothing but took a sip from his own mug.

"Head for that stack then," he said, a moment later, pointing towards a needle of rock that stuck up out of the water beyond the nearest headland. "We'll go around the outside of the rocks."

Alice knew the way perfectly, she knew the bay they were headed to. She'd been there hundreds of times, but she allowed Jamie to give her directions and leaned on the tiller until the yacht was sailing the course that Jamie wanted.

It took them an hour to get parallel with the stack of rock. Alice was more used to thundering past here at 30 knots, but it was refreshing to travel so slowly. And, after the drama she had been through the previous day, it was particularly refreshing to travel so quietly. Although she and Jamie exchanged only a few words as they sailed, there was no sense of awkwardness on board. Indeed Alice thought on one occasion she couldn't remember the last time she had felt so relaxed in the silence of someone else's company. Particularly a man.

A while later Jamie took over the steering and Alice relaxed. They drank beers, cold from a bucket of sea water on the floor of the cockpit, and with wedges of lime stuffed into the necks of the bottles. Alice lay stretched out on the padded seat on the low side of the cockpit. Her head was comfortably in the shade and she watched the boat's wake slowly stretch out behind them.

"Tell me again why you have a beautiful wooden sailing boat?" She said.

Jamie was stood up again, holding the tiller between his knees. It was clearly the way he liked to do it. A warm wide smile stretched across his face "She is beautiful isn't she?"

Alice answered by wriggling down deeper into her cushions.

"And comfortable too."

"I told you. I bought her when I was eighteen. I fell in love." Alice felt Jamie stare at her for a moment, and then shift his view back to their course.

"So what's the plan? Are you just going to keep living on her? Out in the harbour all on your own?"

Jamie didn't answer at once but watched her carefully.

"No. I'm going to live on her somewhere else."

"Where?" Alice asked, turning her neck to get a better view of him.

"Africa." He said the word carefully. As if revealing a secret.

Alice raised herself up in her seat at this.

"*Africa?*"

"Yeah. I want to do what my parents did. Once I get my medical licence. I want to work for a charity. Somewhere I can make a difference to people." Jamie looked faintly embarrassed that he'd told her this and quickly turned the conversation around.

"How about you? What are you going to do with your life? Something exciting I bet?"

Alice felt a little hollow hearing this. For a moment the opportunities her mother had suggested to her filled her mind. The PR company run by Dad's old friend, who openly leered at the young women working for him. Or modelling, where it was even worse.

"What do you *want* to do?" Jamie asked, cutting into her thoughts. While plenty of people hassled her about what she should do, hardly anyone ever thought to *ask* her this.

"I like kids," she said suddenly, and without thinking. "I'd really like to be a teacher. In a little primary school. Somewhere out of the way. Somewhere quiet." The words surprised her. They had come from a place so deep inside she'd hardly known herself they were true.

"Is that what you studied for?" Jamie asked. It was the natural question, but she shook her head.

"No. That's not the sort of thing I could really do with my family. You don't make much money as a teacher." She smiled a little bitterly, wondering how he'd take this. But he just shrugged.

"It's your life," he said. "You should do what *you* want." He looked away, up at the sail, as if to show he didn't mean this in a judgemental way, and perhaps he understood. Or at least understood that he could never understand. She looked up too at the canvas pushed into a taught bow with the pressure of the wind. It was so old the colour had faded, and there were patches where the sailcloth had been repaired.

The crazy thought swung into Alice's brain that just possibly she was falling in love with this boy.

When the headland finally drew level, then slipped behind them, Jamie steered the little yacht in towards the bay. Alice felt that the slowness of travel somehow increased the sense of anticipation. She peered over the yacht's bow and saw, to her satisfaction, there were no other yachts in the enclosed little horseshoe. On weekends in the summer you sometimes had to fight for space to drop anchor here, but today was early in the season and a weekday. They were lucky, and had the place to themselves.

They came into the bay under the power of the sail, Alice steering them in. This time Jamie stood on the bow, prepping the anchor. When they were parallel to the cliffs, thirty metres out from the beach, he let it clatter out into the water beneath them, clear enough so they could see the sandy bottom below them. They dropped the sails and stowed them away. Jamie waited for a while, watching the shoreline carefully to make sure the anchor was holding. Then he came back and joined her in the cockpit.

"So. Do you fancy that swim?" He asked. He began to unbutton his shirt.

Alice laughed. "You're serious?" She said. "The water's freezing."

"No it isn't. It was a warm winter. Come on!" He grinned at her to show he wasn't joking. "Lean over the side. Feel it."

Alice did what he said, reaching down with her hand until it touched the water. It was cold, but perhaps not as cold she had imagined.

"You're serious," she asked. He shrugged.

"Why not? You don't often get this place to yourself." He smiled again and continued to unbutton his shirt.

"I don't have a swimming costume." Alice gave him a look, as if this was something he had been planning all along.

"Go naked. There's no one here." Jamie said. "No one to see anything." He kept his face serious for a moment, but then broke into a smile. "I'm sorry, I'm kidding," he said. "I don't have anything to lend you I'm afraid." He had been about to push his shirt off his shoulders but now he hesitated.

"It's okay," Alice said. "I wore sensible underwear. I can use that." Jamie didn't reply, but she could see from his face that he wasn't sure how to take that.

But with the matter decided he walked onto the roof of the cabin, as if to give her some space to change. Alice kicked off her shoes and socks and placed them neatly in the corner. Then she unbuttoned her jeans and pushed them down over her hips. She felt exposed, just in her knickers, but the warmth of the alcohol still flowed through her, and before she could change her mind she quickly unbuttoned her blouse and pulled it from her shoulders. She bundled her clothes together and placed them on top of her shoes. When she looked up Jamie was standing there just in his underwear too. She knew she was wearing the same self-conscious grin she saw in his face.

"Are you sure about this?" She asked. In response Jamie walked past her to the stern of the yacht and undid a bungee cord that held a folding ladder up out of the water. He pushed it away so that the lower part of the ladder now reached down, its lower rungs appearing to wobble and shifting below the surface. Then he climbed outside the guard rail of the yacht. Still holding onto the shroud for support.

"How cold can it be?" He replied, and with that he jumped forward into a clumsy dive. His hands and head hitting the water before the rest of him. Some of the splash landed on Alice's bare skin, and she let out an automatic little scream. But before she could change her mind she too stepped over the rail and looked down at the water below. Through a few metres of pale green water she saw the sand on the bottom. Then Jamie surfaced, among a billion bubbles. The shock from the cold was clear on his face, but he sounded genuine when he encouraged her.

"It's not too bad," he gasped.

Alice raised her hands above her head. And then she dived.

25

Alice brought her hands forward as she jumped, and she entered the water with barely a splash - after all she had had plenty of practice diving from yachts from Monaco to Martinique. But her perfect form was shattered as the shock of the cold hit her. She came up gasping for breath, to find Jamie treading water and laughing at her.

"Not too cold? It's freezing," Alice gasped.

"I know. I was lying to get you in." He sounded as if the cold had knocked the breath from his body, but his face wore an expression of delight.

"I hate you. I fucking hate you." She splashed water into Jamie's face. He kicked away from her, out from the side of the yacht.

"Come on, swim a bit, you'll soon warm up."

She did what he said, following him for a bit, but then giving up and lying on her back in the upper layer of water which was warmer from the sun. The initial shock was gone now, replaced by a numb sensation on her skin that wasn't entirely unpleasant. And the view, of the empty bay, and the classic yacht lying calmly at anchor in the foreground, was both beautiful and somehow comforting in its familiarity. As she looked, a memory came unbidden into her mind. A few months beforehand she had gone with Andy to the Seychelles, just the two of them. They had gone on a boat trip with a local man - she couldn't remember his name, just his beaming smile - but he had taken them to a bay, similar to this one in many ways. Perhaps more beautiful and more vibrantly coloured. But really just another bay. Another swim. Another man. She glanced up at Jamie who was nearby. She felt a layer of guilt settle upon her.

"Come on, let's swim ashore," Jamie said suddenly. Alice looked. It was thirty metres away to the narrow beach set at the bottom of low cliffs. She had explored it many times, there was little there except for an old fisherman's hut. But now - her mind firing erratic thoughts at her all of a sudden - another image appeared, so complete it unsettled her. It was herself and Jamie inside the fishing hut. But in her mind their underwear was gone, and they were making love against the rough workbench she knew was inside. She could almost feel the knurls of the wood as she gripped it to hold herself still against him. For a moment she stared at Jamie, wondering if this was in his mind as well, or whether he could somehow see what she was thinking. But he just smiled. His hair plastered down over his forehead, his teeth still white in the sunshine.

"OK," she said uncertainly. Keen to distract herself she set off before him, concentrating on her stroke.

It became something of a race. Alice was the more proficient swimmer, and had a few metres head start, but Jamie was stronger, and she felt him in the water, alongside and just a little behind. She put her head down and stretched her arms out in front of her, pulling handfuls of water back as she'd been taught by her father. She kicked her legs in a slow, easy pattern. But still Jamie was there, and still he gained on her. And then - perhaps - he let up as they neared the shore, so that they reached the beach at about the same time. Neither was able to claim victory, and perhaps, Alice realised, they hadn't been racing after all.

They both pulled themselves out of the water and lay on the sand. It wasn't cold now, not with the exercise and the warm sun.

"I've not swum like that for a long time," Alice said, drawing in deep breaths, enjoying the sensation.

"You're fast." Jamie replied. His chest was still heaving up and down. Alice was surprised. Perhaps he hadn't been going easy on her after all.

"We used to come here as kids," Alice said. "Teenagers." She eyed the fishing hut. The effort of the swim hadn't quite wiped the image from her mind.

But then, when Jamie didn't reply, Alice felt awkward and unsure of what to say next. It was like she suddenly realised how inappropriate it was to be lying on a empty beach in her underwear, thinking such thoughts about a man she barely knew. Or at least a man who was not her fiancé. A man she had already slept with once. And Jamie seemed to be feeling it too. They lay in silence. Alice felt the sun begin to dry her skin, leaving an invisible layer of salt.

They stayed silent for a long time, and Alice began to relax again. She let the fishing hut fantasy drift away, and the rays of the sun warm her skin.

"This is nice," she said suddenly.

"Mmmm," he replied.

"I wish we could just do this." Alice said suddenly.

"Do what?" Jamie asked.

"Just go places. Just forget about everything and get away. On your boat."

Jamie's head turned to look at her. He didn't answer for a while.

"We can." He said at last. She laughed.

"No, I mean it. We can go, whenever you want. I get my degree at the end of the summer, then I'm going to sail *Phoenix* down before the weather gets too bad. I'll go via Madeira, then head for Sierra Leone. You could come. You could be a teacher there. They always need teachers. They'd love you out there." He propped himself up on one arm and looked across at her. She stayed lying down, not laughing now. Behind him she noticed the fisherman's hut, still there in the background.

Alice realised how they were nearly touching, and how any moment she could reach out a hand and lay it on his firm body. She wondered how he would react if she did so. She remembered how they had made love on the night of her sister's wedding. She found herself breathing lightly, almost daring herself to move her arm. And then, as if he was again reading her thoughts, he jumped lightly to his feet. He held out a hand to pull her up too.

"Come on," he said. "Let's have a look around."

She said nothing, but stood up, and followed him.

He led the way, walking by the water's edge towards the end of the little beach and the small, grassy mound where the fisherman's hut sat. There was a wooden boat next to it, turned over so that its blue-painted hull faced the sky, and tufts of long grass grew around its sides. A few lobster pots were piled here and there. There was a ring of stones where someone had made a fire. Neither of them said why they were going there, but the hut seemed to be drawing them in. A little, dark, wooden building, its lack of windows giving nothing away about what was inside.

When they got to the door, Jamie pushed on it cautiously.

"Hello?" He said, and he grinned at Alice when no one replied. The door creaked as it swung inwards. They looked inside.

"Mind your feet," Jamie said. "There could be fishhooks on the floor, or glass from broken bottles." He stepped inside and Alice followed.

The bench was much as Alice remembered it from looking inside many times before. It was fixed onto the back wall of the little hut, but far from being empty and the sort of place she could imagine laying back against, it was littered with rubbish. And there was a smell, heavy in the air. Possibly something had died in here or maybe people had just used it as a toilet. Whatever it was, the fantasy image she had had in her mind disappeared at once. They didn't stay. Jamie pulled the door shut again behind them.

"I hate it when people do that," Jamie said. "Why do people have to leave things in such a mess?"

Alice didn't reply. She was still unclear why Jamie had led her there in the first place. She didn't even know why she was here with him at all. Other than because she wanted to be, she realised.

A small cloud slid over the sun. It didn't signal a change in the weather, but it was enough to drop the temperature. Alice shivered.

"I don't want to get cold," she said. "I think we should swim back to the yacht."

He nodded, still looking troubled, and Alice felt a sudden desire to make him smile again.

"Maybe you can warm me up when we get there?" She said, and watched his face change. Then she reached out, took his hand and pulled him towards her. She tilted her head back and kissed his lips, wrapping her hands around the small of his back. It felt delicious, it felt right.

"Okay," he said, when she pulled away, his voice was light, his eyes wide. "I think I have some hot chocolate somewhere."

She burst out laughing, delighted with the response, and then ran ahead of him back down the beach until she was level with where the yacht lay at its anchor. He followed and they entered the water together. They embraced again once they were in, they kissed, but the cold was different this time and she wriggled away and began swimming. They matched each other this time, both using breast stroke. Their fingers brushed together as they pulled through the water.

But as they halved the distance to the yacht, a sound interrupted them, an engine. It wasn't like the melodious throb of the diesel in *Phoenix*, but the harsher roar of a high-performance engine. It quickly grew louder, and then, around the headland of the little bay a white motor cruiser suddenly appeared, moving fast.

Had this been the summer there would have been nothing unusual in seeing it appear, although anyone already anchored in the bay would have tutted at the speed it was approaching - it was still raised up on a plane, riding its own bow wave, and sending out a heavy wash behind it.

It was a small Sunseeker type yacht, squat and bulky – the type favoured by those with sufficient money to keep a boat, but not enough for a vessel which didn't need to compromise its elegance with practicality. It was still doing nearly 25 mph as it carved its way into the flat water of the bay. Clearly whoever was driving it hadn't expected there to be anyone else here today, and when they saw Jamie's yacht sitting at anchor, they made a sudden hard turn to swing around her.

Jamie and Alice both stopped swimming for a moment and trod water. Alice felt suddenly small and exposed, about halfway between the shore and *Phoenix*. Alice sensed how Jamie put himself between her and the Sunseeker, though there would nothing he could do if the driver failed to notice them. Then she felt him tugging at her arm, telling her to keep moving. They both fell into a faster stroke to get quickly to the shelter of Jamie's yacht. As she swam, Alice kept expecting the new boat to slow, as good manners and responsibility dictated. But it didn't. Instead the driver kept the boat planing, and swung it into a fast turn that would take it all the way around Jamie's boat.

It meant Alice and Jamie found themselves, still swimming, right in the path of the fast-moving motor yacht. The high white bow of the motorboat thudded through the little waves, already frighteningly close and still turning - so that its course would come straight towards them. She swam harder, but felt a horrible sense of panic. The driver hadn't seen them, was going to run right over the top of them. But then she saw a figure, on the bow of the motor boat, pointed at her and Jamie. She saw the boat change course just a little to pass alongside. The driver had seen them after all. Now the situation wasn't about the danger they were in. It was more the sheer rudeness of what the motorboat was doing.

Jamie reached the stern of *Phoenix* first, but he waited until Alice got there too, a few strokes behind him, and from there he helped her climb the ladder and re-board the yacht. As she did so the motor yacht finally slowed barely 10 m away. Perhaps the driver would have been able to claim he was just slowing as he came into the bay, looking for a place to anchor, but the reality was different, and Alice felt a burst of fury. He had obviously seen them swimming back towards the yacht and decided to check them out. To check *her* out. The reason Alice knew this with one hundred percent certainly, was because she knew both the driver and the young man who had pointed at them in the water.

"Here, let me get you a towel." Jamie said. He stepped past her and dropped down into the cabin. She heard him padding forwards and for a moment it was just her standing, dripping in her underwear in the cockpit of the yacht. Beside her, higher, since the deck of the Sunseeker was twice as tall as *Phoenix's* cockpit, and gave a commanding view, was Robbie Jones.

His eyes travelled up her body and he took his hands off the wheel, put two fingers in his mouth and let out a loud wolf-whistle.

Jamie's head emerged again from the cabin. He handed Alice a towel and she quickly wrapped it around herself. Jamie glanced across at the other boat, still too close. His face was dark and angry. But then Robbie's eyes obviously took in Alice's face at last.

"Alice?" Robbie shouted, looking surprised now. "*Alice* is that you?"

Jamie had turned to face the men, staring them out. But now the momentum of the motor boat had taken it past *Phoenix*, and it was too far to hail. Jamie turned around and looked at Alice again.

"Do you know them?" Jamie asked. There was fury in his face which somehow both matched how Alice was feeling, but scared her as well. He looked away and began drying himself with a second towel.

Alice nodded. "They're friends of Andy," she said, and he froze. When he spoke again he seemed to be working hard to control his voice.

"Well they drive like fucking arseholes."

Alice didn't reply. She didn't disagree, but on the other hand, she had spent many happy days on the foredeck of the ugly little motorboat that was now dropping its anchor just ahead of them.

26

The atmosphere on the trip back was flat. As if the interruption in the bay had punctured something and it now lay deflated and broken around them. They had stayed a little longer in the bay, but there was no talk of warming up, no jokes about hot chocolate. Instead they had dressed - Jamie letting Alice take the cabin while he changed under his towel in the cockpit. Then Robbie had switched on the stereo on the Sunseeker and turned it up loud, so that the brags and curses of a rap artist bounced around the bay, echoing off the cliffs. Without needing to consult with Alice, Jamie had untied the sails, and they worked together to lift the anchor and sail away, keeping as far to the other side of the bay as the wind would allow.

Once they were back out to sea, they had relaxed again, but it was impossible to escape the fact that something had changed.

The wind was still light, and the trip back took another two hours - plenty of time for thinking. And in the long silences Alice found herself thinking. And as they sailed through the narrow entrance into the harbour, Alice finally made a decision. She waited until the yacht was safely moored, the sails stowed, indeed the very last moment, when Jamie was about to help her climb down into the dinghy.

"Thank you Jamie," she said, breaking a long silence.

"That's OK" Jamie replied, looking a little confused. He thought she meant the words for offering his hand, she knew.

"I mean for everything you've done." She went on. She knew what she was going to say would hurt him. But she said it anyway.

"For coming to me with what you found. For not going to the police. Everything. For listening to me going on about my parents." She smiled weakly.

"What else could I have done?" Jamie said. He still had the rope for the dinghy in his hand, but neither of them made any move to climb down into it.

"We haven't really talked about that..." Jamie began, but Alice didn't let him finish.

"No." Alice read exactly where he was going. "I didn't want to bring that up. It's been such a nice day."

Jamie met her gaze for a moment. "Until that Sunseeker turned up," he said. He seemed able to smile about it now. "You've been very quiet since then."

Alice hesitated. "Yeah. I guess that did have something to do with it."

"With what? I don't understand."

Alice looked at him for a moment before replying. He had caught the sun, his cheeks had more colour than earlier.

"I suppose they were just a reminder. Of real-life. My real life I mean."

Jamie waited a beat or two but she didn't elaborate.

"Well this is real life too." As if to demonstrate he tugged on the dinghy's bow line until the little boat bumped gently against the yacht's hull.

"See?"

"No it isn't." Her voice was firm but sad. "My life isn't anything like this. It's clubbing in London. It's skiing in Verbier, being Mum's tennis partner." She looked away.

"It's marrying Andy and being a good little wife."

Jamie's eyes widened, but he kept his voice level. "You haven't talked about Andy much either," he said. "I almost thought..." he stopped.

Alice waited a moment then asked him. "What? What did you think?"

Jamie seemed unsure how to finish his sentence. "I don't know. I thought that maybe you and he..." He stopped, and looked away. "I thought that maybe you were having second thoughts about that." He tried to lock his eyes onto hers but she had no difficulty in looking away.

"You think I'm getting married to someone that I don't seem to care for?"

Jamie hesitated. Seemed about to speak but then didn't.

"Or you're wondering why I'm getting married to someone at all if I'm sleeping around behind his back?"

This time a goofy smile appeared on Jamie's face, like he appreciated being reminded what they'd done. What they'd nearly done again that day.

"Yeah, I guess."

This time Alice spent a long moment considering.

"The thing is, the annoying little thing is, I do love him. And all this - everything that's happened - even with you, it's shown me that I still love him."

The smile on Jamie's face faded away. But he said nothing.

"I'm sorry Jamie, I know you're hoping that something can happen between us – something more I mean – but it can't. I really shouldn't have even been here with you today. It should be Andy I'm speaking to. It should be Andy who helps me deal with all this."

Jamie opened his mouth to respond but he either changed his mind or couldn't think of anything to say. In the end he pulled on the dinghy's line again until the little boat was held close against the ladder at the stern of the yacht. Taking the cue, Alice climbed over the guard rail and down the ladder, settling herself at the front of the dinghy. Jamie climbed down behind her and sat at the stern. He busied himself with the engine, then looked at Alice again. She was holding the painter, ready to cast the dinghy off. He opened his mouth to speak, but instead he shook his head and fired the engine. Alice released them, and Jamie put the engine into gear so that the dinghy lurched forward. He pushed the throttle forward and carved the dinghy around in an arc so that it pointed away towards the other side of the harbour and the mainland.

The whole trip he didn't look at her. She supposed it was because, travelling so fast, he had to keep an eye out for fishing buoys and other mooring buoys, but she sensed the real reason too, the hurt in him. And she felt it too. For her part she watched his yacht slipping away in the background until, as they turned the corner, all she could see of her was the slender wooden mast, nearly camouflaged against the steep green sides of the island.

A few long minutes later Jamie throttled back as they approached the shore. He steered for a low wooden jetty and came in expertly so that the little boat slowed and stopped perfectly alongside. He reached across, grabbed the side, and held them there while Alice wrapped the painter around a metal ring. When she was done, Alice felt the strongest urge to say something - anything really - that would break the horrible atmosphere that had descended upon them. But she didn't. Instead she climbed unsteadily to her feet, and stepped out onto the jetty. Jamie handed her the bag containing her underwear, still wet from their swim.

She took it, and could remain silent no longer. "Are you going back to the yacht?" She asked eventually.

Jamie nodded. There was another silence that stretched. The awkwardness was breaking Alice's heart.

"I'm sorry Jamie," Alice said, feeling tears welling up. "In a different world, things would be different."

Suddenly Jamie looked at Alice squarely in the face, and she was surprised by the depth of the hurt she saw there. But he seemed determined to cover it up, and his words were reasonable and understanding. So much so that she feared if he had got out of the boat she would have been unable to prevent herself throwing her arms around him and telling him she had changed her mind.

"I get it," he said, a quiver in his voice. "I understand, I really do." Jamie tried to raise a smile. "It's alright."

Alice did not dare to open her mouth. She had no idea what words might come out if she did. Instead she told herself over and over that this was the right thing to do. That this was what she wanted.

Still she hoped he would get out of the boat. It seemed appropriate that they might embrace, at least, in parting. But he didn't move, he didn't even turn the engine off, leaving it ticking over in neutral. In the end she settled for bending down from the jetty to hug awkwardly and briefly. As she did so she realised that their touching would only wound him more, so she pulled away. She raised her hand, the plastic bag with her wet underwear still wrapped around her wrist. She waved, held her hand there a moment.

"Good luck Alice," Jamie said. "With whatever you choose to do. With your family. With Andy." He was crying now, not trying to hide it from her. She felt her own tears come too.

"It's been nice meeting you Alice Belhaven," Jamie said. "Very nice."

With that he released the mooring line again and pulled it into the boat. He gave a light shove against the side of the jetty, like he wanted to put some distance between them, so that she didn't see the extent of his tears. They were running down Alice's face now, and she turned away. As she did so she heard the little engine roar. And when she turned back he was speeding away. Alice, still with her hand raised in a wave, watched him go. Regret seemed to pour into her, like a cup being filled to the brim. For a moment she sobbed almost uncontrollably.

But as she walked up the jetty she pulled herself together. Already she felt better. Like the tears had unblocked a plug of emotion, and now she felt nothing. Hollow. She felt in her pocket for her phone. She scrolled through her contacts, a little surprised at how far she had to swipe until she found Andy's on the 'recent calls' list. Eventually she found it though, and pressed the button to call. She waited until she heard a dialling tone before putting the phone to her ear.

She climbed up the angled walkway of the jetty, low in the water now the tide had dropped. The phone's dialling tone rang in her ear. A road ran parallel to the water's edge and she walked along it. Already she felt back in the real world, back in her world. Her house was no more than five minutes walk away. Her parents' house. A house she now knew may have been paid for with money taken through blackmail. That was a new reality she would have to come to terms with.

The dialling stopped. She opened her mouth to speak, ready to inject a false lightness into her tone - but there was no one there. Eventually a generic voicemail clicked in. A robotic female voice told her that *Andrew* wasn't available to answer her call right now. Andy hadn't bothered to personalise his message, only entering his name in a gruff voice so that it sounded like he didn't care if anyone left a message or not. The robotic woman asked if she wanted to leave a message. And Alice knew she didn't. She left only a few seconds of empty time while she thought of all the things she ought to say to him but didn't know how.

And with her attention focused on the mobile phone pressed against her ear, Alice didn't notice the set of eyes watching her with interest from the silver car parked on the road opposite.

27

The thing Kenning enjoyed most about his retirement job was the variety of it. OK, this particular case hadn't been the most exciting so far, but it was nice to be down by the coast. The weather was good, and he'd even had the opportunity to hire a small boat. And the girl - the one who was spending more and more time with the target - she was a looker. He could watch her all day long.

He wasn't in the Jag, he normally found it stood out too much for surveillance. Instead he'd hired a silver BMW three series. He wanted to get the seven series, or even the five, but he knew smaller cars tended to stand out less. Then again, perhaps around here that wasn't so much of a problem. Every other car that came past was a top-of-the-line Range Rover or an open-top sports car. Maybe he should have come down in the Jag.

A movement on the yacht interrupted his musings.

He picked up his binoculars. They were Swarovski EL 8.5x42s, the most expensive he could find. A cool two thousand pounds they cost, and there hadn't been a murmur of complaint when he put the expense receipt in. Kenning had quickly learnt his new employers wanted the best and were prepared to pay for it. When he put them to his eyes the yacht's cockpit leapt towards him, the quality of the lenses still surprised him. They were worth every penny. Kenning watched the young man climb down into his little tender, and cast off. Kenning took a record of the time and wrote it down in his notebook.

19:45

"Now where are you going son?" Kenning asked, of no one in particular.

With the binoculars he tracked the tender as it sped across the water. Kenning had observed the target using various landing stages, depending on what his objective was. He seemed to prefer one, close to a bus stop, when he was attending lectures at the nearby university. He'd used another when he met the girl, or like earlier, when he dropped her off. But from the direction he was headed now, it looked like he was aiming for the pontoon that was just a few minutes' walk from a small convenience store. He was going shopping. Kenning predicted. And he yawned.

The one thing Kenning didn't like about his job was writing reports. He had never been a desk kind of guy, preferring to report in person, and let others worry about filling in the forms. But for this job he was working alone. And in addition, he had very specific instructions on how and when to send his reports. They used a twice-encrypted email with a self-destruct timer built into it. It was clever alright. It meant that, should there ever be any official investigation into what he was doing, or a seizure of files, which his old colleagues could do on the order of a judge, there would be nothing to find. No trace of what he had been doing, and no one at fault for destroying evidence. Kenning rather marvelled at the ingenuity of it, and its simplicity.

But there was one, rather obvious problem with it. Because of Kenning's reticence in report writing, there tended to be a delay in his employers learning what he had observed. Take now for example. He had been actively on the target for three days since his last report. But since nothing of particular interest had happened, the information from those three days hadn't been passed on. It was stored only in his head, and in the part-written report on his notebook computer. Accessible only to him.

Although this flaw in the system had been there for a while, it had never proved of any consequence before. Because he did always send through his report when something relevant happened. But that was the problem with flaws in systems. They never really mattered, until they mattered.

A trio of swans flew over the water in front of where the car was parked. Automatically Kenning's mind worked out the trajectory he would need to shoot to bring them down. When they passed, his eyes returned to the tender. It was now moving much more slowly, nosing towards the pontoon. He picked up his binoculars again and watched. It really was as if he were standing right next to him, Kenning marvelled.

And then something made him swing the lenses a little to the right. A frown appeared on his face.

"Hello... What's all this then?" Kenning said to himself.

On his forehead, above where the binoculars stayed clamped to his face, thick frown lines had appeared. He stayed perfectly still for a long while, watching. Finally, a full five minutes later, he dropped the glasses down and looked away.

"Well that's a fucking surprise." He said.

The investigation he had thought was just a jolly by the sea had taken a new, and highly unexpected turn.

28

Kenning interrupted his chewing to lick his fingers. The shop had boasted of the best fish and chips in the country, but in his opinion the chips were a little on the greasy side. And he still couldn't get used to how they were served these days, in an extruded polystyrene tray, an unappetising pale yellow colour. Not like when he was a boy. When his parents would take him and his brother to Skegness, and they would sit on the seafront eating fish and chips out of newspaper. That was how they should be served. Throwing the odd chip up in the air and watching the seagulls wheel down and catch it before it even stopped going upwards. And mushy peas too. You couldn't even *get* mushy peas here. Too fucking posh.

Best fish and chips in the country? My arse, Kenning thought to himself.

The cod was alright though. It flaked nicely as he ate it and he washed it down with two cans of coke. When he was finished he closed the lid and tossed the tray down into the passenger foot well. The harsh smell of vinegar hung in the air.

Martin Kenning wiped his mouth with the back of his hand and then carefully cleaned his fingers with a tissue. When he was sure he had all the grease off he picked up his small Sony laptop and opened the lid again. He typed his password and provided his fingerprint to the scanner. The computer let him in. He opened the Word file he had been working on since witnessing the events earlier that evening. A timeline, a page of terse text, and an image which he'd taken by telephoto lens.

What he'd seen had been a surprise. But now he'd had time to think about it, not such a big one. Whatever this case was really about, it fit into one simple category: Fucking rich people and their fucking problems. That was fine though - it was fucking rich people who funded his rather expensive lifestyle these days. In fact, you could say he was on the way to becoming a fucking rich person himself. But whatever - what he'd seen warranted a report. An update to his employers, who would doubtless have a view on how and whether to handle this new development. Hence his evening spent hunched up in front of the laptop. He shifted in his seat. The coke he'd drunk with his dinner had left him uncomfortable.

A set of headlights shone suddenly across the side of the BMW. A car, driving into the car park. Kenning was alert but not concerned. It was a popular place to come, even late at night like now. You could drive right up to the waterside and take a view of the harbour and its islands, without even needing to leave the car. This one was some hot hatch or other, he could hear the music playing, even from inside the BMW. Kenning dimmed the screen on his computer and watched in his mirrors, as the new arrival stuck to the back edge of the car park - away from where he was parked - and came to a stop in the far rear corner, in the relative darkness between two lamp posts. No one got out.

He kept watching. For a moment, the interior light came on. Kenning had time to register two occupants, a man and a woman, both in their twenties. He was either attacking her or groping her. Feeling a little bit aroused at either possibility, Kenning picked up the binoculars to find out.

The reason these lenses cost so much was for their performance in low-light conditions. He could see almost as clearly as if it had been daytime. He watched as the boy pawed at the girl's breast through her clothing, then clumsily attempted to remove her top. He saw her pained expression as she stopped whatever she was doing to his crotch - unfortunately hidden below the level of the car's window - and pulled her top off herself. He caught a glimpse of her breasts before the boy's hand clamped onto them and began mauling them out of shape. Then the seat began to wind itself back. The boy slipped out of view. There was a flash of leg. The car started rocking.

Kenning looked away for long enough to note the time, then returned to observing. Soon after the car door opened and something was thrown out onto the ground. The binoculars weren't so powerful that Kenning could see it was a contraceptive, but he guessed. The seat came up again, the vehicle's occupants came back into view and began to rearrange themselves. The girl even leaned forward into the rear-view mirror and adjusted her makeup. Kenning checked his watch again.

"Three minutes forty-five seconds." Kenning murmured to himself. "You little charmer you."

The little car stayed where it was, now with the interior light on, its occupants chatting and finally Kenning had the opportunity to examine the girl in detail. He decided that, even in her post-coital glow, she had a face like a pinched arse.

After that he lost interest.

He turned around, and scanned the target's yacht again. It hadn't moved of course, it was still on its mooring, way out on the other side of the harbour and still tucked into its little creek. And absolutely nothing had changed, the lights still burned from the cabin, with no one visible on deck. Actually no. One thing *had* changed, Kenning realised. The moon, which had hung brightly in the night sky, bouncing light down onto the harbour so that the little wavelets were tipped by silver, had become noticeably less bright. Kenning frowned at that. He could still see the yacht, part-illuminated by its cabin lights. But as he watched, even that became harder to make out. The reason was clear a moment later, when the front edge of a bank of fog overtook the yacht, making it disappear altogether. He checked through the binoculars. There was nothing to see. Just a blanket of grey.

Well that was the end of that.

It wasn't a problem. There wasn't any operational need for Kenning to observe the yacht personally. He was only really in the car park because it was a nice place to sit and write his report. But that was done, or nearly done. Now the fog had come in he may as well go back to his hotel, send the report, and go to bed.

But watching the sex had made Kenning horny. He thought about this for a long while, and then he pulled out his wallet from his jacket pocket. From inside he selected one of the business cards he had come across in one of the few remaining telephone boxes in the nearby town centre. It wasn't entirely sensible to pick up prostitutes this way, but at least Kenning was able to check them out beforehand. *Lusty Lola* (real name Susan White) advertised herself as 25 but it took Kenning only a few moments to discover her date of birth, which made her rather closer to 40. But he didn't mind that, particularly after hacking her private face-book pages and seeing her promised dimensions were at least accurate (even though the photo she used was her face photoshopped onto a different body.). A few nights previously he'd paid her £200 for an hour in a premium room of the local Premier Inn. Since that hadn't left him itching, he was considering ringing her again.

It was a bit late to call, but the thought of those big tits slapped into his face eventually had him typing the numbers into his phone.

"Yeah?" The word was half question half snarl.

"Lola?" He thought about calling her Susan, but that would spoil the fun wouldn't it?

"Yeah baby?" The voice became suddenly different, husky and softer.

"It's Martin. From the Premier Inn. You busy tonight?"

"Not too busy for you honey. You wanna play again?"

"Maybe. Can you meet me in an hour?"

"Sure. I was just getting ready for bed anyway. Same place?"

"No. There's a Travelodge on the London Road. Can you meet me there. Get a room? I'll cover the cost."

"OK. You're a careful one." Lola said. She paused for a moment. "Want me to bring anything honey? Want to play any games?"

Kenning thought about it. Thought about those tits again. "You got any baby oil?" he asked. His eyes flicked to the clock on the dashboard.

"Sure."

"Make it forty minutes. It's late already." He hung up and licked his lips. They still tasted of vinegar. But he shifted uncomfortably again in his seat. The Coke from dinner was pressing on his bladder. He wouldn't be able to pee when he got a hard on. Best go for one now. He cracked open the car door.

Kenning considered walking to the toilets - at the far end of the car park. But there was no one about, and with the fog no one could see anything. So instead he stepped carefully down onto the tiny strip of beach in front of him. There were no steps, just a few rocks that protected the car park from when the sheltered water of the harbour rose too high. When he got to the beach he turned around to piss onto the rocks, just in case anyone else drove into the car park and illuminated him with their headlights, he would be out of sight. He opened his fly and relaxed. He let out a comfortable sigh, and closed his eyes.

The first blow took him entirely by surprise, but even as his head jerked forward and began ringing, he was calculating. His attacker was reticent, the blow had been weak, cautious. Kenning was able to stay upright, but he wasted valuable fractions of a second in registering disgust that he'd sprayed piss on his trousers. Those fractions allowed his attacker to lift the weapon again. And the second blow was stronger, its intent clearer. But this time Kenning was already moving, so that whatever it was glanced off his head, and only impacted his shoulder with a dull thud. Even so it sent a shower of pain flashing through Kenning's brain. He lashed out with his other hand, not an attacking move, just a defensive push away, and he swung through empty air. Then Kenning saw a snatch of light reflected from the surface of the weapon - it was a spanner, the heavy, adjustable type. His brain screamed at him - *concentrate on what was relevant.* Fragments of training returned to him, as it was designed to do. *Be ready to dodge the next blow, or deflect. Where could he escape? Could he get to his gun, inside the glove box of the car?*

He was still thinking when the third blow came. This time it was driven with anger and rage, and Kenning's questions were left unanswered. The heavy metal of the tool smashed into his head, driving broken pieces of skull into the soft tissue inside. And new thoughts into his mind. The curious feeling that his head had become jelly. Then his legs buckled and he dropped to his knees. He stayed like that for a second, like a man praying, and the change in angle meant he finally saw the light from the lamp post reflected on his attacker's face. Kenning's last moments alive weren't spent with his life running before his eyes, they were spent confused.

How the hell did he *get here?*

29

Alice was asleep when the doorbell rang. She had her alarm set for six, to catch the early train for London, and at first that's what she thought the noise was. But there was no light around the edges of the curtains. And the noise was wrong, not the soft chirping of her phone, but the buzz of the bell downstairs. She looked again at the phone. It was 3:45 am. What the hell? The noise came again. Repeated, and then faintly - because the house was well built - the noise of hammering on the door. A faint shouting, she couldn't make out what.

Her next reaction was fear. Whoever it was knocking on her door at this time, it couldn't be good. Unless - Maybe it was friends - on their way back from a bar somewhere? But they'd never do that. They'd phone her. She glanced again at the screen. No messages. She wondered if she could just ignore it. If they'd go away. She wondered about phoning the police.

But instead she twisted out of bed and pulled a robe around herself. She picked up her phone - in case she did need the police - and padded down the stairs to the front door. There was a screen built into the wall next to the door, the feed, a discreet camera that pointed at the step outside. As soon as she saw it she gasped. She thought for a moment, then pulled open the door.

"Jamie?" She said. "Oh my God!" Her hand flew to her mouth.

He looked bad enough in the muted colours of the iPad screen, but in real life he looked shocking. He was dressed in some sort of blue work-man's overall with no shoes. One of his eyes was puffy and purple, his hair was wet and slicked back, revealing a wound and blood oozing on his head.

"Oh my God! What happened?"

Jamie Weston almost collapsed forwards into the house, He took several deep breaths before he managed to speak.

"You've got to get out of here. I've got to get you away. Right now." But he didn't make any attempt to move - it didn't look like he could. One of his hands went onto the wall and Alice saw how it left a bloody palm print as it slipped down.

His words frightened her. "What?"

When Jamie spoke again his voice sounded clearer.

"Alice, listen to me. Please, I don't know how much time we have." He reached out with his blood-covered hand to take her arm. He began pulling her outside.

"Jamie!" She felt panic rising up at being pulled out into the night. "What's going on? What is this?" Roughly she shook herself free, he stag-gered on the step, like he was about to fall.

"What the hell is this?"

He stared at her, wild-eyed for a second.

"They came for me." He said. Her action seemed to have snapped him back to the present. He was panting, as if he'd been running hard. "We have to get away. Before they get here."

"Who gets here? Who's coming?"

"I don't know. But we have to move."

"I can't. I'm... I don't even have clothes on," Alice said. For a second time Jamie reached in to take her arm, but this time there was no strength in it. Alice feared he was going to collapse right there on the step.

"What happened?" She asked, but his eyes rolled backwards into his head. Moving quickly she put her shoulder underneath his, and he part-collapsed onto her, his head lolling onto hers.

"Got to go..." his eyes returned, but he slumped down letting his weight fall against the wall. He rested there a second, panting. Alice looked around at the darkness outside. The security light was on in the front driveway, rendering the street beyond it darker than it would otherwise have been. She didn't know what had happened but suddenly the darkness around terrified her, and she just wanted to get the door shut.

"Come in. Come on." Using all her strength Alice tried to pull Jamie fully inside. It was a struggle at first, with him still resisting, but somehow the insistence in her voice cut through him, and he half fell over the threshold. She let him slump so she could get the door shut. Then she locked it and engaged the deadlock. When she'd finished she stood behind it, she was panting just as much as he had been. She wondered if this was some horrific dream.

When she turned back to Jamie he seemed to have recovered, and was trying to get up again. The wound on his head looked worse in the light of the hallway.

"Jamie what is this? What happened? Do you need an ambulance?"

He seemed to calm himself down.

"No." He touched his head and winced. "No. I'm alright. Is the door locked?"

"Yes."

"Is it secure?"

"Yeah. And it's like the best lock you can buy. I told you, we had issues with burglars a while back. Dad had all this installed."

Jamie nodded, like he understood. "OK. Well I don't think he followed me here anyway. So we've got a little time. But then we have to go."

"*What happened? Who didn't follow you?*" Alice said but he didn't answer. Instead it looked for a second like he was going to pass out. He screwed his eyes tightly shut and then opened them again. His left eye was puffy, the skin around it beginning to bruise. "Can we go upstairs? I could do with sitting down. "

Alice didn't reply. Wordlessly she put her arm around his waist and began to help him towards the stairs. With one hand on the wall Jamie let his weight rest upon her. Her gown fell open, revealing one of her breasts, but she covered herself up, and Jamie didn't even seem to notice.

"What happened? Who did this to you?" Alice asked again, but the effort of getting up the stairs seemed to prevent him from replying.

When they made it up to the living area, Alice helped lower Jamie into a seat. She went quickly to the kitchen and poured a glass of water.

She paused before taking it to him, giving herself the time to properly knot the gown around herself. Then she helped him raise it to his lips, giving her the opportunity to inspect the depth of the injury on his head.

"Oh my God! You need an ambulance. I'm going to call..."

"No!" Jamie stopped her. "No." Wincing he reached up and touched the wound. Gently his fingers seemed to measure it. "No, it's alright. Do you have a first-aid kit? I just need to put a dressing on it to stop the bleeding."

"How do you know it's not..." She hesitated.

"I'm a doctor remember," he said, and he forced a smile. It was the first time he seemed like the man she knew. Like he was fully back with her.

"We've got some stuff in the bathroom. Stay there."

He gave her a half smile, like he wasn't in much state to go anywhere, and Alice walked away. In the main bathroom she pulled open a cupboard and looked inside. She pushed a pack of plasters out of the way and retrieved an assortment of bandages and painkillers from behind it. She noticed a bottle of antiseptic and grabbed that too, then jogged back up the stairs.

"Here," she said. "I'm not really an expert at this." She leaned in close and inspected the wound on his head. Despite the jagged edge to it, she saw it wasn't as deep as she'd feared before. But it looked a mess. She searched among the packets she had brought and found some cotton wool. She moistened it with the antiseptic liquid and wiped gently on his face, clearing away the blood. With a fresh piece she dabbed at the wound itself.

"Sorry," she said, when he winced.

"It's OK." He told her, and closed his eyes again. He held his head still, letting her do the work.

When the wound was cleaned, she pressed a piece of gauze gently against it. "Hold this," she told him, and she helped him hold it in place with his hand. She noticed his knuckles were grazed, as if he'd been fighting.

"So? Are you going to tell me?"

He nodded.

"Yeah."

"I was asleep," Jamie began. "On board *Phoenix*. I was in the fore cabin

- I don't know why, I sometimes sleep better there. I got woken up by this noise. I didn't know what it was..." He screwed his eyes shut as if trying to locate the memory. He shook his head.

"Then suddenly the light flicked on and there was a man there. Just standing in the doorway"

He stopped again. Alice saw how hard he was breathing.

"No. Not the light. It was a torch. A flashlight. I was so surprised I said hello to him. Then I noticed what was below the light. He had a gun."

"A *gun*?" Alice cried.

"Yeah," Jamie replied. "Like a - I don't know - a pistol? It had a silencer on the end. I assume it was a silencer. I've never seen one before, but that's what it looked like. I couldn't believe it. I thought I was dreaming."

Alice wondered for a moment if *she* were dreaming, but it didn't feel anything like a dream.

"I thought he was just going to shoot me. Without saying a word, just - if that was it. But he didn't. He kept the gun pointing at me and then with his other hand he raised one finger to his lips. You know, like telling me to stay quiet."

Alice stared.

"He had gloves on. Black leather gloves. And he was dressed all in black. Balaclava on his head. He was big. He looked like a killer Alice. Like a fucking *assassin*."

For a moment it sounded like he was going to lose it. Alice spoke to try and keep him focused.

"So then what happened?"

Jamie swallowed. Nodded, like he understood what she was doing.

"He started talking to me. He asked me about you. He asked if you had seen the files." He stopped again and breathed deeply.

But his words had a horrible effect on Alice. So far Jamie's sudden appearance had shocked her - maybe even thrilled her a little - but at the mention of her name she felt fear begin to gather in the pit of her stomach. Real fear.

"What did you tell him?" Alice heard herself ask.

"The guy had a gun pointing right at me. I dunno, I've never had that. Alice it's like you can *feel* the bullet. Like you can feel it hitting your face and breaking through into your brain. I swear I've never felt anything like it. I don't know what I said. I think I just answered him. I'm sorry Alice."

Alice didn't say anything for a few seconds. There seemed nothing she could say.

"What did you tell him?" She asked in the end.

"I told him you hadn't. Hadn't seen the files. But that..." He lifted a hand to his wound. He seemed surprised to feel the dressing there.

"I told him that you knew about them."

Alice didn't reply.

"I didn't mean to. If I'd had a bit longer to think, maybe... Honestly that feeling of the bullet caving your face in, the feeling of actually dying..." His words ran out and he stared at the floor. Then he looked up and continued.

"I did tell him you'd decided not to do anything. That he had nothing to worry about... I..."

"What?"

Jamie looked ashamed. "I think I begged him. I think I begged him not to kill me."

For a moment Alice felt contempt, but it didn't last long. Her brain was actively putting her in the same position. What would she have done? Would she have been any braver?

"Then what happened?" She said at last.

Jamie rubbed his face. "The guy seemed to find that funny. He laughed at it. Then he asked what *exactly* you knew."

"And?"

"I was trying to think by then. I wanted him to think you weren't any threat. So I just told him you knew your dad might have been black-mailing people. But you didn't know who." Jamie stopped.

"And? What did he say to that?"

Jamie took a few deep breaths before answering.

"He... he looked confused."

Alice screwed up her face.

"*Confused?*"

"I don't know. Yeah. He held the gun closer to me, like he was about to shoot. Then he asked what I was talking about."

"What you were talking about?" Alice frowned. "I don't understand?"

"I didn't either. I didn't know if I was dreaming - I'd been asleep seconds before. I think I just started telling him everything. About how I'd found the USB and how there were these sex tapes, and how your dad was using that to blackmail people. And..." Jamie stopped.

"That's when he actually started laughing."

"Laughing?"

"Yeah."

"Then what?"

"Then he shot me."

30

"He *shot* you?"

"Yeah."

Alice looked again at Jamie, as if she had somehow missed the gunshot wound when tending to his injuries.

"So..."

"He still had the gun pointing at my face. He pulled the trigger, but it didn't fire. The gun clicked but nothing else happened."

Alice didn't answer. She just blinked her eyes, like this was finally too much.

"The guy was more surprised than I was. Then he tried again. And again it didn't fire. I don't know. I guess there was something wrong with it. Then there was this crazy moment when we just stared at each other. He wasn't laughing any more. Then he went for me. He came forward and hit me around the head with the gun." He pointed to his head wound.

"I guess he decided he was going to beat me to death instead. But he only got that one blow in before I kind of scrambled backwards out of the way." Jamie touched his head again. "There's not much room in the fore cabin, and he was big, a bit clumsy. When he tried to follow me he cracked his own head on the bulkhead. That gave me a few seconds. I just pushed past him. I thought about grabbing a weapon, but I didn't know if the gun would start working again. So I did the only thing I could. I ran out on deck. I just dived overboard and began swimming."

Alice said nothing, and after a few heavy breaths, Jamie continued.

"A few seconds later I heard these 'pops'. There were splashes in the water around me, so I swam down, and tried to put some distance between me and the boat. When I came up he didn't see me. It was dark, it was misty, a bank of fog had come in. I could hear him on the boat. Swearing. Shouting at me. Even with the fog I could see the lights of the land, so I started swimming away."

The effort of speaking was clearly tiring Jamie, and he stopped for a while. Alice waited for a moment, then picked up her phone.

"What are you doing?" Jamie asked, watching her.

"What do you think? I'm phoning the police," Alice replied. She had her phone to her ear, standing by the sofa. She was shaking, not just her hand but her whole body. "Someone just tried to kill you."

Jamie breathed for a minute.

"Hold on Alice. Let me finish first. There's something else."

Alice ignored him, and walked away to the window, but Jamie lifted himself painfully from his chair and began moving after her. He had his hand out in front of him.

"*Hold on Alice.* There's something else."

There was enough insistence in Jamie's voice that Alice slowly brought her phone back down. She cut the call before it connected.

"Why *wouldn't* we call the police? Someone just tried to kill you."

"You can. You should. But you have to let me finish first. Please?" He held out his hand, inviting her to sit down with him back on the sofa. She did what he asked, folding her arms across her chest.

"Well?" She said.

"I told you it was foggy out there," Jamie began. "After I dived into the water and swam away. After the guy had tried shooting the water, he got back into his boat. He started driving in circles around *Phoenix*. Looking for me. There was no wind, it was dead still. So whenever I tried to swim he could hear it, but he couldn't *see* me. So for a while I didn't go anywhere. I was just treading water. And he knew I was there."

"So..?"

"So he kept talking to me."

In the silence Alice could hear the sound of her own breathing.

"What did he say?"

"At first he was still angry, you know, swearing at me. But then he calmed down. He started to find the whole thing funny. He was laughing about his gun. He told me how it had never jammed before. How I should be dead. How I must have someone upstairs on my side." Alice listened in silence. She still had her telephone in her hands.

"But then I think he realised he wasn't going to find me. In the fog. Or maybe he thought I might have already slipped away. And he started warning me. He said that if I went to the police a lot of people would suffer." Jamie stopped. He looked at Alice as if trying to judge her reaction.

"He wanted me to make a deal. He said he'd let me live. But we needed to talk. To come to an arrangement."

"Who would suffer?" Alice interrupted him.

Jamie hesitated again, this time for a long time.

"You." Jamie's blue eyes met hers. "He told me that you would suffer. He was talking about accidents. About how the police wouldn't protect us. They wouldn't protect you." Jamie looked down at the floor, Alice thought he was finished, but then he continued.

"He said you would have an accident just like your dad did."

The words hit her like a fresh blow.

"Like Dad did?"

Jamie nodded.

"Dad's death *was* an accident."

Jamie didn't reply, but his eyes flicked off the floor and back to her face.

"Oh my God!" Alice said. "He said he killed my father?"

"He didn't exactly say it. It wasn't like we were having a conversation. After that I figured I was far enough away to start swimming. I was being pulled by the tide, he was sticking near to *Phoenix*. And I was pretty cold by then."

Alice said nothing.

"When I was far enough away I was able to swim for the shore. I was freezing. I thought I was going to drown. But I made it. Then I found these clothes stashed under a dinghy.

She looked at him, in his strange overalls. She remembered how he had looked on her doorstep. Then she looked down at the phone in her hand.

"I'm still going to call them," she said. But she made no move to do so.

"What is it? What are you worried about?" She asked him, a second later. "You don't believe this guy is actually going to get me if I go to the police?"

Jamie hesitated. "I don't know. I don't have a clue. *I don't know what any of this is about!*"

Jamie's voice rose as he spoke, like he was on the verge of breaking down. Somehow it injected doubt into Alice's mind.

"I'm sorry," he said a moment later. Then he tried a joke. "I'm sorry Alice, no one's ever tried to shoot me until I met you." He tried to smile at her.

"I don't know what the fuck to think."

Alice looked at the phone. Her finger hovered over the button to dial.

"It's..." Jamie stopped smiling. He seemed to be thinking hard, reluctant to spell out what he was thinking. "You're probably right. You have to tell them. Just - before you do - work out *what* you're going to tell them. Get it clear in your head."

Alice looked confused. "I'll just tell them everything. The truth."

Jamie shook his head. "I mean about your dad's blackmail and everything? Maybe there's a way you can tell the police without saying that. Without destroying your dad's reputation. Without destroying your mum."

Alice didn't speak.

"It sounded like your mum had some idea what your dad was doing. So she could get in a lot of trouble. I mean, maybe you should warn her. Tell her to get a lawyer ready or something. *I don't know...*" Awkwardly he waved away his own suggestion, as if it were stupid. He didn't look at her.

Still Alice was silent, staring blankly out in front of her.

Suddenly she slammed the phone down onto the coffee table in front of her. Then she buried her head in her hands. She sat there, curled up for a long while before Jamie moved closer and wrapped his arms around her. At first she resisted, but then she held him back. She began to sob, his strong arms around her felt like her only remaining connection to reality. For nearly ten minutes they stayed there, two figures comforting each other in the dead quiet of the night.

"So what should we do?" Alice said when she recovered. She pulled out a packet of tissues and dabbed at her face. "If we can't call the police I mean?"

"Are you sure this house is secure?" Jamie replied, as if she'd asked a different question altogether. In response Alice walked to the wall where an iPad was mounted. She pushed a button and it lit up, the screen divided into four quarters with each showing a different view of the front and rear of the house. She pressed another button and more views came up. There was no one in sight in any of them. She scrolled around until she came to a master screen with a thumbnail of every feed. A status button glowed green beneath them.

"All the security cameras are on. So are the motion sensors. We've got alarms that sound here and also automatically at the security company. Our front door cost seventeen thousand pounds. I think we're safe for a while." Alice tried herself to lighten the mood.

"OK. Then I guess we've got some time. Like I say, he didn't follow me. He won't know I've come here. We should have another look at the evidence. Try to figure out *who* is doing this. Maybe then there'll be some way we can tip off the police, without involving your family? Or maybe even make a deal with them. If that's what they want to do. Anything to make this go away." He shrugged, like that was the best he could come up with.

Alice considered what he'd said. It didn't sound very hopeful.

"What evidence?" She asked. It was a straw, but she was prepared to grasp at it.

"The photographs. From the *Aphrodite* parties. In the album down-stairs. And your dad's business contacts. We need to check it all again. We need to look again. The answer must be in there. It *must*."

Alice nodded slowly. "OK." She said. It didn't feel like much of a plan. But anything was better than sitting there doing nothing.

"OK," she said again, even if she didn't really understand how it would move things forward.

Jamie smiled. He tried to get to his feet again, and winced immedi-ately at the pain.

"What are you doing?" Alice asked.

"I'm getting the photographs." Jamie replied.

"Stay there," she said. "I'll get them."

* * *

When Alice returned they sat on the sofa upstairs, the pile of albums in front of them on the coffee table. Alice's mother had only begun organising her photographs once the children were born, and she hadn't been very comprehensive. Whole chunks of Alice's life had been missed out, but other events had been recorded in detail. They were mostly family shots, but there were social events too. Including two parties which had taken place on *Aphrodite*. One party had happened before Alice's birth, and only been included because of Joanne's presence there. The other had happened when Alice was still a baby. From the photographs, neither looked to be a particularly wild affair, but on Jamie's insistence, Alice drew up a list of the names of everyone in attendance, or at least everyone she recognised. In each case there were perhaps thirty people aboard the yacht. From the first party Alice recognised ten of them. From the second she knew twelve. All of the names overlapped - the ten people at the first party all came to the second one, a year and a half later.

"So who are these people?" Jamie asked, looking down the list he'd written.

"Friends of my parents mostly," she replied. "Just normal people. No one who'd do anything like this."

Jamie gave her a look, like he was remembering how it felt to have a gun pointed at him in the middle of the night.

"How about that guy?" Jamie pointed an image of a young man with dark skin and a full beard, neatly trimmed. Alice leaned in to get a better look.

"That's Janez. Mum's brother. He came over here for a while after Mum married Dad."

"Janez?" He leaned in closer to the photograph. Alice watched him. "You said he came here for a while... Where from?"

"Slovenia. That's where Mum's from too."

"Slovenia?" Jamie asked. He sounded curious.

"Yeah. She came over when she was twenty. It wasn't Slovenia then. It was Yugoslavia." Alice didn't explain further. It looked like Jamie was going to ask, but then he tapped the photo instead.

"So where is he now?"

"Dead." She said. "Probably."

The interest written into Jamie's face seemed to intensify.

"*Probably?*"

Alice tossed the album back down onto the table. She shrugged. "I don't know too much about it. Apparently he was here for a while, then he went back and joined the army. I don't know how much you know about what happened over there. Mum was pretty happy to put it all behind her. Janez was more the proud nationalistic type. I don't even really remember him that well." She turned the page on the album. It showed a montage of baby pictures. Someone had put a label underneath. "Alice at ONE!"

"So what happened?" Jamie pressed. "To this Janez?"

Alice took a while to answer. "He ended up fighting in the war in Kosovo. His unit were in the way when a Tomahawk missile landed nearby. That was... I was about 13 at the time."

Jamie considered for a moment.

"They ever find his body?"

"No. But you don't find bodies when a cruise missile hits you. But we knew what happened, because none of them came back. None of his unit." She shrugged again, and looked sad. "Mum took it pretty hard. He was her little brother." But Jamie was hardly listening to that. He pulled the list from her and underlined the name Janez Jovanović.

"What are you doing?" Alice shook her head. "Whatever this is has got nothing to do with that. I swear to you."

"We don't know that," Jamie interrupted her. He spoke gently but forcefully. "We just know it was somebody who went to those parties on your dad's boat. And he was there."

Then he sat back and looked again at the photographs they had open on the table. He sighed.

"Maybe you're right. These parties..." He tapped the album again. "They're like *family affairs*. They're not... They're not when those videos would have been made." Jamie shook his head.

"I told you. My parents calmed down when we came along."

"You don't have any others? Any photos from before? Other albums or anything?"

Alice felt a flicker of irritation. She glanced over at her phone. Her earlier feeling - that doing something trumped doing nothing - had faded. Now this felt like a waste of time. They should be calling the police. But she didn't. She *couldn't*. Instead she forced herself to think. And suddenly she remembered something.

"Yes. There are! Not albums. But I know Dad has a box somewhere in his cupboard. I think that's got some old photos in it. Maybe there's something there."

"Well go get it!" Jamie said at once. And he sat up, waiting for her to move.

It took a while for Alice to locate the shoebox. It was tucked away at the back of the cupboard that led off from her father's study, and she had to search long and hard to find the key for that. The cupboard had been a favourite place to play hide and seek when she was growing up, and Dad used it - had used it - to deposit items he didn't want to throw away, but had no practical use for. There were old wooden-framed tennis rackets, a box with Dad's old rowing trophies. A giant teddy bear that had belonged to both Alice and her sister. Alice felt strange touching its worn fur again after so many years. It looked tired and ragged. She wondered why her father had kept it. But then she pushed it out of the way and pulled out the box.

Inside they found coins, keys to locks that had long since disappeared, letters and cards, and a bundle of wallets of photographs, held together with elastic bands. Some had been developed at *Boots*, others were the type that people used to send off to labs - one for *Bonusprint*, one for *Truprint* - names Alice had forgotten she even knew. Jamie commented on how different it was today, when everyone had a mobile phone but no-one printed any photos. Alice didn't really listen, it was like he was suddenly making small talk. Instead she let her eyes explore the images they looked through. Her parents looked young and healthy in the images. Happy too - in almost every one they were laughing, playing up for the camera. But in the pile Alice sorted through, there were no boats, only cars, mountains, a holiday in the States. In this one they seemed to be at a concert. It looked like *Bon Jovi*.

"Here we go," Jamie said suddenly. "Bingo."

Alice looked up and saw Jamie was laying out photograph after photograph on the smoked glass top of the coffee table. Each one showed a scene from an earlier party on the *Aphrodite*. Alice saw at once these weren't photographs she had ever seen before.

31

"Well? Do you recognise anybody?" Jamie said, when he had finished.

Alice put down the photographs she was holding and moved closer to Jamie on the sofa. She peered closely at the first few photographs he had laid out.

"They're dark," she said.

"I know! These look a lot more like it." Jamie sounded excited. "Do you recognise anybody?"

Alice looked again. Although the photographs were clearly taken on board *Aphrodite*, it looked different. She knew her father had bought the yacht second-hand, and a few years later had paid to have much of the interior ripped out and replaced. These photos must have been taken before then.

"I don't know. Everyone looks so young."

Jamie leaned in close with her. "The brother... Janik? Is he in these photos too?"

Alice shook her head. "Janez? No. And I told you, he has nothing to do with any of this."

For a moment she sensed his frustration. Like he wanted her to believe Janez might be involved. She realised how much he wanted to help her. But he reined himself in and went on, a bit more methodical. "Well who then? Tell me the names of everybody you recognise in these photographs."

Alice tried again. Beginning with the first photograph Jamie had laid down on the table, she'd stared closely at every face that was recognisable. Where she knew the name, she called it out, and Jamie added it to the list. In a lot of cases, Alice didn't know the person at all. In other cases she only had a vague idea of who the person might be, and Jamie would take whatever name she gave him and add a question mark to the end. Soon however, the system became unwieldy, and Alice wrote numbers on the back of the photographs which they used to cross-reference with the list they were writing. Half an hour later they sat back, with another 27 full and partial names written down in front of them.

"So?" Alice said. But Jamie ignored her. He was busy writing, drawing lines between the various lists.

"What are you doing?"

"I'm cross referencing. I'm trying to see if anybody was at every party."

"Why? Just because somebody came to three different parties, where my parents happened to have a camera, that doesn't mean anything." Alice said.

But Jamie looked up at her suddenly. "Your Dad didn't just *happen* to have a camera though, did he?" He raised his eyebrows. "That's what this is all about."

Alice didn't reply. She was suddenly tired.

"There." Jamie said a few minutes later. He slid the list across the table so that Alice could see it more clearly. There were two names on a new list he'd created. People who attended every party they had images from. "So who are these guys?"

Alice looked down and read the names. She shook her head and sighed. "This is stupid," she said. "It's not either of them."

"Why not? How do you know? Who are they?"

Alice sighed again. "Well your first name - Clifford Walker." She sighed. "He ran a firm of very successful lawyers with offices in London New York and Sydney, and he was very good friends with my dad."

"And? He sounds *exactly* like the sort of person we're looking for..." Jamie sounded excited again.

"And he died of pancreatic cancer about four years ago. I don't have any DNA for you this time, but I don't think anybody doubts it." Jamie's face fell a little.

"Well how about this other guy?"

This time Alice raised her eyebrows. "You don't know him?"

Jamie frowned. "No. Should I?"

"Well you have *met* him. At the wedding. Don't you remember he came out to see us? When we were sitting by the fountain?"

As Alice watched Jamie took another, closer look at the photograph. But when he looked up at her again it was clear he was none the wiser.

"And even if you don't remember *that,* you should probably recognise the name."

Still Jamie looked confused,

"Oh *come on* Jamie. Don't you watch the news? *Peter Rice-Evans?*"

Still Jamie was blank faced. But now he was beginning to look a little embarrassed about it.

"You obviously don't. Peter Rice-Evans. The MP? The member of the Cabinet? The Home Secretary?"

She watched Jamie's face as the penny dropped. A pretty big drop.

"The *Home Secretary*? Like from the government?" His eyes widened. "You're telling me the *Home Secretary of the British Government* went to these parties on your dad's boat?"

Suddenly Alice felt like Jamie had turned the tables on her. Like she was the one being slow.

"Yeah. I told you. He's like an uncle to us. He and Dad have been friends for years. They went to school together." She continued in a quieter voice. "And he wasn't Home Secretary then. He wasn't even an MP then. Just one of Dad's friends."

"He was the guy with the cigar?" It seemed Jamie had suddenly remembered. The one you said was spying for your mum?"

"Yeah." Alice gave a 'so-what' shrug. "He's been really supportive since Dad died. Mum's relied on him a lot, even though he is ridiculously busy these days."

"Alice..."

"I mean, we don't get to see him as much as we used to. Now that he's actually in government and not just in the shadow cabinet..."

"Alice! What the hell? You *know* the British Home Secretary?"

Alice stopped herself speaking. She took a deep breath. She decided to start again.

"Yes. I've known him since I was little. For as long as I can remember actually." Alice stopped.

Jamie stared at her in disbelief.

"How? How come?" He said, eventually.

"Jamie I told you. He's like, Dad's best friend." Alice corrected herself. "*Was* Dad's best friend,"

"What?" Jamie said, he was still shaking his head, but something she had said had snagged his attention.

"He *was* Dad's best friend, until Dad died..."

"No, I don't mean that. I mean *how come*? How come your dad knows the *Home Secretary*?"

"Oh," Alice shrugged. "They met at school. They both went to this horrible boarding school, up in Scotland. They were in the same dorm. Bunk mates or something. And Peter's always been there. He's been like an uncle to us. That's what we call him: Uncle Peter."

Jamie seemed to be having difficulty taking in this information. He was shaking his head, laughing in disbelief.

"Your *Uncle Peter* is the Home Secretary?" but there was something else in his voice, something that unsettled Alice. It was like, for Jamie, everything was suddenly falling into place. Whereas for her, nothing had changed. It annoyed her.

"Yes! But the idea that he has anything to do with this is completely ridiculous. He's part of the family."

"Tell me more about him," Jamie said quickly, dismissing her concerns. "Tell me everything. Everything you know about him."

Still Alice felt some irritation at the direction that Jamie was taking things, but she humoured him.

"What do you want to know?"

Jamie thought for a second before answering. "What did he do? Before he became Home Secretary?" Jamie interrupted himself in his rush to ask the question. "There was an election a few years ago. What did he do before that?"

"I told you. He was in the shadow cabinet for years." Alice paused, and noticed the deep frown on Jamie's face. She went on. "That's when your party hasn't been elected but you have to be ready to be the government. It's why they call it the shadow..."

"I know that." Jamie cut in.

"Oh." Alice felt like adding how Jamie should probably have recognised him if he was such a politics expert.

"And before that?"

"Before what?"

"Before he was in the shadow cabinet?"

"He was just an MP." Alice shrugged.

"Did he have any business interests? Any dealings with your father?"

"Yeah. Probably. I mean Dad invested for him, obviously."

Jamie stared at her.

"*Obviously?*" He shook his head like there was nothing obvious about it.

"What kind of investments?"

"Everything. Just the usual. But nothing *dodgy*, I'm sure." But for the first time Alice didn't sound sure. She carried on.

"Peter's family has land. That's where his money comes from, but the cost of the upkeep is hard. So Dad supported him. When he stood for election I mean. Dad helped to fund the campaign. Mum even went out delivering leaflets door to door. I went with her sometimes."

"Jesus Alice."

"What?"

"This is it. This *has* to be it." Jamie said. With one finger he was hammering at the photograph of the young Rice-Evans in front of them. A smiling, tall young man, holding a bottle of beer in one hand, the flash bouncing off the shine from the sweat on his face.

Alice stayed silent for a long time. In her mind she was fighting a battle. Her established view of a man she had known her whole life was suddenly under siege, attacked by Jamie's insistence on linking him with all the craziness she had learnt in the last few days.

"No. This just doesn't fit," she said carefully. "Peter wouldn't have any reason to harm Dad. They were friends."

"Except your father had a secret tape of him having sex with prostitutes." Jamie suddenly stared her full in the face - a realisation had come to his mind.

"Can you imagine what would happen if the press got hold of that? It would ruin his career. What would someone do to keep something like that quiet? What would a politician do?"

"But they were friends. They were close."

"Well maybe they were...." He fell silent for a moment, then went on, taking a new direction. "Maybe they were *more* than close. Maybe that's the key to this. Maybe Rice-Evans was feeding your dad information to help his investments. Maybe everything was fine for years and they helped each other, but then suddenly they fell out over something. Isn't that possible? Isn't that what all this might be about?" He stared at her again, his eyes pleading.

"I mean, this has to be about *something*?"

Suddenly Jamie looked back down at the photographs laid out on the table.

"Which one is he again?" Jamie asked.

For a split second Alice was confused. Then she realised he still couldn't pick him out. And somewhat reluctantly, Alice pointed at a young man who appeared in several of the images. In most, he was simply standing smiling at the camera. But in one he had his arm around a woman.

"That's him. But that's Mum he's with there. Not some prostitute. No one is going to blackmail him over that picture."

But Jamie ignored her comment. Instead he scooped up the four photographs where the young Rice-Evans appeared and sat back on the sofa, studying the images intently, his brow creased again into a frown.

After a while he began shaking his head.

"What is it?" Alice asked.

"I'm not sure. I can't be certain." Suddenly he looked up at Alice.

"What?" Alice felt uncomfortable with the way he was looking at her. "What is it?"

"I'm not certain Alice, not comparing them side by side..."

Suddenly Alice knew what he was about to say. And she knew her world was about to collapse even further.

"But I think it's him. I think this is the same man I saw in the sex videos. Alice it's him."

And all of a sudden Alice *knew* he was right. She hated herself for it. Or she hated the situation that had exploded around her. But from the look on Jamie's face she knew it was true. Or maybe she'd known earlier. Maybe even for years, but just hadn't *wanted* to believe. Whatever, she felt a sense of certainty as she looked at the photograph. Every memory she had of Peter began to shift in her mind. To take on a new dimension. Uncle Peter was involved with the death of her father.

"So now what?" She said.

"Well we definitely can't go to the police now."

"Why not?" She asked, but this time she wasn't challenging him, just accepting that he was making the connections faster than she was.

.

In response Jamie got up. The time they'd spent thinking seemed to have helped him recover a little, and he seemed able to move now without pain. "He's the Home Secretary. He owns the police." Jamie gave a short, bitter laugh at the situation they found themselves in. "This is what the guy said. The guy that tried to kill me. When he warned me about going to the police."

"Well what would they do? I mean how would Peter control just an ordinary officer - if we went to speak to them?"

"Christ *I don't know* Alice." He sounded irritated. "I don't know how these things work. But think about it - he's got the power to stop any investigation. And that's if the police even took us seriously... Which they wouldn't. Think about it - when you're a powerful politician you must get nut-jobs making up conspiracy theories about you every day. They wouldn't even believe us. " Jamie stopped walking suddenly. He was silent for a long while. Then he looked up at her, his mouth open, his eyes wide once again.

"What?" Alice asked. The feeling of dread in her stomach was becoming familiar.

"Alice this *explains it.*" Jamie's words were coming fast and rushed. "It wasn't your Mum. It wasn't her who found out about the USB drive."

She looked confused. "How?"

"They monitor emails and phone calls? Right? MI6 or GCHQ or something. I don't exactly know - but they listen in to all our calls, for keywords. Well what if *your* calls were being monitored? For keywords. Related to any videos your dad had. Or USB devices, or anything like that? If you're the Home Secretary you're going to be able to do that, right? And that would flag up right away that there's a major problem. That would explain what's going on here. That would explain everything."

Now Alice laughed. "You think Uncle Peter's spying on me?"

"Probably not directly no, but why not someone who works for him? Come on Alice. Look around you. Someone tried to kill me! What else explains all this?"

Alice looked away, an image had come into her mind, a black-clad man standing by her bed, pointing a silenced gun at her face. She had to shake her head to clear the thought. Then she looked down at her phone, lying innocently on the glass coffee table in front of them. She picked it up, and pressed the home button to bring it to life. The lock-screen appeared, her thumb automatically traced out the pattern to unlock it, and the screen changed - the familiar apps, her email account, her messaging services - so personal to her, but so mysterious as well. Alice had no idea how they worked. She just trusted them. Or she always had trusted them. Now she wasn't so sure.

"I saw this movie," she began, "a while back. I think it was called..." She stopped. "I don't know what it was called. But it was about this guy who worked for some US intelligence service, and how they were monitoring everyone's mobile phone. The guy, he stole the data somehow, then they came after him."

"*Snowden*. I saw it too."

"But that's just Hollywood, it's not real life."

Jamie looked shocked. "It's a true story. Didn't you know that? Alice you laugh at me for not watching the news? The whole Edward Snowden thing, that's all true. It's all real."

A moment later Alice went to reply, but this time Jamie quickly held up a hand to quieten her.

"What?" She asked.

Jamie shook his head. He looked around until he saw a stereo separates system housed on a shelving unit. He went over to it, and a moment later soft music played from hidden speakers all around the room. Jamie turned the volume louder, until it was too loud for Alice to hear herself speak.

"What are you doing?"

Jamie shushed her again. He looked about the room again, then beckoned to her. She got up, and together they walked to the glass sliding doors that separated the kitchen from the ocean-view balcony. Jamie slid the door open and gently pushed her through into the darkness outside. Then he shut the door behind her.

It was cold and dark - the light here wasn't automatic so it didn't come on. The fog had lifted enough so that they could see the ocean heaving gently, lazily spilling waves upon the steep-shelving sand beach. The moon cast a dim path upon the shifting surface of the water. Alice hugged her arms around her. She waited until Jamie explained what he was doing.

"If they're listening into our calls," he said, speaking very quietly, "then we have to assume they're listening *here* too. Everywhere. Your London house. Bugged. Maybe even *Phoenix* too."

Alice was still holding onto her mobile. They both looked at it now.

"Your phone," Jamie said quietly, "Is probably recording every word we say. Right now."

Alice hesitated. The device suddenly felt hot in her hands. Was she imagining that? Or was it because the battery was working, running the microphone secretly? She had noticed the battery wasn't lasting as long as it used to. She had to charge it twice a day. And there had been strange noises on her calls. But then, it was nearly a year old. Didn't that just happen to mobiles?

"You have to destroy it," he said.

Alice stared at him.

"The SIM. You have to destroy the SIM card. *Right now.*"

Silently she held out the phone to Jamie, as if she wanted him to take responsibility.

She watched for a moment as he flipped it over, looking for how to prize the back off, but it wasn't that type.

"You need a pin to get it out," Alice said. "Hold on."

She went back inside, then returned holding a paperclip in her fingers. Wordlessly Jamie took it from her, bent it open, and used that to withdraw the tray. He took out the SIM card.

"You do it." He said, and handed it back to her.

She took the tiny plastic card from him. She stared at it. Was this really tracking her? Was this real? She didn't know any more.

Without really making the decision to do so, she felt her fingers press down against the edges of the card. She pushed harder, and it eventually began to fold. She snapped it, so that the electronic chip peeled off like a scab from a wound.

In the half-light of the moon Jamie looked resolute. He nodded. But then he looked around again, and saw the hot tub, covered this time but still humming where the pump was aerating the water. He strode over and lifted the lid, folding it half back upon itself. The inside was lit up with blue LED lights under the water. He handed the phone back to her. It was still working, its screen a cheerful, friendly array of colourful apps. Each one hiding their ulterior motives and who they really worked for.

"Throw it in," Jamie said.

From inside the music continued to leak out into the night.

"This is insane. This is crazy." Alice said, not moving. "You're crazy."

"No I'm not. *They are.* They're crazy to try and contain this. And they're watching our every move to make sure they do. Listening too. We've got to get ahead of this Alice."

She stared at him.

"They're using it against you Alice. Drop it in."

Suddenly the absurdity of the situation hit her. She laughed.

"Do I really have to throw my iPhone in the hot tub?" She asked. "I mean..." she stopped. She didn't know what she meant.

"You have to. You have to fry the electronics."

Alice puffed out her cheeks. "I like my iPhone," she said. "It's an eighteen month contract. I'm not due for an upgrade for ages."

Finally Jamie sensed the change in her mood and grinned. And moments later they were both laughing. The music still played from inside. To anyone watching from the beach, they would have just looked like any happy young couple in their multi-million-pound beach house. In the middle of the night. Throwing electronics into a hot tub.

With a casual toss of her wrist, Alice threw the phone into the gently bubbling water of the tub.

It sank at once to the bottom, its screen still on. For a few moments it looked normal, and then a black stain began to bleed onto the screen. The colours of the screen wobbled. It's final act was to flash onto the clock app, showing them the time through the eerie blue water: 04.45. Then it went blank. They both stopped laughing.

"We should get some sleep," Jamie said. "First thing in the morning we've got to get out of here."

32

They left the stereo playing, more softly now, and Alice led Jamie downstairs. She opened a door to one of the spare rooms, which Maria left cleaned and ready for guests.

"You can sleep here," she said. He didn't answer but nodded his thanks, then lay down right away on the double bed, watching her. She thought again of how he had dived into the water, an assassin firing shots, trying to kill him. She thought of that man, still out there somewhere. She moved to walk the few steps to her own room, but then she changed her mind. Instead she climbed onto the bed next to Jamie, still with her robe wrapped tightly around him, and she made her body fit into the curve behind his. He reached behind him and found her hand, then gave it a squeeze. Alice flicked off the bedside light.

When Alice woke she was alone and there was a noise she didn't recognise. She reached for her mobile, to check the time, but couldn't find it. Then she realised she was in the wrong room, and then everything that had happened the night before came back to her. The noise she could hear was the shower in the en-suite - different to the one in her bathroom. As she listened the flow of water shut off and then Jamie walked out, wrapped in a towel. She could see bruises on his torso. He'd kept his hair dry and her dressing from the night before was still in place, she hadn't done a bad job. His eye was a deep purple though. He could only half-open it. A little shocked, she went to speak but he raised a finger to his lips. Then he walked to the bedside table. He'd found a notepad from somewhere.

"Clothes?" he wrote, then added something else. "Your dad?"

She nodded and swung herself off the bed. She opened her mouth again, but then stopped and beckoned instead, leading Jamie to her parent's room, and the smaller of the two walk-in wardrobes. Most of his clothes had already been removed and lots of the space had been filled by Lena, but there were still a few racks with his clothes that she hadn't given away or had removed. Alice waved a hand. She reached for the notepad.

"Help yourself," she wrote on the pad, then mimed that she was going to take a shower too.

When she was finished and dressed she found him upstairs, packing food into a bag. He was dressed in a pair of cotton chinos and a shirt with a jumper over the top. From behind he suddenly looked just like her father, until he turned and she saw his face.

"Does it hurt?" she mouthed, pointing.

He shook his head.

"Let's go," he mouthed back. "We can talk then." The clock on the wall said it was past nine o'clock. They'd slept in.

It felt strange leaving the house, like it was both a place of sanctuary, but also somewhere that was now dangerous. Compromised. Tainted. Jamie led the way down the stairs and went to pull open the front door but Alice stopped him. She used the iPad to check the views from all the cameras. The world outside looked normal. Traffic flowed past, birds flew overhead. The postman pushed a red trolley holding his mailbag. Alice nodded, and Jamie pushed open the door.

"Should I lock it?" Alice asked when they were outside. She wondered when she would ever return here.

"Yeah," Jamie breathed, his voice low. "Just do everything like normal."

They set off along the footpath that skirted the edge of the harbour. On one side the light morning traffic swept past. On the other, a few early risers were rowing out to their boats. A dog walker came towards them, his animal a young black Labrador, straining at the lead. Alice felt the fear rise in her as the man made eye contact, nodded good morning, smiled as he stopped the dog from jumping up to greet her. She saw how the owner raised his eyebrows at the state of Jamie's face.

"So can we talk now?" Alice asked, when the man had fallen behind them. "What do we do? Where are we going?"

"I don't know," Jamie replied. "I'm trying to think."

That surprised her. She had assumed he would know what to do. It was Jamie who had chosen which way they took. But now it seemed that was purely random. Something in this encouraged her too.

"I still think we have to go to the police," Alice began. But then she stopped again. Beside her she felt him tense up at this idea.

"Once we've got real evidence I mean," she continued. "More than this..." she tapped the shoulder bag she had taken, with the photographs, a few clothes. Her father's laptop.

"I mean real proof. If we could get something that proves what happened to you, that *proves* Peter's involved, then the police will have to take it seriously. Even if he is their boss."

"But what?" Jamie replied. "We had the evidence on the USB drive, but he stole it back. He will have destroyed it." They walked on a few more paces before Jamie continued.

"There is one thing I was thinking. Perhaps we could search for bugs. In your house I mean. In *Phoenix* as well. If we found the bugs that would be *something* to show the police. Maybe they could track where the signals go..."

"Unless," she interrupted him. "Unless you're wrong."

She walked on a couple of paces before realising he wasn't beside her anymore. She turned and saw him stopped.

"What do you mean?" Jamie asked.

Alice felt a burst of nerves before she spoke again. She'd had the idea in the shower but hadn't been able to decide if it was ridiculous or not. With everything that had happened over the last few days her sense of reality felt shredded. Her father, always a hero to her, was actually a blackmailer. And Peter, her Uncle Peter, had very likely murdered him for it. She took a deep breath.

"You reckon Peter stole the USB drive from your yacht right? Well, probably not Peter himself, but someone who works for him?"

Jamie nodded. "I don't reckon... Alice, you were *there*..."

But she cut him off.

"And you've assumed that he'd just destroy it right away, because of what it had on it?"

"Well. Yeah. Wouldn't you?"

"I don't know what I'd do. But I do know Peter."

Jamie looked lost.

"What?"

"Well you're right about one thing. If it were just a tape of Peter with some prostitute, then sure, he'd want it destroyed. But that wasn't all there was."

He still looked blank. "I don't understand."

"You said there were lots of files. *It wasn't just Peter*. There were other clips. Other men having sex as well. Dad wasn't just blackmailing Peter. Or it wasn't just Peter he could blackmail. He had leverage on other people too."

"So...?"

Alice felt a moment's frustration. So far Jamie had always been one step ahead of her. All of a sudden he was being slow to catch on.

"So... Don't you get it?" She realised she needed to explain.

"All the people at those parties. They were just young men then. But they were all connected. All destined for great things. Jamie I don't just know cabinet ministers. I know judges. I know ambassadors. Right over there." She pointed through a gap in the houses towards the ocean. "There's a private beach there where I used to sunbathe with the daughter of the President of the United States. That USB drive. If it's really what we think it is. It would be invaluable to someone like Peter. Someone in a position to use that leverage." Alice stopped. Feeling herself shake a little.

"What I'm saying is, Peter wouldn't give up an advantage like that."

From Jamie's face it was clear he still didn't get it.

"I'm saying he wouldn't destroy this USB drive. If it was the only copy of these videos. Maybe he'd want to keep them. To use them himself."

Finally understanding, Jamie stared at her.

"OK, but... So what?" he said at last. "It's not like we can just ask for it back."

Alice hesitated again, thinking back to her idea. She'd read about how people are able to think more clearly in the shower. How lots of famous inventions are dreamed up there. Something to do with the water droplets knocking out the negative ions. Or something, she wasn't clear on how it actually worked. But it didn't matter. Even here standing on the footpath in the bright sunlight, she still felt her idea was worth following up. But with Jamie's sceptical face staring at her, bruised and painful, she wasn't quite ready to tell him what the idea was.

"Come with me," Alice said suddenly, turning away from him and setting off again down the path. Jamie struggled to follow before they fell in step together.

"Where are we going? What are we doing?" Jamie asked, but Alice didn't answer at once. She tried to think of a way to explain what she was thinking, but in the end she gave up.

"We need to go shopping," she said.

After a while they came to an area where the expensive homes gave way to businesses. They were mostly expensive restaurants, the offices of financial advisers and the kind of small supermarkets that sell beach goods. Alice led them into one of these and quickly found a stand filled with cheap sunglasses. She ran her hand up and down the rack before choosing a set with large mirrored lenses. Then she pulled them out and handed them to Jamie.

"Here. To hide the mess you've made of your eye."

Jamie slipped the sunglasses on and bent down to examine himself in the mirror. While he was doing so she snatched a red and white base-ball cap and pressed it carefully onto his head. It didn't totally hide the wound, but it made it less noticeable. Then she plucked out another set of sunglasses for herself, and a big, wide-brimmed blue sunhat, and carried them all over to the till.

When they were outside again she fixed her own hat in place, and slipped the glasses from their case. One of the bigger businesses on the street was a car showroom. About ten models sat for sale on the fore-court. They were a mixture of small sports cars and 4x4s, all second hand, and none costing more than ten thousand. It was a strange choice of business, that didn't look like it would last that long.

"Can you go and choose a car?" Alice said. "I just need to go to the bank."

Jamie stared at her. "What?"

"Choose a car. Something quite fast." Alice said again. "I'll be there in a minute with the money."

She pointed to a bank, a branch of Barclays, and went to walk away, but he just stood there, rooted to the spot, so she turned to him again.

"Look. If Peter is really bugging my house we can't stay there. And I don't fancy idly wandering around until we bump into your friend from last night. So let's get a car, then we can get away from here and work out what to do. OK?"

"You're just going to buy a car?"

"Yes. If we hire one they'll probably be able to track it."

Jamie opened his mouth, as if to argue the logic of this, but closed it again.

Then he opened it again. "But where are we going?"

Alice felt frustration again. She'd thought this might be fun.

"You said we need evidence right? I might know where we can get it." She fixed his mirrored shades with a look then turned away and opened the door to the bank. Inside she kept her head down, keeping the brim of her new hat between her face and the security camera.

When she got back outside she didn't see Jamie at first. She looked up and down the street, feeling a sudden rush of concern, but then she saw him, inside the showroom. He was talking to a man in a white shirt with red braces holding up his suit trousers. They were standing over a silver Ford, the driver's door was open, as if the man were explaining the features. From the look of the car there weren't many. She pushed open the showroom door, making a bell tinkle above her head. Both Jamie and the man looked up to see her. Alice took a deep breath and strode over.

"Hello darling," Alice said, taking Jamie in a light embrace and kissing his cheeks. "Have you found me anything?" Her accent was suddenly a flawless American. Wealthy New York. But Jamie looked horribly uncomfortable, like he understood but didn't want to play his part.

"There's this one," he said. He let his voice go up at the end, as if he were attempting an accent himself, and Alice nearly laughed as the salesman walked around the back of the car to greet her.

"It's the cheapest in here," Jamie added in an apologetic whisper.

"Only came in last week," the man said, holding out a hand for Alice to shake. He was holding in his gut as she shook it. "But we've had it checked over and it's very reliable."

Alice looked at the car, a small hatchback. She spun on her heel and looked around the room. In front of the window, in pride of place, was a small red sports car, it's roof folded down.

"How about this one, darling?" Alice said to Jamie. Her accent was even better now. She pushed her sunglasses down her nose and peered over the top. The car had black leather seats. It smelt of air freshener.

The salesman was there in a shot.

"Very you if I may say so," the man began. He smiled a set of white, unnaturally straight teeth. He turned to Jamie and went on.

"Full electrics pack - roof, windows, mirrors. Obviously it's got full service history and I'll throw in a year's warranty. Beautiful little car." His own accent suggested he'd moved to the coast from London.

Jamie opened his mouth to reply but apparently couldn't think of anything to say. "Don't look at me," he said eventually. "I don't even know what we're doing here."

Alice laughed, a sweet sound that rang like a peal of bells.

"Inheritance," she explained. "My granddaddy left me a bit of money but he told me I had to enjoy it. Do you take cash?" she asked.

"Cash?" The salesman's smile wobbled for a second.

"He never trusted banks. Taught me not to either."

"If it's legal love, we take cash." The salesman recovered quickly and beamed. If he noticed the strange beaten-up appearance of the American woman's boyfriend he wasn't going to make an issue of it. Not with a girl as pretty as this one.

Half an hour later they were on the road out of town, with the hood down and music blaring. Alice was driving, going twenty miles an hour over the speed limit in the fast lane.

"What?" Alice said, looking over at Jamie. "I told you. I'd been needing to buy a car anyway. I saw this one last week. I thought it was better to pay cash so we didn't get tracked."

"Don't you think it just made us easier to remember?" Jamie asked, glancing awkwardly at her.

She realised he was right. And suddenly she felt stupid. She put her thumb in her mouth and bit down on the nail.

"Shit," she said. "Well. It's done now."

Neither spoke for a few moments.

"And where did you say we were going?" Jamie asked again.

"I didn't." Alice said. Then, feeling wounded, she turned up the music.

Alice first drove north, then she pulled off the motorway and doubled back on herself. She kept an eye on the rear view mirror, but there were no cars that looked familiar. No one followed them. She considered that a team of trackers might be behind them, using a variety of vehicles. But then she turned onto a minor road and drove until there were no cars in sight. After a half mile she pulled off onto a farm track, and she waited there. A full two minutes later another car came past. It didn't slow down, the driver looked to be an elderly woman. Alice turned back onto the road, double-backing on herself again. With the roof down she had a clear view of the sky. There were no helicopters, nothing suspicious.

"I guess we can't rule out spy satellites," she said, in response to Jamie's frequent questions.

"Alice, please just tell me where we're going." Jamie said again.

"OK." Alice said, but didn't tell him. Now the easy part of her plan was complete, she was feeling a little anxious that the second part was actually just crazy. She waited until they were back on the motorway heading west, then she couldn't put it off any longer.

"OK," she said, breaking the silence. "Peter is the MP for the whole rural part of South Devon right? He's got a house there. But he spends most of his time up in London now, in his London house."

"So?"

"So. Peter has lived in the same house in Devon for years. Since I was little. It's a big old place right out in the middle of nowhere."

"So that's where we're going?" Jamie looked uncomfortable.

"Yeah. There won't be anyone there. And I know where he keeps the key."

"I still don't understand this Alice. How does this help?"

She turned to him. "Look it might not, this might be crazy. But I want to check. Peter has an office in the house, and there's a safe inside. And I also know where the safe key is. At least, I think I do."

"How?"

Alice shrugged. "I told you. We used to stay there when we were kids.

We used to play in it." She turned to Jamie, a pleading look in her eyes. "Look I know it's a long shot, but I just thought that maybe that's where he's put the USB drive."

Jamie stared in disbelief this time.

"Why would he put it there?"

Alice took a while to answer. She had explained the idea as best she could. Did it really sound that insane?

"It's a *safe*. That's where you put things like that."

"But you said he doesn't use this house?"

"No I didn't. I said he won't be here at the moment, he'll be up in London."

"So why wouldn't he take the USB drive to London?"

Alice began to feel annoyed, not at Jamie for pointing out the obvious flaw in her plan, but at herself, for deciding to ignore it.

"There's always people at the London house. Civil servants, advisers. I thought he might want to keep it away from all that." She hoped he'd agree with her, on this at least, but he didn't seem to.

"But why would he keep it anywhere?"

She began to feel silly. "OK, he might not," she conceded. "But he only has two properties, and I can't break into the London one. So why don't we start with the one we can get into and take it from there?"

Jamie appeared to have no objection to this and he sat quietly, even if he didn't look convinced. She indicated to turn off the motorway again.

"It's about twenty miles down here. I told you it's right out of the way."

They drove for a bit, off the main road now, the lane was narrow, with high hedges on either side. Jamie had obviously decided to let it go. He sat impassively, turning occasionally to check that no one was following them. After a while one of the hedges gave way to a long brick wall, high enough that they couldn't see over it and looking like it had been there forever. Alice drove alongside it for a while, then slowed as she approached a gate. Two stone stags stood proudly on pillars either side of the entrance. Alice pulled off the road and stopped. Beyond the gates loomed the tall, mature trees of a rural estate. Normally she felt relaxed here, hidden from the world. But suddenly the natural screening they provided from the outside world felt threatening.

"What if someone's here?" Jamie said, eyeing the iron gates nervously.

"I told you, they won't be. Peter's in London."

"What about a wife? A Mrs Rice-Evans?" Jamie asked.

"There isn't one. Peter never married." Alice said. But suddenly she didn't feel so confident. She had no way of knowing if Peter was actually on his way down right now. Parliament didn't exactly keep normal working hours. She pushed the thought out of her mind.

"Can you open the gates?" she asked Jamie. He gave her a look and got out of the car. There was no lock and she watched as he pushed them open. Then he got back in the car.

"Shouldn't we close them behind us?" She asked.

"What if we need to get away in a hurry?" he asked.

She didn't like the sound of that, but it did kind of make sense.

She drove forward down the drive. She half expected to see Peter's own silver Mercedes, sitting on the gravel in front of the big house - or the big, black chauffeur driven Jaguar that he was sometimes driven around in - but it was empty. The many windows all looked blank. Dark and cold.

"He must have some sort of security?" Jamie protested, as she brought the car to a halt. There were steps that led to the front door.

"He does, but not much." Alice said, but she wasn't sure any longer.

"How do you know?"

"I told you. We come here sometimes." She turned the key to kill the engine and pushed open the door.

Standing outside the car Alice had a strange feeling. It was like the contact between the gravel underfoot and the soles of her feet was less secure than it should have been. Like she might just lift up at any point and start drifting away. It was as if her connection to everything - to reality, and to the very earth she stood upon, had weakened. She held onto the car door longer than she needed to.

"Shouldn't we hide it or something?" Jamie asked, getting out the other side. "Maybe just put it out of sight a bit?" He pointed to a large separate double garage with space behind it. It led to the tennis court.

But now they were here, Alice just wanted to get this over with.

"There's no need. No one's going to come." She let go of the car. She didn't float away.

Instead her feet crunched on the gravel like always. And she walked towards the grand front door, raised up on four solid stone steps. They dipped in the middle - wear from a century of use. Alice ignored them and walked to the side. She dug around in the grass until she found the stone she was looking for.

"That's it?" Jamie asked, when she held up a key. "You can break into the British Home Secretary's house *that easily*?"

"Only if you know where the key is hidden," Alice replied, a little defensively. Then she climbed the steps to a heavy wooden door. She slipped the key into the lock. Then hesitated. Surely Jamie was right. Peter must have more security that she didn't know about.

She glanced across at Jamie. His face did a terrible job of hiding his thoughts on the matter - he was looking at her as if she were mad. He looked ready to run.

"Are you sure about this?" Jamie asked.

Before she could answer the questions Alice turned the key and pushed the door open.

It creaked as it opened, and it was dark inside, the large cool hallway dimly lit by the house's small windows. Alice stepped over the threshold and felt Jamie follow in behind her, her eyes adjusting to the low light. Then a tone began to sound. In the half light a small keypad was illuminated, its orange light blinking.

"Oh shit," Jamie said. He turned to Alice, gripping her by the arm.

"Do you have any idea of the number?" He asked, stepping past her. He moved quickly over to the keypad and leaned in, inspecting it.

"Get out of the way." Alice heard the tone of her voice rise. She pushed him and stepped up to the keypad, where she typed in six digits.

The beeping stopped at once.

"How do you..?" Jamie shook his head. "You knew the number?"

"Yeah. I told you. We come here quite a lot."

Jamie looked away. Like he felt annoyed she hadn't told him.

But now they were inside, Alice felt nervous. She *had* been in this house many times, but always as a welcome guest. Now as they sneaked down the corridor she felt unwelcome. Usually Peter's taste in dark, heavy antique furniture - much of it having become antique in this very house - felt full of character. Steadying. Now it all felt much more threatening. As if the very furniture had eyes and were watching them. As if the house resented them being here. She tried to brush away her nerves, but couldn't remove them completely.

"Come on. His office is upstairs." She led the way. Jamie on the other hand seemed to have increased in confidence. As doubtful as he had looked before they got into the house, he now seemed relaxed, almost like he was enjoying it now. She didn't know what to make of that.

There was a window halfway up the stairway, and she glanced through it, checking the driveway was still empty. Of course it was. She told herself to calm down. No one was going to come.

The stairs creaked under their feet. Somewhere in the house a clock ticked. Funny how she'd never noticed either before. Beams of light shot into the cool air from the windows, illuminating galaxies of dust. They came to Peter's office door. As ever it was shut. Suddenly she wished it was locked - an excuse for them to leave, to forget her ridiculous idea.

"It's this one." She said, but she hesitated as she stood outside it. She placed her hand on the lever and pressed against it. With another creak that tore further at her nerves, the door swung inward.

Another shaft of light from the half-closed curtains cut into the room, illuminating a large antique desk upon which sat a computer screen. Everything else was cast into shadow. But there was something else. There was a chair, facing a quarter turn away from them, but still they could see there was something on it. A crumpled shape was slumped down, one arm hanging limply, draped nearly onto the floor. Alice let out a small scream.

"*Shit*," Jamie said, striding forwards. "I thought that was a body for a second." He sounded almost exhilarated as he turned the chair fully around, letting the light catch it. The shape revealed itself as a tennis bag, the handles of two rackets poking out from the zip, a jacket slung on the back of the chair caught on one of the handles.

"Me too," Alice replied. She must have sounded shocked because Jamie turned around to look at her.

"Are you OK?"

"Yeah. I just... I'm just nervous that's all."

Jamie walked across to the window, moving to open the curtains. More light filled the room, but Alice stopped him.

"Maybe we should just use the desk light. Just in case anyone does see from outside."

He stopped. "OK," he said. He sounded back to normal now. Alice realised how hard this must be for Jamie as well. Neither of them were cut out for breaking into houses.

She tried to shift her focus. Back onto *why* they were here. She didn't really expect to find the USB drive, did she? Surely that was too much to hope for? She thought about it, as she watched Jamie moving around the desk, inspecting the pile of papers scattered across it. Perhaps she had never expected to find it. Maybe that was the real idea she had grasped at in the shower? If they found *nothing* wouldn't that somehow prove that Jamie had this all wrong? That Peter *wasn't* involved? She wasn't sure now. All she knew was the sense of clarity she had felt earlier was gone now. Everything was muddy.

Jamie had given up on his search of the desk and was pulling open the drawers. Whatever he was looking through didn't seem to interest him, because soon he looked up and spoke again.

"Where's this safe? Can you really open it?"

Alice went over to the far wall where two oil paintings with heavy gold frames were hung above the wood-panelling. She went straight to the left-hand one and lifted the whole painting off, leaning it against the foot of the wall. Revealed on the wall was a heavy steel door, recessed into the plaster. There was an inset handle, and a keyhole.

"Behind a painting?" Jamie said. "That's so unoriginal."

"He never really used it for locking things away. That's why we used to play with it. Peter thought it was really funny that it was even there."

"So why do you think he uses it now?"

"I don't," Alice said, her doubts flooding back. "Maybe this is just a really stupid idea..."

Jamie stopped what he was doing and looked at her. He didn't offer an opinion. Instead he shrugged.

"Well we're here now. Might as well open it and see."

She nodded, then walked over to the desk and squatted down in front of the space where its occupant would put their legs. Inside, out of reach and nearly lost from sight in the gloom of the room, there was a hook, and from the hook hung a key. Alice reached in and pulled it out.

Jamie stared at it. She saw from his face that he was nervous too. Somehow that made her feel better.

"Do you really think it might be in there?" he asked. She could see he was hopeful.

"I don't know." Alice replied.

They walked together to the safe where Alice slotted the key into the lock, but before Alice could turn it, she felt Jamie's hand suddenly grip her arm.

"There's no alarm on this one is there?"

Alice swallowed. "I don't know. I don't think so."

Jamie thought for a second.

"When did you say you used to play with it?"

"I don't know. I think I was probably about ten years old."

She looked at him, and their eyes locked together in the dim light of the room. Finally Jamie released his grip. He nodded at her, a conspiratorial smile on his lips.

"You're a fucking wild one aren't you?" He said. "Go on, just do it."

Alice turned the key.

33

There was no sound, other than the dull clunk of the key turning in the lock. It felt vaguely familiar to Alice. There was no alarm, no electronic beeping.

Alice pulled the door open. It wasn't as thick or as heavy as she remembered, and inside it was smaller. She knew it was ludicrous that Peter would really use it to hide anything he needed keeping secret. But then she saw the stacks of cash. A little pile of neat bricks of notes, each held together with red bands, stamped by HSBC bank.

"Jesus," Jamie said. "How much is that?"

Alice counted the ten bricks. "Ten thousand pounds," she replied. Jamie's eyes slid over from the money to her face.

"How do you know that?"

"Because there's ten. And each one is one thousand."

Jamie responded by reaching inside and picking up one of the bricks. Printed in red ink across the band were the words *One Thousand Pounds*.

"Oh right," he said. He flicked his thumb across the end, like it was a pack of cards.

"I see." He said. An uncomfortable thought flicked across Alice's mind. She hadn't needed to read the values. She was familiar enough seeing piles of cash that she'd recognised them, She made the calculation almost *automatically*. What kind of a family had she grown up in?

What kind of life had she lived? She shook her head again, trying to focus on what they were there to find.

"Pile it up on that little table, so we can see what else is in here," Alice said, and Jamie did what she asked, making a neat pile of the cash. Underneath the cash were a few files of documents. Jamie left those on the desk and turned back to the safe. But now it was empty.

Alice stood staring at it.

"There's no USB drive." Jamie said. "It's not here."

Alice felt empty. Was this the point where she was supposed to say *I told you so?* If that was the plan, it seemed pretty stupid now. She wondered what Jamie must be thinking of her. Bringing him here - not even telling him in advance, in case he talked her out of it. She sneaked a glance across at him, expecting him to look angry, or disappointed. But instead she saw he had picked up the files from the safe. A curious look came onto his face. Then he looked back at her.

"Alice..."

"What is it? " Alice replied. She moved closer. "What's that?"

"What was the name of the boat your dad was on?"

"*Sophtec Endeavour* - it was sponsored by a computer company."

Jamie lowered the file so she could see it. Alice took it from his hands and turned it around for a better look.

The top page read:

Marine Accident Investigation Board report #1863/16

*Summary: Person overboard from racing yacht **Sophtec Endeavour** with loss of 1 life*

Date of occurrence: 8 April 2016

Vessel type: Recreational craft - sail

Report type: Preliminary Examination

"This is your dad's accident isn't it?" Jamie asked.

Alice nodded. She hardly heard Jamie as he went on. "So why does he have this in his safe?"

She took the report to the desk and began reading. It summarised what had happened to Charlie Belhaven. How the racing yacht had been sailing east from Cape Town in South Africa to Melbourne in Australia. How it had suffered delays and fallen behind in the race. How the crew of twelve, a mixture of experienced professional sailors, and wealthy adventurers, had run into the first bad weather of their race. How

Charlie had been on watch in the middle of the night, when a part of the yacht's complicated rigging had got caught on the foredeck, and how Charlie had volunteered to go up and free it.

She read on. How her father had been wearing a safety harness, hadn't clipped it on, presumably to help him move around more easily. She read how the other sailor on her father's watch had shouted to him, that a large wave was coming. She read how it had washed over, and submerged the deck, and how - when the yacht resurfaced moments later - Charlie Belhaven was nowhere to be seen.

The report set out how the crew had been woken up, the yacht turned around to try and locate him, but that the strong winds and high waves had hampered the search. She read how he had finally been found thanks to the location tracking from his personal safety beacon, but that by then it was nearly light. How he had succumbed by then to the cold, and been found floating face down in the water.

None of it was new to Alice. Apart from one, small detail. The name of the other sailor on her father's watch. Philip Marshall.

"Why would he have this in his safe?" Jamie asked. She could tell from his face he thought it suspicious. But Alice didn't answer. She put a hand to her forehead. She felt dizzy.

"They have to do a report," she heard herself reply. "It's standard when there's an accident with a British registered boat. If someone dies."

"Yeah but why does he have it in his *safe*? Why is he hiding this?"

That was too much for Alice to make sense of. Needing air, or light - or both - she ignored him again, and this time walked to the office window. She looked out on the lush gardens, bursting forth with the vigour of spring.

"We should take this. We don't have time to read it all here, but we should take it. It might be important." Jamie was saying. Alice glanced back and saw him folding the slim report in half.

"And I think we should get the hell out of here," Jamie went on. His demeanour had changed completely now. Whether she had been right that he looked to be enjoying himself earlier, he looked scared now. She didn't answer, but she saw he was putting the money back into the safe.

"If we still had our phones we could have taken a photo to get it right."

She didn't understand what that meant.

"What?" she said, absently.

"I mean we could arrange the money so no-one would be able to tell we moved it."

Alice stopped listening. Instead her eyes were taken by movement out of the window. Up past the end of the drive a car was slowing as it travelled along the road that led past the house. As it neared the open gates it stopped completely. The orange light of its indicator was flashing. Whoever was driving seemed confused for a few seconds. Alice knew why - the gates should have been shut.

"Oh *shit*," she said.

"What is it?" Jamie asked.

"Someone's here," she said. "Someone's coming." Alice didn't move though. Even though she was in full view of the window, she couldn't make her feet react. It was like she was frozen to the spot. And for a strange moment she didn't even care. Let them see her, whoever it was. Let them explain to her how she had this all wrong. Let them tell her why *Philip Marshall* was on her father's yacht.

She was there long enough to take in some details of the car. It wasn't either of Peter's - not his personal Mercedes, nor the black Government Jaguar - this was a little blue car. It slowed halfway down the drive. Perhaps the driver had noticed Alice's new sports car parked outside the front.

"You're kidding right?" Jamie's voice cut into her thoughts.

Alice didn't reply. She just stood there, watching as the little car began moving nearer, finally coming to a stop next to Alice's. Alice could hear the engine now. Jamie must have heard it too.

"Well get the hell out of sight!" Jamie shouted. He sounded genuinely panicked. He ran across from the safe, across the room, and pulled her to the side of the window. They knocked together into the heavy curtains that hung to each side of the window, and Jamie did his best to still their movement. Alice looked back. In his rush to move her, he'd knocked over the table with half the money on it. The band from one of the bundles had slipped off, the money was scattered over the carpeted floor. Jamie ignored it.

"What are you doing? Just standing there? Did they see you?"

Jamie's questions - or maybe the sudden movement - shook her from her frozen state.

"I don't know," she answered him, not meeting his intent gaze. "I saw someone getting out. A woman.

"What woman? Who?"

"I don't know. I don't think she saw me," Alice said. But as she spoke she knew that wasn't true. The woman's eyes had met hers. Alice had seen the confusion. The further surprise that Alice had just stared back at her.

And then downstairs there was the clear noise of the front door opening. Footsteps, then a pause, followed by a cautious call:

"*Hello?*"

She sounded uncertain, nervous.

"*Hello?*" Louder now, more indignant. "*Who's there?*"

"Who is it?" Jamie hissed. "Do you recognise her. Do you know the voice?"

"No. She looked like maybe a cleaner."

Jamie looked around the room. Alice followed his gaze.

"We've got to put that away, she's going to think we're robbing the place," he said. And she realised he was right. The safe was still open, and there were bank notes scattered on the floor. Even with the few moments she had to register it, that seemed odd. Stacks of notes were usually more secure than that. Just falling to the floor shouldn't have broken the stacks apart. Had Jamie been counting them or something?

There was no time to think about that. The footsteps moved to the stairs. Moving cautiously, but steadily.

"I'm calling the police," The voice called out again, louder now. Well-spoken. Plummy. If she was a cleaner she wasn't a girl from an agency. Alice remembered Peter mentioned the lady who came in. She'd been with him for years.

"I'm on my phone. I'm literally calling the police right now."

"*Shit,*" Jamie began looking around desperately, as if searching for an alternative exit. But there wasn't one. The only way out was back onto the landing, and the woman had already reached the top of the stairs. She would be at the door in seconds. Alice held her breath for a moment. Then she made a decision.

34

"**G**et the money back in the safe. As best you can. Then hide somewhere." Alice said suddenly. "I'll talk to her."

Jamie stared at her, then glanced around again.

"Where can I hide?"

"Just find somewhere. And clear up that mess," Alice said, then she strode out of the study. As she did so she tried to brush past the door so that it closed, but so that it didn't look deliberate.

"Oh!" The woman stopped, one foot on the landing, one on the final tread of the stairs. She was in her fifties, dressed in worn jeans, pulled tight over thick legs. She carried a mobile phone in front of her as if it were a weapon.

"Hello," Alice said. Her voice was croaky but she forced a smile.

"Are you Peter's cleaner? I'm sorry if I've given you a scare. I saw you from the window."

The woman paused. She didn't drop the phone. "And who *are* you?" She demanded. Her voice was cautious. Suspicious. She moved up the final step to stand level with Alice. They were about the same height.

"I'm Alice." Alice said, trying to keep a smile on her face. "Alice Belhaven." Abruptly she thrust her hand forward. "My father was friends with Peter."

"Oh!" The woman seemed surprised by this, but certainly not satisfied. She conceded enough to put her phone into her other hand, and give Alice's outstretched hand a weak shake. But when she spoke again her voice was still suspicious.

"And what are you doing here? I don't mean to be direct, but Peter didn't mention that anyone would be here. And he always tells me if..." She seemed to think of something. She looked around. "Is Mr Rice-Evans here? I thought he was in London..."

"He is. I'm here on my own." Alice said quickly.

"Oh." The woman considered. Her eyes narrowed again. "Why?"

Alice tried to think of a reason to stall the woman. She let her mouth fall open as if to reply, but had no words to fill it.

"Erm... It's a silly thing really," she said. The woman's frown deepened, and Alice sensed she was losing her. The phone began to come back to its defensive position.

"I was here the other weekend. Peter invited us round for drinks, Mum and me," Alice smiled but partly from relief. She had an idea, but no time to consider whether it made any sense. "And I left my phone." She added hurriedly. "So Peter suggested I pop in and pick it up, since I was passing."

The woman took her time evaluating what she'd just heard. She didn't look convinced. A thought seemed to come to her.

"You were passing? All the way out here?"

Alice realised she was right and conceded.

"Well not exactly passing. But I needed my phone."

This seemed to provoke a reluctant change in the woman's attitude. Like she understood how much a young woman would rely on her mobile phone. It showed up first as a twitch in her cheek. Then an awkward attempt at a smile, which the woman seemed to abandon as soon as she began it.

"You're Alice you say?"

"Yes."

"Alice..?"

"Belhaven."

"Oh. One of Charlie Belhaven's girls?"

"Yes." Alice thought for a moment the woman was going to offer her condolences, but she didn't.

"And Mr Rice-Evans definitely knows you're here?"

"Absolutely."

The woman looked away. She looked peeved still. "But what are you doing in Mr Rice-Evans' office room?" she said at last. "I'm sure he didn't suggest you go rooting around in *there*?"

Alice's face broke into a smile again, but this time it was a real effort. She raised her hands in a shrug. "I know. But I've looked everywhere else and... No luck."

The woman looked like she was going to answer, but then made a grunting noise instead. She tried to move forward, past Alice, into the office, but Alice moved position to block her way.

"I'm sorry to give you a fright." Alice went on. "You gave me a bit of a scare as well. It's quite a creepy house to be in alone."

The woman ignored her again, making another attempt at getting by.

"Well never mind that. But you shouldn't be in there." This time she made a more deliberate effort to walk past Alice on the landing, and even though Alice raised her hand, the woman brushed it off. For a second Alice thought that maybe she was just going to shut the door, but no. She was going inside.

"No, it's..." Alice had no idea what she was going to say, but it was too late anyway. The woman pushed the door fully open and strode inside. She flicked the light on, flooding the room with light. Alice looked down at the floor. She screwed her eyes tightly shut, waiting for the moment when the woman found Jamie, the open safe and the money.

It didn't come.

Alice opened her eyes again. The woman was saying something, but she couldn't hear, so she walked back to the study door. Nervously she looked inside. There was no money on the floor. The safe was hidden again behind the painting. Jamie was nowhere to be seen. The woman was now fussily adjusting the curtains, where they hadn't been equally pulled over the edges of the window. Alice stared around, wondering where Jamie was hiding. Whether there was any chance that she wouldn't see him.

"Normally *I'm* not even allowed in here," the woman was saying, "So I don't think you should be. Whatever Mr Rice-Evans says."

Although it was a big room, it was sparsely furnished, and there was nowhere to hide. Alice couldn't work out where he might be.

"And I certainly don't know how your telephone might have gotten in here." The woman stopped, like she suddenly had an idea. "Have you tried calling it?" she said.

Alice blinked. Wondering what on earth she could say to get the damn woman out of here.

"Yeah. Yeah, but I couldn't find it."

"Well would you like me to try?"

No, I want you to get out of here, you stupid woman, Alice thought, but she heard herself say something else.

"Maybe we could go downstairs and you could call it? We had drinks in the den. Maybe it's in there?"

As Alice spoke she sensed the door next to her move. And she realised, at last, where Jamie was. He was standing in the only place with any hope of hiding - behind the door. It offered minimal cover - when the woman turned to walk out of the room again she would see him, and worse, the hinges were warped so that gravity pulled the door shut, revealing him in his hiding place as it did so. Alice gave the door a casual shove, pushing it so it part-covered Jamie again. The woman noticed Alice's movement, but still seemed distracted by her idea. She pulled her phone out again.

"What's the number dear?" she asked. Alice told her, and waited for the older woman to move downstairs. But she didn't. She pressed the digits into the phone and waited, as if listening to see if the phone might suddenly trill into life from somewhere in the room. Of course it didn't.

"It's got a funny tone," The woman said.

"Probably the battery." Alice replied. "Or maybe we should try downstairs."

"Mmmmm."

Alice backed slightly into the door again, to push it back onto Jamie, but also to try and usher the cleaning woman from the room. And, still with something of a mistrustful sneer on her face, the woman did move. Alice felt the door push back into her, as Jamie pressed himself flat against the wall. She could hear his breathing. But the woman walked out of the room and back onto the hallway without a word. Not quite believing Jamie hadn't been discovered, Alice let the door fall shut behind her. The woman took over, pulling the handle and firmly shutting it.

They went down the creaky staircase and the woman dialled Alice's number again. For a second time the call failed to connect. Not surprising, Alice thought, given her phone was at the bottom of her hot tub. Reluctantly the cleaning woman gave up her idea.

"I usually clean for two hours on a Monday. I suppose I can keep an eye out for it." She said. She sounded keener to help now that she'd begun.

Alice thought fast again. Should she insist on staying? Pretend to search for two hours? Maybe she could make out she had found it and leave - but then she didn't have a phone with her to pretend to find. The woman was staring at her. She had no time to make a decision.

"No." She spoke just a little louder than normal, hoping that Jamie could hear her and understand what was going on.

"No, I think I've looked everywhere. You go on as normal. I'll um... I'll just go. I can always get Peter to send it on to me, if it turns up." She raised her voice just a fraction. She realised she had to give some sort of a message to Jamie. "Or maybe I'll just come back later. When you're gone?" She said.

The cleaning woman looked at her as if this was a very strange thing to say, but she didn't comment further. Alice wondered if she might get another chance to send her message to Jamie, but the woman seemed determined now to shepherd her out of the house.

"Could I get you anything? A cup of tea perhaps?" the woman asked when they reached the hallway. There was no mistaking from her tone that Alice wasn't expected to take up the invitation.

"No. No it's OK thank you," she said, smiling again as best she could. She found herself guided outside and down the steps back towards her car. As she reached it she glanced back at the house. The cleaning lady was standing in the doorway, her hands on her hips, and her face still dark with suspicion. Alice risked a glance up at the study window, hoping to see Jamie there, giving her some sort of a signal as to what to do. But there was nothing, just the blank glass and the straight, still curtains. Alice got in the car, swore under her breath, and started the engine.

35

Two miles down the road, she came to a wood. And just before the trees thickened there was a small clearing, a place where dog walkers came to park their cars. She knew it well. She swung the little car off the road, then turned it around, so it was out of sight from any other vehicles driving along the road. Then she waited, first with the engine on, in case she had to make a quick escape, but then with it switched off, after she worried the noise might attract attention. After a long fifteen minutes in which no cars had come down the road in either direction, she relaxed enough to let herself think.

Philip Marshall had been aboard *Sophtec Endeavour.* Peter Rice-Evans' most trusted adviser had been present at her father's death, and she hadn't known.

She knew Philip. Not to speak to - he didn't attend social events, had never really made the crossover from working for Peter - however closely - to part of the Belhaven's extended social set. But she knew him. Knew what he looked like - a tall, thin man, always in a suit. Always serious. And she knew what he did. Or rather she *didn't* know what he did, but understood the nature of it. Philip Marshall wasn't a politician as such, he was just - what exactly did he do? He was a *fixer*, Alice decided. One of those shadowy men that some politicians or businessmen liked to have lurking in the background. There to do what? To protect their masters, she supposed. A warning against anyone who might attempt to stab them in the back. She remembered a time when Peter had been forced to introduce him, at a social event somewhere. *He keeps me honest*, was all he'd said about what Marshall actually did. *He keeps me honest.*

But then what was he doing aboard *Sophtec Endeavour?* Alice thought further back, remembering the start of the race that had taken her father's life. The huge boats ready for the off, dominating the marina with their sponsors logos emblazoned down their sides. Her father had been excited but nervous - it was the second leg of the race, but the first in the notorious Southern Ocean, where huge storms swirled unchecked around the bottom of the globe, unhindered by land. Alice had been nervous too, but she'd teased her father - joking about how his photograph on the race website made him look old. Especially against the younger, professional sailors with their rugged good looks. And Alice had studied all the crew of her father's yacht, the men - and a few women - with the spirit to take part. Back then she had wondered if one day she would have the courage to do the same. And because she had studied them, she was quite sure that Philip Marshall hadn't been among them.

So how did he get on board? And was it *really* possible that he could have been responsible for what happened to her father? Philip was a strange man alright. But a murderer?

The noise of a car interrupted her thoughts. But it didn't slow down, whooshing past the entrance to the lay-by.

Alice thought back to the report they had found in the safe. Why was that there? She wished she had taken it with her, to read it in full, but Jamie must have bundled it back into the safe when the woman interrupted them. And what about Jamie? Would he have the sense to stay put in the study until the damn cleaning woman left? Alice hoped so.

Then Alice remembered she had her father's laptop with her, tucked away in her bag. She pulled it out, and this time, when it booted up, she ran a search for the name Philip Marshall. As expected there weren't many results - she had never seen her father with Marshall, and he had never mentioned him to her. Nonetheless his name did crop up. It seemed Peter had suggested him for occasional jobs - introductions and the like. But there was nothing that looked in any way suspicious. But Alice had the search results set to show the most recent occurrences of the name last. And the final entry made her sit up and pay closer attention. It was an email, from Uncle Peter and sent to her father. Sent just as *Sophtec Endeavour* arrived in Cape Town, and just a few days before the start of the second leg of the race. In it Peter wrote how he had heard a crew member had dropped out of Charlie's yacht. He asked whether Charlie could put in a good word, and help get Philip aboard. Her father had replied and said he would speak with the yacht's skipper and see what he could do. Five days later, the second leg of the race began. A week after that, and Charlie was dead.

She heard the noise of another car coming down the road. This time it slowed as it neared the entrance to the little parking area. Its indicator came on, and hurriedly Alice stuffed the laptop back into her bag as the car turned off the road. It was a green Volvo estate, and in the back Alice could see two large dogs. She relaxed a little, but now everything was making her jumpy. She watched as a man in a tweed jacket climbed out of the driver's seat. He was overweight, with a neatly trimmed white beard. He didn't look to be a threat, but she had her hands on the keys anyway, ready to fire the engine in her car if she needed to get away. The man opened the boot and the two dogs bounded out. She didn't know the breed but they were big. They looked like they would be able to run someone down in the woods. If that's what someone had trained them to do. She felt the man's eyes on her. She hoped he was just wondering what a young woman was doing, sitting alone in her car in this out of the way place. But he didn't come over. A minute later he was out of sight in the trees. Presumably he was soon far away, walking his dogs, but maybe he wasn't? Maybe he had doubled back and was watching her from the cover of the undergrowth.

She didn't feel safe after that. And from the clock on the dashboard, by now the cleaning woman should have gone. So she started the engine and drove back towards the house. As she drew near she half-expected to see the flashing lights of police cars - surely the woman would have discovered Jamie as she cleaned the house? And what would she - Alice - do if that were the case? Should she drive on? Should she try and evade capture on her own, or turn herself in and throw herself upon the mercy of the police. Beg them to protect her? She felt her nerves tighten as she neared the house, but as she passed a gap in the trees that revealed the driveway, she saw it was empty. No police. The cleaning lady's car gone too. She slowed.

The gates were closed again. The two stags gazing out imperiously. She stopped and looked at the house. It was just as they'd seen it earlier that day, no lights on, no signs of life. Alice nervously climbed out of the car to open the gates. But just then her eyes caught a movement from the vegetation - someone coming towards her, fast. She let out a scream.

"It's me. It's only me." Jamie said, as he came closer.

"Jamie! Jesus, you scared the shit out of me," Alice said, her hand on her chest. "Were you trying to freak me out or what?"

He didn't answer that. "Let's just get out of here." He said.

She sensed something was wrong with him as well. "Are you okay?" She asked. "Did she see you?"

"No." Jamie shook his head. "I figured you meant me to stay there and keep my head down, so that's exactly what I did."

"And she's gone?"

"Yeah. I had to run like hell once she'd set the alarm, to get out the back door before it activated. But I made it." He was already going to the passenger door of the car.

"Are you OK?" Alice asked, again sensing his urgency.

"I just want to get out of here. Like *right now*." Suddenly Alice realised that Jamie was seriously unsettled.

"What is it?" she asked. His face was white. He almost seemed to be on the verge of tears.

"Jamie?"

"Let's just *go*. Please." There was something in the way that Jamie was speaking. Something really wrong.

"What is it?" Alice asked, as she got back in the car as well. But he shook his head again and pulled the seatbelt across him.

"Not here. Let's just go." He looked across at Alice, his eyes pleading with her. She felt a shiver as he did so. And started the engine again. She had to turn the car awkwardly to get back onto the road. In the rear view mirror Alice caught sight of the big old house, its windows dark and empty. She shivered again as she fought the steering wheel to get them out of there.

36

A lice drove for a few minutes, expecting Jamie to explain what was upsetting him, but he sat in silence. In the end she told him what she had discovered about Philip Marshall. Jamie listened attentively.

"What does he look like?" Jamie asked when she had finished.

Alice was surprised by the question. She took a moment to consider. "He's about your height. Mid-thirties. Black hair."

"Does he have an accent?"

Alice thought again. "Scottish. I think. But it's not strong. Why?"

Jamie didn't respond.

"Why do you ask?"

"The man who came to kill me had a Scottish accent." Jamie said, staring levelly ahead. This time Alice didn't respond. She felt a chill running up and down her body. All the time she had been thinking about her father, she hadn't even remembered what had happened to Jamie.

She glanced across at his face. He still seemed unusually quiet. Like he was struggling to keep his composure. She wondered if he were almost on the verge of tears.

"Jamie are you OK?

Still he sat silent.

"Did anything happen back at the house?"

She caught him glancing down, his wounded face pale - even where his eye was bruised.

"Jamie just tell me."

"You've worked out how Rice-Evans had your dad killed. I think I found out why."

By now they had reached the roundabout that connected with the motorway. Alice pulled up at the junction, but didn't move off. Through the trees, the bright colours of Exeter Motorway Services were visible.

"Why?" Alice asked. "I thought you said... It was blackmail." Another car pulled up behind them now, but Alice didn't move.

"Is there something more?"

Jamie didn't respond, and the car behind gave an irritated blast on its horn. Eventually Jamie pointed at the sign for the services.

"Let's go there. Get a coffee or... I want to tell you this around other people."

Alice didn't answer, suddenly she didn't even want to know. But she did what he said, following the signs until they arrived in the car park. It was a bright sunny day - it surprised her, seeing people around. Reassuringly familiar logos hung over the doors. Comforting primary colours. She parked, and once again had the floating, unreal feeling as they walked inside.

Alice took a table by the window while Jamie queued for two cups of Starbucks coffee.

He carried them back, set them down on the table and slipped into the booth opposite her. He wrapped both his hands around his drink. His face was still pale. Alice simply waited. He looked down, took a deep breath, and then began.

"So. After you left, obviously I stayed. At first I was hiding behind the door, but then I remembered she said she didn't usually go in the office. I thought I'd try and sneak out. But it was hard to hear where she was in the house. And I didn't want to get caught. Not after how well you'd done. So I figured I should just wait in there. And after a while I had another look around his office." Jamie stopped and glanced around the services. But he didn't seem to take in the gaming machines, the newsagents and the flow of people. His eyes seemed empty.

"And?" She said.

He drew a deep breath. "And, there wasn't much. Like you could see.

It wasn't like an office he uses all the time. More like an occasional one. But the computer was there, so I switched it on."

Another pause.

"What did you find?"

"Not much. I don't think it's a computer he uses a lot either. But the internet worked."

"The internet?"

"Yeah. And I had the idea that I'd see what I could find out about him. So I read his Wikipedia page." Jamie took a sip of his coffee.

Alice frowned. She couldn't believe there was anything on there that would explain everything that was going on.

"And? What did you find?"

"Nothing."

"*Nothing?*"

"Nothing important. I mean it was interesting. But just background stuff. You probably know it already."

Alice waited a beat to see if he was going to give any details. He didn't.

"So?" She said.

"So. When I finished. I realised I should delete the search history. Just in case he noticed someone had used the computer. That's when I found it."

The sense of foreboding that Alice was feeling deepened again. Around her the bright lights, the chatter, the thick blocks of colours seemed to fade into the background. What was 'it'? Was she finally about to understand what lay behind the craziness of the last few days?

"Have you ever heard of a girl called Emily Brown?"

Alice thought carefully for a moment. "I don't think so," she replied. But she frowned a little, the name was somehow familiar.

"I looked though what Rice-Evans had been using that computer for, and that name kept coming up. So I followed the links. And..."

Alice suddenly remembered. She didn't need him to go on.

"She was that murdered girl. The one in the news. Where the neighbours heard screaming but didn't do anything? She was taken from her house. Then about a week later they found her body."

"That's right." Jamie brought his eyes up to meet hers, and for a long moment he stared at her.

"Why was Peter searching for news about her?"

Jamie continued as if he hadn't heard the question.

"Rice-Evans was reading everything about her. I mean *everything*. Every newspaper story. Every day. And it happened nearby. They found her in the woods, probably about an hour from here."

"I remember," Alice cut in. "It happened not far from our house. I remember seeing it on the local news. It was scary." A knot was forming in Alice's stomach. "But I don't understand what's it got to do with Peter?" A thought flashed through her mind. An explanation.

"This is his constituency. He was probably looking into it because of that." She felt a tiny rush of relief. Or maybe hope. Then saw from Jamie's face that this didn't explain it.

"No." Jamie shook his head. "No. You don't understand." He fell quiet again.

A possibility occurred to Alice. The beginnings of a solution to everything. But mentally she brushed it aside. It was too horrible.

"Tell me," she said.

Outside the window a family with kids walked past, Alice could see the children were shrieking, presumably with laughter, but the glass was so thick she heard nothing. That was what had happened with the girl. With Emily. She had screamed and screamed, but the neighbours had all said they thought it was laughter when the police interviewed them later. Once her body had been found.

"I thought it was odd. The way he was reading everything about her. So I decided to check something else."

"What?"

"The dates."

Alice screwed up her face.

"I don't understand..."

"I checked when the girl went missing, and when they found her body. I compared it with Rice-Evans' search history."

Alice waited a beat. A part of her already knew what he was going to say.

"Alice. Peter Rice-Evans wasn't just searching the internet for things on Emily Brown *after* she went missing. He was searching *before* she was taken. He was googling her. He was looking on her facebook page. All *before* she was snatched. Before he could have known about her. Alice, he was *researching her.*"

She had known where this was leading, but the full implications of what Jamie was saying took a moment to hit Alice. It was like repeating waves of horror. Each one heavier and more horrible than the last.

"Maybe he somehow knew her? Maybe there's another explanation." Alice only formed the words because she didn't want to believe.

Jamie shook his head. "No," he said simply.

"You think he took her? You think he..."

Alice broke off, not able to finish her sentence.

"What other explanation is there?"

For a while they sat staring at each other. Not speaking, while the normal comings and goings of the service station continued around them. Alice looked away first. She noticed that the family she had seen arriving were now inside. The mother took the children to the toilet while the father queued up at Burger King. She found her mind focusing on it. It was easier than trying to engage what Jamie had just told her. The woman came back from the toilets, carrying the little boy. They took a table not ten metres away.

She forced herself to concentrate. To think back to the news coverage about the case, it was a couple of years ago, before her Dad died, and she only remembered snippets. But one part stood out. The way the murderer had supposedly ambushed the girl in her bedroom. They said he had tried to frighten her to death.

But could it have been *Peter*? Could her Uncle Peter be a *murderer*? Or that *type* of murderer? Alice thought hard. It was one thing to order Philip Marshall to kill on his behalf. That was - was horrible, horrific - but somehow conceivable. This though?

But then isn't it *always* inconceivable? Isn't that what happens every time a serial killer is caught? Their friends, neighbours, their *family* always say they never suspected anything? And Peter *did* have two sides to him, she knew that. There was how he acted in public, his politician's image. But that was just a mask. He was different in person. He hid one version of himself from the world. Wasn't it possible that he hid yet another version from her?

"It was the dates that got me," Jamie said. Alice was startled.

"What?" She said.

"The dates. Emily Brown was killed in April, then three months later your dad dies. We now know *that* wasn't an accident, and Rice-Evans set it up. So the question is, why? Why does Rice-Evans need your dad dead?"

Jamie stared at Alice. His face was softer now, gently leading her onwards.

"I don't know."

"This is what I was thinking. What if Emily Brown wasn't the first person that Rice-Evans killed?"

Alice held her breath. "That's what they said on the news."

"Right. And what if your dad knew about it? Or realised somehow."

Alice screwed up her face again. Like she wasn't able to really concentrate on what they were saying, because of the pain it caused her.

"Why? How would Dad know?"

But Jamie didn't answer. Instead he looked away, then sighed.

"Jamie?"

He seemed about to answer, but then sighed again. He drummed his fingers on the table.

"Look, I should have said something about this earlier. But it just seemed." He looked back. "I dunno. A little far-fetched."

"What did?"

"The videos. The ones your dad shot."

"What about them?"

"Well we thought they were blackmail tapes, right? And they probably were. At least, that was probably your dad's intention in making them. But what if he accidentally caught something else?"

Alice breathed lightly. "Like what?"

"I told you I didn't watch the whole of the videos. And I didn't. But maybe watched more than I said I did. And the video of Rice-Evans. It wasn't... It wasn't just normal sex. It was more like... Like he was beating her. Again and again. And towards the end... He had his hands around her neck." Jamie stopped.

"What if your dad accidentally filmed Rice-Evans killing someone. Murdering a prostitute?"

Alice was stunned.

"Why didn't you tell me?"

"I didn't know. It didn't make sense then. I thought it was bad enough without... I don't know." Jamie hesitated, but then he went on, speaking quickly.

"But wouldn't it make sense? If they were out on the yacht, and Rice-Evans took things too far? If he accidentally killed a girl? Might they not decide the best thing to do is burn the boat down. Destroy the evidence?"

"Burn the boat down?"

"Yeah. You told me what happened to *Aphrodite*. You said you didn't believe it was just an engine fire. You said your dad didn't want it properly investigated. What if *that's* the reason?"

"No! Dad wouldn't do that." Alice raised her voice. She sensed a few people glancing over at their table and forced herself to calm down.

"Dad wouldn't cover something like that up!"

"Wouldn't he? He'd go straight to the police would he? Who would then blow apart the whole thing, all the blackmail tapes. Everything. He'd ruin all your lives. All because some worthless prostitute died in an accident? Someone no one would miss?"

Alice didn't know what to think. She couldn't imagine what her father would do, if placed in such a situation.

"But this has nothing *to do* with Dad."

"Except it does. Because three months after Emily Brown is killed, your dad's dead too."

Screwing her eyes shut, Alice had to concede he was right.

Jamie seemed suddenly willing to rethink too.

"Listen. You said your dad didn't need to blackmail anyone, that he made plenty of money. So maybe you were right about that. Maybe it wasn't a blackmail tape at all. Maybe your dad kept it for another reason altogether?"

Alice forced herself to concentrate.

"What reason?"

"What if your dad only kept it as a guarantee?"

"Of what?"

"That Rice-Evans wouldn't do it again."

"I don't understand."

"I don't know what you remember about this poor Emily Brown woman. But she was pretty badly attacked, when she died."

As he spoke Alice recalled snippets from the news coverage of Emily

Brown. Photographs of her smiling face, taken a few days before her death.

"Whoever did it put a kitchen knife through each of her palms, pinned her hands the bed frame so she couldn't fight back. But he killed her by strangling. He squeezed her so hard her eyeballs burst out. It was horrible. The police said they were looking for other cases with the same pattern of injuries. The way murderers kill, it's like a signature, and..."

"And it's exactly what you saw on the tape." Alice finished his sentence for him. Jamie just stared at her. Then he nodded.

"There weren't any knives, but he had her hands bound against the bed. Before he went for her neck."

"Dad was on *Aphrodite* when it happened." Alice said. "He would have heard the girl screaming. He would have gone in there to help her. That's why the tape doesn't show her actually being killed. Dad would have gone in there and tried to stop him."

"But he was too late. Rice-Evans had already strangled her by then. So they were left having to clean up the mess. They burnt the boat to hide the body. And wouldn't your dad have given Rice-Evans an ultimatum. Your dad helps him this time, but never again."

"That's why he kept the tape." Alice continued where Jamie left off. "As a guarantee that Peter wouldn't ever do it again."

"But Rice-Evans did do it again. The bastard couldn't help himself. He killed Emily. And he knew your dad would have recognised the pattern of injuries once they were described on the news. That's why he had to kill your dad too. Rice-Evans couldn't risk him going to the police this time."

The pieces finally fit into place. Alice stared at Jamie. "Dad was trying to do the right thing. That's why Peter had him killed. Dad was trying to keep him honest."

37

A lice drew her hands up to her face and covered her eyes.

"Oh my," she said a moment later, not taking her hands away.
"Oh my God. There might be more."

"What?"

"Dad would have been so distracted with the race he wouldn't have
even been watching the news. But Peter didn't know that. He was reading
all the newspapers - you saw that on his internet history, and that's just
on a computer he hardly uses. He would have been terrified that Dad
would have heard about it sooner or later. Then he got an opportunity to
get Philip Marshall onto the yacht. To make it look like an accident."

Suddenly Alice got to her feet.

"Where are you going?" Jamie asked, but she didn't answer. She
walked quickly at first, then broke into a run towards the ladies toilets.
Once inside she burst into a cubicle and dropped to her knees. She was
just in time. Gripping the bowl she leaned forward just as her stomach
heaved. She hadn't eaten much, so not much came out. But four times
her stomach tried to empty itself. Tears - from the pain of the retching -
spilled down her cheek.

When she was done she leaned back against the inside of the door.
Then she stood. She flushed the toilet and tried to compose herself. She
walked to a sink and splashed water on her face, using her hands to

channel some inside her mouth, to take away the bitter taste. She smoothed her eyebrows and stared back at the pale, lank-haired woman who stared back from the mirror. She didn't feel like the same person she had been up to last week. She didn't look like it either.

The door to one of the other cubicles opened, an elderly woman stepped out. She must have heard everything. She came to the sink next door but one to Alice and she glanced across, concern in her eyes. Alice looked away.

"Are you alright dear?" The woman asked. Her voice was kind. Alice turned to look at her. She had deep lines on her face, around her mouth and eyes - a lifetime of smiling.

"Whatever it is, I'm sure it's not as bad as you think it is right now." The lady smiled and began washing her hands.

"It never is."

Alice felt an overpowering urge to start telling her everything. To prove that she was wrong. But instead she turned away and dried her hands. When she was done she turned back to the lady and nodded her thanks. The older lady smiled at her.

Outside Jamie was waiting for her at the table. He'd put his hat and glasses back on.

"Are you OK?" he asked her. She nodded, blinking away the tears that still smarted at her eyes.

"So, what do we do now?" Alice asked, trying to force a grin.

For a long time Jamie didn't answer. He bit his lip.

"I guess we go to the police." He said in the end.

"I guess." Alice agreed. But neither of them moved.

"Now?" Alice said. She looked at her drink, "When we finish this I mean."

He looked at her. "They're still not going to believe us though." He said.

"What do you mean?"

"I mean the police aren't going to believe us."

"They have to believe us. We'll make them believe us." Alice heard her voice rise in tone.

"How though? I mean, think about it. He's the *Home Secretary*. Why would they believe us over him?"

The tone of Alice's voice settled on confusion.

"You've got the proof. You've got the proof from his Internet search history. Did you print it out or anything?"

"No. I didn't want to make a noise. Not with that woman still downstairs."

For a fleeting moment Alice considered they might have to go back there. But just the thought of going near the place sent shivers down her back.

"Well we tell the police, and *they* can go and get it. Raid his house..." Alice tailed off as Jamie shook his head. Still it confused her.

"They're not going to enter his house just because we say so. They have laws about that. They can't act on information that is gathered illegally. "

Alice was silent.

"And that's *if* they believe us. Which they won't. He's a major public figure. There's going to be a dozen weirdoes making nonsense accusations against him every year. They'll never believe us."

Alice screwed up her face in frustration. "So what are you saying? We have to go back there? Print it out ourselves?" She couldn't believe he was suggesting it.

But again Jamie shook his head. "No. They wouldn't believe that either. It's the sort of thing you could easily fake. And even if they did they still wouldn't be able to do anything. We'd have to tell them how *we* got the information - and we did it illegally. We broke into his house. They still wouldn't be able to act."

"But that's crazy. If he killed that girl, that has to be more important."

"Only if they believe he killed that girl. And they won't."

"They'll have to believe us."

"They won't." Jamie's voice was bitter but firm. "They won't Alice. They might just arrest us though."

Alice stared at him, still breathing deeply.

"At least we'd be safe," she said. There was bitterness in her voice.

"Would we?" Jamie asked, a few moments later.

"Well, if they locked us up I mean."

"I'm not even so sure about *that*. Maybe getting ourselves arrested is exactly what he'd want us to do," Jamie said. He lifted his eyes from where he'd been looking, at the table. Alice saw something in his face. She didn't like the look of it.

"Why?"

Jamie took a deep breath. "He's not fucking around is he? He's already had someone try to kill me. And I'm pretty sure you were supposed to be next. If we get ourselves arrested what would happen? We'd be locked away in separate cells. How hard is it going to be for him, or these guys who work for him, to arrange an accident?"

Alice didn't reply.

"I don't want to end up swinging from a light fitting in a police cell. Just another weirdo stalker who kills himself. If we go to the police it just makes it easy for him." Jamie was the one sounding bitter now. It occurred to Alice that none of this was his problem. It had nothing to with him, yet here he was, caught up in it.

"So what then? What do we do?" Alice asked.

For a long time Jamie didn't answer. The two of them stared at each other, while all around them ordinary people lived out normal, forgettable moments in ordinary lives. All of them oblivious to the horror that had suddenly enveloped the two people sitting by the window.

"I've a kind of half-plan," Jamie said at last.

38

They sat for a long time, Jamie talking quietly and Alice listening. At first she interrupted often, with questions, and objections to what he was saying. But as he outlined his idea she interrupted less. Finally she nodded, then sat back.

"And you really think it might work?"

"If you've got a better idea, I'm very happy to hear it," Jamie replied.

"No," she said. Then she went on. "I don't exactly like it, but I guess it makes sense."

They looked at each other.

"So first of all you need to call your mum. Get it set up." Jamie said.

That was easier said than done. Alice knew her house phone number by heart, but when she tried that, using the only payphone in the services that seemed to work, her mother wasn't in. All the other numbers that Alice thought to try were on her mobile phone. And that was still at the bottom of the hot tub in the beach house.

Alice thought of phoning the tennis club, where Lena would usually be at this time, having her weekly lesson. But again, Alice didn't know the number.

"Don't these places have computer terminals where you can use the internet?" Jamie asked, looking around, as they searched for a solution to the problem. But if they ever did, the rise of smartphones had rendered them obsolete and they had been removed.

"Well how about those numbers you can ring, and someone looks up the phone number for you? They still exist don't they?" Jamie tried next.

"The thing is I don't know the name of Mum's tennis club. I need to get online to find it."

Jamie looked around again. He was staring at the family with the kids. They had finished their Burger King meal now, and the mother was trying in vain to entertain the kids while the dad was flicking at the screen of his mobile phone.

"That guy, we could ask him..."

But suddenly Alice got up.

"Fuck this," she said. "Come with me." She led him back towards the toilets. But on the way she stopped. There was a small booth selling phone accessories. Alice spoke to the girl staffing it, and moments later she triumphantly held up a box containing a pre-paid mobile phone.

"So can I get this, or will you make me throw it in a bath somewhere?"

Jamie gave her a look. "Buy two. Maybe we can phone each other from prison," he said.

She paid in cash, and they spent fifteen minutes getting them out of the boxes and set up. It was surprisingly easy. Then Alice googled around the various tennis clubs and quickly found the right one. It took longer to get her mother's number, since she had phoned to cancel her lesson and the woman who answered the phone initially considered it a security risk to give out her number. But when Alice told her she was her daughter and going into labour, she finally got it. Jamie looked impressed at her ingenuity.

Alice dialled her mother's mobile. She waited. Finally she puffed out her cheeks and killed the call.

"No answer."

"Leave her a message."

"She hasn't got her answer phone on."

"Fucking hell Alice. What is your family like?"

Alice gave Jamie a look.

Then her new mobile phone rang.

"Hello? Who is this please?" Alice heard her mother's voice. She sounded nervous.

"Mum, it's me, Alice..."

"*Alice!*" The relief in her voice was obvious, but so was the anger. "Where are you? I've been trying to reach you. Why haven't you answered your phone?"

"Mum. I..."

"And what number is this? I've had Andy going crazy too, he hasn't been able to reach you. We thought you might have been kidnapped or..."

"*Mum, shut-up.*"

Lena stopped talking.

"You haven't been kidnapped have you?"

"No. I'm OK, but I need you to calm down. And I need you to listen."

Alice could hear her breathing hard on the other end of the line.

"What I'm about to tell you will sound crazy, but you have to promise to listen and not interrupt. It's really important."

There was a pause, then Lena replied.

"Is it any more crazy than you accusing me and your father of blackmailing people?"

This threw Alice. "I think I might have been wrong about that," she began, and her mother burst into sarcastic laughter.

"Of course you were wrong about that. Alice I think you've gone quite crazy..."

"Not completely wrong," Alice interrupted her. "But only half right. There's more to it."

Lena was silent. When she spoke again her voice had a suspicious edge.

"Are you still with that boy? That *Jamie Weston*? Has he been putting more insane ideas into your head?"

Alice hesitated.

"No, he's..."

"He's *insane*. That's what he is. He's not right in the head, believe me. You get away from him right now and come home..."

She was speaking loud enough that Jamie could hear her voice, still sitting on the other side of the table in the service station. As she spoke Jamie pulled his sunglasses off in frustration. The sight of him ignited an anger in Alice.

"You're right Mum, he's not right in the head. It's covered in bruises where someone tried to kill him."

Alice's words silenced her mother at last.

"That's right Mum. Someone tried to assassinate him. Someone broke into his boat last night and tried to shoot him. I'm looking at him right now. I can *see* where they beat him. It isn't Jamie who's mad. It's someone else."

Again Alice heard the sound of her mother's breathing, fast and light, like she was out of breath.

"Who?" Lena asked.

Alice wanted to tell her it was Philip Marshall, but she didn't know that yet. Not for sure.

"I don't know. It was a man." Alice thought of when she met Jamie in the café, the couple he thought were following him. That wasn't Philip, so maybe Rice-Evans had other people working for him too.

"He was followed. I saw them too. A couple were following him. This is real mum. This is really happening."

There was a moment of silence. Alice took it for her mother contemplating. Unable to see her face, she didn't see the shadow of fear that passed across it.

"Alice where are you? Tell me where you are and I'll come and get you."

"No." Alice paused. "Actually yes. I do need you to meet me. That's why I'm calling. But not just you. I need you and Peter."

"*Peter*?" Lena found her voice again. "What's he got to do with this?"

"Everything," Alice replied. "It was Peter that tried to have Jamie killed."

When Lena replied she spoke carefully, as if she were suddenly weighing every single word.

"And why exactly would he do that?"

"Because Jamie found the evidence. He found the tapes that Dad made. On *Aphrodite*. The tapes with Peter in them."

"*Peter*?" Lena said again.

"Yes - who did you think it was?"

"I thought it was..." Lena stopped herself. "I've already told you Alice. *If* your father made any tapes like that - and I don't think for one minute he did - they're not the sort of thing anyone is going to get killed over.

You're being ridiculous. Melodramatic. This isn't some Hollywood movie."

"A sex tape between a government minister and a prostitute? That's *exactly* the sort of thing people get killed over."

Alice heard her mother's exasperated sigh. She could almost see the expression.

"You really think it was Peter in these tapes?"

"Yes. I do. But there's more. We're pretty sure it wasn't just sex."

There was another pause, and Alice heard her mother's intake of breath.

"I'm sorry?" she said at last.

"You heard me." Alice said. Her eyes flicked across to Jamie's face. He gave her a supportive nod.

There was an awkward noise, like Lena was moving the phone from one ear to the other.

"Yes Alice, I did *hear you*. I just don't know what you mean. *More than sex?*"

"Jamie didn't watch right to the end of the tapes, but what he saw was pretty horrible. It wasn't normal sex. He said the guy was hurting the woman. He was beating her chest as hard as he could, then he started strangling her. He poked her eyes out. Does that remind you of anything?"

Lena hesitated, as if the sudden question had thrown her.

"Like what?"

"Do you remember the name Emily Brown?"

A pause. "No. What are you talking..?"

"Emily Brown," Alice cut into her mother's question. "She was a girl who was raped, beaten and strangled. Who was found with her eyes pushed in. Blinded. Not far from Peter's Devon house."

Lena hesitated again.

"She was..."

"Yes, yes. I remember." Lena interrupted Alice. "But what has this got to do with anything?"

"Do you remember how they said in the news that the way she was killed, was like the signature of the killer. That they were looking for similar cases?"

Lena stayed silent this time.

"Mum. I was wrong when I thought this was about money. It isn't. It's something much worse. Dad was making sex tapes, just like I said, but he ended up accidentally filming Peter murder someone."

"What? Who? No one ever died on *Aphrodite*. I don't know what you're talking about Alice."

"How about when Dad sunk her? We all knew it was never really an accident when she caught fire. We think that's when it happened. Dad was filming and Peter took things too far with some prostitute. They burned the boat to cover it up. To hide the body. It explains why Dad told us to meet him in a different harbour. It explains why Dad never wanted to push for the insurance money.

"He was *embarrassed*. That's why he didn't pursue the insurance. It was his responsibility as the captain of the boat and he felt he failed."

"Mum..."

Lena was silent for a long time.

"What?" She said at last.

"That's a fucking shit excuse and you know it."

"Maybe it is," Lena said. "But it's quite a leap from that to suggesting Charlie *killed* somebody."

"It wasn't Dad, it was Peter. It *is* Peter. He's still doing it."

"Oh Alice, this is ridiculous. I can't believe you're making these accusations against Peter. Why? And without any evidence."

"We've got evidence," Alice said. "I told you. Emily Brown."

Lena didn't reply for a moment. "I told you, I don't understand the connection. What about her? What evidence?"

"We looked on Peter's computer. He was stalking her online. Researching her. *Before she was taken*. Mum, I know this is hard to take. Believe me, it took me a while to accept it too. But Peter is a serial killer."

"Mum, are you still there?" Alice asked a few moments later.

"Yes. Yes I'm just sitting down. I still don't understand. How does Charlie fit into everything?"

"We think he kept the tape as insurance. To make sure Peter never did anything like that again. Maybe he told Peter he'd go to the police if Peter ever tried to hurt anyone again. That sounds like Dad doesn't it? Sounds like something he'd do."

Lena took a long time to answer.

"He'd tell the police right away."

"Would he?" Alice replied at once. "Would he really? What if Peter told him it was an accident? And the girl was just some prostitute who wouldn't be missed? I don't think he would. Especially if it happened on Dad's boat. He'd be frightened of the scandal of it. It would affect his business. It would destroy everything. I think he would help Peter cover it up. I think he would make sure Peter knew he couldn't ever do it again."

"Alice your father was a decent man. He'd be horrified to hear you accuse him of all this nonsense."

"I know. Dad *was* honourable. That's why Peter had him killed. He was worried that Dad would see something in the way the news reported that girl Emily Brown's death. He was worried that Dad was going to ruin him."

Lena was silent again.

"Now you're slipping into total fantasy again. Charlie fell from a yacht in the middle of the ocean. How could anyone have him killed?"

But suddenly Alice felt exhausted. She didn't answer. She couldn't answer.

"Mum, I'll explain it all tomorrow. I'll explain it all better tomorrow. But now I need you to do something for me."

There was a sigh.

"What?"

"I want you to phone Peter and make an appointment. For tomorrow. We need to meet. You, me, him - and Jamie - just the four of us. But it's got to be somewhere safe - somewhere where he can't hurt us."

"Alice... He's not going to hurt you."

"*Mum*, I just need you to fix the meeting. Please." Alice tried to soften her voice.

"You know how busy he is these days. Peter's diary gets booked up weeks in advance."

"*He'll see us.* He knows we're on to him. He's terrified of this becoming public. He'll drop anything for a meeting. Trust me."

Another sigh

"OK. But what do you want to *do*?"

Alice hesitated this time. She saw Jamie shaking his head - they'd agreed not to tell Lena this part, but Alice kept talking.

"We're going to trap him into giving a confession. We know what this is about, but we don't have enough evidence to go to the police. He stole the USB back from Jamie's boat. But we think he wants to make a deal. The man who came to kill Jamie. He offered a deal. It's worth a try.

"A deal?"

"Yeah He won't be able to discuss it without admitting what he's done, or at least some of it, and we'll record him. Then we can decide what to do - whether to go to the police, or... Or I don't know. But at least you'll believe us."

Alice glanced at Jamie. His face had darkened and he was biting his lip. Suddenly it didn't feel smart to have said all that to her mother. But it was too late now.

"Why would he agree to a deal? If any of this were true?"

"Mum - will you just do it?"

Lena was silent for a moment. For a split second Alice found herself praying that her mother would say no. That she would tell her this was all some terrible mistake, and explain away all the damning evidence. But Lena didn't.

"Alice, is this all real? I mean are you absolutely sure about this?"

"Yes Mum. I'm totally sure."

There was a very long pause, but Alice knew her mother was still there, from the sound of breathing.

"I'll try and call him now. Will you be on this number?"

"Yeah. We'll be waiting." Alice hit the button to kill the call.

Jamie had been watching the entire conversation, still sitting opposite Alice across the plastic table in the service station. She gave him a half-smile, unsure how he'd take her overstepping the mark.

He held her gaze for a moment, then he stretched his hand across the table and rubbed Alice's shoulder.

"Well done," he said. "You did good."

Her smile widened, but it remained sad.

"We better get ready," he said eventually.

39

They got up and wound their way out of the services. They didn't speak as they got back in the car, but Jamie propped his new phone up on the dashboard, already set up with directions to a nearby electronics superstore.

"Do they still sell mini tape-recorders do you think?" He asked. "I don't think I've seen them since the ninties."

It turned out they did, but these days the devices were digital. It made them realise they could just as easily use their new mobile phones, both had apps that made them do exactly what the specialist devices they were looking at could do.

"Let's get one anyway," Alice said, when they'd examined all the products on display. "Peter might insist on seeing our mobiles, to make sure we're not recording him."

"Let's get a couple then. Just in case one doesn't work properly." Jamie replied. Alice nodded and picked up one of each of the two different models. She carried them over to the till and dug in her bag for some cash. The young man serving looked her up and down, then allowed his eyes to settle on her chest. For Alice it was a weird reminder that life went on. She glared at him as she handed over the money.

Outside in the car park again, Lena called back. Alice answered the call then got into the car.

"Well you were right about one thing," her mother said. "I told him you wanted to meet, and he immediately sounded strange. And he agreed to meet you tomorrow morning which is very unusual..."

"Where?" Alice interrupted.

"His office. It's private, and he's got an hour in the morning..."

"Mum!" Alice cut in again. "What did I tell you? We need to meet somewhere safe! In public."

"Alice I hardly think he's going to do you any harm inside the Home Office." Lena snapped back. "And where did you have in mind? He's the home bloody secretary. He's not exactly inconspicuous in public places."

Alice took a breath to calm herself down. "OK. OK, I'm sorry. I'm a bit jumpy."

"When are we meeting? We'll need a couple of hours to get there."

"Eleven. Is that OK? He said he'd come down to the lobby to let us in. Alice where exactly are you?"

Alice ignored her mother's question.

"Where is his office Mum? I haven't been there before."

Lena paused. Alice guessed she was thinking. "I don't know the address. It's that big glass and steel building..."

"Marsham Street, Westminster?" Jamie said suddenly from the passenger seat. He had his mobile in his hand, his face looking at the screen.

"What?" Alice asked him.

"The Home Office? That's the address it gives online."

Alice composed herself.

"OK Mum. We'll be there at ten thirty. We'll meet you outside before we go in. Don't go there early. Whatever you do, don't meet him without us."

"Alice..."

"Mum. Promise me? Promise me you won't meet him without us."

"Alice this is nonsense, Peter isn't going to harm..."

"*Promise me Mum.*"

"OK. OK. I promise," Lena said.

Alice hung up and stared out of the windscreen of the little car. Outside normal people were parking their cars and heading off into the shops. The contrast between how totally normal it looked, and how her world had imploded was hard to take.

"Well I guess we should find somewhere to stay," Alice said. She turned the ignition and backed the little car out of its parking space.

40

It was a three hour drive to London. They decided to get it out of the way so they would be less rushed in the morning. Jamie drove, while Alice used her mobile to look for somewhere to stay. She found a Hilton Hotel three streets away from Marsham Street, and began a reservation. The little screen asked for a name. She was about to enter hers, but something stopped her.

"Think of a name, any name. A girl," she said to Jamie. He looked across at her from the driver's seat, confused.

"Sarah?"

"Sarah what?"

"I don't know. Sarah Jones?"

Alice typed the name in. Then the website asked what room she wanted. She glanced at Jamie again but this time didn't say anything. She ticked the box for two single rooms, then selected to pay on arrival to avoid using her credit card.

Jamie was driving fast, staying mostly in the overtaking lane and creeping behind other drivers until they peeled off to let them through. There wasn't anything aggressive about it, but Alice noticed his knuckles were white where they gripped the steering wheel.

"Are you nervous?" She asked him.

Jamie glanced over at her. Then he let up on the accelerator and indicated to move into the middle lane.

"Sorry. I was trying to get there quick, so we have time to get ready." he said. Then he went on.

"Yeah. I am a little. You?"

She nodded. "I can do it all here on Dad's laptop. Better than getting stopped for speeding."

His eyes flicked across to hers, he smiled, then he turned back to the road.

Alice pulled out the computer and flipped open the lid. She opened a new Word document and began to type in silence. At first Jamie kept glancing over, as if expecting her to read bits to him, but after a while he just drove, and let her work. Finally, when she finished typing, she looked across at Jamie.

"Are you sure they won't just go to the police?" She said. She had been silent for over a half hour and he gave a start.

"Who?"

"These lawyers. Aren't they going to think this a pretty unusual request? Won't they just go to the police?"

"You're not going to tell them anything they can go to the police with," Jamie replied. "Not yet anyway."

Alice didn't answer. She started reading back what she'd written. But Jamie interrupted her again.

"You've written down everything we suspect about Rice-Evans?"

"Yeah."

"And told them we're meeting him tomorrow?"

"Yeah."

"Good. So first thing tomorrow morning, we print that and put it in the post. We include a note saying if they don't hear from you in person, before it arrives, they should make a copy of what you've written, and send it to the police and the editors of every newspaper they can think of."

Alice nodded. "OK," she said.

"That way he can't hurt us," Jamie went on. "He can't risk this blowing up any more than it already has."

"OK?" he asked.

"Yeah." Alice smiled at him.

"We're nearly there," Jamie said. "Another half hour."

41

The motorway was clear, but once they left it, dropping down into the snarl of London traffic, their speed dropped, so that it was actually more like forty five minutes before they arrived at the hotel. Jamie waited in the car while Alice went in, to pay and get the code to the underground car park. From there they took the lift to the fourth floor. Alice gave Jamie his key.

"You're in here," she said, pausing at the first of the rooms. She saw him hesitate for a second, but then nod. Understanding.

"Let's go and eat." She went on. She watched as he opened the door and tossed a bag onto the bed. Alice did the same in her room and they went downstairs before the kitchen closed.

It was late enough that the restaurant was quiet. The lights were dim, up lighters on the wall casting purple shadows. The few other diners in there were finishing their meals. When the waitress came across to seat them, she looked weary too, but Jamie spoke to her. He apologised for being so late and said they'd be happy to eat whatever the kitchen had left. Alice watched, trying to imagine Andy ever behaving like that to the people paid to serve him.

Some wine came. Jamie poured her a glass, saying it would help her relax and get a better night's sleep. Alice pulled some bread apart as they waited. They hadn't eaten all day. She hadn't been hungry until now, what with everything she'd learnt. But the smell from the kitchen now was making her mouth salivate. Blocking out all other thoughts. When the food came they ate in silence. It seemed to fill more than a physical hole. It made her feel better too.

When she'd finished, Alice put down her cutlery. She took a long sip of the wine then wiped her mouth.

"I can't stop thinking about it," she said, breaking the quiet that had settled upon them. "About what we're going to do. Do you really think it could work?"

Jamie took a while to answer. It looked clear he had been having the same doubts.

"We don't *lose* anything." he said at last. "He knows we know the tapes exist. When he finds out we know what was really on them... I don't know. Maybe he'll just confess everything? Sometimes people like this secretly *want* to get caught."

"I don't see that with Peter," Alice replied.

Jamie shrugged.

"Maybe not. But if he made a deal with your dad, I don't see why he won't consider making one with you. And if he does we'll have it on tape."

Alice swirled the wine around her glass.

"What then?"

Jamie took a long time to answer.

"I don't know," he said at last. He began to run his finger around the rim of his own glass. Not hard enough to cause the glass to vibrate or hum, just enough to draw her eyes to what he was doing. Suddenly he stopped. His eyes flicked up to her face.

"But at least you'll know for sure. You'll be able to look into his eyes and know the truth."

Alice considered that for a moment, holding his gaze.

"But what then? What do we do then?"

Jamie's eyes dropped back to the table. "I dunno," he said. "Maybe we should get out of here."

He was about to look up at her again, but at that moment the waitress reappeared to take their plates away. They both fell silent.

Alice waited while the girl fussed around, sliding sideways glances at Jamie. Alice wondered whether her interest was his good looks or his black eye. At least with the shadows in the restaurant that wasn't too obvious. The girl left again. There was a moment of silence.

"What do you mean, get out of here?" Alice prompted. It sounded like a nice fantasy.

"I mean escape," Jamie went on. "You have some money, I have *Phoenix*. We could sail her away. Somewhere that no one would find us. Not even the British government. We could just go where the wind leads us."

Alice didn't answer him. She remembered the day they had spent aboard his boat. The quiet as its bow had kissed through the water.

"We could sail her down to Africa. You told me before how you wanted to teach? Well, you can do it. There's a million schools down there that would love someone like you. Someone educated. Someone intelligent. Beautiful. And I could work in a hospital. We could do something good with our lives. Get away from all this..." he hesitated, searching for the right word to describe everything that had happened, but seemed unable to find one.

Alice smiled lightly at the idea. She felt the alcohol softening everything she was hearing.

"Is she big enough?" she asked. "*Phoenix* I mean. To sail that far?"

"Sure she is." Jamie sounded enthusiastic. Alice remembered how he had sounded that happy once before, when he had been explaining how he bought the boat, before they discovered the USB drive was stolen. That felt a lifetime ago now.

"She's small but she's tough. And she's just had a major overhaul. She wouldn't let us down." He shook his head firmly.

Alice believed him.

"What about Peter? Are we just going to let him go?"

"No. We'll expose him. But we'll make sure we're somewhere safe first. Somewhere he can't reach us." Jamie looked up at her. He sounded so certain. So confident.

"We could do it Alice. It's not just a dream."

She wanted to just accept what he was saying. Even if just for a little while, while the wine relaxed her mind. But she couldn't. The objections kept surfacing.

"Can't they track yachts? I mean, with satellites or something? Won't they be able to find us?"

"Not if we turn everything off. The sat nav, the phones. That's what they latch onto. But with everything off, we'll be invisible. A tiny yacht, just a scrap of wood and sailcloth, hidden in the vastness of the oceans." Jamie replied. "They'll look, sure they'll look. But they'll never find us."

Something in what Jamie said sparked a memory. A time when she - just after news of her father's disappearance - had sat looking at the globe he kept in his London study. It felt like the first time she had really examined it, had really seen how the Southern Ocean stretched unbroken around the entire globe. How even the largest countries were dwarfed by its size. She had cried that day, heartbroken again by how her father had to die out there. Alone. Jamie was right, the oceans were huge.

"But what about you?" She asked. "This isn't your problem. Why would you give up your life to help me?"

He shrugged. "I don't have a choice. I'm involved whether I want to be or not."

She stared at him, unsure what to think.

"And anyway. I wouldn't be giving up my life. I *want* to go to Africa. I *want* to be a doctor. To help people.... "

She cut him off. "But if you go now you won't be a doctor. Don't you have to finish your studies?"

Jamie shook his head. "I've almost finished anyway. Even if I disappeared now, I'd still graduate this summer." He thought for a moment. "And qualifications don't matter out there. What matters is what you do."

Alice opened her mouth to speak, but then closed it again. The question she had been about to ask bounced around inside her own mind.

What about Andy? What about my life?

"Anyway," Jamie said a moment later, his voice still soft and warm. "It won't come to any of that. He's going to say something. We'll have him on tape confessing. Then we can go to the police and get this mess sorted out." He reached across the table and took her hand. He squeezed it gently.

They got up to go. It was close to midnight by then, the restaurant closing around them. They walked to the lift, and it pulled them silently up the inside of the building. They came to the room that Alice had given Jamie earlier. He used his key card to open the door. She held her own card awkwardly. Jamie hesitated before going inside.

"Are you going to be alright? On your own I mean?"

Alice let her eyes flick onto his face. She nodded, then looked away.

"I can sleep in your room, if you like?" Jamie said. "On the floor I mean. Just in case."

Alice hesitated. She knew a part of her had hoped he'd ask. She smiled.

"You know," she said. "If they ever make a movie about this, I bet I'd say yes." She saw his lips curl into a smile. His arm began moving, reaching out to her again.

"No," she said, stepping back. "I'll be fine. And we need to sleep."

The smile froze, then slowly faded. Jamie looked down. He nodded. "I understand." He said. He looked up again, his blue eyes burning into hers. She almost changed her mind.

"Well goodnight," he said. "I'm here if you want me."

"I'll give you a knock in the morning." Alice replied, and she walked down the corridor until she reached her own door. Her bag was still on the bed, unmoved, but somehow the room now felt threatening. She looked around quickly, the words already forming to tell Jamie she had changed her mind - they would be safer together. But instead she swung her own door closed. Slowly she lay down on the bed and closed her eyes.

42

Alice slept badly, unable to prevent her brain from imagining how the meeting would go. In the end she gave up, getting out of bed at five and walking into the room's tiled bathroom. It was warm and windowless, and her bedraggled reflection stared back at her. She took a long shower. When she finished she stepped out. She wrapped herself in a thick white towel, and wiped the mirror to see if there was any improvement. It was marginal.

She went back to the bedroom. She looked at the few clothes she had taken, and considered which to be the most sensible to wear. There wasn't a lot of choice. She laid her selection on the bed, black jeans and a silk blouse, then put on her underwear. Then she emptied her bag to find the recording devices she had bought the day before. She examined them carefully, and looked at her clothes again. The first device was the shape of a credit card, but slightly smaller and thicker. She pressed the button to make it begin recording, and then looked at her body for where she might be able to conceal it. She tried to fit the device underneath her bra, flat against her chest held in place by the bra's strap. The edges cut into the insides of her breasts and she winced and took it out again. She tried again, this time on the side of her left breast. It felt a little more comfortable here and she added the blouse and examined her appearance in the mirror. She turned sideways to see if the outline of the recording device could be seen. She grimaced. It wasn't obvious, but if you looked closely you could definitely see it. She pulled it out again and threw it on the bed. Then she picked up the second device. This one was shaped like a stick, only about an inch long, and so narrow it didn't even have a screen. Alice tried again, slipping this one underneath the middle of the bra. It felt much more comfortable and she couldn't see it in the mirror. She pulled on her jeans, and after a moment's thought she simply slipped the first device into the pocket. Then, after a final check in the mirror, she walked across the hallway to Jamie's room.

She knocked, her bare feet sinking into the soft hallway carpet. When he opened the door he was already dressed, his hair wet from the shower. But he looked nervous. Without a word she pushed him inside the room and shut the door behind them. Then she wrapped her arms around him and kissed him, hard on the lips. He struggled against her for a moment before kissing her back. She began rubbing his chest, putting his hands onto her body, and then, for a long moment their hands were all over each other. Finally, needing some air, she pulled back. Before he could lean in and kiss her again she held up her hand.

"So?" She asked.

"So what?" Jamie gasped. His eyes were wide.

"Did you notice anything?"

"Notice what?"

She didn't answer but stood up. Her blouse was now untucked from her jeans, and - holding up one hand to keep Jamie away - she pushed it right up, uncovering her bra. Then she pulled out the little device.

"I was recording you," Alice said. "A test to see if you'd notice." She grinned at him. It took a while but slowly he smiled back.

"Christ Alice," he said, his forehead creased into a frown. "I think I need some coffee."

* * *

Outside the hotel the noise and fumes of London hit them like a blast. It was Jamie's idea to walk the few streets to the glass and steel building which housed the British Home Office. He said the exercise would clear their heads, but it took longer than they thought to cross the busy roads so that, for Alice, the opposite was true. Or maybe she would have felt increasingly nervous however she approached. Jamie didn't look to be feeling it though. He was quiet, thinking. He looked like he was rehearsing in his mind. As they finally neared the entrance, Alice called her mother's mobile, but they saw her before the line connected, waiting just outside the revolving doors.

"What's she wearing?" Alice said, mostly to herself. "What does she think this is, some sort of job interview?" If Jamie wanted to reply, there was no time for him to do so.

"Alice!" Lena held her hands out to her daughter, but didn't embrace her. Alice realised she didn't want to crush the sequined blazer she was wearing.

"Oh Alice! I've been so worried about you. I really thought..." Now Lena did touch her daughter, holding her at arm's length to examine her.

"Are you OK? Apart from all this nonsense I mean?"

Alice gently shook herself free. "I'm fine Mum." She glanced at Jamie who had so far been ignored by her mother. Now Lena turned to him. The relief showing on her face dropped away and was replaced by a cold stare.

"Mum, this is Jamie," Alice said. He stepped forward, and after a moment's hesitation he held out a hand. Lena looked at it for a while, as if it might not be clean enough for her manicured fingers, but then she reached out her own hand and shook it.

"Jamie," she said.

A motorbike buzzed past, the driver's blacked-out helmet turning towards them as if he were distracted by the two women.

"Well I suppose it's too much to ask that you've changed your mind about all this?" Lena asked, directing the question at Alice.

Alice looked surprised. "How could we change our minds?"

"I just thought..." Lena looked irritated. She made an effort to soften her expression. "I thought maybe once you'd slept on it you might realise how ridiculous this all was."

"No."

Lena bit her lip. She was silent for a moment.

"Well that's a shame Alice. Because I have to warn you. If you actually go in there and accuse Peter of all this..." Lena didn't seem able to find the word to complete her sentence, but she carried on regardless.

"There's no going back. I don't know what will happen - I really don't. But it won't be good."

Alice didn't take her eyes off her mother.

"So what would you have me do?" She asked, her voice cold.

"I don't know. Take some time. Think about things. Maybe take a holiday? Maybe we could go together? Or with Andy. I'm sure he could get some time away for an emergency like this..." Lena stopped again. She glanced at Jamie, making no effort to disguise the dislike on her face. "And I'm sure you can still patch things up with him, whatever you might have done here."

Lena tried to smile at Alice. "That is what you want, isn't it?" she pleaded.

When Alice responded her words were laced with anger.

"You want me to just forget about this? You want me to ignore knowing that Peter is a murderer. That he killed Dad? Just so that I can go on and marry Andy and everything goes back to normal?"

Lena looked shocked.

"Alice..." She began, but Alice cut her off again.

"You still don't believe me do you? You don't believe any of this?"

Lena seemed to refuse to meet Alice's eyes.

"I don't know what to believe." She said. She glanced at Alice again, then her eyes flicked away. She looked guilty. Suddenly a wave of panic washed over Alice.

"Mum? You haven't told him anything have you? About why we're here? What we're going to do? I told you not to."

Now Lena looked flustered. "Of course I haven't. Do you think I want to tell him what you told me yesterday? After everything Peter has done for this family? Over so many years? You really have gone crazy if you think that."

Alice felt herself relaxing. Just a little.

"I haven't gone crazy." She said in a quiet voice.

"Well if you haven't gone crazy, then please, I beg you. Reconsider what you dragged me here to do." Lena said. "It's not too late, but if you go in there and accuse him..." Again Lena seemed unable to finish the sentence.

"If you go in there and accuse Peter of what you told me yesterday. You will destroy your life. I want you to think long and hard about that."

Alice looked down at the pavement. Despite herself, and how sure she had become, her mother's words caused her to think. Everything in the last few days did, on one level, seem like some crazy, deluded dream she had shared with Jamie. She glanced over at him now. He was still wearing his sunglasses, the ones she had bought in the shop near the beach house, and as she looked he pushed them up into his hair, his face full of concern for her. He looked *genuine*, she realised. His wasn't the fake self-interest of her mother, who just wanted her privileged life to go back to normal. And the proof was right there, beaten into Jamie's face. The swelling around his eye had gone down a little, but the colour, the deep purple bruise had darkened overnight.

Then she thought of Dad. Of how he had gone into the water. How he had been pushed. How he must have watched the yacht sailing away into the predawn light. He must have known there was no chance of his rescue. He must have known he would die, either from the cold or the exposure, or if he chose to stop swimming from drowning. He would have known he was being murdered.

And here she was. Standing outside the office of the man who did it. With an opportunity to get her revenge.

"Mum," Alice said. "This isn't about me. Or Andy, or even *you*. And I know this is a lot to take in, believe me I know. But it's quite possible that Peter has been a good friend to our family on the surface, but a lot less than a friend underneath. Peter is a serial murderer. He killed Dad. I know you don't believe me now, but you will once we've spoken to him. After this you'll understand how I have no choice."

This time it was Lena who hesitated before answering. Finally she gave a loud sigh.

"Well I just hope that Peter is in a forgiving mood. That's all I can say." The two women both turned a little, so that they were no longer facing each other. Jamie glanced at his watch.

"We'd better get on with it." He said.

43

A revolving door separated the spacious lobby from the street, and as Alice stepped inside she touched her shirt, feeling for the recording device. She had reset it before leaving the hotel, and it could run for four hours before its memory was full. For backup Jamie had taped the second device to his chest with sticking plasters. Whatever Rice-Evans did or didn't say, they would capture it.

Once through the door Alice paused, waiting for the others to join her. She looked around, feeling like she had entered enemy territory. On the far wall there was a desk, where two men in security uniforms sat, their eyes were fixed at something below the height of the desk, presumably monitors. Various employees hurried around, clutching folders and cardboard coffee cups. One woman in particular caught her attention, an attractive woman in a red dress, her heels clicking on the marble floor. Then Alice noticed something else. And with a flood of panic, she couldn't believe it hadn't occurred to her before. Although she was inside the door, to get into the lobby proper they had to pass through a metal detector - like those you see at airports. Beside it was a table where two more security guards stood, a man and a woman this time. They were checking everyone that entered the building, the people had to pass through the arch of the device, while their bags were scanned by a separate machine. Alice's hand went to her chest again. Metal detectors. She spun around to see if Jamie had seen it too.

But as she did so, something else caught her eye. The woman in red had been walking towards a man, his back turned, hunched over his phone. But as she reached him, he turned around and slipped the phone into his pocket. He stood up to his full height, now much taller.

Philip Marshall.

Whatever the woman had to tell him didn't seem to interest him much. He almost shooed her away with a hand signal. Alice held her breath as she saw him scan the entrance. Felt his eyes lock onto her. She saw the corners of his lips curl in a cruel grin and he stepped forward at once. He ignored the security guards as he walked between their table and the arch, they did nothing to stop him.

"Miss Belhaven, Mrs Belhaven?" Moments later he stood in front of her, a little too close, she could smell his breath on the cool lobby air, it smelt of his breakfast. Coffee and some sort of meat.

"The Home Secretary asked me to come down and meet you," he went on. Suddenly he seemed to notice Jamie, and there was a twinge of irritation in his face. Jamie still had his sunglasses on, trying to hide the damage to his eye.

"I don't think we've met?" He held out one of his big hands. It was steady, and it looked ready to crush anything that was put in it. Jamie pulled the glasses from his face and folded them up. He didn't accept the handshake.

"Are you sure? You look familiar somehow."

Jamie stood his ground, staring right at Marshall, who stared unblinking back. Eventually he dropped his hand.

"I don't think so." He gave his shoulders an amused shrug and turned back to Alice.

"The Home Secretary is waiting. Follow me."

He held out his arm, shepherding them towards the security barrier. Alice tried to catch Jamie's eye, hoping he might have some idea to prevent the disaster that was about to befall them. But if anything he looked more ready to run than offer any help. She felt a trickle of sweat drip between her breasts.

They got to the machine. Alice saw her mother prepare to go

through, but then something happened. Marshall put his big arm in front of her and shook his head.

"No need for that," he said. Through his accent it was hard to tell whether he was being generous, or the security gate was just another annoyance that he wanted to brush away. He said something to the first security guard - Alice didn't hear what it was - but at once the man opened a gate. It looked like he couldn't do it fast enough. The security guard stepped smartly out of the way.

"Follow me please," Marshall led them through, avoiding the security.

They walked to the lift. Marshall punched the button for the top floor. There was a wait before the car arrived, long enough for the silence to be awkward, but Alice hardly noticed, she was still trying to make herself breathe normally again after getting through the security gate without their plan falling apart. The doors hissed open, the lift was empty, then Marshall stepped forward. Now another vision flashed through her brain. Would he try something in the lift? And if he did, could the three of them do anything about it? She didn't have long to think before Lena followed him inside. Then Jamie too, giving her a tiny nod of the head. Alice stepped forward too. She stood as far away from Marshall as she could. The doors slid closed.

"This lovely weather's continuing," Lena broke the silence, as the lift began to slow. No one else said anything, and Lena was quiet again. The doors opened.

Marshall led them along a thickly carpeted walkway with the booths of offices leading off it. Most of the walls were glass and there were people working in some of them, but it was less busy than Alice had imagined. It added to Alice's sense of unease, she had imagined they would be surrounded with people, in case they needed to shout for help, but instead they seemed to be walking away from everyone. Rice-Evans' office was hidden away, hard to find. Eventually they came to another lobby area, where an older woman was sitting behind a desk, typing on a computer. Behind her there was a closed office door. There were some seats for visitors but Marshall ignored them. He spoke to the woman at the desk, then nodded. He knocked once on the door, then threw it open.

"Go right in," he said, standing back from the entrance.

* * *

Lena went first, tutting at her daughter for the way she had shrunk back from the door. Jamie went next, then Alice followed, feeling Marshall come in behind her and close the door. He stayed there, cutting off their exit.

Her Uncle Peter was at his desk, at the far side of a large room. They seemed to have interrupted him working his way through a huge bundle of papers, stacked up in folders. A governmental red box stood open on a side table. He finished what he was doing and set down his pen.

"Lena! Alice! How lovely to see you. And how *unexpected*."

He came out from behind the desk and kissed Lena. Then turned to Alice. She felt his hands on her shoulders, his lips come close to her cheek. Then he pulled back, keeping his eyes fixed closely onto hers, as if searching for information.

"You've not visited me here before have you?"

Alice didn't answer.

"There's no view of the river I'm afraid. I'm not deemed important enough." He smiled at his own joke, his teeth yellow in the light from the window.

"And you must be Mr Weston?" He went on, turning to Jamie. "Abingdon College wasn't it?" He smiled ironically. "How *is* Georgina?" He let the words hang for a moment, then spun around, as if dismissing Jamie again.

"Phil, I don't think we'll need you for this one," Rice-Evans said. Marshall pushed himself off from where he had been leaning on the door. He looked disappointed.

"Could you ask Monica to bring some coffees in?"

Without a word Marshall turned and exited, closing the door after himself. Rice-Evans turned to the three of them, a wide smile on his face.

"Well?" He said. "Shall we?"

Peter Rice-Evans' office was divided into two areas. The large antique looking office desk where he had been working when they came in took up one end. The other was given over to a meeting area, where a low, informal table was surrounded by six chairs. Cups and saucers for coffee had already been laid out, and with a knock on the door, the woman who had been typing outside came in with a silver flask of coffee, a wisp of steam escaping from its spout and curling up into the air.

They all sat. Alice noticed there was a folder on the desk too, in front of the seat that Rice-Evans took. The woman served them all coffees, her quiet voice the only noise in the room. Alice felt Rice-Evans' eyes on her the whole time. Finally the woman was finished, leaving the coffee on a side table, in case anyone needed top ups, she said. Rice-Evans waited until she had left and closed the door again.

"So. Do you mind if we get right down to it?" He asked. "It's just I can only give you until midday. Then I have meetings all afternoon." He raised his hands in apology, then turned again to Alice.

"Your mother is a little worried about you," he paused, then corrected himself. "We're both worried. She says you've got some strange ideas into your head." Peter looked sharply at Jamie. "And I think we're all confused as to how Mr Weston here fits into things."

Alice took a deep breath. A short silence settled onto the room, and she realised everyone was waiting to hear what she would say.

"So," Rice-Evans smiled at her. "What is this all about? Why exactly have you brought us all here today?"

Alice took a deep breath. She and Jamie had practised this conversation - not quite role-playing but discussing how it might go. They'd agreed it was better coming from her. She had grown up knowing Rice-Evans. It was her father who had died. And in the privacy of the car, or the hotel room it had seemed easy - or at least possible. She would confront him, lay before him all the evidence they had accumulated, and he would confess, or make some slip.

But now he was here, in front of her, any confidence they had felt about that seemed like a terrible mistake. She tried to think of all the discoveries they had made over the last few days, wondering which to begin with. But none seemed right. In fact, what had all seemed so clear suddenly felt muddled. Why were they here? She was beginning to panic again.

"Before Alice says anything. You should know we've contacted a lawyer." Jamie's voice rang out suddenly. Clear and confident. "I won't say which one. But they've received a document outlining everything we're going to say in this meeting. And if we don't walk out of here and contact them this afternoon, they're going to forward that document to the police." He hesitated, smiling bleakly.

"And if that isn't a concern, they're also going to forward it to the editors of every national newspaper. Which I think might be a little harder to control." He was silent, keeping his eyes on Rice-Evans' face.

For a long time Rice-Evans just stared back.

"I see." He said at last. "I assure you that's not necessary. Lena has..." Rice-Evans stopped.

"Mrs Belhaven has explained to me the nature of the... concerns you want to address today. Perhaps we can address those concerns themselves." He turned back to Alice.

"I understand they have developed from a discovery your friend made. Perhaps you could explain about that?"

Alice felt a sense of relief to be given a question to answer. Then she worried. He sounded patronising, but in control. Like he did when he was on TV, on those politics shows. Should she try to unsettle him? Not let him lead the conversation?

"There was a tape," she said at last.

"What tape Alice?" his voice was smooth like warm butter. "What tape?"

"When Jamie was working in our house - the beach house - he came across a USB drive hidden under the floorboards. It had computer files on it."

Rice-Evans didn't take his eyes off hers. "And?"

"The files were videos. Of people..." Her nerve went and she looked at Jamie. He gave her a little nod and waited. Then when she still didn't go on, he finished the sentence for her.

"They were videos of people having..." Jamie began, but as soon as he started speaking Peter raised his finger. It was enough to silence Jamie. "I'd rather hear this from Alice herself if you don't mind," he said. His eyes didn't leave hers the whole time.

Alice exchanged another look with Jamie, who gave a little shrug.

"They were videos of people having sex," she said, forcing her own voice to sound firmer than she felt. "Filmed secretly. The people in them didn't know they were on camera."

Rice-Evans said nothing at first, he seemed to be thinking.

"I see," he said at last.

"Jamie brought them to me because he thought they might be black-mail tapes."

Rice-Evans chuckled. "I see," he said again. "Well I think we've already seen how Mr Weston has a tendency to the dramatic." Then he went on at once.

"I doubt that very much Alice. Your father was a good man. I'm sure there must be some mistake." He still sounded calm and collected, as if he were completely in control. Alice felt further frustrated. She wasn't shocking him, she needed to be braver.

"And where is this tape now?" Peter asked.

"We should ask you that," Jamie interrupted. He sounded frustrated too. Sidelined. But Rice-Evans ignored him.

"Alice?"

"It was stolen. A few days ago, someone broke into Jamie's yacht and took it."

Rice-Evans sat back in his chair. He began rubbing his chin.

"We think the files were stolen by somebody who wanted to keep it quiet. Somebody who was in the videos." Alice went on.

"I see," Rice-Evans said again. "Well Alice, I can understand why you were concerned. This is certainly a delicate topic, and not an easy one to address." He was silent for a long moment, then he sighed. When he spoke again he was choosing his words carefully.

"Your mother has already explained something about this, and what it might be that Mr Weston found." He glanced again at Jamie, as if he wished he weren't there, but he had no choice but to go on.

"Your father was a great man, but he was also someone who enjoyed new experiences. A wide variety of new experiences. He was something of a risk taker." Now he glanced at Lena, who was looking uncomfortable.

He smiled at Lena. "I apologise for speaking of Charlie in these terms Lena, but it's not uncommon for some men to keep a little *visual stimulation* in secret. Perhaps these were just videos that Charlie *enjoyed*. A private collection he felt it was best to keep hidden." He turned back to Alice and gave his widest smile yet.

"Whatever it was, I think we can rule out blackmail."

Alice was silent for a moment. She shot a look at her mother, and saw she was nodding now, as if this might explain it. As if they were nearly done here. Dad was just a pervert. Forget the rest. She glared at her mother, trying to tell her how angry she was that she'd just sit here and listen to these excuses.

"So as I say, a delicate issue, but one with a *reasonable* explanation." Peter was saying, the smug, politician's smile back on his lips. Alice remembered a flash of him late one evening, after he'd been on the red wine with Dad, telling him how he'd defended the government about something in the House of Commons. Laughing at the fools who'd believed it.

"Jamie said one of the people in the tape was you." Alice cut in. She watched the smile freeze on his face. *Bastard*, she thought.

"So don't fucking blame all this on Dad."

Rice-Evans' easy smile dropped away entirely.

"That's not possible." He said.

"Isn't it?" Alice countered. "You and Dad went off on *Aphrodite* plenty of times. They were always innocent were they?"

Rice-Evans hesitated. He glanced at Lena, as if expecting her to step in and support him, but she said nothing.

"Alice I can give you my solemn promise. Your father was not blackmailing me." He paused. "Does that satisfy you?"

There was a silence. Then Lena joined in.

"He wasn't Alice. I've tried to tell you. Your father wouldn't do anything like that. And certainly not with Peter. You know they've been friends for ever."

Alice considered again. "But you think he'd do it with *other* people? You think he'd blackmail other people?" A shadow of a doubt crept into Alice's mind. Could she and Jamie have this wrong? Could it be someone other than Rice-Evans who had tried to kill Jamie? No. What about the girl Peter had killed? She forced herself to concentrate.

Get him on tape. Get him to admit something.

"Do you think Dad might have been blackmailing someone else?" She said again.

Peter didn't answer. Alice turned to stare at her mother.

"No," she faltered. But her face said yes.

From the silence Rice-Evans tried to regain control of the conversation.

"As I was saying," his voice was easy and smooth once more. "It's understandable that learning of this... This aspect of your father's life has been a shock. It's understandable why you might have gone off the rails a little Alice. But what's important now is that you let us handle it." He sighed again. "We do need to try and locate where these tapes are now. And rather fortunately, I am able to deploy certain resources towards that. I think it's sensible to go down that route rather than involving the authorities formally. And your mother agrees. This is a matter that is best kept as private as possible." He glanced again at Jamie.

But Alice was only half listening. Suddenly the meeting felt oppressively familiar. And she knew why. She'd grown up around powerful men who were able to manipulate and control all those around them. Truth didn't matter. All that mattered was that they got what they wanted, whatever that might be.

"Fuck you," she said.

"I beg your pardon?" Rice-Evans had the decency to sound shocked.

"*You fucking piece of shit*. It's not just the tape."

He opened his mouth then closed it again. "I'm sorry?" He managed at last.

"What about Dad? What about how he died?"

Rice-Evans took a few seconds to adjust, but he still seemed comfortable. Despite her outburst he still seemed in control. He let out a sigh.

"Your mother mentioned that was on your mind as well. So I took the precaution of downloading the official report into Charlie's death." He opened the folder in front of him and picked up the A4 pages within. He held them out to Alice so that she could see the title. There was the logo she'd seen the day before, from the Marine Accident Investigation Board.

"It's quite explicit that it was a tragic accident. Nothing more."

Alice didn't take it. "I'm sure that's what it *says*," she said. "I'm sure you've made very clear what you want it to say."

"I'm sorry Alice," Rice-Evans said. "I'm not clear what you are insinuating." Rather than leave his hand hanging he pulled the papers back.

"Why are you handling the case? Personally I mean? Don't you have officials to look into things like that?"

A frown came upon Rice-Evans' face. "I'm not handling the case Alice..."

"And does that *official* report say anything about the fact that Philip Marshall was on board Dad's boat?"

Rice-Evans' eyes widened.

"Well? Does it? Because the one I found in your safe certainly did."

Rice-Evans looked stunned.

"In my safe?" he asked, but Alice ignored him.

"You were trying to hide the fact that Marshall was on board. Your fucking fixer. And not only that, he was the *only* person on deck when Dad went overboard?"

"You accessed my safe?" Rice-Evans said again. Any pretence at congeniality was suddenly stripped away now.

"You need to be very careful what you say in the next few minutes," Rice-Evans went on. He was visibly angry now, his hands clenched into fists.

"Mum?" Alice turned away. "Did you know Philip was on board? *Fucking creep.*" She turned back to Rice-Evans.

"And then you send him down to meet us. Trying to send some *fucking* message..."

"If you're suggesting that Philip Marshall had anything - anything - to do with your father's accident you're quite mistaken. And you're totally out of order," Peter spat back. His voice was loud, he was barely in control of it.

"So he was on board then?" Alice breathed heavily.

"Yes."

"Yet the boat had a website, and he wasn't listed there as part of the crew."

"No. Philip likes to keep a low profile. He asked to be left off."

"Why? Why would he need to keep a low profile?"

There was a silence before Rice-Evans answered.

"It was a private ambition of Philip's to take part in a race like that. When he learnt that Charlie was involved he took the opportunity to join him."

"Mum? Did you know? Did you know Peter's fixer was on board?"

They both turned to stare at Lena. She stared back for a while, breathing deeply.

"Yes." She threw her hands in the air. "Yes I knew. Of course I knew. It doesn't mean... Alice it doesn't mean Charlie's death wasn't an accident. Alice..."

"Mum!?"

"Alice I..." Lena was unable to get another word out.

"Mum you've got to see this for what it is! Peter's fucking henchman was on board Dad's boat. When Dad *died*." She heard the desperation in her own voice. "Don't you think that's odd? You can't just take his word for it. You can't just *trust* him!"

Rice-Evans seemed to reset himself again. He turned back to Alice, the only sign he wasn't as comfortable as before was the faster speed of his breathing.

"Look Alice, your father was a very good friend of mine. After his death Lena asked me to ensure that... That everything that could be done was done. To understand the tragedy of his death. To make sure it couldn't happen again. That's why I took a personal interest in the report. I asked for a preview of the report before it was released. That's why I had a copy in my safe. The only reason."

Rice-Evans had a tell. When Alice was eighteen, her sister twenty one, they'd taken to playing poker. And when he came with them on a family holiday to Barbados, they'd stayed up late every night, smoking American cigarettes and drinking rum. Every night Rice-Evans had lost his pile of poker chips - small stakes represented by tiny shells from the beach. They'd all laughed at the irony of how a politician was so bad at bluffing. Every time he tried to pretend he had a better hand than he really did, he would touch the corner of his eyebrow. He did it now. Alice watched in disbelief. How could a man like this climb so high? How come no one had realised? How come no one had stopped him?

"Liar!" Alice said. But then again she didn't know what to say next. Before the list of crimes they could pin on him seemed so clear, so cut and dry. But now again it felt muddied, confused. She reached for another subject.

"What happened aboard *Aphrodite*? Why did you and Dad sink her?" She asked. Rice-Evans' frown deepened.

"Aphrodite?" he asked.

"You were there when she burnt, then Dad refused to claim on the insurance. Why would he do that? Unless he didn't want anyone looking too closely at the wreck?"

Rice-Evans opened his mouth to speak. He looked rattled now. He touched his eyebrow again, then seemed to realise and snatched his hand away.

"There was an engine fire. An accident."

"Another accident? How convenient."

Rice-Evans said nothing, but he stared at her.

"It wasn't because something happened on board? Something you had to cover up?" Alice wanted to spell it out. To demand that he had killed someone. She could feel the words hammering inside her brain, but she couldn't find a way to make them come out.

"Alice this is insane." Rice-Evans said. He glanced at Lena - Alice caught that too - the attempt at communication. But she went on anyway, she was too far gone now, her anger and frustration driving her on.

"Did Dad warn you? Is that what happened? Did he tell you if it ever happened again, he'd go to the police? Is that why he kept the video?"

Rice-Evans kept on staring.

"It wasn't *normal* blackmail was it? Not for money? He was trying to stop you killing again. He told you if you couldn't keep your hands off any more girls he'd go to the police? Was that it? Dad was trying to do the right thing."

She stopped herself, and took a few deep breaths. It was suddenly like being inside a dream. Was she still in the hotel? Was this just a premonition of how the meeting would go?

"No. That's not it." Rice-Evans replied. His voice was precise and clipped but his demeanour was completely different to before.

"We found something else when we went to your house," Alice said. Her own voice sounded mean suddenly.

"What?"

"On your computer."

"What did you find?"

Suddenly Alice didn't want to talk any more. "Tell him Jamie," she said. This time Rice-Evans didn't try to keep him quiet. He turned and waited.

"Emily Brown." Jamie said. His voice sounded nervous. It made Alice realise how much she'd freed up with her anger.

Rice-Evans screwed up his face. "Who?"

Jamie tried to smile. Tried to get control of himself. "You're a bad liar," he said.

"I don't know who..." Rice-Evans began, but Jamie interrupted him, persuasive now. Firm.

"Emily Brown. The girl you murdered last year. Whose eyes you pushed out. We know about that too. Your signature."

Rice-Evans just stared at him.

"You researched her on your computer. *Before* she went missing. That was a mistake."

Rice-Evans looked flustered now. He pressed the heel of his palm against his forehead, his eyes tightly shut, then he turned to Lena.

"This is nonsense. This is... I don't know." He shook his head, then looked back at Alice.

"Let's put aside for a moment what you were doing *in my house.* What's important is what you found..."

"So you don't deny it then? That it's on your computer?"

"Yes of course I deny it!" he stopped, flustered. "No... I don't. Look I don't know, I've not *been* there in a week. If what you say is on there then I have to believe you. But I can tell you it wasn't me who put it there."

Alice was about to reply when Jamie interrupted.

"Let's all just cut the crap shall we?"

Everyone turned to look at him.

"The only reason we came here was to make a deal. When your friend out there tried to shoot me he said you'd take a deal. Well, that's why we're here. We don't care if you win. We don't really care what you've done. We just don't want to be murdered in the middle of the night."

Alice stared at him. Amazed, almost upset at his interruption. But then she remembered, this was their plan. Get him to admit his involvement.

When Rice-Evans spoke again it was obvious he was shocked, but he was calculating too.

"So this is blackmail after all? *You* want money?"

"No. Not money. It's more simple than that. You leave us alone, we'll leave you alone."

And then they all stared in amazement as Jamie began to unbutton his shirt.

"You see this?" he said, tapping the recorder he had taped to his chest. This uploads as it records. Everything you've said in here is stored in the cloud. Every guilty word you've said."

Jamie glanced at Alice, who was staring at him in amazement. Not least because she knew it didn't do that. But he gave her a nod of reassurance.

"Guilty word?" Rice-Evans said, his voice incredulous. "I haven't said anything guilty. I've been extremely careful about what I said, not least because Lena warned me you were going to be recording this meeting."

Jamie smiled, "That's what I thought," he said. Then he laughed. "Thanks for confirming it."

He turned to Alice and shook his head. "We're wasting our time here," he said.

It took Alice a few moments to catch up, but when she did she turned to her mother, her eyes wide with shock.

"You told him *we would be recording*?" She blinked in disbelief.

The first realisation that hit her was what happened down in the lobby. "The security barrier? That's why you sent Marshall down to bring us up? I thought it was just to intimidate us, but you knew the recorders would be picked up by the metal detectors. And you wanted to make sure we got through..."

She stared at Rice-Evans.

"Why? Why not just let us get caught?" She turned back to look at Jamie, whose eyes were fixed on hers, level and steady. Then she answered her own question.

"Because you wanted to deny everything. You wanted to try and make us believe this was all nonsense. And you," she turned to Lena again. "You were in on it." Alice put her hand to her mouth.

"You were in on it. On everything. You *knew* Philip Marshall was on board Dad's yacht. Did you know he killed him? Oh my God," she said again. "Did you know *before*? Did you even help to plan it?"

Rice-Evans began again. By now any sense that he was in control of the meeting had gone. He was as wild-eyed as Alice was. "Alice, I don't know where this has all come from, but I'm horrified you believe this nonsense. Horrified."

She ignored him. She didn't even hear him. "Why Mum? Why are you protecting him? He wants to kill me! *I'm your fucking daughter*."

"Alice..." Lena had her hand over her mouth. "Alice this is nonsense. You've got this all wrong. The only thing Peter wants kept quiet is that we've been having a bit of a thing for the last year or so. He doesn't want the press to get hold of it."

Alice stared at her. "You're seeing him?"

"Not in an official capacity," Lena tried to explain. "We've always been fond of one another. And we've grown close..."

"Mum?" Alice interrupted. "He's murdered people. He *murdered* Dad."

She was silent.

"Oh my God. You murdered Dad."

Rice-Evans opened his mouth, then closed it again.

Lena did the same.

And Alice stood up. Her feeling of being in a dream was complete, only now it was a nightmare that trapped her and pressed in on her from all sides. She looked at Jamie.

"Come on. Let's get out of here." She floated over to the door and pulled it open, half expecting it to be locked, or that Philip Marshall would step in and block her way, a silenced pistol in his hand. But there was no one. The old woman had gone. Marshall was nowhere to be seen. Alice looked back into the room. Jamie was halfway to the door now, following her. The others were still sitting in silence.

"You two fucking deserve each other," Alice said. And then she walked out.

PART III

44

When Alenka Jovanović arrived in 1980s London, barely out of her teens, she had a simple plan. Find and marry a rich Englishman, so she would *never* have to go back to Yugoslavia. Life there had become increasingly harrowing after the death of her parents, and that of President Tito, as the struggling country ground its way towards war and disintegration.

Alenka learnt English by day and practised it by night, often in the Soho bar where she found work, serving drinks to wealthy city bankers. From the beginning her Slavic looks stood her apart. This was before an influx of girls from the region made it commonplace to see piercing blue eyes, high cheek bones and slender bodies on the arms of rich white men.

And before too long a handsome, blond-haired young man began stopping by more frequently than could be explained by either chance or simple habit.

At first Alenka refused to go out with him. He would ask, lounging with eyes that followed her around the bar, as if trying to memorise every strand of her spun-gold hair. And she would smile, adjust her long straight locks - not for her the frizzy perms that many girls were then sporting. Sometimes she would stare into his eyes with her own, as deep and blue as the hot summer sky. She would smile as his eyes roamed her body - but whatever he suggested, she would turn it down. It became a ritual that happened as a prelude to their other interactions. He would ask her out, she would say no, and then they would begin to talk, sometimes just a word here or there as she worked around him, but if it was a quiet night, longer chats. He would tell her where he worked, in one of the big banking towers. He'd tell her about how much *money* people there were making. He never said it in a boastful way. Instead his eyes would fill with wonder when he spoke of the money, like it were some deity to be worshipped. And her blue eyes would light up to match his own, like four sapphires lit from behind.

He had money of his own too. Exactly how much was a question Alenka pondered often. But he would come sometimes with a briefcase, and inside it he carried a *mobile telephone*. No-one in Yugoslavia had a mobile telephone, not even the people who worked for the government. There wasn't even a network for them yet.

But was it enough? Would it one day be enough? Or was she being distracted by how young and handsome he was? The question plagued her, as he came more and more to dominate her thoughts.

The inevitable happened one ordinary Thursday night.

"What time do you finish?" he asked her, as he always did. He had his tie loosened that evening, his steel-grey suit jacket slung over the back of his chair, and he looked the kind of tired of a man who had just glimpsed behind a facade, at how the world really works.

She shook her head.

"I told you. I don't date customers," she replied. Her accent was still thick back then, and she played it up, knowing it added to her allure. And of course she didn't walk away.

He sighed. Put his head on one side. Then smiled at her.

"That's such a shame. Because I'm celebrating tonight. I've got a reservation at *Alastair Little's*. Do you know it? It's fabulous. Have you ever eaten lobster?"

"No," she said, although she'd never tried it. It was busy enough that night that she did have to work. So she went to turn away, but he stopped her by putting his hand on her arm.

"Ask me why I'm celebrating."

Alenka hesitated. Looking at the waitresses was perfectly acceptable in the bar - encouraged even, but touching wasn't permitted. She stared at the hand until he removed it.

"Why are you celebrating?" She asked, her accent coming through strong.

The young man smiled. He tipped his head back to stare at the ceiling of the bar.

"I'm celebrating because I made a million US dollars today. *One million US dollars*. In one trade." He brought his head back down and looked at her.

"Actually one million and twelve thousand, eight hundred and forty nine dollars and thirteen cents. What do you think of that?" It wasn't boasting, the way he said it. It was disbelief. Awe.

"In one trade. *In one fucking trade*."

Alenka did her best to keep her face impassive. She shrugged, like it was nothing impressive.

"What's your name? I come in here every night. I tell you my life. You won't even tell me your name?" The man stared at Alenka now, his eyes unblinking.

"One million dollars." He shook his head as if even he couldn't believe it.

Alenka thought hard for a long time, studying the young man before her. He had a nice smile. His head was large and square, the features handsome. The look they wore seemed to communicate so much. So much promise. She bit her lip, not in a deliberate gesture, it was just the indecision in her mind.

"Lena." She said at last. It was the first concession she made to him.

Charles Arthur Belhaven didn't answer at once. Instead a wide smile grew over his face.

"*Lena*. That is a very beautiful name. Tell me Lena, if you don't like lobster, what *do* you like?"

* * *

Thirty-four-years later Lena Belhaven stared at her former husband's closest friend in the world. A man she had first met soon after that fateful day, and who was now a minister at the centre of the United King-dom's Government. A man who her daughter had just accused of being a serial murderer. And a man who was her lover. She felt a chill, as the air from the air conditioning swirled around the room from the force with which Alice had slammed the door. She watched Rice-Evans pull his palm across his face, she was close enough to him to feel the rasp of his stubble, breathe in the subtle smell of his sweat. Their eyes met. His were like a pair of black marbles, impenetrable and hard.

The telephone on Rice-Evans' desk rang, and he quickly stood up, strode across and answered it. He listened for a while then said a curt *hold on* and turned to Lena.

"It's Philip. Asking if I want him to go after them."

Lena didn't answer. Her mind was spinning, unable to think.

"Lena?" Rice-Evans said again.

"No. Tell him not to," she blurted out suddenly. "Not with what they think he's done. They could panic. Make a scene." She stood up as well, feeling like she was floating on a cushion of air. "I'll call her later. I'll straighten this out. She just needs time."

She saw Rice-Evans talking into the phone, a while longer, but his voice was low so she didn't hear what he said. When he replaced the receiver she found she had walked over to his desk. She sat in front of it.

"Well," he said. "You said it would be hard, breaking it to the girls about you and me." He offered her a smile. "But I hoped she'd take it better than that."

Lena didn't feel like smiling back. She sat ashen faced in front of him.

The smile on Rice-Evans' face dropped away too.

"She's always had a weakness for drama."

Lena's eyes flicked onto his, then away again. She ignored his comment.

"What are we going to do?" She asked.

Rice-Evans sat for a moment, considering.

"I told you, I have meetings this afternoon I can't get out of." He said at last. "You should go home and wait there, it's likely she'll come to her senses and she might look for you there. But call her too. Try and get in contact. And most of all, make sure she doesn't talk to anyone."

Lena nodded.

Rice-Evans reached out and laid a hand on Lena's.

"Don't worry. We'll sort this out."

45

When the taxi dropped her at home, a small upwelling of hope bubbled up inside Lena. She slipped her key into the lock and twisted it. She found herself holding her breath. She pushed open the door.

"Alice?" She called out. There was no reply.

"Alice, are you here?"

Lena walked to the main living area of the house. The lights were off, and when she flicked them on the room lay mockingly light and empty. Quickly she went around the house, calling into and opening all the rooms. Alice wasn't in any of them.

The hope dissolved away. But what emotions came to replace it, Lena couldn't tell. Doubt, confusion, anger. Whatever they were, they were negative. Black thoughts.

She returned to the kitchen, opened the freezer and pulled out a nearly full bottle of Beluga vodka. She pulled the cork and poured a glass, then took a long slug. The liquid, thickened by the cold, clung burning to her throat. There was a mirror on the wall nearby and she stared at the woman reflected in it. A well-dressed middle aged woman that her teenage self would never have dreamed she could one day be.

The image almost made her vomit, but the heat that now raged in her stomach felt more real, more tangible, than anything else that had occurred that day, so she drank more, until the whole glass was gone. Then she refilled it again.

She tried to call Alice again. On both her numbers, her usual one, then the one she had called her from yesterday. But in each case the calls failed to connect. She tried Andy, and was surprised when he answered at once. He hadn't seen Alice either, and she hadn't responded to his calls. Lena was forced to deny that anything was wrong, and then quickly pretended there was a caller at the door to get away from him. She hung up as he was speaking, and saw her hands were shaking as she put the phone down. She drank more of the vodka as Andy tried to ring back. She didn't answer the call, leaving the mobile to vibrate on the table, as if she were too scared to touch it. It went silent, and he didn't call again.

She drank from the vodka again.

But then her phone rang again. This time she picked it up - meaning to switch it off, but she noticed in time that the screen carried a different name. Lena's eyes widened. Connections fired in her mind. This time the shake in her hand was due to how anxious she was to connect the call.

"Jonathan? Do you know where she is? Do you know where Alice is?"

The man on the other end sounded taken aback.

"Lena?"

"Have you heard from Alice? Please tell me she's with you...."

"No. No she's not with me. Are you alright?" He sounded different to normal. His voice - usually so calm and smooth and collected, sounded tense. Stressed.

Lena didn't reply.

"Lena I need you to listen to me. I need you to listen very carefully."

Lena did so, staying quiet while the man spoke. At one point she put her hand to her mouth in shock and left it there for a long time. When he had finished speaking she asked several questions in a quiet voice. Finally she hung up the phone and sat staring blankly into space.

There was a coffee table in front of her, the corner of an iPad poked out from its lower shelf. She reached out hesitantly and pressed the button to bring it to life. On the browser window she typed in the address of a website she sometimes visited - the local newspaper that covered the town where the beach house was located. The story she was looking for dominated the news.

Body in burnt out car was ex-cop

Police have named the man found this week inside the burnt-out wreckage of his car as Martin Kenning, a former detective with the Metropolitan Police. It's believed Mr Kenning was here on a short holiday when he was attacked on Monday night. Police believe he suffered significant head injuries before being placed into his car, which was then set alight. They are appealing for witnesses, particularly anyone who was in or around the harbour view car park late on Monday night to contact them.

She stared at the photograph. She recognised the car park at once, it was on the waterfront, barely a mile from the house. The wrecked hulk of the BMW was less easy to identify, surrounded by the blue and white police tape and officers in blue overalls. Lena's hands trembled as she read the rest of the story.

Murdered...

She typed another name into the search bar. Moments later the smiling face of Emily Brown appeared in front of her.

Murdered...

What the hell was going on?

46

The vodka bottle seemed to taunt her. Drink me, it said. Drink me then you won't have to *think*.

But she pushed it away. Thinking was what she needed to do. To make sense of this. Her life had been turned upside down before, more than once, but each time she had found a way through it. And she would do it again. She just had to think.

The one thing she knew for sure: Alice had this all wrong. About Charlie. About Peter. About her. The conclusions she had come to - been pushed into by that common young man - were insane. That much was obvious. But how could this all be explained? She tried to calm herself. To break it down into manageable chunks. Was there anything in Alice's theories that made any sense?

She began with Charlie. From the way they had met, and those crazy, wild early years when the money had started to flow and they had realised it was a tap that need never be turned off. Did she need to re-examine those parties on the boat? Could Charlie have been making tapes to hold against people? No. It wasn't possible. It wasn't *necessary*. And besides, she knew what the tapes really were.

Was there anything else about Charlie she may have missed? There had been other women, she was sure of that. Not many, and he had been discreet, but she knew there had been some. From the subtle hints of perfume on his clothes, and the occasional innuendos of his friends, that she wasn't supposed to catch. But he wasn't the worst of them, not by a long way - he was more interested in his expeditions and conquests of mountains than chasing girls. And besides he had her - a woman who dedicated her life to maintaining and improving her looks, and a woman who believed it her duty to open her legs whenever he desired.

But could there have been financial impropriety she didn't know about? She didn't think so. Their fortune may not be moral, but it was legal - or so she believed. Wherever the money came from, and however it was hidden, it was beyond the reach of any authority that might come looking for it. Could that all be wrong? She had heard of pyramid schemes, banking scandals, investors that scammed their clients of millions. Could something similar lie behind this? She didn't know.

Her phone vibrated again. This time it was a text from Peter.

Still in bloody meeting, can't talk. Have you heard from Alice?

She replied, her fingers dully tapping out the words.

Not yet. When do you finish? We need to talk.

He answered at once.

Later. I'll come to you. I have my key.

The words came through devoid of tone and she stared at them for a while. For reasons she didn't quite understand, the words chilled her.

She found her mind turning to Peter. Charlie's closest friend, right from the beginning. She had known he liked her. It was obvious - he would even joke about it, saying how he wished that he, Peter, had been the one to come across the young Lena in the bar. She'd wondered, over the years, if it contributed to Peter's failure to ever marry. No, she'd *known* that his feelings about her contributed to it. But it hadn't seemed important - not to her. But then she was the one with the family. Had it been more important to him?

He had never been anything but a gentleman to her throughout the years when Charlie was alive, and that continued when he died - at least at first. And yet their relationship had inevitably changed. While before there would rarely have been a reason for her to spend time with him without Charlie around, then it was common. And with their long years of friendship it seemed natural that he be a shoulder to cry upon - literally. Physical contact between them became common, yet none of it made her uncomfortable. On the contrary, she found herself yearning for more of it.

The first time they slept together was three months after Charlie's death. The pool room in the basement of the London house had been finished - Charlie's project - that he never saw completed. The girls were away when the workmen finally left. There was no one to show it to, so she called Peter.

She remembered how she had spent forever deciding what to wear, and how to light the shimmering underground pool. She'd nearly panicked at one point, fearful he might be expecting to be attending an opening party - when in fact he was the only person invited. But if anything he'd seemed pleased when he turned up. And looking back at that evening now, she felt her face flush hot with shame at how planned the whole thing had been. She'd led him around downstairs with her hands over his eyes, as if it had been Peter that fought with the local authority for planning permission, not Charlie. They'd opened a bottle of Champagne, letting its spume fizz onto the tiled surface of the spa bath. The lighting was low. Soft music was spilling from the hidden speakers. And when they'd drunk, Lena took his glass and put it down, then pushed him into the steam room. At once her hands had been over his body, and after only a moment's delay his were too. They'd undressed then fucked in the hot mist, and somehow it felt like a tribute to Charlie, rather than an insult to his memory.

Once the dam was broken they fucked often and urgently. But with Charlie still barely in the ground there was no choice but to keep their relationship secret. Her from the girls - and the women at the tennis club - who would gossip relentlessly. Him from the press, who - although they had no public interest in who a single man might chose to date - were happy to ignore this fact for a man who held one of the great Offices of State. So they were forced to act like teenagers. Sneaking around behind everyone's back. She gave him a key so he could come to the house late at night. He would text first to be sure the coast was clear - and the girls were usually out. The sex was carried out in silence, then in the mornings, he'd sneak out before they got up. Yet beyond this he continued to come around in his capacity as a friend, supporting Lena in her grief. They'd eat meals together like a family - a cover story Lena hoped would ease the girl's shock when she finally broke to them that this was, already, her ultimate plan.

Had been her plan. Surely there was no way now that they would ever sit around a table as a family. Not after the horrific accusations that Alice had made against him. Horrific and obviously untrue.

And yet... Charlie was dead. Martin Kenning was dead. Emily Brown was dead. And Alice... Alice wasn't really the over-dramatic type. If anything that better described Joanne. Could there be anything in what her daughter had said?

Asking the question was like pulling the door open, just a crack, on a room where a violent black storm was raging. Like glimpsing a dark vortex of horror. The only possible reaction to doing so was to slam the door shut again.

She knew who Peter was, and he was no killer. And yet Charlie was dead, and what had Peter's text said?

I'll come to you. I have my key.

Hadn't this all worked out rather well for him?

Oh this was crazy. She got up and strode to the kitchen again, putting the vodka back in the freezer. She was beginning to sound like Alice now.

She would go to bed. She was tired, she would go to sleep. Peter would get here when he got here, and in the morning everything would get sorted out. Alice would call, realising what a terrible mistake she had made. And at least now, she and Peter could stop sneaking around.

She went to leave the kitchen, but her eye snagged on something. The rack of knives they kept by the sink. There were six of them, each stored in its own slot in the cherry-wood holder, the smooth crafted wooden handles sticking out, inviting her hand to pull them out. They were beautiful knives, German-made, a present from Charlie when Lena had announced she was going to learn to cook, properly this time. Of course that never happened.

Lena reached out and slipped one of the knives from the block. The handle was smooth to her touch, the wood merging seamlessly into the steel of the blade. It was new enough that the edge was visibly keen, the blade ended in a vicious point.

She wrapped her hands around the handle and - not even sure why - she made a stabbing motion with it, as if experimenting with how it might feel to stick it into something. Into someone. How hard would she need to push? It felt crazy, unreal to be doing so, even though she was alone and no one could see. And yet, it felt no more or less unreal than anything else that had happened that day. There seemed no way of holding it that seemed natural, so she shook her head and smiled at her silly actions. She went to replace the knife, but then something stopped her. It was as if every thought she had experienced that afternoon came flooding back at once. And instead of replacing the knife, she turned it upside down, so that the blade was flat against the inside of her wrist. It felt better there, and in the mirror she saw it was nearly completely hidden.

She turned off the light and went upstairs.

47

The darkness felt like staring into the vortex. Sleep was impossible, and though she tried to empty her racing mind, the same thoughts chased each other around. Demons playing tag inside her head.

She didn't hear him come in. Didn't hear the press of his steps on the stairs. But when he came into her bedroom she heard his breath. From the darkness she flicked on her bedside light.

Rice-Evans froze. "You're still awake?" he said, he seemed to force his features into a smile. "I thought you'd be asleep."

By then she had expected him to be armed, but he was empty-handed, or if he wasn't, he was hiding a weapon. She shook her head, one hand resting underneath the pillow, her fingers curled around the handle of her knife.

"I couldn't sleep," she said.

He thought about this for a moment, before stepping forwards.

"Have you talked to her? Is she here?"

Lena shook her head.

Rice-Evans sighed. "We'll get to the bottom of this. Then she'll come around. I don't know how exactly, but she's a sensible girl. She'll come around." He gave her a watchful smile, then sat down on the bed to remove his shoes. His back curled away from her. Lena felt the opportunity of the moment. But she didn't move.

"What a day," he said, putting his jacket on the back of a chair. "You wouldn't believe the afternoon I had - I got drawn into this ridiculous debate about fishing quotas."

She only half-listened as she watched him undress. His body still strong and powerful, yet weary. She had been surprised when they first got together how big he was. Not just taller but broader than Charlie. He peeled back a corner of the duvet and climbed in next to her. He reached over her to turn off the light. His hand brushed her breast through her nightdress.

The touch may have been accidental, but it seemed to turn him on. Or maybe that's what he wanted her to think.

"God, what a day," he said again. He put his hand on her side and began to move it slowly across her stomach.

"Actually I'm glad you're still awake."

He leaned over her again. His hand creeping up to the underside of her breast, bunching up the silk. He gave a little moan. She felt him kiss her, the skin of his cheek rough against her face. His other hand touched her shoulder, sliding toward her neck. She stiffened, wondering if this was how he intended to kill her. His hands wrapped around her throat, in the darkness. Her own hand wrapped tighter around the handle of the knife. Her body tensed.

He persevered for a while, his hand rubbing over her breast. But eventually he sensed her resistance.

"Are you not in the mood?" he asked.

"No. Not really," she tried to keep her voice level. "Are you? Because that's a bit weird."

"What?" He lifted his hand off her completely, so they weren't touching at all. "Are you OK Lena?"

"I'm fine. I just think it's a bit weird you want to have sex on the same day that Alice accused you of being some kind of serial killer, that's all."

They both lay silently on their backs, not touching, for a long time.

"I just... It's been a difficult day. I wanted some release," he said at last. "I'm sorry."

Lena didn't respond to this.

"Do you want to talk?" Rice-Evans asked.

Lena wasn't following any plan now. If there ever had been one it was long gone. She tried to think now. She pulled the knife a little closer. She imagined the movements she would have to do to whip it out. To angle it against him. Was he a killer? Was she crazy?

"Are you lying to me?" She said at last.

"What?"

"Is this all a lie? Is Alice right?" Dimly Lena knew she was being reckless, she had no idea if she could really pull out the knife and stick it into him. If that's what she wanted to do. But *some* action felt better than inaction. She had to ask him.

"Did you kill Charlie? Or get Philip to do it for you?"

"Lena? Not you too, *please*?" His voice was pleading rather than angry.

"Did you? And don't give me a politician's answer."

There was shock this time, and the beginnings of anger. "No. I didn't. Why would I kill Charlie? He was my friend."

"A friend whose wife you were sleeping with."

"After. That was after. And you were the one who..." He stopped and was silent for a few seconds.

"Lena I loved Charlie. I would never have done anything to hurt him."

"Well maybe he *was* blackmailing you then? After all you fed him plenty of information about where to invest. There must have been some reason for that?"

She felt him sit up in the bed. Moments later his light came on, flooding the room with light. It made Lena feel more vulnerable, without the cloak of darkness should she need it. She pushed the knife further under the pillow and twisted her body to cover it.

"We helped each other of course," Rice-Evans was saying. "But that's just what friends do."

The light distracted Lena from her thoughts. "Your advice made him rich." She said.

He stared at her. "Maybe it helped, but there was no blackmail. You must believe that. We both benefited from the arrangement we had."

"Until he died."

Suddenly he exploded into anger.

"For Christ's sake Lena. Charlie's death was an accident."

He sounded so sure, so convincing, that Lena was confused again.

"So why do so many people suddenly seem to be dying?"

Rice-Evans turned back to her, a frown set deep in his face.

"What? Who else has died?"

"A policeman. Martin Kenning." She watched him as she spoke.

"Who?"

"The man I hired to follow Jamie Weston. He was found dead. Burned to death in his car. Murdered."

"Say that again." Rice-Evans said at last.

"The man I hired to look into Jamie Weston has been..."

"You *hired* someone to spy on that young man?"

It was the indignation in his voice that took her by surprise. She felt herself flushing, heard the sudden defensiveness in her voice.

"Yes. Of course I did. You don't know what it's like having two daughters like Joanne and Alice, I have to look after them..."

Rice-Evans cut her off. "What?"

"What do you mean, *what*?"

"What *the hell* were you thinking employing someone to *spy* on him? What possessed you?"

"What possessed me? What possessed you to *kill him*?"

At this he burst out laughing.

"I didn't kill him Lena. I didn't even *know about him*."

Again there was something in his voice, in his face, that made Lena believe he was telling the truth, about this at least. The confusion in her mind deepened.

"You didn't kill him?"

"Of course I didn't kill him." He laughed again. Somehow it lightened the mood. He put his hand to his forehead, still smiling at her.

"Lena. Why exactly were you having Alice followed?"

Lena's face was red now.

"I told you. I didn't like the way he was hanging around her."

"You told *me*? You've never mentioned any of this."

"Yes I did. At Joanne's wedding. I sent you outside to check up on her. She spun you some story about him being the brother of her old school friend. I never believed that. And then I saw him coming out of her room in the morning."

Rice-Evans was silent, not laughing anymore. Lena could hear him breathing.

"So I phoned Jonathan and asked him to have someone keep an eye on him. That's all. Is that such a crime?"

"Jonathan Herring? Charlie's lawyer?"

"Yes. He helps me out sometimes, with issues like this."

"Jesus Christ."

"Oh don't give me that. He's a handsome young man. Underneath that black eye. I couldn't have him getting his hooks into Alice."

"Does Andrew know?"

"*Andy?* Know what?"

"About Alice, sleeping around?"

"I don't know. That's hardly the main issue here. I'm more worried that the detective Jonathan used was *killed*. Someone *murdered* him. Like that girl in the woods. That's what I'm wondering about. Someone's going around killing people. That's what I'm worried about, *Peter*."

There was silence. Lena watched him. Massaging the side of his head.

"Surely you don't believe I had anything - anything to do with that poor girl who was killed?" He looked pitiful, sitting there in bed, his shoulders slumped. Lena realised at that point he would have been an easy target for the knife. She could pull it out and stick it into him before he even had the chance to react. She wondered, if this might even be what he wanted? Part man part monster, who secretly wanted to be put out of his misery. But although the muscles in her forearm were tensed, there was no way she was going to use the knife.

Suddenly her eyes filled with tears.

"I don't know. I just don't bloody know anymore. I just want my daughter back."

Abruptly she pushed the knife away, not wanting to feel it. Not wanting to face the choice it gave her. The opportunity. She pulled herself to a sitting position, her chest heaving from her sobs. She felt his arms slip around her, and this time she didn't resist, burying her head into his shoulder. A fleeting thought passed through her mind - was this the moment he would attack her? The knife was out of reach now, his strong arms pinning her hands to her side. But she let him. And for a long time he held her.

Eventually her sobs stopped. Rice-Evans let her go. He slipped down in the bed so that he was lying on his back. And he began to talk.

"There's a reason I'm late tonight. I looked into what Alice said. I looked into the girl. Emily Brown," he began. "If there's something on my computer search history about her, then someone must have put it there. I don't know how... But." He looked at her.

"There's something else."

Lena stayed quiet, waiting for him to explain. He took a deep breath, held it in for a while then exhaled.

"She was last seen alive on the 24th September the year before last. Her body was discovered two days later." He stopped.

"So?"

"So I was at the Party Conference. In Manchester. For the entire week. I was surrounded by journalists. Surrounded. I was doing interviews from seven in the morning until midnight for those two days. There's no way I could have got down to Devon." He gave a laugh again.

"And that's quite apart from the fact that you *know* I would never do anything like this. If it's someone trying to frame me they didn't check their dates."

Lena thought for a moment.

"What about in the night? You could have driven down. It's the perfect alibi."

"Oh for Christ's sake Lena, get real. It's a four hour drive each way. I'd need a time machine, not a car."

Lena thought about suggesting a helicopter, or a private plane. But the stupidity of it reached her brain before the words left her mouth. Instead she felt a sense of hope.

"So that wasn't you?" was all she said.

"I still cannot believe I'm having to say this to you. But no, that wasn't me."

Again, Lena thought for a long moment.

She propped herself up on one elbow. It pushed the pillow a little further up towards the headboard. Just a tiny sliver of silver from the knife's handle became visible. Lena noticed, but did nothing to hide it.

"What about *Aphrodite*? Alice was right about when she sank. It *was* odd he didn't want to claim on the insurance."

"No it wasn't." Rice-Evans said. His voice was resigned.

"How do you mean?"

Rice-Evans passed a hand through his hair.

"Charlie was pissed as a newt that day. We both were. We'd been drinking all day. He'd taken some coke. We noticed that the engine was overheating - the warning lights were on, but he just ignored it. When we got picked up it was fairly obvious so we thought it better if the insurance company didn't launch an investigation into what happened."

"So there were no girls on board?"

"*Girls?* No. The idea was just to get away from everything for a while."

He was quiet for a moment.

"Lena, I have to sleep now. But come to the office tomorrow. I'll explain everything then. I promise."

Without waiting for her to reply he leaned to his light and switched it off again, plunging the room back into darkness. She felt him roll onto his side, facing away from her. And quietly she pulled the knife from beneath the pillow. She looked at it for a moment, as if in disbelief it were really in her hands. And she leaned over and slipped it beneath her bedside cabinet. Then, turning her own body away from Rice-Evans she too tried again to sleep.

48

It was gone three before she finally dropped off to sleep. And when he rose, at five-thirty, and padded into the shower, she woke just enough to register what was happening, then sank back into a deep sleep. When she next opened her eyes there was light streaming through the curtains, and the time on her phone said it was past ten. There was a message on the bedside cabinet.

Didn't want to wake you. I've cleared my diary. Come to my office. We'll figure this out.

She read it twice then pushed it back onto the top of the cabinet. And then, in a sudden fright of panic, she checked on the floor, to see whether the knife would have been visible when he left the note. To her relief it had fallen onto the floor under the bed, where it still lay, looking absurd against the carpet.

She showered and dressed, but skipped breakfast, realising she hadn't touched food for nearly twenty four hours. It turned out paranoia was great for the figure.

It was nearly midday when she arrived at the offices of the Home Office. She found a woman she didn't recognise waiting for her in the lobby.

"Mrs Belhaven?" She smiled a cold professional smile, as if Lena were just one on a long list of jobs for the day. "Would you follow me please?"

She took her to a different part of the building than they had gone the day before. They stopped outside a door, where the woman knocked briefly but opened without waiting for a response.

"Go right in please," she said. It took Lena a moment to realise the woman wasn't coming in with her.

The room - which looked like some sort of meeting room, with a large conference table and a screen pulled down to cover the wall at one end - was half full of people. The first that Lena noticed was her lawyer, Jonathan Herring.

"Lena, thank you for coming." Rice-Evans spoke, he had been deep in conversation with another man, a man wearing the uniform of a high ranking police officer.

"Allow me to introduce everyone. Lena Belhaven, this is Barry Williams, Assistant Commissioner from the Metropolitan Police." The uniformed man nodded.

"Over there is Detective Inspector Dominic Parker." A second man, in a suit this time, glanced up at the mention of his name. He mouthed the word hello.

"And of course you know Jonathan Herring. Associate at Wray & Alderney LLP." Rice-Evans gave a grim smile. "The law firm."

"We've been able to piece together something of what's going on here. Lena, would you like coffee?"

Lena nodded. The flask was closest to the lawyer and he poured her a cup, confirming how she took it with his usual quiet confidence.

"I'll let the Assistant Commissioner explain if I may," Rice-Evans said, when he had finished.

The man in the uniform had a precise, clipped voice, like he was used to speaking in public.

"The Home Secretary called me yesterday afternoon and explained that a number of accusations had been made against him, and to some extent yourself too, by a young man named *Jamie Weston*. He asked me to look into the situation with the highest urgency. And in the strictest possible confidence" He hesitated and glanced at Jonathan.

"I understand from Mr Herring here that you were also interested in the young man?" He paused to open a slim folder in front of him and withdrew an A4 colour photograph. It showed a close up of Jamie's face. From the bruising around the eye, Lena recognised it must have come from the CCTV when they arrived at the building two days ago. Lena stared at it, then looked up.

"Yes."

The Assistant Commissioner went on.

"It's a relatively common name, but we weren't able to find any records of this particular Jamie Weston anywhere. Not just any entries on the crime database, but no records at all. No National Insurance Number. No entry on the Electoral Roll. No records of paying taxes or claiming benefits. Now when that happens it's usually the case that the person we're interested in is operating under an assumed name." He coughed lightly.

"Which - we've been able to establish - is exactly the case here. We were able to recover some fingerprints from the coffee cup he drank from in the meeting in the Home Secretary's office. And from those we've been able, quite quickly, to understand some of what this is about." He paused to pull another set of photographs from the folder. He glanced at them himself, then slid them across the table to Lena. They showed Jamie, front-on and showing both profiles. In all three images he was standing against the backdrop of a height scale. They were arrest photographs, and in all three he was smiling as if he didn't have a care in the world.

"His real name is Ryan Riggs. He's got a rather unusual record."

Lena looked down at the paper, but she found it hard to concentrate.

"Quite a lot of juvenile stuff, but we'll skip that for now. It gets interesting about three years ago, when he was caught breaking into the house of a young woman in Exeter. It was while he was being questioned that it became unusual." The Assistant Commissioner began to look a little uncomfortable.

"He was interviewed under caution, but during the course of that interview he managed to cause a degree of confusion. That and..." He glanced up at Lena. "Frankly *panic* at the situation." He paused and looked pained.

"I don't understand," Lena said after a silence had stretched for a few seconds.

"No," the Assistant Commissioner replied. "I'm struggling to understand myself." He checked down with his notes now.

"It seems he's an unusually persuasive individual. In this case he managed to convince the arresting officer that he was a minor member of the British Royal Family. Specifically a second cousin of Prince William." The Assistant Commissioner glanced at the Detective Inspector, who was nodding at this clarification.

"Now it's not uncommon for suspects to lie in interviews. Either to hide their guilt, or - sometimes - to confess to crimes they didn't commit. But this was something different. This was an entirely fabricated false story that was so convincing it left our officer unsure how to handle it. This man was convincing. Extremely convincing."

"What happened?" Lena asked.

"The issue was escalated up the ranks, right up to the then Commissioner. And even he wasn't sure what to believe. He took the precaution of checking the story with the Queen's Private Secretary." The Assistant Commissioner drew in breath to show how shocking he found this. "I understand the Queen herself was very nearly informed of the situation. But fortunately the Private Secretary was quite insistent that Prince William does not have any second cousins - or at least, none who have taken to breaking into houses." He paused again. "As far as we know."

Lena listened, but she couldn't make sense of what she was hearing. She turned to Rice-Evans. "I don't understand. Peter? What's he saying?"

Everyone in the room now turned to the Home Secretary.

"He's a fantasist, Lena. Ryan Riggs is a fantasist. An unusually persuasive one, but still a fantasist. And probably a professional confidence trickster as well. Everything he told Alice he invented, or manipulated."

"Why?"

At first no one answered, then Peter cleared his throat.

"It's not clear if he even knows that himself. If you'd like to continue." He flashed a brief look to the Assistant Commissioner, who nodded and turned back to Lena.

"Despite the confusion Riggs caused, we weren't able to charge him with any offences. Or perhaps, there was an unwillingness to do so. A degree of embarrassment perhaps. It also transpired that he had been involved with the woman in question. She had invited him into the house on several occasions before, which made it more difficult to build a case that this was anything other than a domestic disagreement - albeit an unusual one. He was released with a warning. And after that he disappeared." The Assistant Commissioner took a deep breath before going on.

"That was until eighteen months ago, when the same woman was abducted from her home, and later found buried in a shallow grave in nearby woods."

"The woman's name was Emily Brown." Lena blinked.

The words rung ominously around the room.

"Naturally it became a priority to interview Riggs, but to date we haven't been able to track him down. Detective Inspector Williams here has been leading the search. If you wouldn't mind Detective Inspector?"

Williams cleared his throat now and took up the story.

"We've been able to put together a fairly comprehensive background on Riggs. We first became aware of him aged seven, when his father was convicted of child sex offences. It's unclear the degree to which he was abused himself - there was no physical evidence, and he denied it at the time - but that's not uncommon, and with what we now know about him, he may have been quite expert covering it up. Unfortunately he continued living with the mother - but the court ordered her incapable a few years later, and at the age of ten Riggs went into the care system. He was placed in a number of foster homes but never settled. Similar story every time. Everything seemed fine at first, but then the parents would request he be returned. None of them would ever give detailed reasons why, except one couple who went on the record to say he was *poison*."

"Poison?" Lena checked.

"That's the word they used." The Detective Inspector didn't seem to want to expand.

"His record at school always seemed to follow the same pattern. First he'd be so quiet his teachers didn't notice him, then he'd be so smart they thought he was a genius. Then they'd discover almost everything he said was a lie. After that he'd either leave or get himself expelled. He left school at sixteen with no qualifications. Yet by the time he was caught in Emily Brown's house, he was somehow attending Exeter University. Studying Law. That's where he met her by the way. They were in some of the same classes."

"After her death everything about Riggs was re-examined. It turned out he'd faked his way onto the university course. He had the admissions department so tightly wrapped round his finger they gave him a full scholarship to attend. He told all his friends he had nothing to live off, and conned them to give him somewhere to stay rent free. He even started a fake charity. He raised several thousand pounds for Romanian Orphans. Needless to say, it was never registered and no one knows what happened to the money. Anyway, no one was able to trace him. The assumption we were working on was that he was abroad somewhere. Until he turns up the day before yesterday in a meeting with the Home Secretary. And your daughter."

There was silence in the room. All around her Lena saw stern faces.

"The Home Secretary informed me yesterday that a specific accusation was made by Riggs about the internet search history on a computer in his constituency address," the Assistant Commissioner went on. "Specifically that searches were made for the name Emily Brown prior to her disappearance."

Lena nodded.

"We've had the computer examined overnight. There's no record of any such searches at or around the time of Emily's death. Only searches made last week. We subsequently learnt from Mr Rice-Evans' cleaning lady that she surprised your daughter in his Devon house just prior to when these took place. We believe Riggs would have been with her, and that when she left, he stayed in the house. We believe he made a crude attempt to plant this information."

"Do you think Riggs killed Emily Brown?" Lena asked.

"We're not investigating any other lines of enquiry," the Detective Inspector said.

Lena looked around the room. At Peter, at the Assistant Commissioner, the silver on his uniform so polished it was flashing in the light. The Detective Inspector looking gravely back at her. She remembered the doubts she had been going through. How certain Alice had been. Wasn't this exactly what Rice-Evans would do? Bring in a weight of officialdom to make himself look innocent. Were all these people somehow in on it?

She remembered the bruises on Weston's face. Riggs' face. Whatever his damn name was.

"What about the bruises? They were real. And he said someone tried to *kill* him? Alice said it was Phillip Marshall? He came to his boat and tried to shoot him."

The two policemen glanced at each other, their eyebrows raised, but it was Rice-Evans who answered. He looked faintly embarrassed too. Ah," he said.

"*Ah*? What does that mean?"

But it was the Assistant Commissioner who went on.

"We believe we have an explanation for that as well." He looked at Rice-Evans and nodded lightly.

"Lena, I understand your daughter is engaged to be married? To an..." he consulted his papers again. "Andrew Sullivan? I hear he's the grandson of Charles Sullivan, the former Chancellor of the Exchequer?" He flashed a smile at this, as if to congratulate her. "And I understand he's currently attending Sandhurst Military Academy. Officer training?"

Lena nodded.

"That's right."

The Assistant Commissioner sighed.

"It appears some of Andrew's friends saw Alice with Riggs, aboard his yacht earlier in the week. They believe they... they may have interrupted them in some kind of *romantic* moment. And as a result they thought it appropriate to... Well to teach him something of a lesson. Army types do tend to stick together." He stopped, and tried a smile.

"They confronted him," he explained, adding in a hurry, "they claim the idea was only to warn him, to scare him off. But Riggs' reaction was unusual..."

Lena waited for him to go on, but the policeman didn't. Instead he glanced at Rice-Evans, who nodded.

"And?" She said. "What happened?"

The Assistant Commissioner turned back to Lena. "The incident was captured on the CCTV system of a nearby marina. It's not that clear but..." He used a remote control to light up a projector that was mounted on the ceiling. It lit up the screen on the far wall.

"It tells the story."

Lena turned to look.

At first she couldn't work out what she was seeing, but then, in a corner of screen she noticed five men walking down a pontoon out into the harbour, some distance from the camera. At the end another man was tying up a small dinghy. They moved together and met halfway down the walkway. There was no sound, but from the postures of the men it was clear it had become some sort of confrontation. Then the single man suddenly launched himself upon the group, punching so fast it seemed to blur the image. There was a moment of chaos, but then the group were able to pull him off.

"They claimed he was goading them, shouting insults and threatening to kill them." The Assistant Commissioner went on, as the tape continued to play. Now the group of men were pinning Riggs down, apparently trying to talk to him.

"This is the point they warned him to stay away from Alice. They claim he seemed quite calm at this point and appeared to agree. Then they tried to leave... Then this."

On the video the group began backing away, leaving Riggs still lying on the decking of the pontoon. The incident looked over. But as they turned their backs, Riggs got to his feet and ran at the group again restarting the attack. This time two of the other men landed punches on his face and body, and a third man picked up a coil of hose that was nearby. He swung the nozzle, hitting Riggs on the head, and apparently finally knocking him senseless. This time when they moved away they did so more carefully, not turning their backs on him.

"The injuries appear to match those that Riggs claimed to have received on his boat, from the mystery 'assassin'. We're guessing he realised he could use a damaged face to convince Alice that someone had tried to kill him." The Assistant Commissioner paused again.

"He seems to be extremely skilled at improvising." Rice-Evans took over. "I think we saw something of that for ourselves, no?"

Lena said nothing, but she stared at the men in the room, her breath coming fast and laboured.

"So where is he now?" Lena asked, then changed her question. "Where's *Alice*? We need to get her away from him."

Everyone in the room nodded at this.

"Yes. Yes we do."

So?" Lena asked. "How are you going to find her?"

It was the Assistant Commissioner who answered.

"We're working on that. But there's one more thing we need to explain."

"What?"

The Assistant Commissioner's eyes flicked across to Lena's family lawyer. She had almost forgotten he was there.

"I understand you employed Mr Herring's services here to undertake some surveillance of Mr Riggs? Or Mr Weston as you then believed him to be?"

Lena hesitated, nervous suddenly.

"It's alright Mrs Belhaven. No one here is judging you for that," the Assistant Commissioner quickly went on.

"I understand as well that Mr Herring has already informed you that the man he then employed to carry out the task was found dead this week?"

Lena nodded.

"His name was Martin Kenning. He was beaten to death before being set alight in his car. An appeal for witnesses resulted in a couple who said they saw a young man leaving the scene in a small dinghy. Similar to the one you've just seen Ryan Riggs owned. In the water nearby we found a wrench with traces of Mr Kenning's blood on it. The only finger-prints on the wrench belonged to Ryan Riggs. We believe Riggs somehow became aware that Mr Kenning was following him. And subsequently attacked and killed him."

To Lena it felt as though all the air in the room had been sucked out.

"I want Alice," she said. "I want her found. *Right now.*"

"We're already doing everything we can," the Assistant Commissioner said.

"What?"

"We've issued the highest level of alert to find them. We have officers at every airport, every station, every ferry port. We know Alice has a car which she bought two days ago. If that moves anywhere it'll be picked up on the ANPR system. We also have images of them both loaded into a national facial recognition CCTV network. They won't get far. We'll catch him and we'll find her."

Lena just stared.

"What can I do?" She asked.

Rice-Evans interrupted at that point, speaking gently. "The Assistant

Commissioner thinks the most likely outcome is that Alice will now realise that Riggs is lying, and that she'll return home." He paused, to give what he seemed to think was a reassuring smile.

"He's just told me this bastard convinced the police to contact *the Queen*. How is Alice going to know what he really is?"

He didn't answer this. There was an awkward silence.

"There must be something I can do?"

Rice-Evans and the Assistant Commissioner exchanged glances.

"The Detective Inspector would like to interview you. To try and understand if there's anything we may have missed. Are you OK to undertake that interview now? It might help."

Lena was wild eyed, breathing deeply. "Is that it? Is that all I can do?"

Rice-Evans nodded. "Believe me Lena we're doing everything we can."

"Alice is smart. She'll see through him. I know she will."

49

The interview with the detective passed in a blur. He was joined by a woman named Laura Smith who introduced herself as a Counselling and Trauma Adviser. Together they seemed to ask the same questions over and over. They were either unwilling or unable to answer any of hers. When they were finally satisfied the Detective asked Lena to return home in case Alice tried to make contact with her there.

The woman drove her, and when they arrived Lena found more officers were already there, doing something to her phones and searching the house. Someone explained that both numbers Alice had called from were currently switched off. But if they were activated, even for just a few minutes, the police would be able to triangulate their location.

By mid afternoon Lena was informed that Alice's iPhone had been discovered, at the bottom of the hot tub in the beach house. Then her car was discovered, in the underground car park of a central London hotel. This cheered the police, who assured Lena that there was no way they could escape the Capital. Yet the news she yearned to hear didn't come.

The Counselling and Trauma Officer - who insisted Lena call her Laura, offered to stay overnight, and armed officers were stationed outside in case Riggs turned up. Peter kept in constant contact, updating Lena on the progress of the search. They agreed he wouldn't stay with her that night.

Sleep was impossible. Every creak of the house jerked her to full consciousness, and anyway, she feared falling asleep and missing a call from Alice. In the end she realised she must have dozed, because the clock on her bedside table said it was five am. But when she snatched up her phone from the bedside table there were no calls. No emails. No attempt at contact. She called Alice again, despite the hour, but nothing had changed. The call went straight to voicemail.

The next morning dragged by too, no one seemed to know anything, and Lena tried to make herself busy making coffee for the numerous officers who seemed to have set up base in her house.

And then, at eleven thirty she finally got some news. It began with a knock on the door, which was then answered before Lena could get there. Then Detective Inspector Parker and Peter Rice-Evans walked downstairs into the house's main basement. They looked awkward, their faces tight.

"What? What's happened?"

Rice-Evans let the DI explain.

"I think we explained yesterday how Riggs had managed to avoid detection by living on a yacht? I believe he normally keeps it moored in Poole Harbour?"

"Yes," Lena replied.

"We made the decision to search the yacht late last night, but it wasn't practical to do so in the dark. So we prepared to do so first thing this morning. That's when we ran into a problem. It's gone."

"Gone?"

"Yes."

"I thought you said they wouldn't be able to leave London?"

"That's what we thought, but somehow they do seem to have managed it. Perhaps if they stole a car... It's possible they may have disguised themselves. We're not sure at this point." His voice faded to nothing.

"So you think they're on this boat?"

"It's the scenario we're favouring at the moment, yes."

"So where is it now?"

"We don't know. But in many ways this makes the search easier. A small boat like that... It moves slowly, and it's hard to hide. We've alerted all the ports and harbours both here and within a five hundred mile range. We'll know the moment they make landfall."

She turned to Peter.

"You've got satellites and technology? Can't you do something? Can't you just find it now?"

He sighed. "Unfortunately no. There's no tracking equipment we're aware of onboard. Even if there was they could simply turn it off."

"Well, radar? Surely there's something."

"There's a slim chance they'll be spotted by a ship."

"Is that it?"

"No. Of course not. But..." If there was more, Peter Rice-Evans didn't specify what.

50

But they weren't spotted by a ship. The rest of the day crawled by, with no news. And then the next day. And then the day after that. At first Lena pushed again to be allowed to make a television appeal, she felt a desperate need to do something. But the now team of officers who shadowed her were adamantly against it. The odds, they argued, were better if Riggs wasn't fearful of coming into port and being recognised by anyone who saw him. An alert still went out, to every harbour and port in the country, the Channel Islands and the Atlantic coast of France, to alert authorities if they spotted a twenty-seven foot classic sailing yacht, painted blue, and which may or may not be called *Phoenix*.

But as the days passed, the potential range of the yacht grew, and the number of destinations it might be heading towards expanded with it. A week after the yacht vanished there was a change in the weather. The warm early summer the country had been enjoying was replaced by four days of rain and strong winds. And for the second time in her life, Lena became an expert on low pressure systems and high winds. For the second time she found herself fixated upon how it might feel to be stuck on a small boat in the path of such weather. Around her technical experts were called in to analyse how it might impact upon where a small boat at sea would go.

And when the gales blew themselves out? Nothing. No reports of distress signals. No sightings of the yacht. Nothing from the ports or harbours.

Looking back on those days, Lena would wonder at the malleability of time. Not only did those fourteen days seem longer - far longer - than just a fortnight, it was as if her mind *and* her body experienced the lengthening of every moment. Her hair thinned and the rate it was greying accelerated. She lost weight - but not in a good way - it dropped off her face, so that the reflection that stared back at her from the mirror was like a skeleton that someone had tried to pad out with bags of putty - the handiwork of expensive plastic surgeons suddenly laid bare and exposed.

But all the time the police, Peter, the few friends she had been able to confide in, they all said the same thing. They would be found. A yacht couldn't just disappear off the face of the earth. Alice was somewhere, and they would find her.

51

W hen the news finally came things moved fast. The officer assigned to stay in her house received a telephone call at seven minutes past ten in the morning. Not long after a car arrived out front to collect Lena. The driver knew nothing, only that his instructions were to take her to the headquarters of the Metropolitan Police in Curtis Green. He left the siren off, but drove fast.

Once they arrived Lena was led quickly through the building and into an operations room. Inside Detective Inspector Parker was fiddling with a laptop computer. In front of him on the desk was a cardboard takeaway coffee mug, and a greasy bacon pastry with a large bite taken out of it. The next to arrive was the Assistant Commissioner, along with Peter Rice-Evans. They looked grim faced, but Peter gave Lena a nod, as if to reassure her that this wasn't the worst possible news. Then there was a final knock on the door and Philip Marshall came in. He also nodded towards Lena, then sat down.

They were in a small room, with no windows facing the outside, which gave the proceedings that followed the strange feeling of not really happening in the real world. Lena felt like she could say something quite absurd, and it would have no consequences. It was like being in a dream that she couldn't wake up from.

"You'll remember we said we were placing a watch on Alice's financial affairs?" DI Parker began, moments later. The pastry was nowhere to be seen, Lena noticed. He must have hidden it in a pocket.

"Lena?" She was shaken from her thoughts. She didn't remember, but she nodded anyway.

"Normally this is done to identify where and when credit or debit cards are used. It's a way of narrowing down the location of any individuals at large." Parker stared intently at Lena's face. She felt a moment's curiosity as to whether he found her newly sunken cheeks disgusting. It wasn't that she cared - he was a short man with a face shaped like the pointed features of a rat. No, it was more just curiosity. Just the symptom of an exhausted mind.

"In this case however, something different has been flagged up." He paused and Lena realised she was supposed to say something here, at least if she wanted to give the impression of behaving normally.

"What?" Lena asked.

The DI gave a tiny nod. Like she'd passed some sort of a test he'd set.

"It appears that a young woman has visited a bank and accessed the account of Alice Belhaven. She was in possession of all the requisite password information, so was able to gain access. The bank was on the island of Madeira. Here."

He pushed the laptop towards her. The image on the screen was a still from a bank security video. A young woman could be seen, wearing a hat and sunglasses, her shoulders hunched over. Lena's heart leapt.

"Apparently Madeira has quite a big banking scene..."

"That's her. That's Alice!" Lena interrupted him. Suddenly all the fatigue from her brain had dropped away.

"Are they still there? Who's going to get her?" To her surprise Lena realised she was standing up. Everyone in the room was staring at her.

"That's her," Lena said, unsure why no one else was moving. "I'm sure."

"Yes. Yes we think it almost certainly is. The image is too obscured to run it through the facial recognition software, but..."

"Well? Can you go and get her?"

There was a moment's hesitation. Parker looked at the Assistant Commissioner before continuing. He looked at Rice-Evans.

"We're organising a flight now. You should let the Detective Inspector continue though," Rice-Evans said.

DI Parker picked up his drink, tried to take a sip and decided it was too hot so put it down again. He sighed.

"I understand that Alice was left a considerable sum of money? After your husband's death. That was the account that Alice was accessing."

"That's right. I suppose they needed money for food?" Lena went on. She was smiling now. She had both her hands pressed against her chest. "Alice is alive. Oh thank God."

"It seems she transferred the entire amount." Parker continued.

Lena's smile cracked a little.

"The whole amount? There was..."

"Two point six million pounds was the sum transferred."

"Transferred where?"

"To a new account. That she set up at the same time. But the money has subsequently been moved again, to a third account."

"Where? To whose account?"

"We're not sure. Although Madeira is not exactly a tax haven, it's still regularly used by companies and individuals looking to secure their money offshore. I'm not an expert in these things, but apparently it's one of the easier places in the world to make money disappear."

Lena opened her mouth to reply, but closed it again. Charlie had made frequent trips to Madeira for just such a purpose. She'd accompanied him more than once. So had the girls.

"So? She's trying to hide her money? So what? That just means she still believes what Riggs is telling her. It doesn't matter. We just have to get her away from him. Then we can explain. You've got to get out there."

The Assistant Commissioner took up the story.

"I agree. A European Arrest Warrant for Riggs is already in place, and the Madeiran authorities have a good record of complying. If Riggs is spotted he will be apprehended. But these things take time Lena. And, there is a further problem..." He waited to see if she had already worked it out.

"What?"

"The arrest warrant doesn't apply to Alice. She hasn't committed any crimes, and therefore we're unable to require the Madeiran authorities to detain her. We can ask them to speak to her on a voluntary basis - and we've done so - but if she still believes Riggs' story..." He winced, as though the money transfer proved this to be the case, "she may just refuse to speak to them. And there's nothing we can do in that event."

Lena stared at him. "Nothing? Nothing you can do? You're just going to leave her with him?"

"No. I'm simply explaining the circumstances we're facing. Our power to request the detention of Riggs does *not* apply to your daughter. In theory we can't even require the authorities there to search for her. He waved his hand. "In practice we can expect a little more cooperation than that. But there are limits." The Assistant Commissioner fixed her a look.

Lena said nothing. She just stared at him.

"At this stage we can't even say for certain that Riggs is actually there with her."

"Well he must be! How else would she get there?"

"Correct. We think he probably is. We know they disappeared together on Riggs' yacht. And DI Parker's team have found no records of Alice - or anyone who looks like her - arriving on the island by air. So yes. In all probability she arrived by boat, and therefore Riggs arrived at the same time. But there's no record of a UK registered yacht by the name of *Phoenix* arriving in the last two weeks. So..."

"They could have changed the name? How hard would it be to put a new name on the boat?"

"Not hard at all, and that's probably exactly what they have done. But all of this uncertainty causes delays. It all makes it less of a priority for the authorities out there, who have their own problems, their own missing people to track down. Now we believe, from the way Alice moved the money around, she expected us to learn of it. We also think the timing is significant. The money was moved just before the bank closed for the day. We believe this was in the hope that the information wouldn't get to us until the next day. All of which makes us think they don't intend to stay long on the island. We need to move fast to get to them before they disappear again."

"Good. So what are you waiting for?"

The Assistant Commissioner glanced at Rice-Evans, before continuing.

"Mrs Belhaven, in normal circumstances we wouldn't ask a civilian... But this is a highly unusual case..."

Suddenly Peter cut him off.

"Lena, the Assistant Commissioner is saying we can bypass a lot of the bullshit by getting you involved. The yacht is probably renamed, possibly sailing under a different flag, but we know what it looks like - they can't change that. And there are only three marinas on the island. If we can get you there before they move on, there's a good chance you can find Alice, speak to her and clear this up. All long before the cogs of international cooperation grind into action.

"You want me to go?"

"We have no power to detain her. Any conversation has to be voluntary. And we think you're the person she's most likely to talk to. Now, we'll provide you with a comprehensive file of evidence against Riggs, we think she'll believe..."

"When do I go?"

Rice-Evans stopped. Then he nodded.

"There's a car waiting downstairs to take you to the airbase. There's one more thing."

Lena looked up. "What?"

"I want Philip to go with you. Just in case she's with Riggs and..." Rice-Evans didn't finish the sentence.

"I'd go myself but it's not possible."

Lena blinked. She looked at Philip Marshall, who had observed the meeting but not said a single word. He met her eyes and didn't look away.

"Sure," Lena said. "Whatever. Sure. Let's just get on with it."

52

They travelled in the same car, this time with its blue light flashing, and arrived at RAF Northolt one hour later. Armed soldiers in combat fatigues opened the gates to allow them to drive directly onto the tarmac, and an army jeep accompanied them until they arrived at a mid-sized jet. Its engines were already on, hot shimmering air spewing out of the back.

As they left the car Lena felt her senses assaulted by the smell of hot rubber and aviation fuel. Marshall began shouting at her, something about how the plane was normally used by the RAF to transport top military officials and politicians, but when Lena gave no indication that she was interested, he took the hint.

They climbed the steps in silence. It was a relief to get into the shelter of the cabin. To her left the two pilots broke their preparations to greet Lena, and to her right the passenger cabin was empty save for plush seats arranged around small tables.

"We should have plenty of time to go through all this," Marshall said, dropping a thick document folder on one of the tables.

"Sure," Lena said. But suddenly she didn't want to.

"Can we wait until we've taken off?"

"OK," Marshall nodded.

Lena went to the rear of the cabin and took the window seat on the left hand side. She strapped herself in, then watched as they taxied to the end of the runway, as they barrelled down it, and as they climbed up into the clouds, and then pulled clear of them. But when they levelled out and Marshall walked back to ask if she was ready now, Lena wasn't watching any more. She was fast asleep.

She dreamed as well. Of walking through a busy harbour, and catching a glimpse of Alice ahead of her in a light crowd. In her dream she ran to touch her daughter on the shoulder, but when Alice turned around Lena saw it wasn't Alice, but another girl that looked like her from behind. And yet, *there* was the real Alice again, just a few paces in front of her. But when she caught her up, again it wasn't her. Over and over it happened, until Lena let out a cry, and woke herself with a start.

She looked around the plane's interior, blinking in surprise. Bright sunlight was beaming in through the aircraft's starboard windows. Far below them the ocean stretched blue-black flecked with glints of white. The door to the cockpit was open, and the two pilots sat in their crisp white shirts, they were drinking coffee, sunlight glinting off the steam. Marshall was in his shirtsleeves too, facing her and working at a laptop. He looked up and smiled.

"You must have needed that," he said. He got to his feet and walked past her to a small galley area. "Coffee?" He asked. "There's food too if you're hungry."

Lena nodded, then tested her voice.

"Just coffee. Thank you."

She watched as he poured the black liquid into a cup and carried it to her. "It's a good idea to get some rest," he told her, handing her the drink. Just the smell of it made her feel better.

"Where are we?"

"Nearly there. Just about to start our descent."

She nodded. "Is there any news?"

He shook his head. "Nothing certain. I understand we've got quite the reception party lined up to meet us, but let me handle it." He watched her for a while, then turned his laptop so she could see the screen.

"There are three marinas in Madeira open to visiting yachts, and then a small number of anchorages they could be using. The most likely place is here in Funchal. It's not far from the airport so we'll visit that one first. We've been monitoring all yachts leaving the island. We don't think they've left yet. Here." He minimised the map window, and pulled up another image.

"We've found these images of Riggs' yacht from when it was last sold. It may not look exactly the same now, but it's a distinctive enough boat."

Lena looked at the small yacht that filled the screen. She had worried that Charlie's sixty foot racing yacht looked far too small to tackle an ocean. This boat was less than half the size. It looked tiny.

"Oh, there was one other thing."

Lena glanced up. "What?"

"We're not sure what to make of this..." Marshall's eyes flicked across to Lena. "I understand you've been trying to get information to Alice by leaving messages on her mobile, and sending emails to her account, explaining who Riggs is, that she's in danger..?"

She nodded.

"We've had word from the tech team, one of them was opened."

Lena's eyes widened. "She's read them?"

"We don't know that. It's just as likely to be Riggs. But someone read one. Late last night. On a mobile device. They were logged in for twelve minutes. They haven't been able to identify where the log in occurred, only that it's consistent with being on the island still."

Just then one of the pilots turned around and called back to them, explaining they were going to start their descent now.

"It's pretty windy down there," he said. "And we're kinda light, so be prepared to be blown around a bit."

They strapped themselves back into their seats, and the conversation lapsed into silence. They dropped quickly as Lena caught her first glimpse of the deep green island. At first it looked to be nothing but mountains, but as they descended tiny settlements revealed themselves, clinging to precarious ledges on the land. Huge swells, clearly visible even from so high up, battered the coastline. Narrow roads snaked their way around, occasionally marked by a vehicle, crawling along.

They levelled off and banked hard, the ocean filling the windows. The plane began to judder as the flaps extended and bit into the air. Then there was a grumbling sound below them as the landing gear extended. The plane rolled from side to side as they lost height. Suddenly there was land again. Craggy, green ravines and mountains that were now alongside them, now above them as they slipped down, still shrugging off speed. It looked impossible that there might be enough flat land to land an aeroplane, even when they were no higher above the ground than a block of flats. They were crabbing in, the plane twisted sideways to beat the strong crosswind. Lena felt how tense she was, and wondered - with a bitter sense of irony, if they were actually going to crash. But just before they touched down they straightened up, and the wheels hit down, hard on the tarmac. The plane shook so violently as the brakes bit and Lena felt the strap pulling her body back. She breathed again.

They slowed further, and the pilot taxied them away from the terminal building, where three fat commercial jets filled their bellies with passengers. While normally Lena would shudder with horror at the thought of being squeezed into such a plane, this time she felt a pang of jealousy for the queues of ordinary people and their unbroken lives.

Marshall unbuckled himself and walked forward to the cockpit, speaking with the pilots. After a while Lena released herself and followed him, as the jet stopped beside three cars, close to the perimeter fence. Two were white with blue markings down the side, and blue lights turning lazily on their roofs. The other - a Mercedes saloon - was black with darkened windows. Four men in military uniform stood around it, holding automatic weapons while another man stood with his suit jacket whipping against him in the wind.

One of the pilots came and pushed open the door, then lowered a set of steps. The wind blew in, a gale of cool, fresh air scented with pines and the ocean. Marshall went out at once, telling Lena to hold on for a moment. She stood in the doorway though, looking out over the island. The airport seemed perched on the edge of the land. The perimeter of the airfield was the rocky coast itself and large waves crashed against it. In the distance she could see the masts of a few yachts in a small harbour. Could one of those mark where Alice was? Perhaps getting ready to leave right now. Lena glanced down at Marshall, talking to the man in the suit. She wished he would get on with it.

Another three men joined Marshall and the man in the suit. They seemed to be arguing. Then two of them left again. Lena wanted to descend and listen to what was being said, but wasn't sure if she should. Eventually she decided she didn't care and walked down the steps to join them.

Straight away it felt like walking into an argument, or at least a wall of frustration. All four men stopped talking in acknowledgement of Lena's arrival but Marshall touched a hand to her shoulder. He introduced the first man, as Senhor Rui Fonseca. Marshall explained that he was in some department in the Government, but the wind was so strong Lena didn't catch which.

"They found the boat." Marshall told her.

Lena's pupil's flared. "Where?"

"The marina in Funchal," Marshall sniffed. "At least, it *was* there. It left last night. At midnight." He scratched at his cheek, the frustration was written on his face.

"Do they know where it is now?" Lena asked. Marshall shook his head. From the look on his face this was what he'd been asking when Lena joined them. Lena turned to the Government man.

"Where is the boat now?"

"We do not know," he replied. "So far we have been unable to locate it." He spoke with a strong accent, and with the wind it was hard to hear.

"Well do you know where it's *going*?" Lena felt panic build inside her.

The man shook his head. "We cannot even say for sure if this is the boat you are looking for. Only that it matches the physical description provided, and that the name given when it arrived does not appear to exist on any records."

At this point Marshall turned back to her. "It's the right boat, it's gotta be." He made a fist, and Lena wondered if he was going to strike the car with his frustration.

"Well what happens now?" Lena asked. "How far could it have got?"

The tall man turned to his colleagues and spoke in rapid Portuguese before answering. Eventually he turned back.

"The yacht is seventeen hours out. Assuming an average speed of six knots, they could be a hundred nautical miles away. In any direction." His eyes met Marshall's as if in challenge, but Marshall looked away.

"Do you have helicopters? I mean that isn't that far? Is it?" She turned to Marshall too, only to see he was shaking his head. Angrily he pulled out his phone. He held up a finger to Lena, telling her to wait, and then stepped away. But Lena just turned back to Fonseca.

"Do you have helicopters?" She repeated her question.

It took him some time to answer.

"Yes Madam. There are a number of helicopters on Madeira. That is not the issue. The issue is we do not know which *direction* the yacht has sailed in. To undertake a search we would need to examine an area of thousands of square kilometres. And growing."

Lena stared at him in amazement.

"Well hadn't you better get on with it?" she said. Fonseca glanced away in irritation, and when he looked back he spoke as if explaining to a child.

"I don't think you quite understand. To search such a large area we are talking about thousands of hours of flight time. Hundreds of thousands of Euros of cost. Better to wait and see where they end up next."

Lena opened her mouth to reply, but dimly she began to understand. This man just didn't want to be involved. He was more interested in shifting the problem to someone else's jurisdiction. She changed her tack.

"Sir," Lena tried to fix him in the eyes. "I don't know if you understand but my daughter is on that boat with a *killer*. If we don't find it. If I don't find her..." She screwed up her eyes then tried again. "She might not make it to wherever they're going next."

For a moment the man's face didn't change, but then he frowned.

"Mrs Belhaven, you have my sympathy but it does not change the fact..."

At that moment Philip touched her shoulder again.

"I've spoken with Peter," he interrupted. "There's a Royal Navy frigate coming back from the Falklands. It's about four hours out from here. We can use it as a base for the search. They're sending a helicopter to meet us." He hesitated a second. "I'm sorry. Peter did tell me you don't like flying in helicopters."

Lena stared at him for a moment. "It's fine. Let's go."

Marshall nodded, then turned to the official.

"Mr Fonseca, I have the British Home Secretary on the line. He's prepared to give you a guarantee that Her Majesty's Government will reimburse all costs. Please launch your helicopters." He held out his phone to the official, who looked doubtful at first. But he took the phone.

Lena waited in the jet out of the wind. Below her the cars waited too, but from a hanger nearby she watched a pair of small helicopters wheeled out and fuelled. Still they didn't take off.

"There are no search and rescue helicopters stationed on the island," Marshall said as he climbed the steps back to the cabin. "But Mr Fonseca has pulled some strings and we have a couple coming down from Portugal. There are two choppers aboard *HMS Courage*. Put together with the couple of civilian choppers we've just rustled up, we've got a chance."

His words startled her.

"Fonseca is the man in the suit? He said it would take thousands of hours," she said.

"He's wrong. With the wind this strong we can discount the idea they're sailing against it. That cuts the search area by half. We've just got to get the search going fast. The longer we leave it the further they could go. And once it gets dark it's going to be twice as hard." He hesitated. "Are you ready?"

"For what?"

"The chopper's here. To take us onto *Courage*."

They opened the door again, and this time a large grey military helicopter was landing, a hundred feet away from the jet. Marshall shepherded Lena down the steps to the concrete, just as the helicopter touched down. The noise was deafening and stayed that way as the chopper kept its engine on.

"Keep your head down," Marshall yelled at her. Lena nodded and prepared to run towards it, but a hand touched her arm. She turned around and found Fonseca standing there. It was almost too loud to hear what he said, but she read his lips.

Good luck

At the helicopter door a woman in a flying suit helped Lena aboard, and showed her how to strap herself in. Marshall sat beside her, and at once the engine began to whine as the pilot lifted off. Moments later they dipped forwards and began to race out over the ocean.

53

The chopper took Lena further south, at a much lower altitude than the jet. Rather than stretching out below them, distant and possible to ignore, the ocean now rolled and swelled close underneath them. The higher waves seemed to reach up to try and touch them, to pull them out of the sky and devour them. The little white flecks, seen from high, now revealed themselves as great scars of broken water. And as they pulled further away from the island of Madeira, the colour of the water changed too, from the sort of deep blue that looked good in travel brochures to a thick, impenetrable black.

Eventually the endless expanse of the ocean was suddenly interrupted, by a shape that was both familiar and absurdly alien - the grey outline of a fighting ship, its guns and radar dishes like some surreal decoration. It looked impossible to land on - too thin, but as they drew closer Lena saw the helicopter pad by the stern. They circled in so that they appeared to be chasing the ship for a few moments before overhauling it and descending the few final feet to the pitching deck. The landing was surprisingly smooth, the pilot seemed to mirror the ship's movement, and when the wheels touched down four men in orange overalls raced to lash them down. When they opened the doors the wind screamed.

The men in orange led them across the landing pad, rolling and wet with spray, and through a thick steel door. There they were passed to other crew, dressed in smart navy shirts. It was warm inside and it hummed with electronics. From somewhere there was the smell of fried food. Lena and Marshall were taken to a small room and invited to sit. Lena did so, but found that Marshall had disappeared. The roll of the table was disorientating. People came to speak to her, telling her things she didn't understand, and offering her food and coffee. Somehow she found herself eating soup. At first she didn't want it, but found herself finishing the bowl.

Then Marshall returned, alongside an officer in a white shirt with the sleeves rolled up. He seemed absurdly young, and Lena felt a stab of panic that her daughter's life was in the hands of children. But when he started speaking Lena revised her opinion. He explained how *HMS Courage* was coordinating the search, directing the four helicopters currently available, and how it would liaise with the Portuguese Navy once their search and rescue aircraft were in range. He talked about grid patterns, refuelling procedures, the estimated course of the yacht and more. Lena sat, quickly dazed and overwhelmed.

"What are the chances of finding them?" She asked, when he seemed to have finished.

The man didn't answer at once. "There's a good chance," he said at last. "It's helpful that Mr Marshall here has arranged the additional choppers. The more eyes we have up there the better."

"We just have to wait," Marshall added. "They'll find her. I'm sure of it," Marshall said. He took her hand and squeezed it. For a moment she let him, but then she pushed him away.

"I don't want to just wait."

Marshall frowned at her. The young officer turned to look.

"I want to go in one of the choppers," she went on. "I can't just sit here waiting. I've been waiting for weeks. I need to do something. I need to help."

"Lena the air crew onboard are trained to the highest level..."

"I'm not saying I want to take their place. I just want to go with them. You said the more eyes the better?"

The officer exchanged a look with Marshall and his face took on a pained expression.

"Mrs Belhaven I don't think..."

But she hit the table, not letting him finish. "What if they see the boat? I'm here to try and talk to Alice. If I'm there in the helicopter I can do that. I can talk to her. I can't do that if I'm sat here."

There was a silence in the room.

"Please?" Lena turned to the officer, who suddenly looked out of his depth, as if directing air sea searches was one thing, but dealing with a terrified mother quite another. He turned to Marshall and gave a half shrug. It looked for a moment if Marshall might argue, but instead he just nodded.

"OK. But that means I'm coming too."

Less than fifteen minutes later they were airborne again, in the same helicopter as before, but this time dressed in borrowed flying overalls. Although Lena had travelled often in the helicopters before, they all tended to resemble luxury cars or first class seats on airlines - plush leather seats, mini-bars stocked with caviar and Champagne. Thick sound insulation so that the noise from the rotors and the engines that drove them was muted and almost whisper quiet.

This one was very different. It was almost bare inside, the seats sparsely padded and worn. The two pilots sat side by side at the front, and she and Marshall were the only other people aboard. The helicopter seemed to be built for carrying people, or equipment, as there were seats missing and the metal floor rattled as they flew.

One of the pilots - the co-pilot, Lena assumed, since she didn't appear to be the one actually flying them - explained that they would search the outermost limits of where they estimated the yacht could have reached, and from there work backwards, flying sweeps of an arc. The other choppers would do the same, on different sections of the same arc. The idea was to minimise the risk of the yacht moving beyond the search area before it could be examined. The problem, the co-pilot went on, was the time. It was seven in the evening by then, and sunset was nine thirty. Once the light was gone searching would be impossible. But the yacht would keep sailing, and in the morning the expanded search area would be huge. If they were going to find the yacht, they would have to do so quickly.

It took them forty minutes to get into position to start the search. For the entire time they saw nothing out of the windows but ocean, yet the streaks of white had an eerie knack of looking like something solid, and several times Lena began to point excitedly, only to realise her mistake. The only noise was the thudding of the rotors, the rattle of the tie points on the floor. Inside her flying suit, it was cold. Although she was searching the entire way, it was when the pilot turned and announced they were now flying the first of the search arcs, that Lena leaned closer to her window and peered out. There was nothing, nothing but the rolling waves below them, some cresting and collapsing into a creamy smear of white, but most just chopping and rolling and ever-changing as they tumbled on their epic journey south.

They turned, suddenly swinging around, so that Lena's window was pointed briefly toward the sky. She looked across at Marshall.

"Second arc," he said. She nodded and turned back to the window.

An hour later they were on their fifth arc, with nothing to show for it. Every now and then there would be a burst from the radio as the pilot reported in. And then he would turn towards Lena and shake his head. Nothing. Once, at the end of another arc, they spotted one of the other helicopters, but it was in the distance, and it turned quickly around and disappeared.

It was difficult to stay concentrated. The ocean had a mesmeric effect, the patterns of the waves becoming eventually familiar. At one point Lena wondered if it were as hard for the pilot to stay alert, if it ever happened that they became disorientated and simply steered their craft down into the waves. She began to wonder about the person who had sat in her position when Charlie had gone missing. She was dimly aware that helicopters *had* gone looking for him - although it had been the yacht itself that picked up his body. She glanced across the cabin at Marshall. Funny that he had been involved then. Funny how things worked out.

They turned again, the manoeuvre now familiar to Lena, and she took the opportunity to rest her eyes.

"This is our final arc guys," the pilot called back to them. "We're getting low on fuel. And the light's going too."

Lena felt like arguing, but suddenly it felt hopeless. She searched her mind for something to distract herself with.

"Why are you here?" she said suddenly to Marshall. The question clearly surprised him. If anything it surprised her too.

"I mean, I know Peter asked you to come, and I'm glad you're here. I could never have organised all this. But why? Surely there's lots of people Peter could have asked."

They were seated far enough away from the pilots that their conversation couldn't be overheard.

"I volunteered," he said. "I asked Peter to let me come."

"Why?"

"I let you down once, I didn't want to let you down again."

Lena felt suddenly uncomfortable. Not for the first time she wondered how much he had been told about the terrible things Alice had accused him of. It was something she hadn't felt able to ask. But now it felt wrong that she *hadn't* asked. She remembered it wasn't Alice. It was Riggs. He was the one who had caused all this.

"Did Peter tell you?"

His eyes flicked to hers. "Tell me what?"

"What Alice said? What Riggs made her believe?"

It took Marshall a while to answer, and when he did so it was with a subtle nod of the head.

Lena smiled, an apologetic smile. "You always were the strong silent type. But I can't really imagine you as an assassin."

In reply he simply gave a small, sad smile, then turned back to the window to continue the search. Lena turned too. But the ocean hadn't changed, the same never-ending expanse of black. She glanced at the pilots, saw that their heads were scanning still. She turned back to Marshall.

"You know there's one thing that still bothers me," Lena said. "One thing where I've never thought Peter was telling me the whole story."

Marshall turned again to look at her.

"What?"

"What really happened on Charlie's yacht? When he died?"

From his reaction Lena wondered if he perhaps hadn't heard properly. Lena was unsure whether to repeat the question or pretend she hadn't asked it, but then he suddenly began speaking.

"That's because he wasn't. Telling you the whole story," Marshall said. He took a deep breath and Lena waited.

"On the night it happened there were four of us on watch," Marshall began. "One professional sailor, a guy called James Alum, and a woman, like Charlie and me, just on board for the experience. But they weren't all on deck. Alum was down below. There was an issue with one of the pumps and he had it in pieces. And the woman was ill. Seasick. It was the first real weather we'd been in.

"And the weather was... It was exciting. It was windier that this," he cast his eyes out the window at the ocean below. "We were going like a train. And Charlie was loving it. They'd had mostly calm weather on the first leg and he'd been looking forward to his first storm. I was... I was more scared. But I appreciated having him there. And you know Charlie..." he stopped.

"What?" Lena asked.

Marshall took his time to continue.

"The way they ran the boat was pretty strict. It wasn't just about giving people an experience. We were there to win the race. I'm talking about what we were allowed to bring on board. How we were supposed to act." He paused again.

"No drinking for example. Somehow Charlie had smuggled a bottle of Scotch on board. But up to that point it had been impossible to drink it. If Charlie had been caught he'd probably have been thrown off the crew. Certainly the Scotch would have gone over the side. So that night, with just Charlie and me on deck, we were taking the opportunity to drink it then. Riding out this storm, swigging from a bottle." He smiled.

"Can you imagine anything Charlie would have loved more?"

"We weren't drunk. Not really. That didn't play any part in the accident. But afterwards I told Peter about it. He decided it would be best to keep the drinking out of it. There was no need for that to come out. Peter said it would change the way the accident was reported. How everyone remembered him. I don't know, maybe it was a bad move. But he was always looking out for Charlie."

Marshall was silent for a long time, still staring out the window, but it was clear he was seeing nothing. Suddenly he turned to Lena and seemed surprised.

"What is it?" he asked.

Lena was crying silent tears. "I always thought it might be that." She tried to blink away the tears, and steady her voice.

"The Scotch was from me. It was a present. I smuggled it onboard for him." She said.

Marshall was about to reply, when suddenly there was a shout from in front of them.

"What's that? Ten o'clock? Looks like a sail?"

54

Lena's attention snapped back to the pilot. She followed his
outstretched arm and squinted through the gloom. The dark was
coming fast by then, and they were flying through a squall of light rain
that peppered the windows of the helicopter. Below them, and about a
half mile away, she saw a white triangle rolling with the movement of the
waves. The co-pilot was on the radio at once, relaying coordinates, and
for a few moments no one else spoke. Then the helicopter swung into a
tight roll and began flying directly to the boat.

"Is that them? Is that the one?" The pilot asked.

Between the pilots, clipped to the instrument panel, was the photograph of *Phoenix*. In it she lay at anchor on a sunny calm day, and looked
stable and inviting. The contrast between the boat in the photograph,
and the tiny vessel that pitched and rolled below them couldn't have
been more stark. Here she looked like a scrap of driftwood lost in the
ocean. The tip of her mast drew huge circles in the sky as the waves
passed underneath her. She was sailing under heavily reefed mainsail
and storm jib, not travelling fast. The helicopter was overhauling her
quickly, but with no deck lights it was still hard to make much out.

"Well? Is it?" The pilot asked again, when no one answered.

"Looks small enough. Right number of masts." Marshall replied.
"You're not going to get many boats that small this far out."

"There's a guy on board. A figure," the co-pilot said.

"A guy? Or a woman?" Lena heard her voice call out.

They were close enough now for all of them to see the figure, dressed in yellow yachting jacket, and turned so that he was watching them. The pilot flicked a switch and a spotlight flashed on, throwing a cone of light at the yacht and the surrounding ocean. At once the man raised his arm to shield his eyes from the light. He seemed to cower before it, but they only had a moment to see before the helicopter overshot, sweeping over the top of the yacht as it did so.

"Shit. Sorry. It's windy out here."

The pilot banked them around into a hard turn and came in again, slower this time, until they were manoeuvred into a hover just off the port hand side of the yacht. They were low, but high enough to be well clear of the rolling tip of the yacht's mast.

"Man," Marshall said. "Too far away to say if it's Riggs for sure, but it's definitely the right boat. Can we raise him on the radio?"

The co-pilot was already speaking into her headset.

"*Phoenix*, Phoenix, Phoenix, this is *Rescue Tango Two*. Come in please."

There was no reply, and the man on the deck didn't move, except to adjust his position enough that he could watch them from the shelter of his forearm.

"Yacht *Phoenix* come in please. This is *Tango Two* from the Royal Navy Frigate *Courage*. Are you receiving, over?"

When there was no reply again the pilot shook his head. "Maybe they don't have it on. Switch to loudspeaker."

But before they could do so, the man on the yacht below moved his position. He put the tiller arm, with which he was steering the boat, between his legs, and he clearly raised one arm to the helicopter, his middle finger held aloft. This time the light shined upon his grinning face.

"That's him, that's Riggs. The fucker," Marshall said.

The co-pilot tried again to raise the yacht, this time through a loud-speaker.

"Yacht *Phoenix* this is *Tango Two* from the Royal Navy Frigate *Courage*. You're instructed to heave to immediately."

In response Riggs raised the index finger on his other hand, to match the first.

"I guess that's a no," the pilot said.

"Why can't we see Alice?" Lena said. "Ask him where Alice is."

Before the pilot could do so Marshall had interrupted. "Put it on again, let me speak to him."

The co-pilot didn't hesitate. She pulled off her headset and passed it back. "Talk into that," she said.

"Ryan Riggs," Marshall's voice was sent blasting out into the growing night this time. "Riggs it's over. We have your location and a Royal Navy frigate is on its way here right now. It's over. Give it up."

Riggs responded by dropping his hands and doing something to the rigging. The jib, which had been mostly furled upon itself, unrolled, increasing the sail area, and - marginally - the speed the yacht was travelling. It made no difference to the helicopter's ability to hold its position.

"Riggs - Where is the girl? Where is Alice Belhaven?"

The man went back to the tiller now and they watched him lash it in place.

"Riggs you're not going to be able to escape. You should give up now."

Then Riggs disappeared below.

"The fuck's he doing?" the pilot said. And at that moment an alarm sounded on the instrument panel. The two pilots looked at each other. Then one of them pressed a button and silenced the noise.

"What's that?" Marshall asked.

"Range warning," the pilot said. "We've got fifteen minutes fuel left. On top of the twenty-five minutes it's gonna take to get back to *Courage*. Whatever happens here is gonna have to happen quick."

"Can anyone else get here in fifteen minutes?" Marshall asked. The pilot got on the radio, asking with the control room back on the frigate.

"Negative. They're all on the outer edges of their arcs. And running low on fuel themselves. The closest is the Portuguese navy SAR chopper. They're refuelling now. It would help if we could get that bastard to... *SHITTTTTTTT.*"

From the companionway of the yacht a streak of red-yellow light suddenly launched towards them. Acting on reflex the pilot pulled up on the controls and the helicopter rocked backwards. They were just in time. An explosion of light lit up the sky in front of the helicopter, so bright that Lena was momentarily blinded. More alarms sounded. Lena remained aware enough to expect that any second they were going to crash into the boiling surface of the ocean. She braced herself for impact.

But somehow the pilot levelled them up.

"Jesus fucking Christ," the pilot said. His co-pilot began punching switches on the instrument panel. They were talking so fast that Lena didn't understand any of it. Finally the alarms muted, but three lights remained lit up.

"What happened? Are we OK?" Lena asked.

No one answered.

"Are we going to crash?" She asked again.

"We might if he does that again." The pilot replied. He shook his head.

They were level again now. Outside the sky was suddenly lit up into a yellowy version of daylight. A light was dropping down towards the water, like it was being slowly lowered by a crane.

"What was that? What happened." Lena asked, still not understanding.

"Your man fired a parachute flare at us." The co-pilot said. She got on the radio again, reporting what had just happened, then interrupted herself.

"Look out, there's another."

Below them Riggs released a second rocket flare, but this time they were further away and the pilot had time to edge sideways so the flare simply lit up the area of sea between the boat and the helicopter.

"This guy's a fucking arsehole," the co-pilot said on the radio.

Riggs came back out on deck now. They were too far to see clearly now, but he seemed to be grinning. Then he bowed elaborately to the helicopter. Marshall still had the loudspeaker controller. He answered him.

"Riggs, don't make this harder for yourself. You need to heave to immediately and await further instructions. I repeat, you are not going to escape. Don't make this harder than it needs to be."

Below them Riggs clearly and slowly shook his head. He *was* grinning they saw this time.

"Where's Alice? Ask him again where she is." Lena pleaded.

Marshall hesitated but he did what she asked.

"Where is the girl? Riggs don't make this worse for yourself."

He disappeared again below.

"Look out," the co-pilot said. "He may fire again." But he didn't. For a few minutes they hovered thirty metres off the empty deck of the yacht, yawing and rolling its way down the swells.

"The fuck's he doing now?" Marshall said. But they didn't have to wait long to find out.

When Riggs reappeared he was dragging something. It was hard to make out what at first, with the yacht's movement, and the lip of the cockpit obscuring their view. But eventually he got it up the steps and Lena gasped. It was a second figure, a woman, not moving. But then they realised this was because she had her hands and feet bound. Lena gasped again.

"Alice! Oh my God, it's Alice." Without thinking she grabbed Marshall's arm.

But Riggs wasn't finished yet. He disappeared again into the cabin, and this time put the lights on below. The yellow light spilled from the companionway and the windows. For an instant it made the scene friendlier, until you took in the woman tied up in the cockpit, either unconscious or dead.

"She's moving," the co-pilot said. "Look, her head's moving." And it was. They could all see it now.

"Oh thank God," Lena said. "We've got to get her away from him. Can't we shoot him or something?"

The pilots glanced at each other, then the co-pilot answered her.

"I'm not confident we can eliminate him without sinking the yacht. And even if we avoided that it would leave the girl tied up and unable to maintain steering. The yacht could swamp. It's too risky."

"Well can't we go down and pick her up?"

The co-pilot didn't get a chance to answer, since the alarm sounded on the instrument panel again.

"Five minutes fuel, then we're outta here."

Riggs didn't keep them waiting. He climbed out of the cabin again, pausing only to wave an arm at the aircraft. He was carrying something else but with the lights below it cast the deck into shadow, meaning it was hard to make out what. They saw him give Alice a kick as he passed her though. And then they saw what he was doing.

Below them Riggs opened the top of a jerry can, and began pouring the contents onto Alice's prone body. They could see how she twisted and fought to escape him, but tied up she had no chance. Then Riggs began splashing the decks and the cockpit. He threw some down the stairs into the yacht's cabin, then slowly and carefully, he began making his way forward, across the top of the yacht's pitching cabin roof. As he went he splashed more of the contents of the jerry can, over the ropes that fed up the mast, over the parts of the sail he could reach, and finally, he emptied the can over himself, dousing his clothes and his hair. Then he tossed the can over the side of the yacht.

"Shit," someone on the helicopter said. Lena didn't know who.

Riggs reached into his jacket. He cupped something between his hands.

"Oh no," Lena still couldn't place the voice. It didn't seem to match anyone in the helicopter.

Riggs struggled to get the lighter to ignite, but then he did so, and held it aloft, away from his body, a tiny blue flame. It was the type designed for outdoors, that sent out a flame like a miniature blowtorch. Charlie had one just like it, Lena thought. It was strange the things you thought of at moments like this.

He was grinning again. And slowly, very slowly, he bent his arm and touched the lighter to his chest.

"It's not going to light. It's too windy," the voice spoke again. And this time Lena realised it was her speaking all along. "It's not going to..." But she was wrong. Whatever had been in the jerry can must have been plenty flammable, because it was alight now, a ghostly blue flame wrapping around his body, growing yellow tongues and reaching up to his neck and face. Seconds later his hair was alight, his clothes and arms too, the flames strong now. He held out his hands in the shape of a cross and slowly began to rotate, like some flaming barbecued Jesus. He tipped his head back, and opened his mouth. It looked like he was laughing, but Lena realised he was screaming. There were flames coming out of his mouth.

The mainsail caught next, and then the flames began to lick along the top of the cabin. The fire climbed the ropes and rigging, like so many fiery monkeys swinging through a jungle. Riggs dropped to his knees. He was almost impossible to see now, just a black shape, more and more obscured by flames as every second passed.

"We've got to get her off there." Marshall said. "We've got to move now." Lena didn't speak, her hands were covering her mouth.

"I said we've got to *move*. Can you get me on there?"

The pilot stammered. "The boat's too small. The rotors would hit the mast. There's no way..."

"Can't you winch me down?"

"This is a transport chopper. You see a winch?"

"*Shit*," Marshall said.

The front of the yacht was well alight now. What had been Riggs was just a black shape sprawled on the roof of the cabin. It may have been the fire, or the movement of the boat, but it seemed to be squirming and writhing, in flames that now reached up a third the height of the mast. But the wind, pushing the boat forwards, had also kept the fire towards the bow of the yacht. The cockpit, where Alice lay, had yet to catch. And Alice was doing her best to wriggle further backwards to the very rear of the cockpit. But the flames were coming.

There was a whoosh, and fire dropped down into the cabin.

"We might be able to use the downdraft to blow the fire out," the pilot said, and without waiting for anyone to reply he began to move the helicopter forward. They turned side-on, so that the yacht was almost immediately below them. They were close enough now to see Alice's screaming face.

"Three minutes Jack," the co-pilot said. Her voice was dark.

Marshall had moved to join Lena on the left side of the aircraft. "It's not working, you need to get closer," he said.

"I can't," the pilot yelled back. "We'll hit the shrouds holding the mast up. *Shit!*"

"We need to be out of here Jack," the co-pilot's calm voice interrupted. "I'm sorry Mrs Belhaven, there's nothing more we can do."

"What? You're just going to leave her? Leave her to burn?"

"*There's nothing more we can do.*" Her voice cracked. "Jack we're going to fall out of the *fucking* sky if you don't get us out of here right now."

The pilot made no movement. But then he smashed a fist against the window of the cockpit.

"Fuck it!" he screamed.

Suddenly Marshall began fighting his way out of his jacket.

"Can you get me on there?"

"Sir?"

"I said can you get me close enough to get on there?"

"No, I told you, we've got no fucking winch on this helicopter."

"The other chopper, the nearest one. Do they have a winch?"

"Yeah, it's the Portuguese SAR. Yes, they have a winch. What are you thinking?"

In response Marshall ripped open the door in the side of the helicopter. At once an explosion of noise and wind flooded in.

"Sir you cannot do that," the co-pilot said. "Close the door sir!"

Marshall ignored her and spoke directly to the pilot. "Just get me as close as you can!"

He put his hands on either side of the void and braced himself. The yacht was fully ablaze now. It was just possible to make out Alice, still bound, but pushed up against the stanchions at the very stern of the yacht.

"Just tell that Portuguese chopper to hurry the fuck up." Marshall said.

And then he jumped.

55

No on spoke as he dropped to the water. The splash when he hit was audible even over the wild noise of the motor, the wind and the fire.

"There's one minute of reserve fuel left Jack," the co-pilot yelled. "We've got to get out of here. Now." She struggled out of her seatbelt and climbed into the rear of the cabin. She pushed Lena out of the way and pulled the door shut. The maelstrom calmed a little.

"Jack! Right fucking now please."

He did what she said. As the helicopter turned away Lena just had the chance to see Marshall's arms moving as he swum through the waves towards the back of the yacht. And then the scene disappeared behind them as the chopper turned away and the nose dropped. They increased speed to one hundred knots and blasted back across the now dark, ocean towards *Courage*.

"We have to stay!" Lena heard herself say, although she understood. "We can't just leave them."

Both pilots ignored her now. The man flying was speaking fast and urgently into the radio. The co-pilot punching buttons. But then she turned to look at Lena. Her face was white.

"The Portuguese SAR chopper is ten minutes away. It's a search and rescue helicopter. They've got winches and a diver on board. They're absolutely the best chance your friends have right now. I'm sorry but there is nothing more we can do. If we don't go back right now, we will ditch in the ocean? Do you understand that?"

Lena nodded. The co-pilot turned back.

The minutes crawled by. The tone of the engine seemed to have changed, as if the flow of fuel was no longer smooth. Ahead of them the dark ocean seemed endless. No one spoke.

Five minutes later the pilot requested an update from the Portuguese helicopter. They took a while to answer, then replied they were ten minutes away from the yacht's reported position. Lena moaned. An animal sound.

They flew on. The co-pilot giving readings on the fuel every minute. Her voice was sickening. She turned again, and this time made Lena put on a life jacket. She told her not inflate it until she had escaped from inside the helicopter airframe.

"You'll know we're going in when Jack yells *ditching* into the radio three times. If that happens you put your feet flat on the floor. Not under the seat, that might collapse and trap your legs. Do you understand that?"

"Repeat it to me please. Where do you put your feet?"

"Flat," Lena replied. "Not under the seat."

"That's right. Now most of the weight of this bird is on top of us, so it's likely to roll before it sinks. Just before we hit, take a breath and keep your eyes closed. The water may be clouded with hydraulic fluid that could burn them out. Focus on staying calm. You got that?"

Lena nodded, but she knew she hadn't. She wouldn't survive a crash in the cold water below them. She would be trapped in the helicopter as it sank. As it dropped a a mile, or maybe more, to the bottom of the ocean. She felt a new wave of panic at the thought, not hearing the co-pilot as she continued her instructions.

"The latch to the emergency window is positioned next to your hip. You bring your hand down to the hip, and then straight out to find the latch, OK?" Repeat it back to me. "Straight out to find the latch. Try it now."

Her hand shaking, Lena did what the co-pilot said. On the radio there was an interruption.

"We have visual on the yacht. Quite a bonfire. Stand by."

"Can they see them?"

The pilot relayed the question.

"Negative. There's no sign of anyone alive on board. The whole thing's alight like a firework."

On Lena's helicopter there was silence. But then, up ahead of them there was a sliver of yellow light in the gloom.

"*Courage*," the pilot said. He checked the fuel again. "Oh fucking hell," he said.

"Come on baby. Sip it. Fucking sip it." The co-pilot said. Lena didn't say anything. Her face was wet. When she touched it she found it was soaked with tears.

The yellow of the light grew, and took on the outline of the Frigate. The two pilots were focused totally on getting the aircraft to it now, before the engine sucked empty on the fuel tank and they dropped out of the sky.

"One minute away," the pilot said.

"Fuel's gone. We're on fumes," his co-pilot replied. "You ready back there?"

The ship was large now in front of them, and they were still flying fast towards it. The helicopter pad, on the stern, was lit up. They aimed directly for it. Seconds later they were flying past the superstructure. The engine gave a sudden howl, and then began juddering.

"We're gone, get her down Jack."

He didn't need telling. With a sickening lurch they began dropping sideways and backwards out of the sky. Below them the ship's stern dropped into the hollow of a wave, which just gave them a few metres more height to position over the landing pad. They hit it hard, with a massive bang. The chopper nearly tipped onto its side, then came back upright. They were down.

Moments later they were surrounded by figures dressed in orange, grabbing hold of the sleds and lashing them on.

The pilot pushed the control stick away from him and dropped his head into his hands. Then he vomited into his lap. The co-pilot turned to Lena, her eyes were wild.

Then there was a message on the radio. The accent Portuguese.

"*We're seeing a figure in the water here, maybe two. We're going to put our diver down and pick them up.*"

A fuzz of static. A very long wait.

"*We have them on board now.*"

56

"I need to see her. I need to see Alice!"

"I understand that Mrs Belhaven, but you're in severe shock and the helipad needs to be checked for damage. I cannot authorise anyone to fly at the moment."

Lena was still on board *Courage*, but this time – without Marshall to assist her – she felt she was fighting against a system that existed to resist.

"Where is she now?"

"We understand she's being transferred to a hospital in Funchal. We'll get you there as soon as we can."

Lena put her fist to her forehead and pushed. Hard. "I need to see her," she said in a quiet voice. "I need to be with her."

But, for a long time, she didn't.

The helicopter that hauled Alice and Marshall from the roiling waters carried them to Madeira, where they were taken to the main hospital in the island's capital. Alice was treated for exposure, shock and burns to her legs and feet. Marshall for the gash to his head he had acquired when trying to board the burning yacht.

The damaged helicopter was cleared from the stern of the frigate, and the Navy doctor finally authorised Lena to board another one. But by the time it landed at the Cristiano Ronaldo airport on Madeira, Alice had already been put in a specialist medical repatriation flight bound for London Heathrow. Lena missed it by less than twenty minutes.

The earliest commercial flight was the next afternoon, so she was forced to spend the night in a hotel, where every minute seemed to take an hour. She couldn't sleep, and lay staring at the ceiling. Eventually the time passed, and she joined those queues of tourists she'd watched the day before, as they wound their way through the airport, through the air, and finally back down to British soil. The only relief came at Heathrow Terminal Four when things sped up. She was met at the aircraft door by a woman who called herself Jennifer. She explained she would take Lena directly to the Royal Brompton Hospital where Alice was now being treated. They took a back route through immigration, and out to a Government Jaguar that was parked in a no parking zone. As they walked Jennifer spoke in a quiet voice, updating Lena on everything that had been discovered about Riggs, how the yacht had sunk shortly after Marshall and Alice had been pulled from the water. How Marshall's head wound wasn't serious. But Lena found it impossible to concentrate on what she was saying.

Once they were in the car they fell into silence. The traffic was typically thick, and many times they slowed to a painful crawl. Eventually they pulled off the road and stopped outside the hospital.

Alice's room was up on the top floor, and buried away down what felt like miles of corridors. When they finally stopped walking there was a uniformed police officer at the door. He wore a pistol strapped to his body armour. As the two women approached him he stiffened and saluted.

"I'll wait here," Jennifer said, and stepped back. Lena nodded. She prepared herself and pressed gently on the door.

Alice lay propped up against a pile of pillows, her eyes closed. Her legs were exposed, and partially wrapped in bandages. A machine measuring her pulse beeped quietly beside her. As Lena entered the room, Alice opened her eyes. There was a flicker of something – pain perhaps? Shame? She smiled but there was no depth to it.

"Mum."

"Alice."

There was a silence. A moment of terrible quiet when Lena wondered if this would be it. If too much had been said, too much damage done for them to go back.

"I'm sorry Mum," Alice said.

"Oh darling *I'm* sorry. I'm *so, so* sorry," Lena heard herself say, and suddenly she was leaning in, trying awkwardly to squeeze Alice's shoulders. It took a few moments for Lena to realise that muffled sounds Alice was making were attempts to get her off.

"Ow," Alice said, smiling a little.

"Are you hurt badly?"

"No. The doctors said I was lucky. But I'll have scars on my legs."

Lena nodded like that was no small thing. A moment passed between them. Lena sat down. She looked at Alice's hand as if she wanted to touch it, but she didn't.

"So what happened. When did you know?"

Alice glanced across at Lena. She seemed to prepare herself for an explanation. Lena just waited.

"I don't know exactly. When we walked out of Peter's office I was so angry. I just let Jamie take over. We took a coach back down to Poole and onto the boat. We didn't know what to do. At least - I didn't. Jamie said it was the safest option, that we had to get away. And somehow I agreed. But those first two weeks. Just him and me on that little yacht. It was such a long time.

"At first we didn't even talk about it. We both tried to pretend there was some other reason we were out there, sailing without any lights on. But eventually we had to. And when we talked together he somehow made it all make sense. But then, when I was trying to sleep, there were bits I couldn't understand. So I'd ask him the next day. And I'd understand again. But..."

There was pain written on Alice's face.

Lena didn't reply, but she glanced at her daughter's hand again.

"Then what?"

"We were going to Africa. We weren't going to stop at Madeira, but I saw it on the charts. We'd talked about the money by then, how useful it would be. And I told him if we went there I'd be able to get it. I'd be able to put in an account that no one could reach. At first he refused, but I persuaded him. He really wanted the money. And I don't think he *really* knew where we were going anyway.

Alice was talking freely now.

"When we got to the island, he was wary. He didn't let me out of his sight. It had to be me going into the bank but he was right there too, watching everything. And then afterwards I wanted to check the news websites, to see what was happening. But he wouldn't let me. He always had some reason why it wasn't a good idea. He just wanted to get moving again. Straight away."

There was a distant look in her eyes. "We bought another phone, a pay-as-you-go one, to check that the money had gone through properly. He kept it with him, he didn't let me use it alone. I think he realised then, that I was beginning to doubt it. Then, after we left, he was on deck, sailing the yacht, and I was putting provisions away, I saw he'd left it below. The phone. There was still signal - we were close enough to the island I suppose. So I used it to log onto my emails. I read what you sent Mum," She turned and looked at Lena.

"I read it as we sailed away. How it was all him. How he'd killed that girl, and blamed it on Peter." She bit her lip for a moment. "That's when I understood. When it all finally made sense.

"I read how he'd killed that man too. The one that you sent to watch us." Lena's eyes flicked up as Alice said these words. And another moment passed between them. This time there was meaning in it. Some kind of recognition of how bad things must have got between them that Lena thought it appropriate to hire someone to spy on her daughter. But then Alice went on, as if acknowledging that that discussion would wait for another day.

"And then, as I was reading who he *really* was, that's when he found me.

"I don't know how he knew, but he did. *He knew* I knew. This totally different look came onto his face. Like all that time he'd been playing a character and now he didn't have to act any more..." Alice stopped. She didn't seem to want to go on.

"What happened?"

"He grabbed some rope. There's a little locker by the steps. When he walked towards me I was so scared. I thought he was going to strangle me. So when he just gently took my hands I just let him. I knew what he was doing but I let him tie me up." Alice looked at one of her hands now, as if it had betrayed her. Lena noticed the dark red marks from where they had been tied.

Alice continued. "And then, when he was finished, he looked at the phone too. He read it all, nodding, like it kind of made sense to him somehow. There was nothing I could do to stop him.

Alice hesitated, and when she went on her voice cracked.

"And then he raped me."

The words made Lena wince. She sunk down further into her chair.

"All the time he told me it was my fault. That I shouldn't have looked. That I'd ruined everything. Then afterwards, when he was finished, he smashed the phone to pieces with a tin can. He wouldn't talk to me then. He wouldn't listen when I tried to talk to him. To ask what he was going to do next. It was like I didn't exist after that.

"I don't know how long I was stuck down there. With the boat moving all around me. He came down a few times and sometimes he looked at me, like I was this problem he had to solve. But he wouldn't talk. He was going to kill me. I know that, he was just working out how to do it. Then he started siphoning fuel from the engine. He had these jerry cans. But he was nervous. He was scared to do it. And then I heard the helicopter."

"I think he was pleased to see it. He was screaming. Laughing. He came down and told me everything was going to be OK. The cavalry was here. I told him he had to turn himself in. That it would be better. But he eyes were wild. He wasn't ever going to turn himself in.

"Then he fired at it with the flare gun. I couldn't see much, from down below. Just this explosion of light, so that I thought for a moment he'd hit it. But then I heard Marshall's voice again. And then he was dragging me on deck. And I knew what he was going to do, but I couldn't stop him. He kept talking about how he'd be famous. How they'd be filming in the helicopter, and he'd be known in the newspapers as the man on the burning boat. That was all he wanted then. Some sort of recognition. He said that was the best way to end it. Through immortality.

Alice turned to Lena, and was about to say something else when there was the sound of voices outside. A moment later there was a knock on the door and a doctor entered, she looked at Lena, surprised to see her there.

"Hello." She turned to Alice.

"I just need to have a look at you. Check how you're feeling."

Both Alice and Lena waited while the doctor read the chart hanging at the bottom of the bed, and then spent some time examining Alice's legs. After a few minutes she seemed satisfied.

"She's very weak, you shouldn't stay too long."

Lena nodded. And when the doctor left the room, Alice smiled at her mother.

"I guess you know the rest. I can't believe you were actually in the helicopter. I thought you hated helicopters?"

Lena smiled back. "Neither can I. And I still do. Even more now."

Alice smiled. She turned to look properly at her mother.

"I'm sorry Mum. For believing him over you..."

"No." Lena stopped her. "Don't. There's nothing to say sorry for."

Finally she picked up Alice's hand and, softly at first, she traced down each of her fingers. There were a hundred things she wanted to say about family, about how they had to find a way forward, and about how everything would be OK. But at that moment it was all she could do to squeeze her daughter's hand and try and fight back the tears. But in that moment. It was enough.

It was enough.

The End

AFTERWORD

Hello!

Thank you for reading *The Girl on the Burning Boat*. I really hope you enjoyed it, and I hope I managed to lure you in to believing the good characters were bad and the bad ones were good. I love a story that does that...

If you did enjoy it, I'd be incredibly grateful if you could leave a short review on Amazon (and anywhere else). Reviews make a huge difference to authors in their struggle to gain visibility. It's easy to do, just visit the book's Amazon page and follow the links to leave a review. Thanks!

And while you're in the mood, please consider signing up to my mailing list. I really enjoy keeping in touch with readers, and feel I now have friends all around the world as a result of the books. I also try my best to make my emails entertaining (and never spammy). If I'm wrong, you can always unsubscribe at any time! But if you'd like to hear more from me, and especially about upcoming releases, please visit www.greggdunnett.co.uk and you can sign up there)

Finally, it took me a long time to get around to writing, but now I've started I plan to stick around for a good while longer. I may mix up the genres a little, but I'm sure they'll all have a couple of common themes - they'll be books set on or near the sea, or the beach, or the coastline.

Books that mix mystery and adventure, with thrills and twists. If that's the sort of thing you enjoy too, I'd love you to stick around too.

Following this note you'll find a page on each of my other books, in case you'd like to read more, and a thank you to everyone that helped with writing this one.

Thanks to you again for reading. I really appreciate it. 😊

Gregg Dunnett

Oct 2018

THE THINGS YOU FIND IN ROCKPOOLS

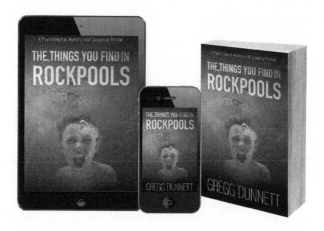

How do you catch a killer - when you're just a kid?

A teenage girl disappears from an island beach town. Two months later the police have no leads. So quirky local boy Billy Wheatley steps in to help.

At just eleven years old, he's a little young to play detective, but he's confident of success. After all, he's kind of a child prodigy - at least - he *thinks* he is. Either way, he's got one very good reason to want the police off his beach.

With an investigative style like nothing you've seen before, he follows the twists and turns of the case. But when the clues start pointing in just one direction, Billy knows he's in trouble.

Because the person who took the girl is someone close to him. Someone he thought he could trust. And when they find out what Billy is up to, they're going to have to make Billy disappear, just like that girl...

The Things you find in Rockpools is a gripping and twist-filled psychological-thriller set in a fictional island off the east coast of the United States. In 2018 it reached the top 50 in both the US and the UK Amazon charts in 2018, with over a thousand five star reviews across the two sites.

Available in print, on Amazon Kindle & KU and as an audiobook.

THE WAVE AT HANGING ROCK

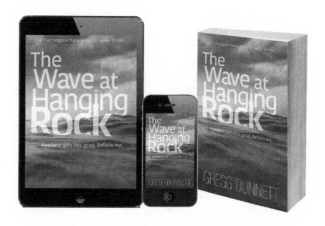

Natalie, a young doctor, sees her perfect life shattered when her husband is lost at sea. Everyone believes it's a tragic accident. But a mysterious phone call prompts her to think otherwise. She sets out on a search for the truth.

Jesse, a schoolboy, is moved half way around the world when his father is blown up in a science experiment gone wrong.

Two seemingly unconnected tales. But how they come together will have you turning the pages late into the night. And the twist at the end will leave you reeling.

The Wave at Hanging Rock is the debut novel from British author Gregg Dunnett. With over a quarter of a million downloads it became an Amazon bestseller and was shortlisted for the Chanticleer Award for Best Mystery or Suspense novel of the year.

Available in print, on Amazon Kindle & KU and as an audiobook.

THE DESERT RUN

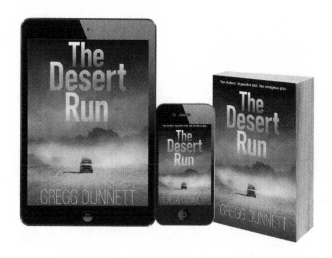

Two students' impossible debt. One outrageous plan.

Jake is just out of university and right out of cash. His former classmates are off on adventures or getting on with their lives, while he's stuck in a dead end job and can't get a break. Until his best friend comes up with a plan to reverse both their fortunes.

He's smart enough to know it's madness. But then - he's also smart enough to calculate the odds of getting caught. And just how much money they'll make if they don't. The harder Jake tries to dismiss the idea, the more the pieces fall into place.

Until one day he finds himself queuing at the border while armed customs officers search their van - packed with enough dope to put the boys away for twenty years.

Yet Jake hardly even cares. Because - by then - prison is only Jake's second biggest problem...

The Desert Run is a refreshingly unusual thriller from Amazon UK and US bestselling author Gregg Dunnett. If you like nail-biting suspense, jaw-dropping twists and ordinary people facing extraordinary events, then you'll love this fast-paced read.

Available in print, on Amazon Kindle & KU and as an audiobook.

THANKS TO...

Books take a lot of work and a lot of people play an important part of making them happen. I'd like to thank a few of those here.

Firstly thanks to Rob Earp of Coolwatercreative, who took my ideas for a cover (hashed together from photos illegally sourced from the internet) and made them beautifully shocking, beautifully designed, and most importantly legal!

Thanks to lots of people for their comments on early drafts. To Lucy Clarke (the brilliant, bestselling author, yes *that* Lucy Clarke). To Clyde, Arancha, to Maria's boss (for saving me from an inadvertent Spandau Ballet reference - Oh and I made the boat bigger - did you spot that?) Particular thanks to my Mum, my Dad and my brother. I don't think my brother actually ever *finished* the book - but then he is two years into an epic mission to windsurf alone around Europe. And if he couldn't quite find the time, well that told me something needed fixing, in that draft at least.

A huge thanks to my team of beta readers who scoured the text for typos and errors. I tried not to leave them too many, but they all found lots. I hope I haven't missed anyone out here, but thanks to: Sue Soderlund, Dave Evans, Kristi Van Der Lelie, Melanie Banton, Elsa Hoffmann, Ann Underwood, Andy Pearce (for pulling my military language into rank!), Susan Rasdale (for the much needed final chapter) and Jackie

Porter. It goes without saying, but any errors that are still here are entirely my fault (not least as I couldn't resist tweaking the final text, and probably introduced a whole host of new ones!) If you've spotted any, please do let me know. I love nothing more than fixing typos and can always update the ebook. Drop me an email at hello@greggdunnet-t.co.uk

Thanks to my lovely children, Alba and Rafa (currently aged 6 & 4). It would be misleading to suggest they helped in any meaningful way, but I enjoyed having them here. And a huge, massive thank you to my partner Maria, who has encouraged me, advised me, put up with my worrying and generally been just about the perfect editor/coach/proofreader, and lots more besides. Thanks!

Thanks also to anyone who has read any of my earlier books and either contacted me, left a review or just enjoyed it. It's an amazing privilege (and slightly terrifying) to know I can write a book these days and people all around the world will actually read it. Gulp.

Finally, thanks to Grubby, my ever faithful dog. He plays two vital roles in my process. He keeps my feet warm while I'm writing (saves a fortune in slippers) and with an unerring sense of when I've got stuck, he'll leap up and insist on some exercise to walk out the problem. Works every time...

I hope you enjoyed the book.

:-)

Gregg

Made in the USA
San Bernardino, CA
29 March 2019